500 numbered and 15 lettered copies were printed. This is number ___393___

BLOOD HARVEST
James A. Moore

BLOOD HARVEST
James A. Moore

EARTHLING PUBLICATIONS - HALLOWEEN 2011

FIRST EDITION, FIRST PRINTING
October 2011

Blood Harvest is the seventh book in Earthling's Halloween Series

ISBN-13: 978-0-9838071-0-0

EARTHLING PUBLICATIONS
P.O. Box 413
Northborough, MA 01532 USA
Email: earthlingpub@yahoo.com
Website: www.earthlingpub.com

Printed in the U.S.A.

PROLOGUE

What's in a name? Had it remembered its name it might have pondered that question. Instead it considered only the hunger that had been building through endless months of darkness.

Once it had a name; it knew that. Once it knew the sunlight and the touch of warm skin — wanted and unwanted alike — and the comfort of a bed. None of those things had mattered in longer than it could easily fathom. The darkness was all. The end, the beginning, everything in between. The darkness ate the world and stole away memories and comforts along with warmth and the notion of companionship.

There had been others once, just as lost and just as imprisoned in the darkness, but the hunger had been too much and in time it had decided to sate that hunger — had, in fact, consumed the others, devoured their forms completely, even chewing away their bones until there was nothing left but the crashing, booming noises and the dank, dark, endless cold.

How long had it wrapped itself in the meager comfort of the darkness? How long since it had heard any sound aside from the drumming beat of the endless cycle of — it struggled for the right word or concept and finally smiled as the term came to mind — the surf. The smile felt wrong, distorted and obscene, but then everything felt that way, had for as long as it could remember.

It crawled, hands and feet and knees and elbows scraping the hard ground and then the walls and then the damp ceiling overhead. Distant thoughts said that crawling on the ceiling was impossible, but that was wrong. Impossible no longer existed as a concept. There was merely the darkness, and in the darkness all was possible.

And as it lay in that mothering womb of darkness, it changed, became more than it had been, perhaps, or became less. How could it say? It had nothing to compare itself to any longer. It could see in the darkness now, could hear the voices of people far, far away, through stone and dirt and the roots of trees. It could see differently: light came not merely from the sun and moon and stars, not only from electrical devices, but also from all living things. The light was good. The light made it hungry.

The darkness owned everything, except, of course, for the hunger. How long had it starved? Surely not as long as the darkness had held it, comforted it, loved it as only the darkness could. Had someone asked it what the darkness was, it would have pondered the notion for a very long time and sought the right word to encompass the concept of how powerful the darkness was. Eventually, it would have explained that the darkness was God. That, or it would have eaten the foolish thing that asked it questions.

Yes, that. It was so very hungry.

Desperate fingers pressed at the stones above it, sought a way to escape the prison, and for the first time in eternities, the attempt was rewarded. The darkness above it crumbled. That, or it became one with the darkness. It was hard to say, because there was nothing to use as a comparison.

It had been alone for such a long time. There was nothing, no way to weigh the difference in the darkness against what had happened before. All it knew, really, was that something was different.

It attacked the difference with a ravenous hunger.

It moved slowly upward.

And the darkness bled as the drumming noise thundered all around.

CHAPTER ONE

Surely towns endure. Most of them, at least. A few grow tired and diseased and die, sometimes with quiet dignity and sometimes in flames and ashes. But most towns, most cities, survive the tragedies that try to crush them.

Surely their people do, too. Tragedies occur and sometimes loved ones are lost, but the survivors have to go on, they must live and remember. In Black Stone Bay that was as true as anywhere else, but there was also the matter of appearances to consider, wasn't there? The mansions along the Cliff Walk had seen their share of tragedy well before the incidents of five years earlier, and the residents of those vast, opulent homes had continued on. The recession that the president had called the "worst economic disaster since the Great Depression" had bashed and beaten at the country, but Black Stone Bay continued, unflinching despite the financial losses. The same is true of the universities that dominated the center of the town and of the shops that adorned the quaint side roads near the institutes of higher learning.

Adversity does not always destroy. Sometimes it brings a town closer together and binds neighbors with ties of shared tragedy and loss. And even if it does not always unite neighbors, it can still create the illusion of solidarity.

Regardless, Black Stone Bay endured with quiet strength and stoic dignity. No one would have expected anything less of the town or its citizens. If there were old wounds that had not healed, then surely it was best to let them fester in silence, hidden away like a shameful secret.

Five years had passed since the worst tragedy of recent times, and most would never know the truth of that event. A fraternity house had burned down with no survivors. A school bus had collided with several other vehicles in the road, the driver likely confused by the deep fog that rose off the ocean that dreadful Halloween night, and there had been other fires, explosions, and bodies burned beyond recognition. Somewhere along the way Halloween pranks had gotten out of hand and buildings were destroyed, houses of God were desecrated.

People died. More people disappeared, presumed dead by some, assumed to have run away by others. In the long run the difference was negligible. The Bay had suffered, and the community had come together to help the wounded heal.

Five years is the blink of an eye in the history of a town like Black Stone Bay. Buildings were restored, businesses rebuilt, trusts that had broken were carefully recreated, and in no time the town was alive again, vital and healthy.

People are not always as quick to recover. Families were gone, sometimes completely, and occasionally they were merely wounded. Others continued on, seemingly unscathed by the events that had wrought so much damage.

Sometimes towns heal. Sometimes people do not.

Sometimes appearances are deceiving.

***

Are we there yet, Mommy?

"No." Her back hurt from carrying his weight. She'd carried him for so long and there was no way to set him down.

When?

"Soon, sweetie."

Are you tired?

"Mommy's always tired, baby. You know that." She spoke softly as she drove, and looked at the skin on her arms where it flaked and peeled as if recovering from a bad sunburn. She doubted she'd recover from this one.

Tell me about home. His voice was so wistful, and she smiled. She loved him so much, as only a mother could.

"You'll like it. There's plenty to eat, and the people are nice."

Will Daddy be there?

"No, baby. Daddy won't be there."

Will I ever see Daddy?

Only in Hell, she thought, but kept that opinion to herself. "I don't think so, my sweet angel."

The pain in her back moved across her stomach, her abdomen, pushed slowly through her until she had to pull the station wagon to the side of the road and gasp as it grew and pulsed and twisted her insides. "Oh, baby, please…"

I'm sorry, Mommy. I don't mean to hurt. I'm so hungry.

"I know. I know. I'll fix it. Mommy make it better, okay?"

She climbed from the car and looked at the parking lot just ahead. A convenience store. It hadn't been there the last time she'd been to Black Stone Bay. Then again, she'd seldom been on this side of the town. This was the area that led to the north and the last time she'd been this way she was going home to see her parents. The pain grew worse, and despite the love she felt for her baby boy, Angela Fremont growled in her throat.

I'm sorry, Mommy. I'm so hungry. His voice was growing desperate.

From fifty yards away she could see the people inside the Smart-Mart. The clerk was talking to a girl who was far too young for him, staring hard at the cleavage she displayed proudly in her too-small shirt. While he was busy trying to see more of her breasts, her boyfriend was slipping a large can of beer into his jacket pocket. For just a moment she felt her lips pull down in a disapproving frown. Who was she to judge? Back when she'd had a good body, before she married and got pregnant, she'd used her charms the same way. She chastised herself. Being a mother changed everything. She wanted better for her baby boy. She wanted everything for him. Everything that she had never gotten out of life, he would have. That was the way it was supposed to be, right?

The teenaged girl smiled and flirted with the teller, who looked ready to drag her into the back room and violate her. Angela moved closer, her eyes fixed on the cashier. He reminded her of Brian: always with his mind on getting laid. He could have had Angela five times, and two minutes later he'd be ready to nail whatever piece of ass came his way. The thought enraged her, and her hunger flared as she moved faster. She had intended to walk into the store casually, but the anger and the baby's desire to feed spurred her into a hard run.

Hungry, Mommy!

Five years she'd been carrying him inside her body, and she was getting very, very sick of his whining. Most women endured nine months. This? This was Hell!

"Shut the fuck up, you parasite! You're as bad as your goddamned father!" She spat the words and immediately felt bad for saying them. Her baby might not understand the words, but he got the gist of her tone and what she was saying.

He did not cry, but she felt his sadness.

"I'm sorry, honey. Mommy's sorry. But she's hungry, too." She pushed open the front door of the shop impatiently, ignoring the sound of glass exploding. "Mommy's hungry, too!"

***

Courtney Deighton was beginning to think the pig at the counter was actually going to try groping her tits—a thought that disgusted her, thanks just the same. This wasn't the first time Billy had asked her to distract the guy, and it probably wouldn't be the last. She hated it, but she loved Billy, and so she did what she had to. The guy was looking at her tits like they were the sweetest things he'd ever seen, and she pushed her chest out as hard as she could, hoping he wouldn't see that she'd padded her bra with tissues to give the proper view. Billy was going to have to start groveling a bit and that was all there was to it. She didn't even like beer and wasn't going to drink any of it. The beers were for him and his douche bag friends. He'd had enough time to grab three or four, and she wasn't going to stand here much longer.

The loser in front of her licked his lips nervously and started to ask her a question—he'd actually asked for her phone number last time and she'd nearly laughed in his face—when the front door of the shop crashed open and shattered. For just an instant she thought a car had come through the front of the building. Her mind flashed to the cop shows she'd seen where that sort of thing happened, and she tensed, waiting for the impact even before she looked toward the flying glass and the bent door frame.

Her hand moved instinctively, trying to block the shower of fragments that tore the air to shreds. Modern safety glass is designed to break into small squares rather than sharp shards, which was a blessing in this case, as the tiny pieces blasted her before her hand got anywhere near the right spot to protect her.

Courtney was screaming, expecting the worst. Instead she survived with minimal damage to her nearly flawless skin. Everything seemed to happen too slowly. Her hand was too late to protect her face. Her body tried to curl in on itself, but not fast enough to shield her from the missile that pushed into her and knocked her through the air.

Courtney, at all of sixteen years of age, was fairly sure she understood how the world worked. She'd seen enough guys staring at her to know that she could probably get her way with a lot of them. She also understood that Billy liked her, but that he was using her. She thought that summed up the level of pain she could suffer in her world. She was wrong, of course, but no one could have told her that. Some lessons have to be learned, rather than merely explained. Regardless, she got over her opinion of her own invulnerability around the same time her left shoulder impacted with the metal shelves of candy bars and twisted away from the socket meant to house it. She had just long enough to wonder if she was okay before the pain slammed through her and she hit the ground, blinded by the unexpected agony.

The clerk let out a scream that ended very abruptly, and Courtney looked toward him as he was lifted off the ground and thrown completely across the store, his body sailing over the four-foot-high shelves as easily as a football thrown by Billy or another of the players on the team. His scream stopped when he crashed into the cooler door five feet from where Billy was trying to pocket another beer. The door shattered. Unlike the front door of the Smart-Mart, the glass front of the refrigerated glass case was not shatter-proof. Thick blades of glass hacked into the clerk, cutting through muscle and sending a spray of blood from a hole in his flabby neck.

Courtney would have screamed if she could have. Billy screamed for her, his eyes wild and shocked and trying to look everywhere at once. Finally he looked toward the thing that had thrown the clerk in the first place.

Courtney looked, too, barely able to grasp what had just happened past the nauseating pain emanating from her left arm. It took a moment, really, because what she saw made no sense. There was a woman standing where the clerk had been. A pregnant woman. She didn't look right. It wasn't just the snarl on her face, or the fangs she bared as she growled. No, it was also the way her skin was shedding away like something peeling off a snake, and the bald patches where the hair had fallen from her head. And her skin tone, which was pasty white most places and gray in a few others.

She looked dead, give or take the way she was moving and screaming.

"Mommy's hungry, too!"

"What?" Courtney was trying to make sense of the words, but nothing much was getting past the pain.

"Ahhh. What the fuck?" Billy's voice. She looked toward him, rolling her eyes because moving her head hurt too much. The room seemed to jitter as she sought the comfort of his sweet face. He was so cute it hurt sometimes.

One breath. That was all it took. She exhaled and then sucked in a deep breath. And by the time her lungs had filled—was she going to scream? She thought that yes, maybe she was—the pregnant dead woman was standing in front of Billy. Her hand lashed out and grabbed Billy by his face, his perfect, sweet, kissable face, and her nails ripped into his cheeks and drew hard lines of blood as they sank deep past skin and peeled him down to the bone.

Billy tried to make a noise, but before a sound could come from his ruined mouth, the woman bit him in his throat and sucked violently at the wound she'd caused. There was no passion, no affection in the act; there was merely violent, savage biting. Billy thrashed and his hands lashed out, slamming against the woman's head and face and shoulders, but nothing he did made a difference. She sucked noisily at his neck and grunted, moaned as she drank his blood.

The word came easily enough. She'd lived in Black Stone Bay for her entire life, and though she'd never seen them before, she'd heard the stories that all the other kids heard after Halloween, a few years back. Vampire. The full potency of the word was still rocking into her brain, cutting through the pain and driving for her sense of self-preservation, when the woman threw Billy aside. Billy, who smelled so sexy, who had a million dimples when he smiled, who felt so damned good when he was holding her.

Billy, who collapsed on the ground and stared at the ceiling tiles without seeing a damned thing.

Oh yes, Courtney was going to scream.

The clerk beat her to it. He let out a girly shriek as the pregnant woman grabbed him and snarled in his face, her cheeks and chin covered in blood, her lips peeled back from teeth that shouldn't have fit in her mouth. He tried to fight, too, and she held him easily, tearing and biting and clawing at him with her hands, drawing lines of blood from him with brutal ease.

She made him suffer. That was all there was to it. Even through the shock that was trying to pull her away from the world, Courtney knew the woman deliberately made the clerk hurt as she killed him, fed on him.

And then she threw him again, hurled him across the store a second time, launching him through one of the unbroken plate-glass windows and looking after him as he rolled and bounced and flopped to a stop in the parking lot, right next to Billy's Kia.

The scream didn't get out of Courtney's mouth, so she blew out a deep gust of breath and sucked in again, ready to cut loose for all she was worth. Oh, my, yes, it was screaming time. No time like the present.

And then she stopped again as she looked at the woman turning to face her. She could see the changes as they took place. The blond lady's skin took on color, grew tinged with healthier tones, and the peeling flesh sank into her, merged with the skin beneath. Hell, her hair grew back right before Courtney's eyes.

And the woman looked at her with blue eyes that seemed to sparkle. Her face was so pretty, her very essence was vital. Courtney couldn't look away.

"I know you liked him, but I was doing you a favor." The woman walked closer and Courtney forgot about the pain in her shoulder as she formed a weak smile. It was just a misunderstanding, really. The lady hadn't meant to hurt anyone, that was obvious. "A guy like him? He'd just use you and throw you away. You don't know, but I do. I was married to one just like him. I'm saving you from that."

Courtney was vaguely aware of the explosive pain that ripped into her as she pushed to her knees and then stood up. Her left arm hung uselessly, but it was all right. None of that really mattered, not when the pregnant woman was looking at her and smiling so sweetly. Had a woman ever looked more amazing? What they said about pregnancy was true in this case. She positively glowed.

Courtney tried to speak, but her mouth didn't seem to want to work. The blond lady's fingers pushed Courtney's hair from her face, and she couldn't help blushing a bit, as she was unused to having a woman look at her with such intensity.

And the lady leaned forward and Courtney felt her lips part. It was crazy, but if the woman wanted to kiss her, she knew she'd let her. Did that make her a lesbian? She didn't know. Didn't care, not as long as it was the woman in front of her.

"I'm sorry. He's still hungry."

Courtney shook her head. "No, 'sokay. Baby's gotta eat."

"Exactly. And he's so hungry, all the time." It made perfect sense, of course. So Courtney bared her throat and sighed as the woman's lips touched her skin. She didn't even scream as the teeth punched through her skin; Courtney merely closed her eyes and drifted into a contented sleep.

***

"I'm not saying they were *actually* fired from a catapult, Richie, I'm just saying it looks like they could have been." Danny Holdstedter shrugged as he looked over the crime scene. In his defense, his theory was as sound as anyone else's. That didn't make Boyd any happier about it.

The Smart-Mart looked like a war zone, complete with shattered glass, broken bottles, blood, and bodies. Richard Boyd chewed on the end of his unlit cigar and scowled. He'd liked his world better when he was just in charge of Missing Persons. Of course he'd said the same thing about Vice when he was over in Missing Persons and he'd always hated working Vice.

"You know what the problem here is, Danny?"

"What?" Danforth Edward Holdstedter looked like a model. He was tall, muscular, blond, and handsome. Even his dimples had dimples when he smiled, and most every woman and a few men wanted to sleep with him. The fact that he reeked of old money didn't hurt either. To Boyd he was just Danny or Holdstedter and while there was some serious truth to the notion that he wanted to do bad things to his partner's sister, the man did nothing at all to Boyd's libido.

"You can't get a catapult through the door, or even through the broken window there. You'd have to fire the victims from inside to get that sort of clearance and it just wouldn't work." Most people listening would have thought they were serious. That was one of the reasons the police captain had moved them to Homicide. There were less people to listen to their banter when the crime-scene tape blocked off easy access. The other reason was that they were very good at solving crimes.

"You always have to punch holes in my theories. Always. Do I go messing with your theories?"

"My theories have some connection to reality." Boyd looked down at the clerk's body where it rested in the parking lot. He'd been wrecked. His face was destroyed, his body was broken, and his head had almost been torn from his body. His was the only body they could look at clearly, because the county coroner hadn't shown up yet to declare the victims dead. Like there was any fucking doubt.

"So, if I were to accidentally move the body, you think the captain would be pissed?"

"Was she pissed off the last time?"

"Well, but you have an in with her. She wants to suck face with you, Richie." Behind him Tom Burton, a uniformed officer who had been on the force long enough to know the history between the detective and the captain, coughed into his hand to hide his muffled laughter. Boyd shot a glare at him that would have melted steel, which just made the man smile a bit broader.

"Swear to God, Danny, you start that shit again, I'm gonna cut your balls off." Burton let out a full-scale laugh and actually slapped his hands against his thighs. None of the other uniforms were close enough to hear. Captain Nancy Whalen was a damned good cop. Before her promotion she'd been in charge of Homicide. These days she was in charge of the precinct, and as much as it annoyed Boyd, there were plenty of people on the force who knew that he had the hots for the woman, and at least as many who swore that she felt the same way about him. She was short, mean, smart, and sarcastic and had a body that distracted him from thinking clearly. It was an extremely annoying situation for Boyd. Whether or not he wanted her, or she wanted him, there was a serious problem with that notion. She was married. That was all he needed to know.

Still, Danny poked at that sore spot every chance he got, knowing Boyd would never actually do anything about it.

Danny looked his way, eyes too wide with false innocence. "What? I'm just saying that you're her favorite detective."

Instead of answering, Boyd crouched closer to the body of the clerk. The man looked familiar, but he couldn't come up with a name. This was the part of town he seldom bothered with, and the man he was looking at was at least fifteen years younger than he was. "This guy look familiar?"

Danny walked over and loomed above him. It wasn't hard. Danny was a giant at six-four. He was taller, broader, sleeker, and richer than Boyd. He had more hair, fewer wrinkles, and was younger, too. His suit was probably worth a month's salary, which was a little irksome, but other than that, the rest could be forgiven. Danny squinted for a moment and nodded his head. "Ryan Colquitt. Picked him up for drugs once and buying hookers three times." Danny shrugged. "Seemed like a nice guy other than that."

"Yeah." Boyd rolled his cigar around and thought hard. "Look at his neck."

Danny crouched in one smooth motion, as opposed to Boyd's grunts and groans and popping joints as he'd lowered himself down. "You gonna say it?"

Boyd pulled the pen from his coat pocket and came dangerously close to touching the ruined flesh. He traced the rough texture of the wounds with the tip. "No. Neither are you. But we're gonna look at the other two bodies before we leave here." His eyes flickered over to where Burton was very studiously not looking back in his direction. That was good. Some things weren't discussed in public. Not ever. Burton had survived that night, too. He hadn't been there to see how things ended with the cause of the problems, but he knew what went down as well as anyone else did.

Damned if the wounds didn't look a little too much like someone had been biting all hell out of Ryan Colquitt's neck.

Danny didn't have any smartassed comebacks. That was okay. Neither did Boyd.

Danny stood up and stepped back. "Where the fuck is the coroner?"

"He'll get here."

Danny nodded. "Good. I want a closer look." He pulled out his digital camera and snapped pictures of the wounds that could be seen. Boyd walked carefully around the closed convenience store, his eyes looking again at the trail of destruction that surrounded each of the victims. He would have preferred the idea of a catapult to the thought that a vampire had come back to town and started feeding.

Catapults were easier to destroy.

***

Some stains are harder to remove than others. You can scrub them, whitewash them, sand the spot repeatedly, but some stains never seem to go away. Mary Margaret Preston understood that notion. She stared out the window of her house on the Cliff Walk and looked at the ocean where it continuously pushed against the black rock and tried to come closer to where she waited. Ben was in the next room, and the rhythmic sound of his fingers typing away on the keyboard was almost as constant as the surf's efforts.

Ben knew her as Maggie. These days he was one of the only ones who called her that. Most people called her Ms. Preston, with just a small edge of worry in their voices. That was fair. She seldom met anyone these days who didn't work for her, and even when she did, she had a certain presence about her that convinced most people to be on their best behavior. Ben said it was the mark of the predator with an extra flair of drama that almost always put a smile on her face. Five years together and he could still make her smile. How amazing was that?

She closed her eyes for a moment and simply listened. Down the street Mike Carver was working on his '57 Ford Fairlane, a juggernaut of a car that he'd decided to restore around the same time he retired from the bank. He had preposterous amounts of money and could have easily hired a dozen mechanics to do the work, but that wasn't the point. He wanted to get his hands dirty, wanted to remember what his life had been like before he sat at a desk and then spent his years acquiring money and power. She could understand that.

Two houses down from him, she could hear Marley Thompson giggling with a few of her friends. They were having a tea party along with their mothers, basking in the sunlight and laughing with the sort of abandon that fades with childhood. It was Marley's sixth birthday, and the notion of dressing up in floppy hats, sipping tea, and eating tiny cakes had her and all of her little friends laughing. She envied them that. Part of her wished she could be a part of that world, even knowing full well that she would never be accepted into their social gathering.

Best not to think about that, wasn't it? But that was the problem with stains. They never really go away.

The Hendersons were walking slowly along the view afforded by the cliffs, enjoying each other's company and savoring the weather that hadn't yet become too bitter cold for their comfort. They'd be heading for Florida soon, as they did every year before the end of October. They always left before November showed its face. Every year for the last five, just in case.

She couldn't hear them, of course, but she could imagine the sounds of the planning committee working out the details of the Phi Kappa Gamma memorial services. Five years and there was every reason to believe the damned celebration would go on forever. There would be speeches, tears, lamentations about how the wonderful boys had been killed, had burned in tragedy before their lives could really start. Maggie knew better. They hadn't burned. The building had burned. They boys had been taken away before their house blazed down into cinders. Of course before that happened, she'd killed every last one of them. Five years and her full lips still curled into a sneer of contempt. She was supposed to feel guilty about it, she guessed. And there was a part of her that occasionally felt pangs of conscience at their deaths, but the rage over what they'd planned to do to her normally crushed that nonsense before it got out of hand.

Deep inside her, the memories stirred and the first distant flares of discomfort started. She'd have to eat soon.

Ben's chair rolled softly away from his computer and she heard him sigh as he stood up. His work for the day was done. The sneer on her face smoothed away and was replaced by a small smile as he started walking toward her. She didn't have to see him to know that he was looking her over from head to toe. She could hear his pulse increase just a little at the thought of touching her, and as he moved closer still, she reached back with her hand, groping blindly for his. His fingers entwined with hers, and he moved closer behind her until she could feel his lean form pressing to her back.

"You okay?" His voice was soft. Five years together and he always sounded like he was in awe of her. Maybe he was. She could have reached into his mind and taken the information, but she preferred to simply guess.

Maggie pushed back against him, and his arms moved, hugging her closer still even as he held her hands within his. She let herself relax against his body and felt him respond. Five years and he still hardened at her touch, but as always he didn't pursue the matter. For Ben it was just his body responding to her presence, and his self-control was as solid as ever. He wouldn't push the issue. There was too much history for her, too many things she'd done in the past. He never made the first move, but waited for her. Most times that pleased her, but now and then she wished he'd show a little initiative.

Benjamin Kirby loved her. That she knew. He'd said it more than a few times and shown her more times than she could count easily. He'd saved her life both figuratively and literally and she loved him back. At least she thought she did. Her teeth worried at her lower lip for a moment at that notion.

"You okay?" Ben repeated himself, his voice barely above a whisper. He always spoke softly when they were alone, knowing how sensitive her hearing was.

"Yeah." She made her voice sound properly pleased. She was really a very good actress. "I'm fine. How about you?"

"Done for the day. Your fashions are selling very well, Ms. Preston." He got bold and nuzzled his lips against the dark curls of her hair, breathing against the lobe of her ear.

She rewarded his bravery by pushing back against him, slowly, steadily, and heard his sharp intake of breath, felt his growing excitement. Rather than merely tease, she pushed harder still, urging him on. Ben didn't quite growl, but it was close. His hands released hers, moved to her sides, held her softly against him, and then slowly began to explore the shape of her, the curves that he already knew better than any man ever had.

She had never been with any man for five years. Most men couldn't afford her rates and those that could normally paid by the hour or the night. Ben did not pay. She was his and he was hers. She knew that as surely as she knew her name. There had been a time when Maggie sold her sexual favors and was paid very well. That was long past. Ben had taken care of her financial needs as surely as he watched over her.

His breaths washed over her neck, his lips followed, kissing, tasting her skin. His heart pounded, his blood flowed, the scent of his arousal was the finest perfume.

Maggie turned and kissed his mouth urgently, her hands moving, peeling at his clothes, stripping him down, ignoring the fact that someone walking past might get to see more than they should if they bothered to look through the windows.

"Uhnn. Maggie…." His voice shivered. Five years and she still made him weak with the promise of the pleasures she offered. He would die for her. He would kill for her. She knew that. Her hands urged him to stand still, and her mouth began the slow, pleasant task of exploring his body.

For five years he'd made working out a part of his regular life, and while he was slim, his body was muscled and a delight. Her hands caressed, her mouth tasted, and Ben shuddered and moaned a symphony for her.

Just for her. He loved her.

And she loved him. At least she thought she did. Really, she had nothing to compare the feelings to. At the very least, she needed him as much as he needed her.

"I love you, Maggie." His voice broke as he made his confession.

For a moment she rested her forehead against his abdomen and looked down at the plush rug beneath his feet. "I love you, too, Ben."

The words didn't quite feel like a lie.

***

Jason Soulis knew the moment that everything changed in Black Stone Bay. He knew because he had sentries posted, as it were, and because he could feel what was happening with all of the offspring from his experiments.

First, he knew that Maggie was feeling doubt again. She often felt doubt about herself, about her existence and whether what she'd become was a good thing or a bad thing. He found that amusing and depressing both. Amusing, because in the end it didn't matter, she was what he had made her, and only death would change that. And death did not come easily to one of their kind. Depressing because he'd expected better from her. He had given her a great gift and she was still wondering what to do with it instead of enjoying it.

And really, that was probably the fault of her pet boy, Benjamin. He did not like the boy and never had, but she had to make her own mistakes in the world and he had to let her make them if she was ever going to grow into what she had the potential to be. Keeping a pet human was never wise. They started expecting things, making demands, and then you had to get rid of them and find replacements. It was rather like taking down a rabid dog, he supposed. You felt bad for it, but it was a necessity.

Second, he knew that the girl was coming back to town to deliver her child. He'd made sure she was safe for as long as it took to let the creature come to term, and now he was going to see firsthand what happened to the progeny of a vampire. He'd heard of such things, of course, but never seen one up close. This would prove interesting. He did love his experiments.

Jason considered these things while he packed, carefully folding the clothes he planned to take with him and ignoring the girl that was currently sleeping in his bed. Amber, that was the name. A pretty piece of fluff, but little more than that. She had all the intellectual might of a carrot, and about as much personality. Still, she satisfied certain urges.

Amber rolled over and mumbled in her sleep. He stared at her face for a moment, finding flaws that he'd deliberately overlooked before. She was sufficient for his needs, yes, but only barely.

The house he was currently staying in was on the West Coast, in Oregon. A beautiful location. A boring place, to be sure, but with plenty of acreage to hide an occasional body. The crows would make sure work of the meat and hide the bones for him.

Jason stopped packing long enough to break Amber's neck and then to throw her body out the window of the master bedroom. The crows were already heading for their latest meal by the time she hit the rocks below.

It was the last of the experiments left that he was most interested in. Jason knew that the detectives had blocked off the only way out of the underwater caves where he'd stashed most of the bodies of the people he'd fed on in Black Stone Bay. In due time they'd changed, risen from the dead and become vampires, as they all did if they were not taken care of. Leave a corpse in a clearing, let the sunlight take care of the second death, and all was well. Remove the head from the corpse, or tear out the heart, and the same end result. But leave the corpses alone and within a few days they rose, hungry and desperate to feed.

Even then, most vampires didn't last long. They lacked the necessary cognitive skills. They might understand that the sun burned them, but they'd think about the pain and not how to escape it. They came back from the dead with damaged minds. That damage eventually healed, true enough, but only if they survived long enough. Most did not.

Not until Jason decided to experiment. The vampires were left in the darkness, locked in a cave under the water's edge and imprisoned there for five years. They were, for lack of a better term, germs on a perfect Petri dish. He left them to grow and fester as they would, and now his patience was being rewarded.

He closed the last suitcase and smiled to himself. This should be delightful. This would justify his invested time and efforts.

"I have no idea what you will be, my friend," Jason spoke to the air, knowing full well that no one save his crows were close enough to hear him. "But I suspect you will be interesting at the very least."

He carried the bags down the stairs to the main foyer. The trip to the airport would be a simple one, and he felt no need to call a limo service.

Outside, the crows hid the remains of his latest paramour, feeding quickly, tearing away gobbets of meat and squabbling over who would get the best parts. They were his special friends, and he was glad to keep them well fed. Perhaps he'd convince Maggie to try her luck with animal servants. They were far less petty than humans.

CHAPTER TWO

What's in a name?

It didn't know anymore. It only knew hunger. It had been hungry for so long that the very concept and word had become a part of its identity.

The ground was not moving, not sliding as it had thought. No, the ground stayed where it was, but it was still moving forward, going somewhere after so long in the darkness. It wanted to scream, to push, to fight for every inch, but instead made itself be calm. Once upon a time it had been a patient or it had been patient. The words, the concepts, they were foreign these days.

As it pushed and slowly rose, it did its best to remember. There were important things that it needed to know, to understand. The desire was more than merely curiosity; there was a need to puzzle out the past, because that past would be important to the future. At least it thought it would be.

Frustration burbled through the thoughts of the creature as it struggled ever so slowly through the darkness and resistance. The darkness had always seemed so solid before, but now it could move through the hard black, could push and swim and rise as long as it was careful. When it tried too hard the resistance came back and so it made sure to relax, even though it wanted nothing more than to fight through.

Long claws cut at the darkness and then broke past the darkness into something different. The tension that had held it prisoner for so long was suddenly gone. For a moment it thrashed, tried to push harder, and then remembered it had to be calm, to remain patient. It pushed again, and the pressure left its face, its neck, its shoulders.

Air. It felt air. Had it needed to breathe, it would surely have gasped at the notion. Eyes that had not seen anything but darkness for a very long time were assaulted by colors, images; an information overload that almost resulted in panic. Calm. It had to stay calm. It squinted until most of the light was gone, and then it felt a new sensation, the darkness slid upward, wrapped it in a shroud of pleasant calm until it could see without being overwhelmed.

It looked around, slowly absorbed the sights that surrounded it, assessed them and tried to remember the symbols, the words that made sense of what it experienced.

It kept rising, pushing through the black granite of the cliffs, puzzled by the notion. Stone was impenetrable. It had been buried in stone. The darkness was the rock, which even now it rose through. Impossible? Apparently not. There were houses nearby, and it knew the houses, knew the location.

Black Stone Bay. Yes. That was the place. The Cliff Walk, which it had roamed for years before the darkness took it. Buried alive? Was that possible?

No. It had died. It knew that. It remembered the teeth, the biting, the pain heaped upon pain, the heartbreak, the suffering. None of that mattered. All of that was inconsequential when compared with the endless hunger that had been the only companion to the darkness over the years.

There was something else that was more important, so much more significant, and so it rose the rest of the way from the hard ground, and set its…the word was missing….foot…its foot upon the lush lawn that started where the black granite ended. Joints protested after so long remaining still, muscles that had barely moved in months groaned their discomfort, and it matched the sounds, aching everywhere. It fell forward, caught itself on hands and knees, and shivered, twitched, and finally rose back to its feet. Crawling had been the only way to move for so long that walking was nearly alien. Still it had to try. It had to learn all over again. Concentration was key. Small steps. It walked, slowly at first as the notion was almost completely unfamiliar after so long in the darkness, bound by the stone and shadow and the endless pulsing of the waves that even now crashed against the cliffs.

Words and symbols, images and memories tried to flood its mind, but as with the steady climb through the hard earth, it made the concepts and recollections come back slowly. There would be time. Surely there would be time.

First it would go back. Back. Where family waited. Family. The thought would have made its heart race, had it had a pulse.

The wind whistled and shrieked. Being so long in darkness, lost to almost every sensation, had made it far too sensitive to everything; like the teeth of a man chewing on tin foil and ice, everything was painful.

Unsure of how to handle the assault, it collapsed in on itself. Moaning in agony at every small impact. Pale hands covered ears that felt wrong, obscured a face that wasn't the same as it had been back before the great darkness. The memories were sporadic, but the features it remembered were softer, different. That was a niggling concern, however, and not as important as the pain that cut into its mind. The pale skin of its hands shivered — no, that wasn't right. The flesh twisted, changed as it looked on. The same darkness that had covered its face spread across its body, across its arms, muffling the noise, the pain, until they were tolerable.

It was enough. The silence was not complete, but the wind no longer roared, and the surf merely whispered. It felt the darkness around its body taken by the air, pulled and snapped. It held its arms out, looked at the protective cover that surrounded it. The breeze billowed out its protective veil like a cape and it smiled at the notion. Were the breeze any stronger it might have taken flight. What a delicious thought!

Less overwhelmed, though hardly at complete ease, it moved again, heading for…Home? Was that the place? Possibly. Yes. Home. Where the heart is. Where they have to take you back. Those concepts overlapped like the dark weave of the shroud that grew from its skin and soothed its senses.

Home. It was time to go home.

But first it had to feed. The hunger came back with a screaming vengeance and it sniffed the air hoping for the scent of food.

***

Late again. Melinda was going to kill him. Ron Caulfield hated being late, but he almost always managed to remain in that state, and his girlfriend was getting a little tired of it. Tonight they had plans to get together for dinner with Victor and Sarah, two of Mel's friends, and if they were more than ten minutes late, he'd be hearing about it for months.

Not this time. He gunned the engine a bit and looked around, making sure there weren't any squad cars hiding in the usual spots. They'd been cracking down again, because now that football season was in full swing, a lot of the high school crowd was driving like they wanted to get busted, and the cops were happy to accommodate.

The cell phone played a snippet of the song "Baby Love," the ringtone he'd selected exclusively for Mel, and he reached for the device, taking his eyes from the road for a moment.

Just long enough, really.

Ron saw the black shape from the corner of his eye. It was long and angular, twisted into an uncomfortable stance as it turned its head toward him and bared too many teeth in an otherwise obscured face. He tensed for impact and slammed on the brakes even as his fingers wrapped around the phone. The impact rattled the car, and the deep thump of the vehicle hitting the black thing echoed to his ears with an unsettling finality.

Ron dropped the phone. "Oh, fuck! Shit! No!" A thousand notions fought for dominance: *I've just killed a man (surely it was a man, it was too big for anything else); I've just totaled the damned car and I can't afford higher rates; I'm going to be sooo late!* They all fought for his attention. He looked down: the car was damaged, he knew that, but it didn't look too bad. On the other hand there was someone pinned under him and he had to check, had to make sure — please God! — that the person he'd hit was okay. Around the same time, the adrenaline kicked in and he gasped, shivered as the fight-or-flight desire swam through him.

He couldn't run. He had to call for help. Ron reached for the cell again and saw the picture of Mel wearing her oversized novelty sunglasses and blowing a kiss looking back at him. Somehow he'd managed to answer her call when the impact happened.

Melinda's voice cut the air, "Ron? Are you okay? What's wrong? What happened?"

"Mel, baby. I think I just hit someone. I have to call the police." His voice sounded wrong. His lips felt numb, and his heart was hammering away in his chest, pounding too hard, too fast.

"Wait, what? You hit someone? Why are you fighting?" Her voice went up half an octave and took on that nagging note he hated so much. He didn't have time to bitch about it though.

"Fighting? No. I think I hit someone with the car. I have to go." He was reaching for the door when the thump came from beneath him.

"Ohmigawd, are you okay?" Her voice was even higher now, more shrill, but the concern for him took away a lot of the irritation.

"I'm okay, but I can't see the guy I hit." He pushed the door open and even as he did, the car shifted under him and the door promptly slammed itself shut. Ron strained and pushed the door open again, tried to step out and was stopped by the seat belt. He'd never unfastened the stupid thing. He reached for the release and almost dropped the phone, had to scramble to keep it.

"Ron, you have to call the police!"

"I can't call the police, Mel! You're on the line!" That tone in his voice? It was going to cost him. He knew that, but couldn't stop it from coming out of his mouth. He loved Mel, but sometimes she was so damned clueless.

Mel didn't respond. Instead she killed the call on her end. He stared at the phone for a few seconds while he contemplated how badly she was going to tear into him. No time. He had to check on whoever he'd hit.

The sounds coming from below him didn't sound promising: there was a hissing noise—radiator?—and then a loud crunch that sounded expensive as all hell. Yes, he was worried about whoever he hit, but what the hell was happening to his engine? BMWs were great cars, but not exactly cheap to get repaired. Guilt caught him under the chin. *What if someone's dying under the fucking car? What does the cost of repairing the damned thing matter?*

He tried pushing the door open again, caught himself on the seat belt again. "Come on already!" His anger flared and he fought with the seat belt release and below him something else crunched, the vibrations running through the soles of his feet and halfway up his calves. What the hell was going on? Was the engine block falling out?

The seat belt finally popped free and he started to stand when the floorboard at his feet exploded. Ron had enough time to look down at the pale things sliding through the ruptured metal and carpeting before long fingers grabbed his ankles. Thick, dark nails cut through the denim of his jeans, punched past the socks on his lower legs, and drove hard into his skin and, just that quickly, all of his disjointed thoughts clarified. He wasn't worried about the man he'd hit, or about the car, or even about how pissed Mel was going to be if he didn't find the right way to apologize for his attitude. Instead he focused solely on the pain that rode up his legs like fire. "Ahhh?! What the fuck?"

The hissing sound came to him again even as the hands (long, wicked fingers, too long and too pale, and so unbelievably strong) clawed savagely at him, pulling meat and tendons away from bone with unsettling ease. The adrenaline in his system might have let him overlook a minor boo-boo or two, but it had no impact at all on the screaming assault on his pain receptors that came with the violent attack.

Ron stopped trying to think and focused on getting away. He kicked with his legs, whimpering at the pain every movement caused, and tried to lever his body out of the car, pushing against the steering wheel — and now the fucking horn was screaming at him, just to add to the fun — pulling at the open door jamb. He didn't make it far. The hands that held his legs ruptured more of the flooring, and he saw the shape of a face, a body as whatever it was he'd hit forced its way into the car from below.

The hands were deathly pale, but the rest of it was hidden, wrapped in a dark cloak. All except for the eyes which glittered brightly and the mouth, the horrid mouth, filled with too many bloodstained teeth.

The claws and fingers hurt.

The teeth were so much worse. They barely took the time to chew before they swallowed meat and bone alike.

Ron managed to scream for almost two minutes before he died.

***

"Okay, seriously?" Danny was staring at the ruined floorboards and the trails of blood that covered almost half of the car's interior. Antifreeze, brake fluid, and motor oil were mingling under the vehicle and spreading slowly across the street and down to the next gutter. They mingled with an unsettling amount of blood. Pieces of the car's undercarriage were scattered here and there as well, torn and twisted into so much confetti. Whatever the car had hit was nowhere to be seen.

Boyd crossed his arms and shrugged. "I'm thinking maybe he hit the world's meanest Rottweiler or something."

Danny shook his head and moved in a slow circle around the car. Boyd had already done that a few times, but he didn't mind letting his partner look a second time. Two sets of eyes were always better than one, especially if the second set belonged to Danny Holdstedter.

"Coroner already take the body?" Danny was frowning.

"No body to take. What you're seeing is exactly the way it looked when I got here."

"I'm hearing that tone, Richie."

"What tone?"

"The one that says you got all lonely and shit without me." Danny's voice was teasing.

"More like I got tired of waiting for you to show the fuck up, asshole."

Boyd was teasing too, but most strangers would have thought he was serious. Boyd didn't look like a practical joker, and his voice only had one tone: gruff.

Danny dropped down on his palms in a flawless execution of a push-up. Not surprising. Boyd figured his partner probably did a hundred or more push-ups a day. He was disgustingly physical that way. The end result was that women still tended to glue their eyes to his body and start imagining what he'd be like in bed.

"Stop looking at my butt, Richie. You know it makes me uncomfortable."

"You're the one makes it flex like that, Danny. I just sit back and watch."

"I'm telling Nancy on you."

"Swear to God, I'm gonna bust your fucken knees for that one." Boyd pulled out a cigar and prepped it for smoking. Maybe he'd leave his partner's knees and just burn the side of his face.

"What? Sexual harassment is a serious offense, Richie. I have to tell the captain if I feel I'm being harassed by my senior partner, don't I?" As he spoke Danny held out a hand and snapped his fingers. Boyd slipped a surgical glove over his partner's fingers. "You do that like a pro, Richie. You put a lot of condoms on? Is that how you get all the practice in?"

Boyd shook his head. It had been a while and Danny knew it. "I keep hoping you'll take the hint, Danny."

"I don't need condoms, Richie. All the girls I'm with are as pure as the driven snow."

"You're gonna have a kid that way."

Danny didn't answer for a moment; he was too busy straining to reach something under the car. "No kids for me. I'm saving all my sperm for the right girl." That was a lie if ever he'd heard one. Boyd knew too many of the women his partner had slept with.

"What? You hold it in?"

"It's a special technique. Your mom taught me how." Danny climbed up without his usual grace, but there was a smile on his face as he held up a thick, black strand of cloth. "Look, Richie. I got a clue, just like you always said I should."

"Yeah? Wanna get a few hundred more?" He put away his cigar, as yet unlit, and pulled out a couple of gloves. Best not to taint whatever evidence they could find.

Danny held the stuff for him to see, a thick, coarse fabric, like handwoven linen. Boyd gripped one edge of the stuff and spread it along his opened hand. It looked…wrong. That was the only way he could put it. A moment later the stuff was tagged and in an evidence bag.

"You should check the bottom of this car, Richie. It looks like a badger was trying to chew it apart. Only, you know, a really big badger, with a chainsaw."

Boyd shook his head. "Naw. See, you come from a rich family, Danny. I come from a blue-collar family. What that means is that I can look at you crawling around in all that shit on the road in your six-hundred-dollar suit and I know it barely bothers you to ruin it. No dry cleaner on the planet is fixing that thing. Me? My fifty-dollar Goodwill suit is still clean and I have the information I need without having to ruin it."

"You have a good point there." Danny looked down at his suit and sighed. "Of course, I still have four times the suits you do, and losing this one doesn't hurt my wallet." He smiled brightly as he examined the mix of fluids soaking into the fabric of his jacket.

"I've always admired your optimism, Danny."

"Yeah, well, it comes easily. You know why?"

"No. Why?"

"Because I'm fuckin' rich, and you're not." He dug in his pocket for his digital camera and when he had it, he took a picture of the glower on Boyd's face. "Also, I'm a lot better looking. No offense, Richie."

"None taken, douche bag."

They'd have probably continued on that way, but the wrecker came to take away their new toy. They watched while the ruined car was hoisted into place, and Boyd took the time to look at the underside of the vehicle while it was lifted, successfully avoiding ruining his suit, which had actually cost him substantially more than fifty dollars, but still managed to fit like it was a cast-off. Something about his shape never seemed to fit the jackets he liked.

When the car was gone, Holdstedter took pictures of the fluids cast across the ground and shook his head. When he spoke again, he was far more serious. "I don't like this, Richie. This is starting to feel like it belongs in the Red Lady File."

The Red Lady File. It was their own code for the impossible. They'd witnessed a few things in the past, including a very buxom woman soaked in blood who moved at impossible speeds and did horrific damage to a pimp who richly deserved it. There were things that happened that couldn't be explained easily, but that still had to be handled. Red Lady stuff.

Boyd shrugged and pulled back out his cigar. He took the time to light it before he answered. "Been five years without that shit, Danny. I don't even like to think about it, but I'm gonna have to agree with you."

"The ones yesterday. They were bit. Are we doing anything about that?" Danny's voice was very soft.

"Yeah. We are. Just not quite yet."

Danny put his camera away and looked around the area. A small group from the sanitation department was waiting to wash the street clean of any potential health hazards. Boyd nodded for them to come over and do their stuff, and then he headed for the Cliff Walk.

It was October, but the lawns were still immaculate. Gardeners who probably made more than he did in a year were busy around the Cliff Walk. They sculpted hedges, trimmed trees, maintained flawless lawns until the last moment, until the snows came and covered over their work areas in blankets of white. Then they decorated for Christmas or found other ways to keep themselves occupied. So of course the lawns were perfect.

Except that the grass ahead of him looked wrong enough to make him stop and raise a hand to halt his partner, who he knew was already following him.

They moved forward together, looking at the grass where it had withered away to gray, lifeless blades in a pattern. Danny pulled his camera back out and took pictures, moving slowly, carefully, taking images of the individual spots and several of the entire length of the pattern together.

"Dead grass normally goes brown, doesn't it, Richie?"

"Or yellow. Especially this stuff." He waved at the grass, indicating with his gesture what was already obvious to Danny. The grass was a hybrid, bred for the sole purpose of looking good and staying green for as long as the elements permitted. The damned stuff was hardy and cost a fortune. Holdstedter's entire front lawn was coated with the stuff.

"Shit ain't cheap, Richie."

The pattern told a story, but it wasn't a story that made any sense. There was a large patch of dead grass not far from the edge of the cliff, and from that point on the markings were distinctive enough to let them count the long shape of each foot, even the number of toes on each footprint. Near the larger spot was a different marking. It had four fingers and a thumb.

"So, something that can kill grass with a touch fell down here, got up over here and walked over to the road." Danny's voice stayed low and soft. "And it got into the road right near where somebody in a car got into a wreck with something that tore up the car and took the driver away."

"Yeah, it looks that way."

"Know what I like best about this, Richie?"

Boyd looked over at Danny. The man was looking back with a shit-eating grin on his face. "No. What?"

"It's your turn to do all the paperwork."

Boyd sighed. Sometimes Danny was a pain in his ass. On the other hand, at least he didn't need to buy a new suit.

***

She bit her hand to avoid screaming, tasting the black filth that passed for her blood these days as her teeth broke skin and sank deep. Loathing filled her, hatred for the thing that filled her belly and churned inside of her, struggling, moving, pushing at her insides and causing her wave after wave of pain and nausea.

It did not speak to her now, but struggled.

And there was nothing she could do about it. How the hell did any woman ever survive this nightmare?

Angie Freemont groaned and stopped chewing on her own limb as the pain faded away again. She looked at the wounds in her palm and winced.

This wasn't going to happen. It wasn't going to work. She needed to feed. She'd ruined three people just yesterday and it didn't matter in the least. Enough to sustain her with ease and it was gone, drawn into the child in her womb.

Impossible.

She rolled over onto her hands and knees, ignoring the pain that flared in her recently bitten palm. She had to feed now, before the pain started again. If she didn't give the damned thing what it wanted, it would tear its way free of her, and she knew she couldn't possibly survive that.

Five years of this, she'd gotten very good at surviving. It was what she did.

Her skin was breaking down again. She could see it happening. The soft flesh started flaking at first, and then it got worse. Decay.

She hated this part, maybe most of all. The pain was brief, because as the flesh rotted, the nerves died. She'd grow numb to almost everything but the hunger if she waited too long, and though she knew she'd never let it go that far, Angie wondered how it would feel to actually die. No. There was no part of her that wanted to succumb to that. Her momma didn't raise any kids that were quitters. Of course the old lady might have regretted that after she invited Angie into the house the last time. There was no regret over killing her parents. That was for human beings and she'd stopped being human a long time ago. These days she had memories and she had instincts and little room for anything else.

Intellectually she considered the idea of suicide. She thought from time to time about the moral implications of what she did to survive and the number of creatures she'd killed in the last five years. Emotionally there was nothing. She did what she had to do to survive, that was all. She had to take care of herself and she had to take care of her baby. That was the imperative that drove her on.

She didn't kill every day. If she had they would have found her by now. They'd have connected the dots and realized that there was a predator among them. She remembered what had happened in Black Stone Bay when she was changed. There were dozens, maybe hundreds of vampires and they'd been killed off quickly, either by humans or by their own stupidity. She was lucky. Instinct had saved her from most of the mistakes that the others made. So instead of glutting herself, she moved from place to place and took only what she needed, careful to kill in the hours before dawn and to leave her victims out in areas where the sunlight would take care of the evidence.

Sunlight. That had been an unpleasant lesson to learn. A few seconds of direct sunlight and the body died for real. A few hours of indirect sunlight and the same thing happened. Lessons learned the hard way were seldom easily forgotten. The flesh healed eventually, and took all evidence of what had happened along with it, just so long as there was enough blood. If there wasn't enough blood, the flesh decayed and stayed that way. Curiosity had made her leave one of her victims in the sunlight as the dawn came. When she rose for the evening the body had still been there, but looked as if it had been rotting for a week.

Blood was everything. She could eat other foods until she turned blue in the face, but they did nothing. She wasn't even sure they digested inside of her, so much as rotted away. Whatever the case, food didn't taste like much of anything to her these days. Blood was the stuff that did the trick, but even that was just sustenance. If she was completely truthful, it was the baby inside her that took priority.

She shook the thoughts away. They were doing her no good. What mattered was the food. She had to feed the damned baby before the hunger grew too bad. Because she could feel something was different inside of her lately. What used to be enough food to hold her for a week or more was sometimes barely enough for a single night, and worse, there were the times when no matter how much she consumed the hunger only grew worse.

There was only one answer. The baby wanted to come out. It was done with her. It was done.

She accepted it. She didn't much care one way or the other aside from the fact that she would finally be free of the damned thing. *Liar! My baby! Mine! My little one!*

"Enough." She groaned as she crawled to the doorway of her storage shed. There wasn't much to see beyond the threshold and that suited her just fine. The small, corrugated steel room held the light at bay and also had a dozen old tarps crammed into the corner. It wasn't much of a room for the day but it kept the sun off her until the night came back.

The darkness outside was new, the sun only recently set, and she felt herself smile as she started moving. The yard she'd found to settle into was unmown, abandoned, exactly what she'd expected. The woods surrounded the house where she'd died, but Angie wasn't scared of the darkness or whatever animals might hide in the forest at the edge of town.

The slumbering thing that hid inside of her sighed and made mental noises of discomfort. Running always made the baby grumpy. How ludicrous did she look, she wondered, running through the woods with a ponderous belly swaying in front of her? Brian would have laughed at her.

Or just slept around behind her back again. He did that a lot, something she found out when she met the women he'd raped. She thought about her husband, about the women he'd terrorized, the lies he'd told her and finally she felt something other than hunger again.

She felt rage blossom in her chest and spread through her, a warmth that brought with it a modicum of comfort. And that comfort allowed her to move faster, to hunt faster.

And hunt she did, for she was so very hungry.

***

Depending on whom you talked to about it, the Allan Phillips Hartshorn Bayside Academy was either the best damned school known to man or just another failed attempt at being progressive. The academy sprawled across twelve acres of property, and came complete with stables, a small farm for the care and observation of farm animals, a complete dock with multiple rowboats and a few larger craft—all of which had been put away for the season already—and a total of three hundred and fifty students.

Here's what can be called fact: the kids who went there had a lot of fun for the most part, were stuck wearing uniforms to school every day, and by and large went on to excel in their educations. That last could be blamed on their early teachers, or on the fact that most of the students came from families with money who could afford the very finest tutors when things went wrong.

Most of the kids who were doing so well never had to resort to tutors. Lora Angela Dowling was a teacher at Hartshorn. To her students, she was Miss Lora. She never had any problem pointing out the lack of tutors. She was also one of the very first to state that she was proud of the work she did and the kids she taught.

Third graders, to Lora's way of thinking, were pretty darned cool kids to work with. They were like sponges waiting to absorb information, and she was among the first to give them enough knowledge to drown them, but she was also a firm believer in life preservers. She provided those too, in the form of an open policy regarding questions.

Lora also believed that one of the secrets to teaching kids was making sure they had fun. To that end, the kids were writing their own spooky stories to be read in front of the class. Mark and Tina were both looking dreadfully nervous about the idea of telling their stories in front of everyone, but she knew they'd do well enough.

The class was mostly quiet — as quiet as eight-year-olds can manage — when she looked outside and saw the insane swarm of birds flying overhead. They weren't migratory birds, and even if they had been they were heading in the wrong direction. She almost pointed them out to the kids, but then held her tongue. The last thing she wanted at that particular moment was all of the glorious silence being destroyed when it looked like her class was actually going to finish their stories on time.

A quick look told her most of the kids were engaged in their stories — Todd was drawing a picture, but she decided to pretend it pertained to his story for the moment and let him have his peace — and so she looked at the birds again. Crows. Lora found herself frowning at that notion. Crows.

There had been times in the past when crows seemed to become far too prevalent in Black Stone Bay. Most recently was a few years ago when everything went to shit and a lot of people "disappeared."

Her stomach got that nervous feeling, what her dad always called "butterflies," and she shook her head. There might be no correlation at all, but she wasn't willing to take that chance. She made a mental note to let Simon Bradford, the head of security, know that something felt wrong. Simon was big on trusting your instincts, and he'd take the warning with more than a grain of salt. That was one of the many reasons she liked the man. The biggest reason was probably that he was great with the kids.

Anyone that liked children and treated them well was okay in her book.

As she watched the crows, a stream of black birds broke away from the great flowing cloud of them and drifted lazily down toward the school, looking almost like a spiraling run of leaves falling from a black tree. The took their time but eventually drifted down until they were positioned on the west wing of the building, where they lined up like soldiers along the wall that faced her classroom.

Not a one of the birds made a noise, as if they were fully aware that the children shouldn't be distracted from their work. She didn't find their courtesy the least bit comforting.

***

Black Stone Bay was the sort of place people dreamed about moving to, with pristine streets, well-groomed lawns, and a population that was used to the finer things in life. The citizens paid handsomely for the privilege of living there, though some paid with more than cash.

The New Harbor docks were loaded with boats, most of which were in the process of being prepared for the winter. A few were still active, the occasional yacht or, more often, a fishing vessel, but by and large it was time to call it a season and dry-dock the fleet, so to speak. The weather was already getting cold earlier than it had for the last few years, and very few of the people who'd truly earned their sea legs were expecting pleasant weather for the winter.

Frank Preston knew his way around the docks better than most, which was hardly surprising as he was the Harbor Master. He checked the area over regularly, because his livelihood depended on it. He had no delusions about his position in Black Stone Bay; he was replaceable. He kept his job exactly as long as the people who paid his salary were pleased with his performance, and for that reason alone he made good and damned sure that everything was kept properly.

So of course he noticed the smell before anyone else. He'd served in both the Navy and the Coast Guard in his time and during the quarter century of military service he'd learned a few important facts, like what death smells like. One whiff was enough to have him calling on Dave Burke to come investigate the situation. Dave didn't mind. If there were strange things to investigate — and there were almost always oddities coming into the area via the ocean's waters — Dave was the one who got to look into them. Frank's health didn't allow him to do a lot of things he'd done when he was younger and Dave was his right-hand man, so to speak.

Dave looked around for his boss until he spotted the older man standing at the end of the breakwater closest to the docks. He took four steps in the man's direction before Frank waved for him to stay where he was. Dave nodded his head and pulled a stick of gum from his pocket. Juicy Fruit. Not his favorite, but it would have to do.

Dave Burke had never been in the military. He wasn't fit for service. He'd tried his luck with the Police, the Fire Department, and the Army and been turned down in every case, because his left hand was a mess and had been from birth. There was nothing to be done about a hand that was built with only half the bones it should have, but Dave was fine with it. He'd had it for all twenty-three years of his life and Frank was good enough to give him a good job when no one else would even consider it. Long as he wore his gloves, Frank didn't care. Frank didn't mind the deformity, but some of the clientele were bothered by it. Frank was very careful when it came to offending the locals. Fair was fair. They paid the bills, after all.

At fifty-seven years of age, Frank still struck an intimidating figure.

He had the ramrod-stiff posture of a long-time military man and still managed to walk in a way that was positively predatory. The back was because of a few fused vertebrae. The predatory gait was because he was still a soldier at heart. He had a weathered face and short, salt-and-pepper hair, and an expression that said he took exactly no shit off of anyone. It took Dave about two years to realize the man wasn't in a bad mood but just had a face that wasn't made for smiling. If his lips curled upward, it was the same as most people bellowing laughter.

Frank nodded as he strode closer. "Still chewing gum instead of smoking?"

Dave nodded and smiled easily. "Yuh. Gum still costs less."

Frank slapped him lightly on the shoulder. "I don't know what the hell is going on over there, but the smell is about to make me gag." He indicated the breakwater with his chin. "I can't find a damn thing. I thought maybe you could take a look along the water line."

Dave patted his hips. He was wearing his fishing gear for exactly that reason. The rubberized overalls covered most of his long body, and while they wouldn't keep him warm, they'd at least keep him mostly dry. "First beer's on you tonight, and before we head for the Kettle I expect a damn big coffee, fresh and hot."

One corner of Frank's lip pulled upward. "You drive a hard bargain, boy."

Dave chuckled. "I'm gonna freeze my balls off, I need something to warm the rest of me."

"Here's hoping it ain't another floater." Frank headed toward his office and pointed. "I'm gonna start the coffee. Might find a little whiskey to put in it, too."

"Won't break my heart." Dave watched the older man walking away for a moment, noticed that the limp he tried to hide was showing again, and shook his head. It was driving Frank crazy that he wasn't as young as he used to be, but he did his best not to let it show. It wouldn't have been all that long ago that the old man would have handled the examination of the breakwater himself, but the weather as cold as it was, he'd have been damn near crippled by swollen joints by the time he was done. Arthritis or some such. Dave didn't envy him.

He sighed and started into the water, squinting against the glare from the sky above. The sun was sinking fast, and it wouldn't be long before the glare faded and the dark snuck in to make it harder to do anything at all. That was okay; he'd brought the halogen flashlight along just in case.

Dave was wearing a coat that should have been too thick for the season, but as soon as the water passed his knees he was grateful for it. Still, the coat didn't help at all when the water passed his testicles. Sure enough, they shrunk down to the size of marbles and he felt a shiver run through his body. The water lapped against him, gently pushing and pulling at his body. He took his time, making sure his feet were planted carefully before he took another step. It didn't take much to let the tide fool you, especially this close to the stone outcropping. He'd seen a few bodies pounded into the rocks over time — animals, granted — but the same waves that shattered a dog's carcass would pulp a human body. Best to respect the water and its attitudes.

Fifteen paces out, he caught the smell that had bothered Frank so much. Decay has a unique smell, and while the human animal is nowhere near as good as a bloodhound for telling the difference between scents, it sure as hell wasn't rotting fish he was smelling. Fish had a very different stink to them. This? It smelled like a mammal left to rot and fester in the summer sun.

Dave's light shone along the edge of the thick stones that made the breakwater, and because it was waterproof and designed for scuba diving, he didn't hesitate to put the light under the water's surface and aim it along the foundation. The light showed nothing at all that could have caused the smell for the first thirty feet. By that time the water was high enough to make walking a challenge. His body wanted to float, and he had to use his free hand to brace himself against the rocks to avoid getting tossed around.

He was about to call off his investigation when the water drew back as the tide pulled away from the shore and revealed the hole in the breakwater's side.

It happened from time to time. Erosion caught a few of the smaller rocks and pulled them out of place, and the next thing you knew there was an undercurrent that cut at the sand and left a cavity in the side of the otherwise solid structure. As he was in the water and not looking from above as Frank had earlier, he could see where the stones had been pulled out of place by the tide. The sun's glare didn't protect the water's secrets from a good flashlight. Damnedest thing, because he'd seldom seen rocks moved that far by the waves in that short a time.

Whatever was going on, this was the spot the stench was coming from. It was bad enough that his eyes nearly watered and he had to resist the urge to gag.

"Better be more than one drink, Frank. Especially if I find a floater." According to Frank, if you waited around the docks long enough you were almost guaranteed to see a corpse. People fall off of boats or try to swim out too far or maybe just throw themselves off the cliffs, and sooner or later the bodies wash up. The natural tendency of the tides in the area meant a lot of debris found its way to the harbor and the New Harbor docks. The Old Harbor side maybe wasn't as pretty, but at least it got less driftwood.

Dave looked at the hole in the breakwater and licked his lips, tasting his own sweat and the spray from the water. Something was under there. He knew that. Now he had to find out what it was. The easiest way to do that might be to look, but he didn't have a diving mask with him—he was smart enough to remember the flashlight, that was about as good as it got—and that meant he'd have to reach in there to find out. His right hand—the good hand—was holding his flashlight. That meant he had to use his south paw this time around. No one was around to see, so he pulled off the heavy glove that normally covered the malformed fingers and took a deep breath as he reached down to feel under the stone shelf.

The water promptly slapped across his face and shot halfway up his nose. Dave was expecting to get wet but the force of the wave caught him off guard and he spluttered as he coughed brine from his mouth and nostrils.

So he almost missed the way the hand he encountered wrapped around his wrist and squeezed. Dave yanked back as quickly as he could, gasping from the cold, the sudden contact, and the feel of frigid, wet flesh clutching at his weaker hand.

He could not pull back; he was caught. He hauled with all of his strength, braced his foot against the black stones of the breakwater, and pushed himself away from the structure, but instead of freeing himself, he felt the pressure increase on his wrist. Dave looked at the water, at the dark shape that held him, but the moving water distorted what he saw, made it impossible to see clearly.

The water rushed forward and slapped against his face again, stinging into his eyes and trying to slide down his throat, up his nose. He closed his eyes and pulled harder, doing his best to ignore the stinging tears that burned and watered past his eyelids.

The water came in harder, pushing him back, and he let it, embraced the notion, because maybe it would let him escape from whatever was holding his hand, his wrist, in a vise grip. Rather than trust to that, however, Dave braced both feet against the rocks and tried to pull his wrist free again, gritting his teeth at the pain that flared from his captured hand. The water drew back again and he could breathe for a moment, could see the fingers on the pale hand that held him in place, and could see where the thick nails of that hand were starting to sink into the flesh of his trapped limb. Lines of crimson ran from different spots around his hand, and the pain of fresh wounds mingling with the salty brine was startling.

"What the hell? Lemme go!" That was all he could manage before the water sloshed back toward his face. As the water came in and lifted him again, he pushed harder still against the breakers and felt whatever was pinning him — he could not accept that it was a hand; the notion was ludicrous! — slide, coming toward him. Emboldened by the notion, he pulled harder still, letting out an involuntary whimper as the bones in his hand creaked and the biggest joint in his thumb popped with a hot flare.

Desperate times can lead to desperate strength. Adrenaline kicked in and Dave pulled harder still, his neck and arms corded with the strain, and he let out a prolonged groan as he felt the mass holding him slide even more. One more good tug and he knew he'd be free.

Dave pulled.

The stench from the water exploded outward in a roiling mass of gas bubbles, and at the same time, the thing holding on to him rose from the water. Dave fell backward as the crushing pressure on his arm eased, but did not disappear. He stared at the hand he could see clearly for the first time, and it was a hand, no denying it: long, thin fingers reminiscent of spider legs and claws that were preposterously long, even with a good portion of those claws buried in his skin. The flesh of that hand was dead white, save where the tracery of veins and arteries dyed the skin a dark gray, and even as Dave took in the predicament, he saw drops of blood spill from the spots where the nails were digging deep in to his weaker hand.

He wanted to scream, but his voice was gone.

He wanted to back up, but the hand still held him too tightly.

He looked at the arm above the hand, saw where it got lost in the black membrane of fabric that seemed to wrap itself around the flesh too tightly. The thing he looked at made a noise and Dave looked at the face of the thing, where the face should have been, at least, and saw the wet cloth that covered the long, thin shape. He could see the hint of facial features, sockets where eyes should have been, a cavernous indentation where the nose should have hidden, and then the gray lips, the dark gray gums, the yellowed teeth—so damned many teeth, a forest of bone knives—stained pink in spots as the mouth opened and hissed a spray of bloodied froth in his direction.

Dave tried to pull back. He did. But it didn't matter. The thing yanked him forward, lifting him easily from the water as it rose to a height that made Dave seem small.

Oh, how he wanted to scream. He almost made it, too. But then the mouth full of teeth was clamping down on his face, covering his lips, his chin, and biting down, carving into him with frightening ease. He'd found Frank's problem. Sadly, this time he could not fix it.

***

Names meant nothing. Memories were useless. All they brought with them was confusion and pain. Betrayals can do that.

Blood drooled from cadaverous lips, and it dropped the man it had been feasting on, ignoring the cold wash of seawater that splashed across its body as the corpse hit the surf. Though the red fluids took away the worst of the hunger, there was more that it wanted. The last one, the screaming fool in the car, had been a mistake. Eating flesh was not the way, as it learned when the time came to vomit back out the bones and gristle of the body. Hours spent curled in a fetal position and hacking up shards and fragments had taught it a very important lesson. Still, it hungered.

The body had been drained of blood. The eyes of the dead man stared sightlessly at the waves that sought to take the body away. Perhaps it was instinct, what happened next. Maybe it was something else at work. Whatever the cause, the dead thing reached down and covered the face of the corpse with one hand and concentrated. There was nothing to see, but it felt the energies drawn from the corpse and pulled into itself. They were weak, the sputtering flames of a nearly exhausted fire, but they were there and they sated the deep, hollow hunger that had been gnawing endlessly inside of the creature.

On the off chance that there might be more of those odd energies inside the body, it lifted the corpse and walked toward the docks, trying in vain to pull still more of the sweet, ethereal force from within the empty shell. Sadly, there was nothing to be taken.

Frustrated, it dropped its new toy and moved away, heading once again for the place it had sought the night before. Heading for home.

Had it waited around, it might have seen the thin trail of black pustules that slowly rose on the dead face of Dave Burke. They blistered the dead skin like bubbles rising to the surface of a stagnant pond, and slowly took the shape of an elongated hand across the dead man's mouth and lower face.

Had it remained to see what it had done, it might have been fascinated, might have been concerned, but really, that wasn't very likely. It had little concern for anything but the need to sate a hundred different urges, the worst of which was taken care of for the moment.

Instead it moved across the docks and then up the side of the road that led to the rest of Black Stone Bay. There was so much that bordered on familiar, so much that seemed like it should have been clearer to the mind of the thing. Déjà vu was its nearly constant companion. There, that spot along the road, it had been there before, with others, but it had been something different then, unafraid of the sunlight, unconcerned with the hunger of starvation, the cold ache of death's touch. And smaller. It had been smaller. That thought was enough to make it stop and look down at its hands again. They were not the same. They were longer, pale, powerful things, and the twisted vines of vein and artery had not been visible then as they were now. There had been pale blond hairs on the arms and hands it knew from the past, but those were gone now, replaced by the hairless, slightly greasy flesh it bore now.

Curious now, for the first time since it had found a way to escape from the darkness, it moved its hands across its body, feeling the differences. It closed its eyes as it felt the contours and structure of its body. There were hard muscles just under the skin, corded and powerful, but as unfamiliar as its new height. The bones were close to the surface; thick, hard bones and nearly bulbous joints. The skin was cold and retained that odd, greasy feel to it that was simply wrong. The flesh of the man it had just consumed had been warm, supple, closer to what it should have felt. Not this. This was…well, it was lifeless.

Long fingers and sharp nails pulled the thick caul of darkness from its face and carefully felt along the angles and planes of its skull. There was little hair here, not as much as should have been across the skull and below that the skin was stretched in ways that made little sense, that felt as wrong as the texture of its flesh. The angles were too prominent; the nose was gone, replaced by a wrinkled mass of collapsed skin and cartilage. The meat beneath the skin was nearly gone, offering only more hard bone. The lips had been full once, possibly pleasing to others? Did that make sense? Yes, it thought so. It had been pretty once, and now?

And finally something came to its mind that overtook even the hungers of its new existence. Its fingers caressed the withered lips, moved past them to feel the teeth that filled its mouth. They were many, and they were wrong, long and sharp instead of smaller and rounded.

It moved along the road, leaving the darkness drawn away from its face, looking for a reflective surface in which to examine itself. Curiosity was a powerful thing, almost as potent as the hunger that had held it earlier. It moved to a car parked on the side of the road and stared at the glass of the driver's side window. The surface was clean enough, and the distorted reflections of the street and the trees and the sign leading to the docks were all visible within the surface. What was not visible was the shape it knew should have been there. There was no face to see, and even when it moved its arms closer to the glass, there was no sign that it stood before the glass.

It made a noise. Not quite a word, for it had forgotten how to form words and its lips weren't quite up to relearning, but a sound. Just to be sure of what it was seeing, it reached out and tapped the glass with one long finger. It saw the nail scrape the glass, but no reflection of that finger existed.

Rather than think any longer on the puzzle, it shattered the glass, swinging one hard fist at the offensive surface. The shards tinged across its body, and a loud screaming noise immediately started from the vehicle.

A car alarm. It understood that one immediately.

No reason to stay. It moved, sliding up the long road away from the docks and the car that continued its cries of protest over being violated. It felt...cheated. No reflection. How could it ever see what it looked like without a reflection?

Above it, behind it, the winds picked up and howled. It opened its mouth and let out a low howl of its own.

Enough. It would head home now. That was all there was to do. It would head home.

Was it clear memory or instinct again? In the end it did not care. It merely moved, following the desire to get to a place of comfort and safety, of pleasant memories and warm recollections.

Five years earlier it has been buried in the side of a cliff, left to rot and die. It had survived that hell, had come back stronger than it had ever been before. It had earned the right to a place of its own, a place of safety. What it had not expected was that the place where it was most comfortable would no longer be there.

It stopped to stare at the spot, then slowly circled around the location again and again, ignoring the frantic barking of the dogs in the neighborhood that heard it approach.

The house was not the same. There were aspects that were similar, but the color was wrong and new parts had been added. Also, the cars that should have been in the driveway were gone, replaced by several vehicles that were in poorer states of repair and covered with political slogans and the names of bands. It stared long and hard at the vehicles and the house, trying to understand the changes. They were like the lack of reflection: they made no sense.

Music came from inside the home, a heavy bass that pulsed in its ears and stirred distant memories. Enough. This was home. That was all that mattered.

Finally it stepped toward the house and stopped only when it felt the resistance in the air before it. There was nothing there, yet it could not move forward. It pushed harder and the resistance remained, unaffected by its best efforts. Finally it roared in frustration and struck at the air, pounding its fists against the barrier that held it at bay.

The dogs in the nearby houses howled in response or barked challenges, a German shepherd in the next yard shoved itself against the closed front door of the house and growled a warning to stay away from its family. It did not remember the dog from previous times. Like the house, things had changed around the area and there was a growing confusion caused by that notion.

The barrier held, refusing to allow admittance. It fretted, paced, tried to puzzle out the existence of the resistance. A car pulled into the driveway and it moved away from the offensive car lights. A moment later the driver killed the engine, cut off the headlights, and stepped out. A young man, unattractively overweight, with clothing that it knew it had seen before. Rather than approach the house immediately, the driver moved around the car and opened the passenger's side door, pulling out a dark container, and it nodded its head. Pizza. It remembered pizza fondly though the notion of trying to eat the stuff now was repulsive. Thin, cold lips pulled up in a smile. Cognitive flashes ran through its head, and it once again found itself wondering if what it felt was a memory or a new instinct.

It moved to the side and slid into shadows, standing still, waiting patiently.

And as it waited, the driver walked past, oblivious to its presence.

And it waited. Had it been breathing, it would surely have held its breath in anticipation.

***

Malcolm Dunbar heard the knock at the door and shook his head, the dreadlocks running down to his shoulders rolling gently as he did. He was mostly done with his essay and didn't feel much like looking up from his laptop. "Can you get that, Randy?" he called over the sound of Cee-Lo Green crooning out a cheerful tune about a girl who didn't love him back.

His brother looked at him for an instant and called out, "Come in!" instead of moving. He was currently being distracted by the girl sitting across his lap. In his defense, she was a good-looking thing and doing her best to be a distraction. She was very good at it. Blond and thin and dressed for weather about forty degrees hotter.

"Dude, seriously. I can't stop now." Malcolm's voice took on a warning edge that Randy knew well. Still, Randy smiled and shrugged as the door was opened. The girl did not move. Randy reached into his pocket and pulled out a wad of bills as the pizza guy came into the house. Same guy that had delivered yesterday and the day before. What was his name?

"What's up, Scott?" Randy to the rescue. The pudgy kid smiled, delighted to be recognized. Randy pointed to the table with his chin and Scott obediently set the pizzas down on the table and then walked toward Randy, wise enough to stay well away from Malcolm as he typed furiously. Randy handed the kid a twenty and a ten and told him to keep the change. Scott nodded his thanks and headed for the door.

"Thanks, guys. Have a good one, right?"

Malcolm grunted and Randy nodded and the girl — what the hell was her name, anyways? It was gonna bug him until he remembered — waved and smiled prettily at the delivery boy.

"You hungry, man?" Randy finally stood up, carefully sliding the shapely girl off his lap and standing stiffly. Not surprisingly, he had an erection from the last half-hour of the girl doing her best to keep him distracted.

"In a while, dude." He had a few more paragraphs and he'd be finished with the paper on religion in the modern world. He typed furiously, the words flowing easily from his mind to the computer. He loved the rare occasions when he could write like that. Most of the time he had to fight to get the thoughts out of his skull.

Randy offered to the girl — seriously, it was going to make him crazy if he didn't remember her name — and she accepted eagerly. Skinny as she was, it looked like she never ate a damned thing. Malcolm had always preferred a girl with a little meat on her bones. Randy liked the ones that looked like they could pass for anorexics. This one had breasts, at least. It was a step up from the last one, who looked like she was the offspring of a broom handle and a twig.

Done. He saved the file and leaned back, grateful to have finished the first draft. Later, after he'd eaten and maybe taken a nap, he'd do the edits.

He reached for the pizza box and pulled two slices with olives and onions, ignoring the pie covered with three different types of meat. Mostly he was a vegetarian. Now and then he broke down, but mostly he behaved.

Carly was supposed to be coming over, if she remembered to. He wasn't going to hold his breath. Most of the time, when they got together, he had to go to her place. It wasn't that she had a problem with Randy, or even with any of Randy's girlfriends, but she seemed to really not like the house. Or maybe she was just more comfortable on her home turf. He hadn't sorted all of that out yet, he just knew she was cool to be with.

The girl repositioned herself on Randy's lap and chewed daintily on her slice of pizza for a moment. Randy slowed down on his chewing, trying to concentrate despite the fact that the girl was basically giving him a slow dry hump. Malcolm did his best to ignore it. They were brothers, but they definitely had different ideas of what was right and what was wrong. Malcolm would have moved the show to the bedroom. Randy didn't care who saw him doing anything unless their mother was around, and she was back in Louisiana.

The dog that had been going insane for the last half-hour let out a yelp and stopped barking. That probably meant the losers who left the poor animal out in the cold every day had finally let it inside and that was a good thing. It didn't look like the fur on the animal was going to stop the sort of chill that was getting stronger every day. Of course, being from New Orleans, Malcolm was hardly the expert on cold weather. It went below sixty degrees and he wanted to put on an arctic parka. But Sacred Hearts had the best department for his particular field of studies and the cold weather was a small price to pay.

"Damn, Vikki…" Randy's voice was part purr and part plea for mercy. Well, at least he knew her name at last. Malcolm looked over and saw the blond girl's lips teasing along his brother's earlobe. Her tongue flitted out and traced the curls of his inner ear. Randy's eyes were closed and a small smile of pleasure took the lines of stress from his face. Randy was a hedonist. No two ways about it. Not that Malcolm could blame him.

The front door slammed open with enough force to rattle the windows, and Randy, the blonde, and Malcolm joined together in a communal squeak of surprise. The air that came into the room seemed cold enough to freeze water into instant ice, and Malcolm stood up and headed for the door instantly. He wasn't as tolerant of the cold as his brother, and he also didn't have a girl in his lap. He grabbed the door and pushed it shut harder than he meant to, the resistance he expected was not there, and the breeze that had forced the door open in the first place was gone. So, too, was the bitter cold that had hit him as he stood up. It was chilly out there, but no longer felt like an arctic front coming through hard and fast.

Randy made a face. "What the hell is that?"

"What, baby?" Vikki looked at him with wide blue eyes and then her pretty face screwed up, her nose wrinkled, and she shook her head. "Oh. Damn. Never mind." She waved her skinny hand in front of her face, hoping to blow away whatever stench the two of them had caught. Malcolm had no idea. He shook his head, locked the door to prevent any more unexpected door openings, and moved back toward his pizza. On the way he caught the smell himself. It was vile, but short-lived. He'd have thought his brother was pulling a fast one with a surprise fart or two, but not even Randy's gas smelled like something dead.

"Ugh. Maybe a dead rat in the vents?"

Randy shook his head. "I'm not looking."

Malcolm shot his brother a withering look. "Better think again. I just covered your half of the rent. Again. It's on you this time."

He might have argued, but Randy took one serious look at his expression and reluctantly nodded his head. "Fine. But later. Me and this fine young thing have other plans for now." Vikki giggled as he playfully swatted her hip.

A moment later they were headed for Randy's room, which suited Malcolm just fine. He didn't need to see his brother getting ridden hard. He watched them leave, his brother as dark-skinned as he was, and the girl with him as pale as fresh cream, except for where she was peppered with freckles. They made a cute couple, though he was sure their mother would have disagreed.

A chill danced up his back and across his neck before dissipating. Without even thinking about it, he let his hand drift to the crucifix around his neck. A moment later he felt warm again and settled in to eat his pizza. The music changed to the Black Eyed Peas. He closed his eyes and listened to the lyrics, letting himself relax for a change of pace.

Fifty feet away from him, his brother and his sibling's lover started the process of dying while he tapped his foot to the music, oblivious to the change in his environment.

Fifty feet away from him, Black Stone Bay started to show the first signs of its decay.

CHAPTER THREE

Ben Kirby drove down the long stretch of back road effortlessly, his eyes checking the mirrors, the shadows around the vehicle, everywhere. It was his job after all. The radio was playing softly and Maggie was on the phone, talking to her date.

Ben managed not to scream at that notion. Barely. He knew the score. Maggie needed to feed, the urge was getting too strong for her to resist, and for that reason they were driving down to Hobb's Point, where she would meet with a man she'd known back before she'd been changed. This was a necessary evil. This had to be. That did not mean he had to like it in the very least. He made his jaw unclench. She'd see, and she'd be upset, and he couldn't stand the thought of Maggie being upset because of him. She had enough to deal with in her world.

She killed the call and dutifully handed him the phone. He smiled his thanks. "All set?"

"Yes." She smiled at him, a cool, distant smile that she normally employed when she was getting ready to feed. She'd changed in the five years they'd known each other, but not so much that he couldn't predict what she was thinking or how she was feeling. Mostly what she was feeling right now was a need for a fix. That was the only way to put it. She needed to feed, and soon, or she would lose herself in the hunger. He'd heard her once talking to herself, when she called it going into the Red. He understood. She's explained to him once that when the hunger got to the point of no return everything went a dark red color. Everything, her sight, her senses, her emotions.

Hobb's Point was a little fishing town, really, not much of anything special, except that it was far enough away from Black Stone Bay that no one would look for a connection. That was important, too, because if she went too far, if she lost control and drank too deeply, they'd need the distance. He tried not to think about that, tried to pretend that this was just going out for dinner. That felt better than murder.

"What are you thinking about, Ben?" Her voice was soft. He looked quickly into the back of the car and smiled. Five years together, two years before that where he basically adored her from a distance, and he still got lost in her every time he saw her. "Just going over the details in my head. In case anything goes wrong." She frowned just a little. He knew why. "Nothing will go wrong, Maggie. And if it does, we'll deal with it." He looked back to the road. "No worries."

"No worries." She sighed the words out and rocked softly in the back seat. She allowed herself to relax a little, because she trusted him. That was important. That made everything worthwhile in his eyes.

A sign up ahead stated that Hobb's Point was the next exit. Good. Excellent. He cut to the right when the time came and decelerated onto the main street for the small town. To the left he could head to the private academy and the worst part of town. To the right, he could head to the lavish homes of the wealthier people in town. He moved to the right.

As he parked the car, he looked at Maggie in the rearview again. Beautiful. He watched while she checked herself in the rearview. "You're perfect and you know it."

"You have a bias, Ben. Best to double check." She rolled her eyes and actually blushed.

"I'll give you that one." He smiled and made himself sit still. He didn't want this. He didn't want her going up to deal with the man that was up there. She didn't want it either, but it had to be. There were no choices, really, unless she wanted to become the same sort of monster that had created her in the first place.

Jason Soulis. He could still see the man's thin smile, his predatory eyes, the cold, intense expression that he wore when he spoke to Maggie and looked at Ben. He would never like Jason. Never.

Ben opened his door and swung to the back of the vehicle, opening the door for Maggie as she stood up. He kept his face expressionless. She mouthed a thank you and he nodded curtly. From this moment forward, it was strictly business until she'd fed. His senses seemed to expand, to cover the whole area. He made himself aware of everyone around them, the ones in the houses close by, and the ones walking along the street. They didn't mind walking after dark in this area. They knew they were protected. That was good. That was for the best. He liked the extra security.

His eyes tracked Maggie as she walked to the house and rang the doorbell. He was aware of her every move, even after the door was closed and his view of her eliminated. Gift or curse, there was a connection between them now and there was nothing he could do about it. Most times he was fine with that, but now and then it was agony. He didn't see her as she moved into the man's house, but he knew exactly where she was. He didn't watch her as she made her moves and he certainly had no desire to feel it when she kissed the man, or when the man took her in his arms. Even the feeding was something he didn't want to know about, but he got all of it in an odd, muted way.

Nothing like feeling the woman you love fucking another man to put you on edge. Maggie always slept with them. They got hot and heavy and well involved in what she was capable of doing to give them pleasure, and she in turn took what she needed from them, drinking their blood and satisfying them sexually, and somewhere along the way, the men always enjoyed every part of it, even when they woke up exhausted for a week and anemic as a result of her needs. To be fair, she was worth a little blood loss. He knew that from firsthand experience. Which was exactly why he hated this so damned much. Down the street he could hear a couple arguing at the threshold of a house that bordered on being a mansion. College age, the two of them. A few years younger than him, maybe, and no doubt convinced that the entire world revolved around their relationship, which sounded like it was in danger of falling into shreds. He didn't let himself listen to the words, though he could have heard them if he'd wanted to. Instead he listened to the sounds, the pattern of their words and breaths. The girl's heartbeat was steady, but her voice shook just a bit. The boy? His heart was doing a double-time march and his voice shook, too, with grief. Yes. A breakup. A tragedy in the making.

In the house behind him, he sensed Maggie kissing her way across her lover's body. His hands clenched until they shook, but he did not move. He would say nothing, do nothing, but be here, waiting, watching, protecting his one true love. And he would hate the man inside that building with her. He'd do nothing about that hatred, but it was there, a dark coiled thing that nestled in his heart and spat venom.

In the distance a couple fell apart. The boy staggered away, punch drunk with grief, and the girl watched him go, her lower lip trembling with what? Grief? Relief? He didn't know. Not far away the woman he loved more than life itself pleasured another man and sated her own hunger. He felt the hunger fade down to a tolerable level and then finally expire, though he knew it would resurrect itself soon enough. Maggie shuddered in pleasures both physical and spiritual, and he felt her orgasms in that same muted fashion and hated his existence through each of several.

When she was finished with her lover, her prey, she came back to him and Ben opened the back seat for her, never saying a word. They would not speak of this dirty little secret. They seldom did, and when it came up, they handled it as clinically as they could, carefully skirting around her pleasure and his pain in an effort to pretend that everything was just fine.

And in a few days he'd convince himself that everything was hunky dory. Ben Kirby loved Maggie Prescott with all of his heart and soul. He was hers. So everything would be fine, because it was better to endure this than to risk losing her.

Sometimes love is a harsh bitch.

***

Boyd chewed slowly at his cigar, and Danny watched him. His partner was doing his best to stay calm, but Danny knew the signs. There wasn't a calm bone in either of their bodies. He didn't need a stethoscope to know their hearts were beating too fast, their breaths were too harsh.

Finally Boyd let out a soft sigh and Danny moved. He reached for the body bag and pulled it from the back of the old station wagon, not letting himself think about the fact that the contents had been a person once.

"I hate this shit, Danny."

"Preaching to the choir, Richie." He'd have gotten all of the bodies out by himself and Boyd knew it. Still, his partner didn't make him do all the dirty work. That was why they were such good partners. They worked together on the good stuff and on the heavy shit, the things they didn't like to think about when they were sober and didn't dare speak about when they'd been drinking.

Boyd looked around, his eyes checking their surroundings with hard intensity. They were committing a crime, after all. Best not to get themselves caught. Not that they'd get into any trouble, not really. Someone had to do this shit after all.

Whalen knew about it. She'd have been there if she could, but they'd agreed a long time ago that it was best if she didn't get her hands dirty with this particular sort of task. Back when the nightmares had started there had been a dozen cops to do this stuff. Now there were five. The rest had left the force, left town, left the world, whatever it took to not be a part of the insanity.

Danny reached for the last body before Richie could make a grab. Boyd wasn't a weakling, but he was smaller than Danny and he was getting older, too. Shame about that last part, because Danny knew good and damned well that his partner wouldn't settle down any time soon. Wouldn't even consider retiring, either, not as long as Whalen was in charge. It would have been funny if it hadn't been so damned sad. Two people who had the hots for each other in a bad way, and neither of them did a damned thing about it.

Boyd pushed Danny's hands away from the zippers on the body bags. He might let his younger partner handle the lifting, but he still intended to get his hands just as dirty, even though both of them were smart enough to wear evidence gloves to avoid contaminating their packages.

Three bodies, all of them bagged, tagged, and waiting for autopsies. You had to do autopsies on the murders, didn't you? Had to make sure that the cause of death was identified, the evidence recorded, examined, and carefully cataloged.

Only not always in Black Stone Bay. Sometimes the medical examiners left the bodies for a day or two, carefully forgetting to identify them, neglecting to call the next of kin, avoided starting a paper trail that might bite someone in the ass later. The previous lawsuits had taken care of that nonsense.

The girl's body shifted on its own, and a soft moan escaped past pale lips.

Danny managed not to scream. Boyd let out a soft curse and spit at the ground.

It was like someone had set an alarm clock for the dead. All three of them started making noises, started moving. Danny stepped back to the rear of the station wagon and reached for his ax. Shit was not going to happen on his watch.

Boyd held out a hand to make him wait and pointed to the lightening sky. Sunrise was just a few minutes away, tops. Danny sighed and waited, repulsed by the entire affair.

The heavyset man rolled over in his body bag and grunted, his eyes rolling beneath closed lids. His face didn't move properly, but twitched as if trying to decide how it should work, trying to remember which muscles to move. He remembered the store clerk well enough. Even when they'd busted him a few times he'd been amiable. Was that a small pang of grief? For a perp? He shook his head. He was getting soft.

When Danny stepped forward the second time and hefted the ax above his head, Boyd didn't stop him. One hard blow was enough. He cracked the fat man's skull open and the store clerk fell forward onto his face. He didn't stop moving, but he didn't seem to have the strength left to get to his hands and knees.

Danny shivered. The air was cool, but not really cold. The shakes didn't show up because of the weather. Something about dead people moving just screwed up his sense of right and wrong.

The girl crawled to her hands and knees, her head hung low, her eyes still closed, and moaned out a sound that bordered on being sexual in nature. The notion was almost enough to make Danny gag. He took one step toward her, his throat working to force down the dry lump that had manifested behind his tongue, but stopped when the sunlight lanced out from the horizon and struck the dead girl's body. She didn't quite scream. She wanted to, he could see that, the way her dead mouth opened and her pale throat strained to find a noise big enough to encompass the pain as her skin started to blister and burn. The other two made noises, but Danny couldn't make himself look away from the girl. She was pretty, or at least she had been before some sick fuck killed her.

She cringed and tried to get away from the sunlight, tried to find a place to hide, but Danny didn't give her the chance. When she sought shelter in the thin plastic of the body bag he lunged drunkenly toward her and ripped the semi-transparent caul away from her, watched her cringe and roll her dead eyes toward him, confusion twisting her dead features mutely into a mask of tragedy.

Someone's little girl. Somewhere out in the town there were a couple of parents who were wondering where their daughter was, why she hadn't come home and why the police couldn't find her. Maybe they were still asleep; maybe they still hadn't managed to find slumber after she didn't come home. Maybe they were holding each other, and maybe they were accusing each other of doing something vile to their own little one. He'd seen goddamned near every reaction over the years and he hated that more than he hated almost anything else. He was repulsed. He was horrified as he watched the dead teenager crawl around and whimper and burn. It wasn't like the damned movies made it look. There wasn't anything poetic about it or fast. No, this was a slow torture. It took the girl almost three minutes to finally stop moving. Two minutes after that the sun had finished cooking her into a fine powdery ash.

That first time, they'd found the bodies scattered everywhere, dead and decomposing, but not burnt to ashes. It took them a while to figure out it was the clouds that kept the bodies from roasting away. These days they waited for the sky to be clear when they could. If not, they had a funeral pyre waiting nearby, or in a pinch they went to the Sanderson Crematorium. Whatever it took, really.

Boyd moved forward and kicked the first of the thick stacks of ash, scattering the gray dust through the air and across the ground. They were near the cliffs, and the wind was strong. In another hour there'd be no proof that three bodies had ever been there.

They didn't have to worry about witnesses. Danny owned the land and the house. One thing about Black Stone Bay: you wanted privacy and you had money, you could get the privacy with ease.

Danny gathered the body bags together and threw them in the back of the station wagon

Boyd moved to the front of the car and pulled out a thermos with around two cups of coffee in it. The coffee was properly spiked. They drank in silence, both raising the cups to the memory of three poor souls that would never be properly reported as dead.

Another thing about Black Stone Bay. There were a lot of missing people over the last five years. Ridiculous numbers.

"Well. I guess that settles that." Boyd's gruff voice was not pleased.

"Yeah. Got another one."

"Better get some sleep, Danny. Looks like we're working nights again."

Much as he wanted to have a smartassed comment for his partner, Danny couldn't think of a thing to say.

***

Marcus's eyes flew wide as the alarm clock screamed at him. He reached over and swatted blindly until he found the right button to make the noise fade. Then he groped around with more care until he found his eyeglasses. It was too early in the day to even consider contact lenses. Besides, Carly said the glasses made him look like a sexy professor. He smiled to himself. Thinking about Carly did that to him every time.

The sun was pushing gently into his room, and he was glad that he hadn't fought as hard as he could have for the master bedroom. His brother was the one who got the full force of the sunlight from the east. He just got a little collateral damage. Considering that he'd heard Randy and Vikki going at it like porn stars all night long, he suspected his little brother was currently burrowed deep under the blankets and pillows. Randy had always hated waking up to the bright light of a clear morning. He was just too thick to consider that when he fought for the master bedroom's ten extra square feet.

He stretched as he rose from the bed, moving with careful skill to avoid the piles of clothes scattered across the floor. If Carly ever came over he'd be worried, but knowing that she preferred her own place gave him a perfectly good reason to be a slob.

A quick shower later he was drying off and going over the list of things he had to do today. Most of them revolved around spending time with Carly as soon as he was done with school. That was why he did all his studying as soon as he could. He wanted to spend the time with the girl who was making his life interesting, and if he didn't get the work done first, he knew he'd never get it finished at all. Randy waited. That was why he was smarter than his brother.

He was dressed and out the door fifteen minutes after his shower was finished. He would have called out to make sure his brother woke up, but Vikki was still over and even though he still wanted to protect his younger sibling from everything the world could throw his way, he had to let Randy make his own mistakes.

Five steps out the front door and his cell phone quacked at him. Only one person had been assigned the sound of a duck chatting away and he smiled as he answered. "Good morning, Carly. How are you?"

"Better now." Her voice was low and pleasant. "I was just dreaming about you sleeping with that bitch, Lianne, so I had to call and make sure you were all alone." He had no idea who Lianne was. It didn't matter. She had dreams about him sleeping around almost every night. Or at least she said she did. He couldn't tell if she was serious or pulling his leg.

"I'm afraid there were no Liannes in my room last night. And no Sallys, Maureens, or Tablthas, either." He smiled and squinted against the sunlight. "I was hoping for a Carly, but the best I managed was a Vikki in my brother's room and believe me, the door was closed."

"Better be."

"If you came over, you could check for yourself." He could hear her hesitating. She wanted to say something, but couldn't articulate the reason for her unwillingness to stay over. "I'm just teasing, baby girl. I was busy until almost one, finishing up all my school work."

"Oh? What were you working on?" Her relief at the out he'd offered was obvious.

"All of it. I wanted to have my night free."

"Really? Why?"

"There's this darling girl I know, name of Carly, and she said I could stay at her place tonight if I played my cards right." He slipped into the driver's seat of his car and tossed his book bag in the passenger's seat. It rolled off and fell on top of the overnight bag he already had stashed on the floorboard. Fresh underwear, a clean shirt, and deodorant, along with a traveling kit for shaving and brushing his teeth. They hadn't quite reached the stage where he got to keep anything over at her place, not yet.

"What makes you so sure she won't change her mind?" She did love to tease.

"A man has to have hope, doesn't he?" She laughed and he started the car. A moment later he was pulling away from the house, completely unaware that his brother and Vikki were curled up and shivering in Randy's room. Unaware something had moved in and made itself at home.

It would be over a day before he learned about the changes in his world. By the time he made the discovery it would be too late.

***

Carly Winters shoved her cell phone into the back right pocket of her jeans and smiled briefly before she started worrying the metal post that pierced her tongue. She was glad that Marcus was coming over. She just hated having to keep secrets from him. What secret? Simply that his brother was a pig. Three times she'd come by the house he rented with his brother, and all three times Randy had managed to hit on her as soon as Marcus had his back turned. A little flirting was one thing, but he'd been working it, trying his best to get into her pants, up her skirt, or under her shirt depending on the moment.

Marcus adored his brother. She didn't want to be the one to cause all sorts of insane troubles between them, but there was no way she would leave herself open to any more attempts by Randy. It was okay when he was just looking, but one time he'd kissed her hard and tried to push his tongue into her mouth, while Marcus was in the next room.

She'd slapped him, and Randy had just smiled, his dark eyes drinking her in, daring her to call out for Marcus. She'd almost done it, too, but in the end she'd chickened out, afraid of hurting Marcus, maybe, or maybe, just perhaps, terrified that the nicest guy she'd ever been with would choose his brother's side in the argument.

Carly had a long history of picking losers to date, guys just like Randy, or even worse than him. The sort that liked to use an open hand across her face to explain their opinions, or in the worst of the cases, the sort who didn't believe "no" was a word that should be in a woman's vocabulary. That had been Bill Marsden's philosophy. He'd raped her.

She'd had the good sense to take herself to the hospital as soon as he was done and had rolled over to go to sleep. She hadn't even been thinking about whether or not he was a bad person at that point. He hadn't used a condom, and all she could think in her state of mind after he'd finished was that if she were pregnant with his child she'd have to kill herself. She hadn't been rational. She knew that now.

She also knew that the police did more than just hand out speeding tickets. They'd visited her at the hospital as soon as she reported what had happened to a nurse in the emergency room. And after that, they'd visited Bill at his apartment and arrested him.

If it was true that she'd made bad choices for romance, it was equally true that Bill was a little too sure of himself and a lot too ignorant of the way the laws work. He'd declined his right to an attorney and had also explained to the police who arrested him that he was merely putting Carly in her place. Since then he'd been behind bars. She hoped he stayed there for the rest of his life, and that his life was short and violent.

Two years and a lot of therapy later, Carly was feeling better about herself, but that didn't mean she didn't dread the idea of looking at Randy ever again. He wasn't a good person. He knew that in her heart, just as surely as she knew that Marcus was one of the best people she'd ever met. He was sweet and he was patient and he was gentle. She trusted him, and that was a very rare commodity in Carly's world.

She grabbed her backpack from the passenger's seat of the car and started across the parking lot, shaking her head and trying to push the thought of Randy out of her head. He was a pig. He was not Marcus. Marcus was a much better person. She thought about that, about him, as she headed for class.

He was coming over tonight. That was about the best news she could think of.

The university was full of activity, students moving across the campus at different speeds, ranging from frantic jog to slow, steady mosey. Carly took her time. She always got to school early because she hated to feel rushed. Chad Remington saw her and smiled, moving at the same leisurely pace. "Hey, Carly…" his words tapered off in a slow fade, as they always did, and the long black bangs he had obscured his eyes as surely as a funeral veil. Still, despite his black leather and the makeup he wore — often prompting her to think of him as Emo-Chad — his face lit up in a smile. They were lab partners and they were friends. The partners was coincidence. The friends was because they worked together at Plaza Pizza Palace, and had discovered along the way that they had a lot in common.

"Hey, Chad! Ready for the test?" She smiled at him, and it was a genuine smile. He was a good guy and he was in a steady relationship with a girl who probably outweighed him by thirty pounds. Lollie. The girl called herself Lollie and she dressed in clothes that would have made the standard Goth feel awkward. Lollie was chesty, and she liked to show that fact off, even if to prove it she had to ram herself into a corset that nearly cut off her ability to breathe. Still, Lollie was nice enough once you got past the odor of clove cigarettes and patchouli.

Chad tapped his temple with one long, bony finger. "Got all the answers right here." He wasn't bragging. Chad was disgustingly intelligent. He worked the pizza place for spending money. He was actually attending the school on a full academic scholarship.

Chad moved closer, his slumped shoulders and bowed chest making him look almost like a question mark when seen in profile. The coolest thing about him? He genuinely didn't care what anyone thought of him. The other coolest thing? He was a good listener, and had been dealing with her crap ever since they started working together. He was, in other words, a great girlfriend. Not that she would ever say that to him, of course.

They moved into the classroom, sliding into step with each other unconsciously.

It was good to have friends. There had been a time when Carly had believed firmly that she would never have friends again. She'd lost so many of them before, when she was younger and foolishly went to the circus in her hometown of Serenity Falls. There had been a fire. And clowns. And death.

Sometimes the world gets better when you aren't looking. Carly was grateful for that.

***

Lora's class sat in a semicircle, their chairs and small desks rearranged so that they could all pay attention to the student who was speaking.

Currently Bernadette was doing her best to read her story without stuttering on each word. The girl could normally be counted on to interrupt class a dozen times a day with her loud musings about the world around them, but when she had to read in front of the class she lost her way every time. She had no semblance of a speech impediment; she was just nervous. Her ponytail shook as she stood in front of the class. Lora smiled a silent encouragement but otherwise left her to tell her story. She certainly had a good imagination.

The story she told was about a little boy named Dave Darkly, who had a lame hand that made the other children tease him. Dave got angry one day and decided to have his revenge, so he stole the shadows from other children. Once he had their shadows, they had to do what he said. Everything worked just fine until the shadows rebelled and wrapped him up like a fly in a spider's web. Most of the kids told stories that fell apart or dissolved into absurdist comedies. Bernadette's was the exception. Though simplistic in approach, it was genuinely creepy and Lora got a kick out of watching the other children as they listened.

She resisted the temptation to scream BOO at the top of her lungs. The odds were good that Todd would wet himself again and there would be hell to pay.

Lora could take or leave Halloween, but it was always fun for the kids. When they had fun, they learned better. It was also a good chance to make the shy ones, like Bernadette and Mark, work past their nervousness.

Bernadette finished her story and Lora smiled and applauded. "That was a great story, Bernadette, and spooky!" Several of the kids nodded their agreement and a few even clapped their hands together. Bernadette smiled shyly and slid back to her desk, looking a little shell-shocked but no worse for the wear.

Dina Whittman stood up next, looking like man walking the final mile before his execution as she headed for the center of the class. Lora smiled her encouragement and barely faltered at all when she caught the crows once again waiting outside of her classroom.

Nowhere else. Just her classroom, as if they were keeping an eye on the students and waiting to see what would happen next.

She made herself smile. Maybe they just liked Halloween stories.

Dina's story was about a lonesome black cat who befriended a scarecrow. Lora wondered how the crows would feel about that story as she listened to the little girl recite her tale. It was cute and harmless and a little endearing, much like the little girl who told it.

If the crows had any opinion on the matter, they kept it to themselves and merely waited, as silent as the grave.

***

The house had been her palace once. Now it was merely an empty building, covered with dust and rat droppings, littered with the things that had meant something to her once upon a time. Like the life she'd once had, the house was devoid of anything that mattered, abandoned and discarded.

Angie Freemont screamed as the pain tore at her again. Had anyone ever survived childbirth? If so, she couldn't imagine how. The damned thing inside of her mewled in her head, and she growled in response, baring her fangs and hissing as the blood dried to her skin. Four bodies lay around her, filling the house where she'd lived with Brian in the past.

Dear, departed Brian. She was glad she'd killed him. If she could have brought him back to life, she'd have killed him all over again, just for the pain trying to deliver his child was causing her.

There was no mistaking it, this was the end game. The kid was coming and there was nothing she could do to stop it from showing its face to her and the rest of the world. Just to make her point clear, the damned thing twisted inside of her and she felt something vital rip inside of her. Blood forced its way up her throat and she choked it back down, afraid that if she lost so much as a drop of what she'd consumed she would surely dry up and die.

The sun was up outside of the house and she had to bite off another scream. Five years ago the house had been in the middle of nowhere, with a couple of acres between them and the closest neighbors. She'd liked it that way and so had Brian. Privacy was a lovely thing. Now she didn't have that luxury any longer. Whoever had owned the land around them must have finally broken down and decided to sell, because there were newer houses all around the half-acre lot. There were children moving about, heading for school or to their bus stop. Children, little demons like the one growing inside of her. She wanted to scream her hatred to them, but any extra noises might get them calling the police or worse, and she didn't need the interruptions, not when she couldn't go outside without burning.

The baby ripped at her insides again and Angie fell on her face, unable to even bring her hands up in time to catch herself. She rolled herself over, falling heavily across the floorboards and clawing at the wood as the pain reached a new level, a crescendo that shattered every belief she'd ever had about how much pain a body could endure.

"Get out of me! Just get the fuck out of meeeeeee!" Her voice carried; she could no longer help that. This was too much. In the last five years she'd found herself in numerous occasions where she'd been injured — bullets, knives, dogs, sunlight, and fire had all been used against her body with varying levels of success—and she knew how resilient her vampiric body was. But this?

Something moved inside of her, pulling, tearing and this time she bucked upward as the pain carved a trench through her.

And then the blood came again, spilling from her stomach and lower as her body tore open, bursting like a rotted fruit. For five years Angie had managed to recover from every injury, no matter how grievous. There was pain, true, but in short order she'd recover from the injuries, she'd heal, and she'd adapt. It was, she believed, the nature of what she had become.

And now she endured still, as the thing that had festered inside of her for too many years slipped from her abdomen and spilled feebly across the floorboards, carried along in a tide of blackened, clotted blood and withered placenta.

"Aahhuuggg." It was all she could manage, the sound half-strangled in the blood that filled her throat. She turned her head and vomited, spilling still more of the precious fluids across the floor, emptied of the vital life force that she'd eagerly stolen from the dead bodies around her.

Angie lay back, shuddering, unable to do anything at all but stare at the ceiling without actually seeing anything. She heard no sounds at all for a while—she did not have a heartbeat and felt no particular need to breathe—and she might well have stayed there for the rest of the day—hell, forever—but eventually she did hear a noise: the sound of her child moving, struggling through the sluice of viscera spilled from inside of her body.

It took so much effort to move, to do anything at all. Still, she managed to move her head until she could see it as it crawled, slithered toward her. How silent the world seemed now that she could no longer hear its voice within her skull, calling, whining, demanding so much of her time and energy.

She missed that connection more than she would have ever thought possible.

"Why can't I hear you anymore, baby?"

Through the veil of drying blood and ichor that coated it, the infant looked at her with bloodshot eyes that seemed to have no irises, merely thick black pupils. It did not speak, did not move, but merely stared with a face that barely moved.

Movement from beyond the child caught her attention and Angie looked at the window in the living room, where the sun would shine later in the day and burn her if she didn't move before then. If she could move, if, by some dark miracle, she found the strength to do anything at all after all the blood she'd lost.

A great black shape settled on the ledge and stared at her with eyes even darker than her child's. A moment later another landed with a heavy rustling of obsidian wings. Not much later a third found space, nudging the other two to make room.

The three crows watched Angie as she lay still, wishing she could make herself move. They also watched as her child crawled toward her face, moving until her view of the birds was completely blocked.

And they continued to watch, making no noises whatsoever, as the child's hands reached for Angie's bloodied face.

***

Jason watched avidly as Angela Freemont birthed her spawn. He was amazed by how much she'd endured. It was one thing for him to survive catastrophic wounds, because his kind were, well, they were heartier than the average vampire. They were stronger, faster, and better equipped to survive in every way. Sunlight was an inconvenience, not a deadly thing. Blood was necessary, yes, but not the only possible means to an end. He'd heard of others that had adapted, found other ways to feed. That was one of the many differences between the Undead and vampires. The Undead, like him, like Maggie, were simply better at adapting.

That was one of the reasons for his experiments. Okay, that and boredom, because after a while almost all of the experiences the world had to offer grew tired.

The infant crawled around in the remains of its mother and then curled into a fetal position. Jason curbed his disappointment. There was no guarantee that it would simply wait there to die. There were too many unknown quantities.

"In due time," he cautioned himself. "Patience, old boy. Patience."

CHAPTER FOUR

October in New England was hardly shorts weather. The mornings started cold and the days warmed up a bit, but most people quickly figured out it was time for sweaters or jackets. In Black Stone Bay the wind off the ocean was harsh; it cut across the lawns of the wealthy and the less fortunate alike, and it dragged a chill with it that managed to slither past almost any coat or jacket.

Boyd and Holdstedter stared down at the waves of the bay, watched them slam themselves into the black cliffs and heave themselves against the jagged teeth of stone that rose from the water, and waited patiently for any and all items that might fall toward them.

"It's fuckin' cold, Richie." Danny was whining. It was what he did when the weather was cold and he hadn't had enough coffee to warm his bones.

"You're the douche that wanted to come look at the water, Danny. I'm just humoring your latest stupid theory." Boyd was cold, too, but he faked being warm and lit a cigar, watching the smoke scatter itself into a faint ghost as the wind tore it away. Better not to let Danny see another weakness he could exploit. The little shit liked to pick at any possible wound.

Danny sighed and looked down at the water, watched the way the waves slapped and shifted and sighed again. "It just isn't the same anymore." After the night they didn't like to talk about, the two detectives had blown the hell out of an underwater cave in the cliffside. Right after that, the deaths had stopped.

Boyd shrugged and squinted as the smoke came back around and slapped him in the face. That was what he got for sucking on a stogie in a high-wind zone. "It was worth a shot anyway."

"Then why did you call it a stupid theory, Richie?" Like he didn't already know the answer.

"Because you came up with it first."

"We ever find a good expert on the bloodsuckers?"

"No." Boyd spat. "Couldn't find one. Couldn't find anything on the Internet either, except for porn and a billion sites that sold fake fangs to sad little Goths."

Danny shrugged. "I liked the porn part, at least."

"'Course you did. You're a pig."

"Said the swine."

"True enough."

Danny kept looking over the side, studying the waves and maybe hoping they'd tell him a secret. Once upon a time there'd been a college girl they'd been fond of who took a swan dive off the cliffs. Kelli something or other. She was good people. Since then, Danny never made jokes about the fact that the rocks turned people into jelly. Mostly because it was true. Also because the cave that they'd sealed off had been a haven for nightmares and Danny was maybe just a little afraid of giving the nightmares a reason to come back.

Even though it seemed they already had.

Boyd suppressed a shiver; he wasn't about to give Danny the satisfaction. "Let's get the fuck out of here." He looked away from the waves and toward the houses along the Cliff Walk. He'd lived in Black Stone Bay for decades, but he never got tired of looking at the mansions or the great old trees that stood like sentinels around them.

The flutter of wings caught his attention and Boyd froze, staring as the first of the great old crows settled on the closest tree and stared at him, head craned cockily. It was a big bird, bigger than most of the black birds, and it hopped to the left as it looked his way. Despite himself, he felt a flutter of dread in his stomach.

Danny turned and stopped next to him, looking at the sky above. He reached with his hand and slapped lightly at Boyd, not saying a word. Boyd grunted an acknowledgment, watching as several more crows spiraled down from above, riding the air currents until they could settle themselves on the branches of the same tree. The first was the biggest of them, but there was no doubt in Boyd's mind that they were among the largest crows he had ever seen. He'd seen what the birds could do to a corpse in a very short amount of time. He'd seen it firsthand, in fact.

He resisted the urge to draw his service pistol and open fire. Instead he stared back, looking the largest of the birds in one eye as it looked back, unblinking.

"Richie?" His partner's voice was tight.

"Yeah, Danny?"

"Remind me to load up the trunk with fresh shotguns, okay?"

"You got it."

Without another word Danny started moving walking along the path that took them within ten feet of the tree that was currently housing a dozen of the carrion eaters. Just as he reached the closest point to the tree that the path allowed, the birds exploded into flight, leaving their perches in unison and flapping into the wind, rising high on the air currents in a matter of seconds.

Boyd and Holdstedter looked at the crows as they vanished into the sky.

"I fucken hate those birds." Boyd was barely aware that he's spoken aloud.

Danny patted his shoulder and started walking again, his face clouded over in thought. "Preaching to the choir here, Richie."

Neither of them said the name. They didn't need to. The last time the crows had come to town, they'd shown up at the same time as the individual they were fairly certain had brought the nightmares to town in the first place.

They didn't say the name. They didn't want to. If they said the name, it might act like an invitation, and no one in their right mind invited a vampire to visit. Ever.

***

Lora was in a strange mood all day long. She felt sluggish, and no matter how hard she tried, she didn't seem capable of getting warm. She blamed her dreams, which were about a boy who had a bad hand and stole shadows. The notion almost made her muster a smile. She remembered the story, of course. If she'd told Bernadette that the girl had given her nightmares she'd never hear the end of it.

The crows at the school waited until the last bell of the day before they took off in an explosive wave. Lora might have been impressed by the show, but by that point the first of reports of a stranger lurking around the buildings had come about.

Absolutely no one took that sort of story lightly at Hartshorn Elementary. No one. Not ever.

The three security guards looked around the entire school, but found nothing.

If the crows knew anything, they weren't volunteering the information.

***

Ben stood in the kitchen and chopped onions with a speed that would have shamed most chefs. It was an advantage of too many years spent playing video games and writing code: his hand-eye coordination was unsettling. That didn't stop him from blinking back tears. Onion juice was a killer.

The onions went into the sauté pan, followed by the green peppers and the jalapeños. The meat was already searing away in the pot at the back of the stove. This meal had to be a good one. Maggie's family was coming over and she was starting to feel the tension.

Maggie loved her family. Very much. The problem was that they loved her, too, and could not stand the changes she'd made in her life. Among those changes, as far as they were concerned, was Ben. They liked Ben just fine. He and Maggie's father, Frank, had enjoyed several conversations ranging from movies to music to politics. They could discuss almost anything civilly, excluding only sports (of which Ben knew remarkably little) and Maggie (of whom Ben knew far too much for Frank's comfort). The biggest problem they had was not Ben, however, or even the fact that she and Ben lived in the same house. No, the biggest problem was Maggie's absolute refusal to attend church with them. Even when Maggie had been turning tricks as a method of paying for school and saving for the future, she'd still attended church on Sundays. Sometimes with her family, sometimes without, but she'd attended.

The problem wasn't that Maggie had given up on God. It seemed, however, that the same could not be said in reverse. Maggie had been raised in the Catholic faith. She'd gone to church right up until the time she became a vampire. Afterwards she had issues, not the least of which was that her actions were partially responsible for the churches' being desecrated and nearly destroyed on Halloween a few years earlier. She'd been paid to seduce the clergy in Black Stone Bay and she'd done her job very well. What she had not known then, had not understood at the time, was that her actions were paid for in a very successful attempt to break the faith of those clergy. Priests, preachers, rabbis, and others of faith had that faith tested by Maggie's seductive skills, and most of them failed. With their faith broken, the houses of God were no longer the sanctuaries they should have been, and the vampires had little trouble shattering the very locations that should have offered haven against them.

And whether she liked to say it or not, Maggie blamed herself for the fall of the sacred places.

Even that, however, was only a small problem. Because once the troubles had ended in town, the churches got back to being churches. New clergymen were sent for, who then took the place of their predecessors and did the work of spreading the Word of God to the best of their ability. And their best, apparently, was quite good.

Maggie hadn't understood why Jason Soulis wanted the clergy taken out until after their replacements showed up. She'd heard the stories, same as he had, about how vampires could not abide the cross. As it turned out, that was so much rhetoric. Maggie had and wore several crucifixes. She was in her room at that very moment and there was a good chance that she was choosing which one she intended to wear.

No. It wasn't the cross that was the problem. It was the faith behind the cross. Or behind the Star of David or for that matter behind the belly of a good, fat Buddha for all they knew. The churches and synagogues and mosques weren't the issue. It was what they fostered. Though the faithful were not as numerous as they surely must have been in different times, they still existed and their presence wasn't exactly painful, but it was decidedly uncomfortable as far as Maggie was concerned. Faith and the faithful weakened her, made her more vulnerable and even slowed her down. That was the only way she could describe it. Everything about her was lessened in the face of the faithful.

In light of the situation, going to church with her family was an issue and one that her parents couldn't see past. She could hardly tell them what had happened to her, either. *By the way, folks, I drink blood to stay alive and I'll never die.* Not exactly words that make parents proud of their little girl.

He stirred the vegetables together into the pan and then stirred the meat. Chili for dinner. He made decent chili and he wasn't in the mood for anything more difficult to cook. Garlic was another of those things that proved untrue about vampires. He was grateful for that. Garlic went into almost everything he cooked. Cans of tomatoes, tomato paste, more seasonings, all of them were ready to go into the stew pot with the meat and would soon. In the meantime he turned off the heat on the vegetables and stepped outside for a moment to escape the onion juice that was still stinging his eyes.

The backyard of the house on the Cliff Walk stared out at the ocean and the waves that heaved and sighed the day away. Nearly a full acre of land stood between the house and the edge of the cliffs. That entire area was covered with crows. Hundreds of the great black birds sat in the grass, crouched on the branches of the two ancient trees that lurked in the backyard, and perched along the railings that stopped the foolish from merely walking off the land and into the waters below.

Ben stared at the birds, his mouth hanging open for a moment. The birds looked back, making him the center of their undivided attention. Not a one of them made a noise, nor did they move much.

"Shit."

The crows did not respond to his profanity, but merely kept their positions.

The crows were familiar enough. He'd seen them from time to time over the last five years, though never in this volume. They were the harbingers of darker things, violence and death and worse. They were the familiars of Jason Soulis, the creature that had changed Maggie from human into what she was now.

"Maggie." He was barely aware of his lips moving, still, there was that connection and he knew in an instant that she'd heard him. He felt her moving through the massive house, stepping gracefully from the room where she was dressing herself for the appearance of her family and heading down to where he stood looking out across the ocean of black feathers that separated them from the actual ocean that drove against the cliffs again and again in an endless dance.

Ben kept his eyes on the birds, as if they might decide to disappear if he blinked. He couldn't have that. It would be like letting Soulis win an argument without having ever said a word.

Maggie was next to him a moment later, her hand on her cell phone, already dialing the numbers she had programmed in to let her speak to Soulis.

"Jason." Her voice was surprisingly calm. "You could call, you know. I have company coming over and I really don't want to explain to them why there are a zillion crows tearing up the lawn." Her voice held a tinge of humor, but the expression on her face was a quiet challenge.

Ben rolled his shoulders and hated the feeling of helplessness that was building around him. At the end of the day he was human, and that left him at a distinct disadvantage when it came to the man Maggie was speaking to. That didn't make him hate the man any less.

"And while I'm sure this is amusing to you, Jason, I still have guests coming over. Please get rid of your damned birds, before I ask Ben to go after them with a shotgun." She nodded her head a few times, short, curt nods, and Ben wished he could hear the words the man was saying on the other end of the line. "That's very nice. Yes. We'll talk soon, but for now I have plans that include my family."

Maggie sighed and paced away from the window. As she did, the birds took off, lifting into the air in a nearly solid wave. Even knowing that they were merely birds, knowing what made them act so strangely, the sight was unsettling.

Maggie walked into the other room and Ben forced himself to stay where he was. He wanted to follow her, to listen in, to help, but he also knew that she needed to handle Jason on her own more than she needed his assistance. Just like he knew his tendency to want to dote drove her a little crazy from time to time.

When he realized he'd clenched his hands into fists, he made them relax and moved back to the kitchen. There was still a meal to make.

And if he resented his placement as the cook and servant in the house, he knew there was no one to blame but himself. Still, sometimes he hated the way his life was unfolding.

The lawn was clear again, as if nothing had ever happened. That didn't lighten his mood in the least. Jason Soulis had that effect on him. The reason was easy to understand and he was exactly honest enough with himself that he had to admit it, too.

Maggie was at Soulis's beck and call. He didn't know if that was because the man had caused her transformation or if there was more to it, but Soulis could call and she would come running, even if she was putting on a good show of being independent. And it was a show. That was the part that was bothering him the most right then. She left the room to talk with Jason because she didn't want Ben to hear the conversation. It was exactly that simple.

He moved back into the kitchen and back to the food he was preparing. What he wanted to do was simply leave the house, and there was a small part of him — small but vocal of late — that thought leaving Black Stone Bay wouldn't be a bad idea at all, even if that meant leaving Maggie behind.

No. He crushed that notion as quickly as it flashed into his mind. The thought scared him more than he wanted to realize. Maybe what they had was love, maybe not, but either way she meant too much to him to ever want to let her go.

It's possible that he might have let himself follow the darker train of thought, but for now, for the moment, he needed to finish dinner. Maggie's family was coming over, and she needed his support to deal with them.

She needed him. In the end, that would have to be enough.

***

Maggie stared at Ben over the bowl of chili. The meal was as delicious as ever, and Ben was as charming as could be while they entertained her family, but there was something going on in him that she couldn't quite get a handle on. Normally she could sense what was going through his head with ease — he was the proverbial open book — but just now he was hiding from her and while she might have been able to force the issue, it would have been uncomfortable.

She could guess, of course. It was Jason's sending his birds and her responding.

A look around the room and she tried to push all of that aside. Her family was here, and they were all acting that little bit off that they always acted since she'd stopped going to church. There had to be a way around that, but very little was coming to mind.

Unless she took care of it the way she had before.

No. Best not to think that way.

When she'd met Jason Soulis he'd hired her for the simple purpose of seducing the clergy in town. She hadn't understood why until he explained it to her later, but the idea was to cause them to question their own faith. By betraying their vows to church or significant others, she made them doubt themselves and their connection to their god. The end result? According to Jason that lack of faith made it easier for him to move through Black Stone Bay. All she knew with absolute certainty is that the Houses of God were not easy for her to be around. She wasn't sure she could physically enter any of them at this point, but there were still things she didn't completely understand about her current condition. Jason was the only reliable teacher she'd encountered, and he wasn't exactly forthcoming with most information.

Her father's hand touched her wrist. Frank Preston was a big man, weathered and tough, and he was like putty in her hands. Her father loved her and she knew it, even though his disappointment was still there, an undercurrent to remind her that she was failing to meet the guidelines she'd been raised with.

How does one explain that one has become a monster?

Maggie smiled for her father. He had an expectant look on his face. Ben sent the thought straight into her mind; his voice, clear as a bell, but his lips didn't move and his eyes were looking toward her mother, who was engaged in an animated discussion about Maggie's company. *He wants to know if you're going to your cousin's christening.*

"Of course I'm going." Maggie smiled for her father, even as she lied directly to him. Really, she'd become adept at lying over the years. She sent a mental wave of thanks to Ben, who nodded acknowledgment, even as he answered her mother's questions.

Her mother was always surprised by how well the dresses she designed sold. Maggie was not surprised. She had a good eye for fashion, she sold to the right people, and she also had the advantage of a great deal of money to start the company with. Ben was the one who'd set that up, taking the money he'd stolen from her pimp years ago and carefully funneling it into the company to make sure that everything looked and stayed legitimate. The first year the business might have failed, but Ben was there to make it work. The recession came around and a lot of businesses that were better built than hers fell under the weight, but not hers. Ben worked his miracles again and while the company didn't exactly thrive, it stayed above water. And now? Well, now her designs were gaining in popularity and her mom had seen some of her dresses for sale at Macy's, and suddenly Maggie's silly little dream of being a dress designer was a reality even in her cynical mother's eyes.

Ben did that. She reminded herself of that fact every day.

It helped her keep her mind off of Jason. She didn't love Jason. She knew that, but she obsessed over him. He crept into her thoughts at the damnedest times, and he lingered in her mind's eye like a puzzle she couldn't quite solve. Jason Soulis was very annoying that way.

She shook thoughts of Jason out of her head, like shaking away cobwebs, and smiled for her father. He smiled back, doubly pleased that she was going to make it to the church and the christening, and just like that she knew what she had to do. She had to corrupt the priests at

Sacred Hearts. If she could break their faith, she could once again attend the church as a member.

Ben laughed at something her mother said and whispered something back with a conspiratorial look on his face. Her mom swatted his arm playfully and blushed. Maggie would have never thought Ben capable of flirting when they first met, but he'd eventually caught on to the idea.

There are moments when decisions are made. Sometimes a person can look back and know exactly when all that was good and right fell apart. Later Maggie would look at that dinner as the moment when she ruined her life. At that moment, however, she was still happy.

Amazing, isn't it, how fleeting happiness can be?

CHAPTER FIVE

The tide pulled back and Dave rolled from his watery grave, his eyes burning with the salt of the ocean's caress. As he stood up, he coughed out the heavy flow of water that had filled his lungs since the moment when a nightmare had killed him.

Killed him. No mistake. He knew he was dead. He could feel it, the differences taking place within his body, the way that his blood no longer moved, his heart failed to beat. His lungs, well, they'd been filled with brine for the last dozen hours and he was still moving.

He looked around and recognized where he was immediately. Just the day before he'd been pulling a body from the reef where he'd been unceremoniously shoved.

Water drooled from his lips which felt stiff in a way that was puzzling, as if they'd been stung by bees and swollen with toxins—and he spat furiously, desperate to escape the taste of seawater. As soon as he was done with that, the hunger started. It was a deep feeling, locked into his stomach, yes, but more than that. He could feel it throughout his body. His lips were numb, his face felt half-lifeless, but the hunger was a living, breathing thing and it demanded attention.

Dave started from the water, shaking his head and pushing at the waves that wanted to keep him. Each step he took increased his consciousness, and his anger. Frank had done this to him. Perhaps not intentionally, but the man had led him to his death, and Dave was not at all amused by that notion. Frank was a good man, yes, a good employer, but where the hell was he now?

"Frank. We need to talk, buddy." His voice was wrong: it was low and gurgled. Dave took in as deep a breath as he could and felt the fluids burbling in his lungs. A moment later he was coughing, forcing the ocean's remnants from his chest, hacking out brackish water and shreds of something black he didn't even want to contemplate.

"Testing, testing…" That was better. More like what he was supposed to sound like.

The clothes he was wearing were heavy, waterlogged, and cold and genuinely uncomfortable. He stripped them away, not at all concerned about anyone seeing him in his birthday suit. He'd just spent twelve hours being rocked by the tide and pushed against a prison of stone and sand while he considered how badly he had screwed up.

The thing that had grabbed him hadn't been human. He knew that. Maybe once, maybe not, it was hard to tell past the black shroud that wrapped its body. And yes, it was a shroud. He'd seen pictures and illustrations and he could see that the stuff wrapped around the body was pulled tight, a cloak meant to cover a corpse. He'd also seen the dead, gray skin under that shroud and the teeth, damn, the teeth that had sunk into his neck, his shoulder and broken skin, pulled blood from him like a vacuum.

Dave stopped, let his hands move up to examine his neck and shoulder, the places where he'd felt impossible teeth chewing away at him like he was a fucking Big Mac. No wounds. He tried to look over the area, but it wasn't possible, the wounds he remembered were too close to his face. He touched the flesh carefully, examining the spot, hating that his skin still felt oddly numb.

Not far away he could hear people talking in low conversational noises. There was no sense of urgency from those tones, merely people talking and enjoying each other's company. He looked toward the docks and saw them, four teenagers, older, possibly in college, and his hunger flared like a flash of lightning cutting a calm sky in half.

Dave Burke was a smart man. He'd been raised with a minor handicap and knew exactly how little it meant in the real world. He'd studied hard; he'd taken night courses; he'd striven hard to make himself a better man than his station in life might have expected of him. He avoided the lure of drink and drugs and he focused on his studies. He was a sociable enough man in life. He had a few friends and despite the odd shape of his hand, he was handsome enough and quick enough with the charm to have female companionship from time to time, even if he never quite managed to keep a steady girlfriend for more than a few months at a time—and he was smart enough to know that the problem there was not his malformed hand, but his sense of priorities. Had you asked him how it was that he'd managed to avoid a lot of the worst pitfalls for a person who could easily have become a victim not only to school bullies—children can be very cruel to the physically different—but also to the vices waiting to numb a person's palms, he would have said it was good instincts.

It was the same instincts that sent him toward the four teens sitting along the docks. He was hungry. Instinct alone told him how to handle the problem.

***

Stephanie looked around the playground and smiled. In the windows of the school she could see orange and black crepe paper, and on the wall next to the door of Miss Nora's class, a mummy grinned at her from its position next to a witch with a broom and a black cat. She wanted to be a witch for Halloween. She knew that as sure as she knew her name.

The air was cool, but not so cold that it made her nose sting, and she smiled even brighter. Halloween was almost on them and she loved Halloween. Her daddy always told her ghost stories around Halloween and even when Mommy got upset, all she had to do was ask again and he'd tell her another one. She sighed at the thought of her parents. They were getting divorced-but-that-didn't-mean-they-loved-her-any-less. She wasn't sure exactly what all of that meant, except that Mommy was hanging around with a man named Tim a lot and Daddy had moved out of the house.

She saw Daddy on weekends. The weekend was coming soon, and he was going to take her to see a movie. She just had to decide which one they were going to see. He said she could see anything she wanted, as long as they told Mommy it was a cartoon. According to Daddy it wasn't lying if it kept Mommy from yelling.

"Stephanie." The voice was familiar, but she didn't see anyone at first. Stephanie frowned and looked around the schoolyard and the playground. School was out and the buses were about to leave. She would have to hurry to get to the bus on time.

As she stood up and adjusted her pack, a grown-up hand covered her mouth. She struggled, of course, because the stranger had grabbed her by surprise and she wasn't even supposed to talk to strangers.

Turned out it wasn't talking the stranger had in mind.

***

Sometimes life is not kind. Oftentimes it is not fair. And while Jonathan knew those words were true, he knew on an intellectual level and not because of anything he'd ever gone through in his life. He was a college student. He had perfect grades. He was studying what he wanted and with his parents' blessings. He was also enjoying the hell out of himself in the process. At twenty-four years of age he should have graduated already, and he could have, but he was far too busy enjoying the lifestyle to care and his parents didn't mind that he had switched majors again (his new major was physical therapy with emphasis on massage and homeopathic treatments) as long as he behaved himself and, more importantly, avoided any scandals for the family.

There had been a few of those in the past, and he'd learned. These days it was best to follow the rules and stay away from the worst troubles. Currently his hair was stuffed into an oversized knit cap that hid the dreadlocks he was sporting. They'd be going away in another month, of course, because his dad expected him home for the holidays, and they'd shit themselves if he came anywhere near the house looking like he did at the moment. Scraggly beard, dreadlocks, pierced eyebrow — they were all going away. Until then he intended to look the part of an impoverished college student in a school where poverty was more of an intellectual concept than a reality. Why? Because the look attracted exactly the sort of girls he liked to spend his time with, and the best part of his current life was getting laid regularly.

He pushed his glasses back up his lean face and took a pull from his bottle of Fresh Kill Ale. He liked the taste and he got a kick out of the name, but mostly he drank it because it was currently fashionable to drink that particular beer. It should be, with the exorbitant cost. Tanya leaned into him and nuzzled her pretty face against his shoulder. He moved one long, lean arm around her shoulders and rested his chin against her skull. She was cute, vapid, and liked to cuddle. Perfect, in other words. He liked a good intellectual discussion, but not with whomever he was sleeping with.

The docks were nearly empty already, and that suited him just fine. He had a boat that was almost ready for drydock, but in the meantime it would also serve as a great spot for sleeping with Tanya. Brett and Mandy were also going to be using the yacht for the same reason. Why? Because there was a game tonight and the four of them wanted a place a little quieter than the quad for their night of intimacy and minor violations of the law. The Ecstasy would be kicking in soon, and when it did they'd retire to the privacy of Mom and Dad's latest method of reminding him to behave. Until then they were enjoying the chilling breeze from the water and the peace and quiet.

And when the naked guy started walking their way, Jonathan had to wonder if the X had been tainted with something else, because naked men didn't often come waltzing along the docks looking like they were on a mission. At least not in his experience.

Brett said something witty and both of the girls giggled. Tanya's hand slipped along Jonathan's lean thigh and sent shivers through him. She was a good-looking girl, no two ways about it. Her auburn hair was teasing along the side of his face, captured by the wind, and he almost pulled away from her because a stray strand was tickling his nostril, but he stayed where he was, mesmerized briefly by the naked guy.

He was about to mention the strange event—having finally decided he was not imagining things, when Mandy beat him to it. "OmiGAWD!" She pointed, her mouth hanging open and slowly spreading into a grin.

It had to be the lighting on the docks, but the man's flesh was pale, grimy, and gray. His skin looked mottled, with spots where he looked horribly bruised. The Ecstasy must have kicked in, because he knew what it was called when the blood pooled in a body but he couldn't think of the word to save his life but yeah, it looked like that. Like blood had settled in a dead body. Only the colors were wrong and the guy was naked, his

Johnson swinging casually with each stride he took, and his hair was wet, plastered to his body, his skin dripping with water. He wasn't a corpse, so he couldn't have lividity marks. Wait. Lividity. That was the word.

"Dude! What the fuck?" Brett was standing up. He wasn't a jock, not really, but sometimes he acted the part anyway. Mostly he was bristling because his girlfriend was currently staring at a stranger's junk as the guy came closer.

The stranger reached out with one hand and grabbed Brett by the throat. Brett immediately started trying to cough, his face turning dark red, and the stranger lifted him completely off the ground. "Shut your face, Frank. You're pissing me off." He had no idea who the hell Frank was, but Brett was suffering the consequences of whatever Frank had done. The stranger was close enough now that Jonathan could see the blisters covering the lower part of his face, tiny black pustules in a shape like a starfish or a handprint. The X had to be tainted. That was all there was to it, because the naked guy was looking too dead to be on the move otherwise.

Jonathan wasn't a violent man. He avoided fights whenever possible, because it was hard to look properly sensitive when you had a hundred stitches from some asshole with a bad attitude's kicking the crap out of you. He'd learned that lesson a long time back. Just the same he reached out to help his friend.

And the Gray Man moved again, his left hand grabbing at Jonathan's wrist. The hand that clutched his arm was wrong: it felt like some kind of snake, with soft spots that shouldn't have been soft and a few bones that seemed to hold the entire affair together. Maybe the rest of the Gray Man was in excellent shape—including the annoyingly large penis that was swaying as he moved, like Jonathan needed another reason for an inferiority complex, thanks very much—but his hand was deformed. He took a perverse sense of satisfaction from that fact even as he felt revulsion at the cold skin that gripped his arm.

Jonathan tried to pull away, fought hard against the malformed hand, but failed to manage his escape. He looked toward the Gray Man's face and gaped, having trouble accepting the raw strength in the underdeveloped fingers.

The Gray Man looked his way, his eyes lost in pools of shadow, his face seemingly carved from stone it was so damned immobile. A shiver crept through Jonathan, and the man's cold expression changed. His mouth opened in a sneer of contempt. That sneer revealed teeth that were impossible and actually getting more impossible by the second. The teeth were growing, splitting dead, gray gums bloodlessly as they lengthened and thickened within the mouth.

"I'm going to kill you now, Frank." The words were not distorted by the new teeth or the altered shape of the lips holding those teeth in place. They were just as clear as crystal, and Jonathan renewed his efforts to get away as the meaning of those words sank in.

"I'm not Frank! Fuck off! Go the fuck away!" His voice cracked, rose nervously. And he slapped with his free hand, trying to escape the steel fingers crushing the meat of his arm into the bones beneath. In the demon's other hand, Brett had stopped struggling. His eyes bulged widely from their sockets, and his face had turned so dark it almost looked black.

And all Jonathan could think was that things must have been happening very fast, because it wasn't until that moment that either of the girls started screaming. Tanya's voice was so loud and so distorted that he couldn't make out what she said, but at least she was speaking. Mandy just let out a shriek and stared at Brett's unblinking eyes in his darkening face.

The Gray Man dropped Jonathan to the boardwalk and bit into Brett as if he were chomping down on an apple. Brett's head bobbed to the side while the freak sucked noisily. The expression on the Gray Man's face bordered on ecstatic.

In the end, there was only one decision as far as Jonathan was concerned. He stood up, looked carefully at the thing that finished drinking the blood from his friend, and then he ran. Tanya was cute, but she could save herself. Mandy was just, well, she was kind of trashy anyway, so he ran.

Behind him Mandy started to scream again and then stopped abruptly. There were a few snapping noises and he dared a look back, just in time to see the Gray Man bending Mandy backward, several spots on her torso twisted into new shapes by the nightmare's strength.

Tanya was hauling ass in his direction, her eyes wide and frightened and her mouth drawn down in a grimace of terror. Tanya was on the track team; she blew past him like he was standing still, so he moved, pumped his legs harder, wanting to get the hell away from the madness with his body intact. The punch line to an old joke rocked through his head: "I don't have to be faster than the bear, I just have to be faster than you." The boards of the dock slammed and groaned under his feet, adding a staccato to the sound of his heavy breaths.

The Gray Man had other ideas. He risked another look over his shoulder and saw the bodies of his friends, but no sign of the thing that had killed them. He was just getting ready to thank God for that when the thing dropped from above him and caught his arm for the second time.

Nothing could be that fast. Nothing he had ever seen could fly like that, either. Jonathan stared at the Gray Man and froze, unable to accept what had just happened. His mind simply would not process the information. Behind him he saw Tanya dwindling in the distance, not bothering with a backward glance as she pelted to the edge of the docks and the gently sloping road that led to Black Stone Bay proper. His eyes teared and a sense of betrayal cut at him.

The Gray Man blocked his view, its eyes burning with a dark intensity. The eyes were wrong, black and wet, like the eyes of a rat, bulging in their recessed sockets. It was still changing, becoming something else, even as it looked him over. The teeth were thicker now, longer, and the thing's mouth seemed incapable of properly closing. Fine strands of what looked like black hair were floating from the thing, creeping out of its flesh and waving like the slow-moving cilia of an amoeba. He knew all about amoebae, from back when he'd been majoring in marine biology.

"Told you I'd kill you, Frank." The voice was a little slurred past all those impossible teeth, but he could still understand the words.

"I told you. I'm not Frank." His lips pressed together. "My name is —"

That was as far as he got before the Gray Man bit into his neck and face with jaws that opened too far to be real.

The pain of the bite was short-lived. The blood loss saw to that. But far worse was the feeling of loss as something vital jumped from Jonathan to the Gray Man.

***

Three of them died because of Dave's instincts. He fed on the hairy one and dropped the body, inconvenienced by the feel of the boy's facial hairs stuck between his teeth. The last of them, the girl with the rust-colored hair, was running hard and fast and he contemplated letting her go because he was nearly sated.

But really, only nearly sated. For that reason alone he rose back into the air and chased after her. He had never flown before a few moments ago, but that was all right. He'd never been dead before, either. His body was still changing, becoming something else, and he supposed in a distant way that he should have been panicked by the changes, but he wasn't. He was stronger than ever, faster, and his senses seemed to have sharpened to unnatural levels. Take the girl that was running: he could hear her heartbeat, see from fifty yards away that she was terrified, and that she'd broken a hard sweat as she tried to escape from him.

Instinct. Dave followed his again. When he grabbed the girl he lifted her completely off the ground until she was kicking and squirming and fighting without the traction to properly fend him off. Her feet kicked against his legs, even moved up to crash between his thighs but the pain was minimal. Most of him was still unsettlingly numb, almost dead. The thought amused him distantly.

Rather than bite her flesh, he pulled her protesting form closer until he could kiss her mouth with his lips. She fought harder still, screaming even as his lips covered hers. She was still fighting as hard as she could when he drew in a mighty breath, and sucked the air from her lungs, the life from her body. Her body shivered and convulsed and she fell back bonelessly, hanging limp in his hands.

He pulled her dead form closer again and kissed her once more, breathing back a portion of what he'd stolen from her. Her eyes flickered and then she was still.

She was breathing when he set her down on the ground.

His instincts said to leave this one alive, and so he did.

***

Fame comes with a price. Had anyone told Brad Hunter that when he was younger, he would have said he didn't mind paying that price in the least, and he'd have said it with a perfect smile on his handsome face. That was the good old days, when he was younger and the world wanted to know him better.

These days the world was not quite as eager as it had been, and the smile that had charmed so many was a pale shadow of what had been. These days Brad Hunter was a has-been in the eyes of Hollywood, and the girls who'd wanted to know him better and maybe hear all about his latest exploits in the likes of *16 Magazine* and *Teen Beat* had moved on to actors who'd been accused of having more substance than Brad. Mostly he was okay with that; the whole idea of being a celebrity had lost its appeal a long time ago, and he wanted little more than to have a nice, comfortable existence.

He was trying to explain that to Bernie Lapham, who had worked as his agent since he was the ripe old age of fifteen. Eighteen years later, Bernie kept calling him when the occasional offers came in, and Brad kept letting him down gently.

Only this time the offer had a certain appeal. Mostly the offer was for a great deal of money, and that coming at the end of a very long and drawn-out divorce.

"I'm not sold, Bernie. I'm just saying if you can get a really good offer then I'll seriously consider it." He spoke calmly and kept his eyes on the road, not taking any chances with the BMW or the property around him. This was Black Stone Bay, and what wasn't considered a historical landmark was probably painted in gold leaf. Best to be careful when driving.

"We're talking a sweet bit, Brad. We're talking good money and a serious role, not another guest appearance on a cop show."

Brad shook his head. There had been a lot of offers in the past, and for about two years all of them had boiled down to guest-starring on different TV detective shows as a parody of himself. He had no desire to mock his old career or his life, regardless of how nice the monetary considerations.

"I haven't been in front of a camera in eight years, Bernie. And I haven't needed to be in front of one." Which was true enough. He'd been working as a producer for a lot of smaller projects over the years, but that was a different beast. Producer versus actor. He'd tried his hand at directing a couple of times, but it was important to know where your strengths were and where your weaknesses were, too. He couldn't direct. Not any more than he could compose music. It wasn't something he was ever going to get good at.

"Brad, listen to me. This is a legitimate chance to show you've got talent. Added bonus, they want to pay real money."

"I'm all for the real money part, Bernie, and you know it. Like I said, send me something I can read and I'll get back to you." He killed the call. There was nothing else going on. It was just that simple. The divorce was finalized, his old life was gone and he was more than glad to move on, but he wasn't going to jump into the waters without testing them first. The last time he'd done that, his career had taken a nosedive, though to be fair it had been helped along by his falling for the hype that his life had generated at that point.

Three DUIs, a couple of run-ins with paparazzi where he threw fists, and two girls who claimed he'd forced himself on them had all thrown monkey wrenches into his career. He was guilty on all counts except for forcing himself on the girls. The good news was simply that they eventually settled out of court for monetary considerations. But the damage was done and the golden boy of Hollywood quickly became another tarnished example of what happens when you start thinking you're indestructible.

Good PR people had saved him from himself to a very real extent, but they'd barely managed to save his career in Hollywood in the process. He wasn't a kid anymore and he wasn't a child actor anymore, either. Instead he was simply doing his best to get by. He left the Hollywood area and made his money on the sidelines instead, investing in movies and working behind the scenes. He'd made enough to stay comfortable, even by the standards of Tinseltown, but his receding hairline and the lines on his face had taken away most of his worries about whether he'd ever be a sex symbol again. He wasn't ugly, but he also wasn't exactly star material these days, either. That was for the best, maybe. He wasn't as likely to get himself in trouble if he didn't let all the glitter distract him from reality.

And then there was Stacia, and the marriage from Hell. Or, as he liked to put it, the main reasons for his hair loss and the lines on his face. Stacia Dunham had come out of nowhere and made a name for herself working alongside him in one of his last movies, *Because of Her*, a piece of fluff teen romance that was embarrassing at best and a failure even by Hollywood's standards. It broke even, but only after two years of video sales and reruns on Showtime. Those numbers, on top of his continuing spiral into stupidity, had left him stunned and staggering and vulnerable to Stacia's advances.

It wasn't fair to say that she manipulated him, but that didn't stop him from saying it anyway. The fact of the matter was that the two of them should never have married and he should have listened to everyone involved and paid attention to terms like "prenuptial agreement" before taking his vows. He should have also been able to accept that nothing was going to work out, not even after they'd gone to marriage counselors and moved themselves away from California in an effort to save the joke that passed for their marriage.

The one good thing? Stephanie. Their little girl. She was perfect. She made all of the shit worthwhile. Through the epic ugliness of the divorce—which was now finalized and left Brad emotionally and financially close to ruination—he had Stephanie as a balancing point. Despite Stacia's best efforts to keep him from his daughter, the final decision was that they still had joint custody. Not much else mattered after that.

Brad pulled into the driveway of his house and shook his head. At least Stacia hadn't gotten this from him. She would have if she'd been able to manage it, but despite her best efforts the house that had belonged to his cousin was still in the family. Though he now occupied the property and paid the terrifying taxes on the land, it was still technically in his cousin's name for another two years. She and her entire family were still technically missing until then. No one believed they were anything but dead, but without bodies, that was very hard to prove. Brad didn't know all of the details. He didn't want to know them or need to know them. He'd loved Michelle Lister like a sister, had even thought the douche she married—Bill was a bit of okay when he wasn't eyeing every girl he saw like fresh meat, but he also knew his cousin well enough to understand that if she were alive she'd have returned to the house long ago. Brad had spent five years adjusting to the fact that his cousin was dead. He didn't expect any miracles or that anyone would suddenly find her alive and well and living in the Bahamas. But because of the legalities, Stacia couldn't take this from him. Considering that the house and property were worth a couple of million dollars, he was okay with that.

The house was technically a mansion, and it was along the Cliff Walk, possibly the most expensive bit of property in a hundred miles. Opulent didn't begin to cover it. That was okay. After his previous existence in California, a little extravagance was a good thing.

And Stephanie deserved nothing less when she came to stay with him.

Brad parked the car and climbed out, looking down the length of the driveway as he did almost every time, eyeing the property and enjoying the view. So he wasn't taken completely by surprise when the police cars came up the driveway, lights flashing.

The problem with a bitter divorce? In this case it was simply that Stacia assumed the worst of her ex-husband when her daughter disappeared. And just that simply all the goodness and light left Brad's world.

Stephanie was missing.

His little girl was gone.

Taken.

***

"Have you ever seen a ghost?" Leah asked the question with the directness reserved for little children, staring up at Malcolm with eyes that were unsettlingly similar to her aunt's. Malcolm looked at the girl for a few seconds and smiled. This? This little girl was probably exactly what Carly had looked like at the same age. He thought she was absolutely precious.

Somehow the best laid plans had fallen apart. Carly's sister was having some sort of meltdown and that meant that Carly was watching the little girl who looked so much like her. He was okay with that. No misunderstanding here, he'd have preferred a night of snuggling and more, but he was all right with taking Carly and her niece out for a bout of Halloween costume shopping.

Leah was waiting for an answer. "Not around here, but I saw a couple when I lived in Louisiana." That was true. He wouldn't even consider going into details with the little girl, but he wasn't going to lie about it, either. Malcolm disliked lying.

"What did they look like?"

He disliked lying, but he wasn't above it. Explaining that a disembodied head had come screaming through his room was maybe a bit too intense for the average preschooler, and there was no way in hell he was going to talk about the other one, the one that had left him with nightmares for years afterwards.

"Like Casper. Clear, and white and creepy." That was the best she was getting. Apparently it was enough, because she held up the package that had a "Guaranteed Creepy" ghost costume and grinned ear to ear.

"I want this one!" The kid was almost dancing in the aisle. He stared at her, enraptured. Sometimes he forgot how cute kids were. In his defense, there weren't a lot of them wandering around the campus where he spent most of his time.

Carly rolled her eyes and shook her head, smiling all the while. "Then you have to say please."

Leah looked from Malcolm to Carly and then back again, her eyes as wide as saucers in her little face. "Pleeeeeeease?" How the hell could anyone say no to a kid that cute?

"What about you?" He looked to Carly and stared at the bundle in her hands. She was doing a very good job of not letting him see exactly what she'd picked out, but he could see fishnet stockings and that part didn't hurt his feelings at all.

"Oh, no." She shook her head and pouted playfully. "It's bad luck to let you see my costume before Halloween."

"I thought that was wedding dresses on wedding days." He'd never heard that one before.

"It's both."

"Far be it from me to argue with a beautiful woman."

"Two beautiful women!" Leah held out two fingers in a peace sign, and Malcolm laughed.

"Two beautiful women. You win."

"What about you? Are you getting dressed up?" Carly looked at him, one eyebrow raised in a half-challenge. So far he'd been resisting the idea of playing dress up, even for Halloween. His mother frowned on Halloween, called it a day for devils. Malcolm did not agree and never had. He'd gone out every year when he was younger and the Devil had never come around to cause any grief. It was one of the points where he and his mother disagreed after all of these years. He'd have been stuck at home for certain if his father hadn't been around to disagree with his mother back in his youth.

Still, he smiled. "I've got something in mind."

"What are you dressing up as?" Carly stepped closer, her hand moving around his bicep.

"Oh, no." He shook his head and smiled, the thick dreadlocks rolling across his jacket. "You don't tell me, I don't tell you. Fair is fair."

"There's nothing fair about that at all, Malcolm. I think that's cheating." Her tone was playful.

"You'll see on Halloween. Until then, you'll just have to wait." His grin only grew wider as she shook her head.

Leah did a perfect imitation of her aunt and shook her head, rolling her eyes. "That's what you get when you keep secrets…."

Malcolm chuckled and picked the little girl up. She smiled and hugged him, her skin as pale as milk next to him. She smelled of baby shampoo, and her breath tickled along his neck as she hugged, her ghost costume crinkling inside its package. "Let's go get food."

"Chinese! Chinese!" Leah's voice was almost enough to blow out an eardrum, but that was okay.

"So you want pizza?"

Leah's eyes looked at his face, studied him in that way that seemed exclusive to children—without guile, in other words—and she shook her head again. "No, silly, I want egg rolls."

He could see the frown of disapproval on Carly's face. "We don't call people names, Leah...."

Chinese. He could do that. What he could not do, would not do, was stop Carly from chastising the child. That wasn't his place. The thought brought a smile to his face. Maybe if they ever had kids of their own.

It was that thought that made him realize how much he liked the girl he was spending all of his spare time with. The notion that he might someday have children with her should have terrified him, but instead it felt like Christmas, like something special and sacred.

"Chinese it is," he said, making sure not to look at Carly for a moment. That would be foolish when his heart wanted so much to be worn on his sleeve. Instead he carried the little girl to the cash registers and waited in line with child and aunt alike, playing what-if and imagining what might be someday.

He should have been terrified. He knew for a fact that Randy would have been scared to death by the very notion.

If Randy had been capable of thinking at that point.

***

Had he ever felt so cold? Randy Dunbar didn't think so. He hadn't climbed from the bed all day, and now that night was properly surrounding him, he still had no desire. Nor had he left the bed the day before, except once, to empty his bladder.

Today that hadn't worked as well. He'd pissed the bed and so had Vikki. The two of them lacked the strength to do much more than moan occasionally, and much as he might have wanted to change that, he couldn't even generate the interest needed to do anything about it. The cold was too powerful. The smell of something dead permeated the air in the room, so instead of bothering with it, Randy simply breathed through his mouth.

Malcolm should have been home. He should have come in and checked on him by now, but it was the weekend and he knew that meant his brother would be hanging around with Carly instead. Carly had possibly the finest ass he'd ever seen but even that wasn't enough to make Randy care. No. He was, if anything, angry about it. Malcolm was supposed to be there to make it better when things went wrong. He'd always been there, and now when Randy needed him, he was nowhere to be seen. Nothing much mattered beyond the cold that made his joints ache, his eyes burn, and his teeth chatter. Next to him in the bed, Vikki was moaning and nearly curled over on herself, shivering in the cocoon of thick quilt she'd managed to wrap around her body. Her breaths sounded horrible: wet and strained and almost burbly.

He had to move, that was all there was to it. If he stayed still, if he gave into the desire to huddle in the soggy blankets for warmth, he would surely die. Vikki would die. He liked her. Maybe not enough to make their relationship serious, but he liked her.

It seemed to take forever to move his arm, but eventually it lifted from under the covers and reached for the phone beside the bed. His eyes focused almost exclusively on the cellular phone, but he saw the dark shape standing nearby just the same. It was the same form he'd seen the night before when he'd made his way to the bathroom, a towering black shadow that merely stood and observed, never speaking, not even moving save to follow his progress with its cloth-covered head, as if it could possibly see him through the veil that covered its narrow face.

"Got nothing to say to you…." He almost called it by name, but he didn't quite dare. To acknowledge Death was bad, but surely calling the Grim Reaper by its name was worse still. He did not want to die. He wanted to live, even though that notion seemed like an impossibility as he flipped open the phone and looked at the lit keypad, trying desperately to remember what he was going to do. The phone hadn't rung that he knew of, so surely he was going to call someone? Perhaps, but he couldn't think of any names.

The darkness stepped closer to him, looking down from its towering heights with a face of shadows that seemed to have no eyes, merely a drooling, bloodied mouth. As Randy watched, a thin trickle of red spittle fell from the shadows where the mouth should have been, but the droplets never quite touched the ground—they had evaporated before that could happen.

His thumb reached out, tapped the 9 button on the phone, and then followed through with a 1 and another 1. A second later the phone dropped from his hand and he let out a small gasp. In his mind he could see the plastic construct striking the ground, shattering, spilling the battery from its backside as it had done a hundred times before. Maybe this time it would break once and for all. That was almost inevitable, wasn't it?

He never even saw Death move. One moment the shadowy form was several feet away, and the next it was holding the phone in a pale hand adorned with thick claws that could surely peel the flesh from his face with ease. He stared at that hand for a long moment and slowly cringed backward, terrified but too weak to do anything about it.

From the hand in front of him the phone spoke with a tinny voice. "Nine-One-One, please state the nature of your emergency....Hello? Can you hear me? Can you speak to me?" The voice started to sound concerned. Randy thought about speaking, but the darkness looming over him seemed to steal away his ability to talk.

Very slowly, like a flower blooming in reverse, the hand closed over his phone and folded it shut.

Randy tried to move, but he was too weak. He closed his eyes instead, drifting into exhausted, fitful sleep.

***

It fed on the two bodies before it, never touching, not needing to. Great, powerful breaths drew in the life force from the two people on the sodden bed, and filled it with vitality. It could almost see the life flowing from them like mist, and when their hearts barely beat, when their lungs scarcely moved, it stopped taking from them and gave back the smallest breath, little more than a gentle sigh.

And then it stepped back, sated for the moment.

The boy moved, sighed, and rolled over on the bed, his skin blistering around his mouth and nose. The girl did not move, but her skin blistered as well, small red sores starting to form around her nostrils and covering her full lips, then filling with a blackness not long after they formed.

It could have left the house, but there was no need; it had found a good place to hide, and it was no longer hungry. For now that was enough. The sound of distant sirens wailing their way closer made it move. It slipped back into the darkness and crawled down to its safe location.

Deep within it, something was happening, something new and

wonderful, perhaps even miraculous. It was not sure what that something was, but it wanted to understand better, and so it rested and contemplated the feeling that was growing inside its core. Distantly it was aware that the boy it fed on the day before was once again alive and moving. More importantly, that boy was feeding, and in turn, what that boy ate was feeding it as well.

It drifted into a daze, barely moving, certainly not breathing, as the paramedics came along with the police, and eventually broke down the door when there was no response to their urgent requests for entry.

The boy and the girl with the blisters forming on their young flesh were taken away, hauled to the local hospital by ambulance. It wasn't bothered by this knowledge: it could still feel them, drifting into their death-like stupors, breathing, but just barely, living by only the thinnest of threads. If it wanted, it could stop their breathing, stop their hearts, but not yet.

It wanted to learn about them first, and about what they were becoming, the better to understand what it had become over the course of five years lost in the darkness.

***

Stacia Dunham Hunter was doing her best to keep from screaming. It wasn't easy. Stephanie was gone. She'd been taken sometime between the time she left for school that morning and the time she should have come home. According to the school administrators and teachers who'd taken attendance, Stephanie had been there all day long. According to the bus driver, she'd never climbed on the bus after school. Never set foot on the big yellow vehicle that should have dropped her off only a block away from the house.

Stacia had been waiting at the bus stop with half a dozen other parents, ready to take her little girl home, but there was no one to hold hands with, to walk with, and to talk about the day's adventures.

Her stomach was a tight knot of fire inside of her, and no matter how hard she tried, she couldn't get a decent breath.

And she knew in her soul that somehow all of this was Brad's fault. Brad, her bastard ex-husband, who couldn't stand the idea that he might lose custody of their child for even a moment. Brad, the control freak. Brad, who always had to have the final word in everything. Brad, who was currently being grilled by detectives about where he was when his daughter disappeared. She hadn't even waited an hour after Stephanie should have been home before she called the police and told them that Brad might have taken her, that he'd made veiled threats before, and that he'd sent her a dozen text messages and emails that promised he would have complete custody of Stephanie one way or another.

Tim put a hand on her shoulder and she leaned back into that hand like an anchor for a second, drawing strength from his touch. "We'll find her, babe."

"God, I hope so." She closed her eyes, felt the heat of a few more tears sliding free from her eyes. She wasn't even trying to stop them. She was lost without Stephanie. That was all there was to it.

When Stephanie was born, everything in Stacia's world got better. Well, everything but her marriage, but that wasn't important anymore. He'd been the wrong guy. The only thing he'd ever done right was to help make Stephanie.

And now he'd taken her. That thought came back again and crushed her stomach into an even tighter knot, burned her insides with fear and heat and hatred. Brad had done this to her, and she hated him right then.

At that moment, given a chance she'd have gleefully cut his throat wide open if it meant getting her baby girl back safely.

It scared her just a little how easily that thought came to her.

Tim said something. She had no idea what it was. "What? I'm sorry baby, I just…" She couldn't think of the words.

"No. It's okay. I just…" He waved his hands in small circles, as if trying to find the right gesture to make his point known. He always talked with his hands, claimed it was his inner Italian coming out. "Whatever you need, okay? Just tell me what you need. We'll work it out." Tim was a sweet man. He was a bit dramatic, but his heart was in the right place and he loved her. She knew that. He loved her. That was pretty amazing when you got right down to it. That was incredible.

She meant to tell him as much, but instead she started crying again, and a second later he was in front of her, holding her, and she was half-folding herself into him and bawling even harder.

It's possible that the hug might have evolved into something more, certainly they had a strong physical relationship, but instead they were distracted by the phone ringing.

"Hello?" Her heart was pounding in her chest, and Stacia waited to hear the voice of a police officer, prayed that voice would tell her that her little girl was safe, that she'd been found and it was all some sort of mistake.

"You told the police I would hurt Stephanie? You actually thought I'd consider hurting her?" Brad's voice was strained, wounded, furious. In that instant she knew that she'd done him wrong. Her anger, her fear, they'd blocked off the simple fact that he loved his daughter. If the world were a perfect place it's possible that she would have apologized, done something to rectify the situation before it could be made much worse, and certainly she wanted to, but her mouth and her mind disagreed with her heart on that one.

"You'd do anything to get back at me and you know it." She heard herself speaking and wished she could take the words back, but it was too late. It had been too late between her and Brad a long time ago; she'd just fooled herself into believing that they could be civil to each other through the process.

Still, she had to try. Her voice softened, and she tried to backpedal. "Brad—"

"Fuck off, Stacia." Had any voice ever sounded so cold or filled with hatred? "You were supposed to be protecting her. You insisted that you could keep my little girl safe. If she's been hurt, I'll make you pay." He hung up the phone before she could respond.

After that, it was tears again. She couldn't help herself. The divorce, the hatred in her ex-husband's voice, the accusation, they all added to the fear over Stephanie's disappearance and the way her entire world had simply fallen to shreds in the last few months.

She cried again, and Tim held her. Sometimes that's all there is. Sometimes it's enough.

***

"Why are we looking at this one, Richie? Why are we even considering this a homicide?"

"We aren't. We're considering this a 'what the fuck was that thing and who should we stick it with'." Richie chewed on his cigar, wishing he could smoke away on it instead of respecting the crime scene, if that was what they were looking at.

"Oh. Red Lady. Why didn't you say so?"

"I just did, Danny. What? You having trouble concentrating these days?"

It was hard to say, because none of what they were seeing made much sense.

There was a body, yes, but it was old, desiccated, withered away to almost nothing, and what was left was looking decidedly unpleasant. Strands of blonde hair scattered around a skull that still carried some flesh on it, but not enough to make it look human any longer. Whatever had happened, the body had been dead for quite some time. Only that didn't make sense, because the body was positioned on the ground, legs spread wide, arms thrown to the sides, fingers scraped along the floor boards, looking like they'd been clawing at the hardwood, marks trenched into the ground as if fingernails had dragged through the wood and torn it apart. There were no nails to be found, or if they were there, they'd broken away. There was no flesh left on the fingertips, no anchors for the nails.

The skull was turned to the side, looking toward the broken window not far away. The window had been broken from the inside, and the glass was scattered over the wraparound porch of the house that the detectives had last visited five years earlier.

There had been screams from the place the night before. As the house was technically abandoned the police didn't mind opening the door when no one answered their knocks. One look at the corpse sent the uniforms calling for detectives. Whalen, always glad to make Richie squirm, had assigned the task to them.

"You know, if you'd just put out for her, Whalen wouldn't give us these stupid-ass assignments." Danny's voice was low and calm, almost conversational.

Boyd very calmly reached for his partner and drove his fist into the meat of Danny's bicep. He made sure to hit him hard enough to bruise.

Holdstedter looked at him and smiled just as soon as he was done wincing.

"You watch your mouth, Danny."

"You're just pissed because you know I'm right."

"Let's just get back to the body, asshole." Richie ignored his partner and studied the details again, not touching, never touching, because they had to decide whether or not the coroner was getting called on this one.

The body was old, dead, and withered, but there were still obvious signs of violence. The torso was torn apart, blasted through the guts like someone had taken a shotgun to the stomach from the inside. There should have been blood all over the place, but no. Nothing. Or very little, far less than there should have been.

"I think we have a serious problem on our hands." Danny's voice was sober.

"What are you thinking?"

"I'm thinking this is Brian Freemont's place. We know that. And I'm thinking that Angela Freemont disappeared a long time ago, and that she was pregnant when she vanished."

"You thinking someone dug up the corpse of a dead pregnant woman?"

"Don't be dense, Richie." His voice was kind enough, but the admonishment was solid. "You and me, my friend, we saw her when she came for Freemont. She was preggers."

Boyd closed his eyes and suppressed a shiver. They'd begun to suspect that something unnatural was going on when the disappearances started half a decade earlier, but they hadn't known for certain that anything was truly insane in the world until several women who'd been reported missing showed up to take Brian Freemont off their hands after they'd arrested him for murder. A cop, allegedly one of the good guys, had committed rape and murder and maybe even worse, and they'd busted him, had him dead to rights on at least one case, and then the women who'd disappeared came back and dragged him kicking and screaming from their squad car. And chief among the culprits? Angela Freemont, the seven-months-pregnant wife of Brian Freemont, who had reported her missing a few weeks earlier.

"Are you saying she came back here?"

"Maybe." Danny looked at him and shrugged.

"Danny, even if it was her, why would she come back now?"

"Maybe she needed to give birth." Danny shook his head. "Maybe she wanted to come back where she thought she'd be safe."

Boyd looked his partner over carefully. He knew Danny was being serious, but the thought was ludicrous. Just the same, he had to consider it. Red Lady meant anything was possible, and this was definitely Red Lady material.

"I don't want to think like this, Danny." He was serious. He hated this.

Danny pointed out the facts, just in case he'd somehow missed them. "Got a dead body, decomposed and lying in Freemont's house. Got a blown-out belly. Got a busted-out window. A dead body that looks like it's been lying here for a few years, only we know it hasn't been, because you and me? We've been checking this place every few months. Because we're stupid like that. Looks a lot to me like something tore out of that dead body, got tired of waiting around and left through the window. Not like a person would, through the door, but like an animal would, through the window. Maybe it couldn't figure out how to open a door. Maybe it doesn't even know what a door is." Danny's voice was slowly rising, stressing, because he didn't like to think this way either.

"I got it." Boyd raised his hand and shook his head. "I got it."

He squatted closer to the body, looking at the ruined flesh, the torn fabric, the lack of blood that should have stained the wooden floors around them. "Tell Whalen not to call in the coroner." He took the stogie from his mouth and spat. "Tell her we got this."

He pulled on his rubber gloves and looked at the body for a moment. The sun was still up. If this was what was left of a vampire, it should still burn in the sunlight. That much hadn't changed as far as he knew.

Danny grabbed his phone and started dialing, and Boyd caught the ankles of the corpse.

He pulled.

The body reared up and screamed through faded, withered lips.

Boyd screamed, too.

Danny was far more eloquent. He pulled his service revolver and blew four amazingly large holes in the withered head of the thing that was reaching for Boyd and probably planning on chewing him apart.

Boyd clutched at his own chest and staggered backward, far more terrified by the screaming corpse than he was by the gunshots. He knew exactly how well his partner could fire a weapon. He didn't expect the screaming dead thing, and he sure as hell hadn't planned it into his day.

While he was still making sure that his heart was a) still where it belonged and b) still beating, Danny grabbed the leg of the dead bitch on the floor and hauled the body out into the sunlight, ignoring the possibility of being discovered in the process.

Goddamned if the body didn't thrash around and struggle as it was pulled from the house. Those ruined, nailless hands? They left trenches in the floorboards as Danny hauled the wasted body away. The withered legs in his hands? They kicked and twisted and tried to escape him. Danny's face showed the horror he felt, the revulsion. Boyd knew the feeling well enough and would have gladly taken the place of his partner to avoid the poor bastard dealing with any more of the sensations. It might have even managed another scream—headless or not, it might have screamed and that was another thought to turn his dreams into nightmares—but Boyd's ears were still ringing from the close-quarters gunfire and he couldn't really tell.

It burned though, when the sunlight hit it. It burned and it struggled and it might have even managed to get away, but Danny grabbed a weathered, broken chair from the porch and pinned the damned thing in place as it smoldered and then blackened, his face set in an expression of disgust.

Danny paced the warped boards of the porch for ten minutes and then came back inside. By that point Boyd was mostly back to feeling human.

Danny grinned. "I think you might have peed yourself a little there, Richie."

Boyd looked at his pants. They were clean. It was just Danny being Danny. "Nah. That's a trouser oyster from thinking about your sister."

"She'd still eat you alive and spit out the bones."

Boyd thought about it and lit his cigar before he answered. "You say that like it's a bad thing."

"Allegedly."

"You get through to Whalen?"

"I got distracted."

"That's why you're my sidekick, you know. It's because you never follow orders."

"I thought it was because you were old and needed someone to help you in and out of the car."

"I'm gonna put my cigar out in your eye, Danny Boy."

"That threat would work better if you weren't so short, Richie."

"Sooner or later you're gonna sit down, and then I'll get you."

"Isn't that what Whalen said to you?" Again with the wide-eyed innocent expression. Maybe that shit worked on the women, but the only thing that stopped Boyd from punching his partner in the nuts was the fact that the man had just saved his life. Again.

"Let's just get the hell out of here and go look into a real case somewhere."

Danny sighed. "Is that code for let's go get ripped and sleep it off?"

"Of course it is. What else would I be suggesting?"

"A threesome with you and Whalen?"

"That husband of hers would kill us both."

"So I could maybe hook him up with my sister."

"Didn't you say she'd eat him alive and spit out the bones?"

"That's a win-win for you, isn't it Richie?"

A deep sigh and he headed for the door, pausing only long enough to kick the remains of the ruined skull ahead of him.

CHAPTER SIX

The first two patients were brought in before midnight. The doctors in the emergency room looked at the pale skin, the heavy sweat stains, and the odd blisters around the mouths and decided they might be dealing with an infection. The two patients were immediately placed into isolation, and the paramedics who'd dealt with them were pulled aside and held for decontamination. That was bad enough, of course, to generate a call to the Centers for Disease Control, but the third victim was enough to start a frenzy of concern. Like the others, she was feverish, pale, sweating, struggling in and out of consciousness, and, of course, had a face covered with red-lined black blisters. Her lips, her nose, her gums, were covered with the red blisters of varying size, some of which had ruptured.

They were not found in the same places. The CDC was nearly screaming orders about the proper isolation of the patients. By mutual agreement, the doctors decided it was best not to alert the public about the strange incidents without first knowing if there was a common cause.

Neil Brighton was the doctor in charge of the emergency room that first night. He was also very familiar with communicable diseases. He made good and damned sure that every person who'd been in contact with the patients, no matter how briefly, was decontaminated, including himself. The proper protocols were immediately enforced, which meant a complete lockdown of the learning hospital at Sacred Hearts. All medical emergencies and situations were to be shipped to Saint Joseph's instead, until further notice. The only exceptions being anyone else who showed similar symptoms. No one wanted an epidemic on their hands. No one wanted to take any chances. Brighton was right in his decision. He followed all the proper procedures to avoid a major epidemic if they were dealing with an airborne contagion.

That made him just a little more popular than Osama Bin Laden in most people's eyes. No one working at the hospital, and none of the patients, wanted to be locked away and kept from their loved ones. No one wanted to take any chances with getting infected by something that might be airborne and capable of potentially killing them.

Brighton didn't care about being popular. He'd seen the end result of diseases escaping their initial contacts before and he never wanted to see it again. The CDC was on the way and they would take care of matters. Until then the people around him could call him names and send all the hatred they wanted to in his direction. They'd thank him later when their families were alive and safe.

The quarantine was inconvenient at best. Everyone who'd come within breathing range of the known infected was locked down in the same area and given a cot to call a bed. That included Brighton. While people were allowed to make phone calls—and really, who could have stopped them— it was made clear that what they were dealing with was simply a precaution against a possibility of infection. No one was considered dangerous at this time and no one was considered infected. They were merely erring on the side of caution against an unknown situation. The doctors and medical staff understood the situation and they were there to calmly, carefully explain that to the people with them. It was best to avoid a panic, and that was basically the end of the discussion.

When no one showed additional signs of dangerous infection everyone felt a little better about the situation. When the samples taken from the three patients showed no signs of known contaminants or viral infections, another sign of relief was released. By the time the sun rose, the CDC was moving in and taking over, and Neil Brighton and his staff allowed themselves to relax a bit. They still had patients to take care of, but even without backup and replacements, it wasn't impossible to stagger the care between the staff and allow everyone a few hours to rest at a time.

After almost twenty-four hours of non-stop activity, Neil took a three-hour nap and was rewarded with a much calmer environment when he awoke. Everyone was still stressed, understandably, but there was less of a sense of restrained panic. The CDC staff confirmed what Neil already knew: that there were no correlating bacterial strains between the victims, nor viral for that matter. At least none that were detectable.

It was just possibly an allergic reaction. It was always possible that all three of the victims had been contaminated at the same place. Black Stone Bay was a small enough community, and they all attended Sacred Hearts University. But it was also just as possible that all three had been poisoned. Not a comforting notion, true enough, but far less terrifying than the idea of a new and uncharted contagion that might spread through everyone.

There were so many possibilities, really. Sometimes it amazed Neil that anyone at all survived on the planet. He did his rounds with Dr. Lisa Davis in tow. That suited him just fine, as Lisa was a cute piece of eye candy: married and faithful, true, but fun to flirt with and fun to look at. His libido just liked to play what-if whenever Lisa was around. They were in good form through the walk-through of the emergency room. No one seemed much the worse for wear, except John Terwilliger, who'd come to them after a rather severe car wreck and was lucky to be alive at all. Whether or not he'd ever feel that way would depend largely on the amount of permanent damage done to his cognitive skills as a result of the brain swelling he was currently suffering from. Time would tell, in other words.

When they were done with their rounds, Lisa and Neil sat down in his office for a few minutes, the both of them properly exhausted after too many hours on call with too little help. The good news was that Neil had a personal coffee machine and a large selection of coffees to choose from. It was his one vice. Some people had fancy cars, and Neil had an addiction to Starbucks. They agreed on Sumatran—strong enough to slap your tongue into the next week—and Neil started brewing.

"So, turns out the guys from the CDC are assholes." If there was one thing Neil would change about Lisa it was that she was married. If he could go for two, it would be that she had a gutter mouth. As his life went on he was realizing he was kind of a prude that way. Who knew?

"The CDC?" He grinned. "Say it ain't so, Dr. Davis."

"I'm afraid so." Lisa leaned back in her chair, and he forced himself to look at her face instead of the way her chest was defined by the motion. She knew exactly what she was doing to him and reveled in it. Not that he was complaining. "Seems they like to be in control of everything. Murphy said they're going to do full body exams of everyone who's been around the three unknown cases."

"Why?"

"Because the blistering around the mouth and nose is reminding them a little too much of bubonic plague."

"Bullshit." And just like that he was the one using profanities.

"Seriously. Not from the cause, but from the symptoms." Lisa moved her hand through her hair, brushing back a loose strand behind her ear. The way she did it was a "tell" according to his college roommate. That particular Romeo claimed the gesture was a sign of a woman flirting, albeit possibly unconsciously. If he'd believed that was true, he'd have carried her into the back of his office right then and there. Maybe he did believe it, and he was a coward. It was hard to say with any certainty. All he knew was that sometimes she seemed attracted to him and sometimes she wanted nothing to do with him and it was best not to let himself play any of those games.

"Well, I'm still hearing there's nothing showing up in the cultures. For all we know, all three of them are trying a new street drug that causes burning. It would make sense when you consider where the blistering took place."

Lisa stared hard at him for a few heartbeats, just long enough to make him aware of her in ways that he tried to avoid. She was years younger than him, and she was married. He just had to remember that part and the rest would be easier.

"See? I hadn't even thought about that." Was that admiration in her voice? He refused to consider that possibility. Office romances were a foolish cliche that he could do without, thanks just the same. Wallace had slept with that little redhead in Maternity, and that had gone horribly wrong, hadn't it? Oh, yes. Divorce, scandal, and finally a relocation to a different state to avoid the continued threats to his license. Maybe the threats would have never amounted to anything, but who needed the aggravation?

"Well, just because I called for a lockdown doesn't mean I think there are any serious threats. I'm just following protocol and I've seen a lot of truly stupid kids come through here overdosed on designer drugs. Too much money, too much time, and too little common sense." He shrugged off the potential admiration from his peer and reminded himself that she was a peer and nothing more. Anything else was probably just his imagination anyway. That, or a sign that the honeymoon was over at the Davis household and that Lisa needed a reminder that she was attractive. She was, but he wasn't about to be the one to tell her.

For a moment he thought about acting on what he thought he saw in her eyes, but before he could do something that was, no doubt, deeply foolish, her cell phone rang. The tone of voice she used said all he needed to know. Her husband on the phone. Bill? Phil? He could never remember the man's name, despite the fact that they'd met several times. Lisa had nothing at all in common with the man. He'd never understand their relationship. Regardless, whatever the reason for his call, it stopped Neil from making an ass of himself.

Lisa apologized silently and rolled her eyes toward the heavens for patience. A moment later she left Neil's office, heading down the corridor.

That was for the best, surely.

Still, Lisa was a nice fantasy.

Two hours later they were together again and comparing notes, and if Neil stood a little taller when she was around, well, that was just a coincidence. And there was never a good reason to slouch.

At four in the morning, Neil took another long nap in his office. The couch was hardly perfect, but it would work in lieu of a real bed. And it was private, well away from the interns and the rest of the staff who were stacked against the walls in cots.

When he woke up he felt the first of the small blisters around his mouth and nose and knew he was screwed. The lockdown had been a wise precaution. He wasn't alone. Lisa and several other members of the staff also had the damned blisters forming. They were smaller than the ones on the college kids, far less pronounced, but there just the same.

He could barely muster a good panic he was so tired. Still, he had coffee. That would help.

And he was glad of the coffee, because none of them were going anywhere anytime soon. The CDC would see to that.

***

"They shut the fucken hospital down?" Boyd looked up from his cup of coffee and stared at his partner.

"Locked it up nice and tight. No one in, no one out."

"No shit?"

"Hand to God, Richie."

"I thought you didn't believe in God."

"No, you don't believe in God. I believe in heaven and God every time I'm with the right woman."

"Pig."

"Oink," Danny agreed. "But that's not important here. What is important is that we have a serious problem on our hands."

"How does the hospital being shut down affect us, exactly?"

"Now we have to be civil to the perps. It's gonna cramp my style." Boyd chuckled. He knew full well that his partner was deliberately generating scandal. The reason was simple enough: there were civilians in the next booth and they were the sort that liked to listen in on cop conversations. How did he know? Because the two old biddies had actually changed tables when he and Danny sat down, the better to listen in on their conversation.

"I told you before, you can't go slapping around every hooker you meet until they pay you protection. Also, you're not supposed to steal drugs from the dealers. I guess you're just gonna have to start hiding bodies again." He kept his face on the reports he was filling out, never once looking up, even when he heard the gasp from one of the blue-hairs at the next table. Better to let his partner have his fun. The kid was desperately bored, as their waitress was about a pretty as a garbage truck and, for a change of pace, not interested in Danny.

There would be hell to pay, of course. Eventually the reports would get to Whalen, who would have to deal with the repercussions. Shit rolls downhill. Not that Boyd minded. He sort of liked being taken to task by his boss. Not that he would ever admit it.

He felt the floor shake just a bit as the third member of their group joined them. Robert Longwood, who was the anti-Danny of the universe. Just as tall, but seemingly built of flab and homely flab at that. Not ugly, just not pretty either. He was a nice guy and could intimidate a rabid Rottweiler without even trying. Danny slid over because he knew good and damned well that Boyd wasn't about to scoot over even an inch.

"What's up, fellas?" The two little old ladies at the next table leaned toward each other and whispered. Probably they thought Bob was a mob enforcer. He had that sort of comforting aura about him.

Before Boyd could open his mouth, Danny took a jab. "Mostly Richie's cock when he thinks about your ex-partner." Several years ago Longwood had worked with Boyd. They'd handled Vice together and back in the day they'd even ridden together in a squad car. After that, Bob had moved on to partner with Nancy Whalen before she got promoted.

Bob snorted like a bull. It was his way of trying not to guffaw out loud at Danny's latest knee slapper.

"You assholes remember I'm armed, right?" Boyd looked up from his paperwork, closed the thick file he'd been working on, and slid it to the side of the table. Their food would be arriving soon and he was looking forward to his thick stack of pancakes.

"Just checking to see if you're getting more disappearances than usual right now is all." Danny kept his voice low, soft enough that the old ladies at the next table wouldn't be able to get any actual information from them. It was one thing to mess with their withered brains, and something else entirely to give them actual information. That wasn't acceptable.

Bob looked around and stretched, his thick arms over his head and his jacket straining at the shoulders to compensate for the shift in position. His cheap cologne wafted across the entire table, and not for the first time Boyd wondered how it was that the slob was married to a nice woman. Some guys got all the luck.

"Aside from Stephanie Hunter I haven't noticed anything." Bob ignored Danny completely and leaned in closer. "Why?" Stephanie Hunter was all over the news, which wasn't surprising when one considered that both of her parents were b-list celebrities in the Hollywood scene. Three different reporters had tried to get quotes from Danny and Richie alike. Per orders they offered only "No comment" in response. Some things you didn't play with, ever. The fastest way to get relocated from Homicide to school crossing guard was going to be getting quoted by anyone in the media.

Danny took no offense from being ignored. Kind of like he expected it from Longwood, which he did.

Richard Boyd was seldom at a loss for words, but at that moment trying to come up with a proper explanation was challenging. The good news was that Danny was there to save the day.

Danny leaned toward Longwood and spoke softly. "Had a few on the move just lately."

Bob Longwood had been a cop in the Bronx once upon a time. He'd done his time in the Marines, a tour to two in the Middle East to keep things interesting, and he'd been in town five years earlier. The first time when corpses were on the move. He stopped his fidgeting, closed his eyes, and took a few deep breaths.

Danny leaned back and crossed his arms. The look on his face said he knew the older cop wasn't really ignoring him. Boyd resisted the urge to tell him that cocky didn't look good on him.

"Whalen know?" Longwood stared hard at Boyd, almost daring him to keep secrets.

"Don't be a dork. Of course she knows." He took a sip of his coffee. "Nothing on paper. Just, you know, a few passing phrases."

Bob shook his head. Danny stared, nearly mesmerized by the way the man's jowls moved as he made the gesture. Boyd could understand that. The man was never going to be pretty and that hadn't changed in all the years they'd known each other.

When the door to the diner opened, the cops all looked. It was automatic. You don't become a police officer without knowing what's going on around you, and if you do, you get over the lack of awareness as quickly as you can.

From time to time Danny and Boyd discussed the Red Lady. They'd met her. They knew who she was. By mutual agreement, they'd forgotten to talk to anyone else about her, because they'd have had to explain why they let a young woman get away with murder, and in that one case, they'd not only understood the motivations, but they'd also agreed. The man she'd murdered had it coming.

Still, Boyd was surprised when she walked into the diner along with a kid they'd met at the same time, who'd been a terror with computer hacking skills. Ben Kirby. It took him a second to remember the kid, because despite a rocky start to their relationship, the boy had managed to keep his nose clean for the last five years. Same as the girl, at least to the best of Boyd's knowledge.

Danny's eyes widened just a bit, but otherwise he kept his cool demeanor. Richie had to crane his neck to see the couple, but she was worth it. Stunning was the word. Margaret Preston stood a little over five-and-a-half feet tall, but she had presence. Well, and a nearly perfect body didn't hurt anything. Just the right sort of curves to make a man wreck his car if he stared too hard, and a thick wave of dark, curly hair that a guy could easily get lost in. She was wearing a light jacket and a pair of casual jeans, but she still stood out. Next to her, Ben looked almost mundane. Had anyone bet Boyd that the two of them would be together five years after he'd last seen them he would have taken the bet and lost his money. That Ben was crazy for the girl was obvious. That she didn't feel the same way for him was equally obvious in Richard Boyd's eyes. And yet they were walking into the diner together and they were standing close together and then settling in at the table with a comfortable familiarity.

Ben had changed. He was older, obviously, but he'd filled out a good deal and he was sporting a mustache these days. All in all, the kid was growing up. That was a good thing, maybe, but he had hard lines on his face that hadn't been there five years earlier.

Ben's eyes scanned the table with three cops at it, and moved on past, checking out the occupants of each table in a cursory glance. If he recognized them he didn't let it show. Then again, it had been a long time. Boyd was good with faces. Danny was better. Not everyone shared that talent.

The girl—Maggie? Yes, that was how she'd introduced herself before—looked at them and smiled, her dark eyes showing no recognition, but that was okay. They'd only met in passing. Besides, he wasn't really sure if he wanted to be remembered by the sort of woman who could tear a man to shreds the way she had her pimp back in the day.

Danny looked at him and his mouth twitched from the desire to say something. Boyd shook his head, acknowledging the issue without a word.

He wanted to know what was going on in the lives of the two people, but he wasn't willing to make a scene about it. It was definitely a case of guilt by association. The two of them had been seminal in gathering information about Jason Soulis in the past. Soulis, who was as close to unstoppable as anyone or anything that Boyd had ever encountered.

Bob Longwood said something, and Rich looked his way. "Sorry. What?"

Bob shook his head. His eyes stayed glued on Maggie Preston. Boyd could understand that. "I said I might have something. Last night we got a call on four different kids all at the universities. All from the same school. One of them is at the hospital, under quarantine. The others? No sign of them."

"Four college kids didn't show up for class?" Danny chuckled. "Stop the presses."

Longwood ignored him.

"What do they have in common?" Boyd stared at Bob, his gut pulling in on itself a little.

"Not a damned thing. I mean, they knew each other, but that's it. You wanted to know if I had anything, and that's all I've got. Four kids. No. Wait. There's a dock worker, too." Bob frowned. "The one they found? She was at the docks when they called her in as unconscious." He shrugged, doubting there was anything there. Any college kids hanging at the docks were looking for privacy, or they were looking to score weed. The cops in the area knew the score. As a rule the docks were low priority unless it involved someone stealing a yacht. Currently there were no yachts reported missing, so the docks were low priority.

"So what do we do?" Longwood was trying to be a team player, which was rather rare, but Boyd would take it. As a rule he was a contrary bastard, more so if you worked with him.

"Just humor me: keep me appraised if you run across any weirdness." He made it a point to stare hard into Bob's eyes as he spoke, wanting to make sure the man understood the gravity of the situation. There was remarkably little evidence—well, okay, aside from the four bodies they'd burned to ashes in the sunlight—but he was getting a feeling that the worst was still coming. He leaned toward Bob again and Longwood leaned in until they were almost nose to nose. Speaking very softly, he went over the four bodies, the crows, the odd markings in one of the lawns, the ruined car.

Longwood looked at him for a moment and then leaned back. "So, there were some strange discolorations on the grass near the docks. A couple of bushes there looked like maybe they got burned by bleach or something, too. Not dead, but maybe dying."

Danny sighed and stood up. "Come on then, let's go."

Boyd looked back at him. "Go where?"

"The docks, where else?"

"Sit down. I'm not going anywhere until I've had my pancakes."

Danny smiled. "I'm really glad to hear you say that, Richie. I was gonna get all pouty if I didn't get my fried shrimp and onion rings." Danny sat back down and relaxed. Boyd sighed. Now and then if you didn't throw the kid a bone, or let him eat food, he got all whiny. At least he acknowledged that there was a problem these days.

"They have to-go boxes, asshole."

"It's not the same."

Twenty minutes later they said their goodbyes to Longwood—who was much friendlier after Danny picked up the tab—and headed down to look at the discolored plant life near the docks.

It wasn't hard to find. The bushes had apparently continued to die, because when they looked them over there was no color left to them. No green, anyway.

Danny crouched near the base of the plants and shook his head. "They aren't dead, Richie. They are well and truly dead. The trunks have dried out."

"How long should a thing like that take, Danny?"

"How the hell should I know? Do I look like a landscaper?"

"Your mom used to do the gardener, right? I figure maybe he's your real dad and this should all come naturally to you."

"Me and dad, we ain't tight."

"Pretty sure that's what he said about your mom."

"That's it. I'm telling, and she's never putting out for you again." Danny stood up. "These plants look like they've been dead for months. We're talking leftover-Christmas-trees-in-July dead here."

"Suppose the coroners could help?"

"Not a chance. Maybe one of the botanists down at the university?"

"They got any pretty interns down that way, Danny?" Boyd jotted notes to himself in his notebook.

"Probably."

"Then you handle it."

"Oh goody. Jailbait." Danny looked around before he said that. These days even a few off-color comments could get you in trouble. When he realized there was no one around to overhear his comments he looked disappointed. Boyd looked around the ruined bushes and stared at the lawn. It wasn't as manicured around here, but the grass was still stubbornly hanging on to its color, except around the dead plants, where the grass had done gray.

"Okay, Danny. Seriously. We have a fucken problem here."

"Like what?"

"Someone is deliberately killing lawns. That's a dangerous game to play around here, especially in your neighborhood."

"You kidding? My dad would shit himself anything happened to his lawn." Danny paced across the affected grass, looking at the ruined grass and the way it spread out. His feet easily made it from one small island of dead grass to the next. Then again, Danny was tall and had long legs. Boyd would have almost been jumping from spot to spot and they both knew it. "So, I think we can safely say the grass murdering bastard has a long stride."

Boyd stuck his cigar in his mouth again and this time lit it up. "I really don't like this shit, Danny." His voice was completely serious.

"How we handling this?"

"You take the car. I want to take a walk."

"Where you going?"

Boyd pointed at the docks and the beach that ran toward the not so distant cliffs of the Cliff Walk. "I'm gonna see if I find any other signs of dead plants."

"And if you do?"

"Then I'm gonna fucken pack a bag and move to Bermuda, because if the things we're dealing with are killing plants and draining bodies of blood, I've had enough of this."

Danny didn't laugh. It wasn't a joking matter.

***

"What do you mean I can't go back to my house?" Malcolm closed his eyes and Carly studied his handsome face. He was trying to stay calm, but failing in his efforts. "It's my house!" He'd gone home almost an hour ago and come back when he realized that the house had been sealed. Everything he owned was in the house, and he was being forbidden to enter. The policeman outside of the place had been very sympathetic, but also had no answers for him and refused to let him go inside, regardless of how angry he got or how much he begged. Now he was back at Carly's place, and sitting on the edge of her ratty old couch, and staring at the coffee table's scarred surface.

"No, I don't much care about that. I just want to know why I can't see my brother or go into my house." He shook his head, his full lips pressing into a thin line. "No. I really don't much feel like going to the hospital. Why? Because you already told me you're holding my brother and his girlfriend. How do I know you won't hold me, too?" He sighed. "And I already told you, I'm not suffering from any symptoms of anything. Then you come find me. Fuck you." He closed his cell phone and muttered something under his breath.

Between his numerous conversations with the different agencies he'd called after trying his luck with the police, Malcolm had already filled Carly in. Randy was in the hospital, and so was his latest squeeze, both of them suffering from something that had the doctors puzzled and a little scared. They weren't allowed to see anyone and they were being kept until the hospital could be sure that whatever they had wasn't spreading.

At first Malcolm had been worried and furious. Now, after being informed that his brother was in "stable condition," he was just furious.

The knock at the door was completely unexpected and it took several seconds for Carly to remember that she had people coming over to study. Chad and Lollie. Okay, study was maybe too severe a word. They were supposed to hang out. She reached the door as quickly as she could, waving a silent apology to Malcolm.

She was expecting a tall, thin man and his pudgy girlfriend. The two uniformed police officers were a complete surprise.

Malcolm's phone call was cut short. Within five minutes they were both on their way to the hospital for mandatory testing. The only thing that kept them out of handcuffs was a promise to behave themselves on the way to their unwanted destination.

If she thought Malcolm was angry before, she was in for a surprise.

The next ten hours were spent getting poked, prodded, and drained of vial after vial of blood to tell the doctors what Carly and Malcolm already knew: whatever might be contagious about Randy and his girlfriend had not spread to the two of them.

Malcolm stayed remarkably polite and civil as he tore the doctors and the police escorts a few new rectal orifices for their troubles. To show how bad they felt, the doctors didn't actually keep them at the hospital, which apparently never crossed Malcolm's mind until Carly pointed it out to him.

After that he was a bit calmer, but only a little.

***

The weather started off pleasantly warm for the time of year, but halfway through the day a cold front decided to move into the area and took with it both the pleasant warmth and the sunny skies. A little after one in the afternoon the clouds rolled in and anyone who'd left the house that morning with only a light coat was dreading the idea of heading home in the unexpected arctic chill.

With the sun lost behind clouds, Maggie decided she felt like going out. It wasn't that she couldn't tolerate the sun, because she could. It was rather that the sunlight sometimes made her feel weak, and she'd long since grown to dislike the feeling. She liked being in control and independent. She needed that, because the world kept trying to make her dependent on other people and she'd learned to dislike the feeling intensely.

Tom Pardue had tried to make her dependent on him, and she'd killed him for it. Okay, and she'd also killed him because he planned to sell her off for a night of violent rape, but even before that point she'd wanted him dead.

Ben was back at the house when she went out. He'd have asked to come along if she'd told him she was going out and so she slipped away while he was busy on his computer. There were things she needed to take care of that he couldn't help with and she was already far too dependent on him for her own comfort.

There were things she had to do, to take care of, that he didn't need to know about. There were already enough strains on their relationship. Too many, really, even if he didn't want to realize it or admit it.

Which brought her back to the fact that she didn't know what they were, or where they were going in a personal sense. Five years, and she still couldn't say with any certainty whether or not she loved Ben. Needed him? Yes. Liked him? Absolutely. Loved him? She just didn't know.

When her phone rang she answered it automatically. She knew who it was, even before she answered. "Hello, Jason." She could feel him, sense that he was calling.

Of course the crows that were following her were a dead giveaway, too. They hopped from tree to tree, flitted between houses and kept her in their view, and while they were rather subtle, her senses didn't allow much to sneak past her.

"Hello, Maggie. How nice to hear your voice." Damned if her heart didn't beat faster when she heard his voice. Damned if the thought of his hands, his lips, didn't make her ache to be with him. She hated that, that he had such a casual power over her. It made her feel weak.

It made her feel like Ben surely felt around her, like a dog waiting for the master to offer a treat.

"It's nice to hear from you, too. What are you doing calling me in the middle of the day? I thought you preferred to make your calls later in the evening."

"I rather like being able to surprise you." The closest of the crows, a larger bird than she would have thought possible before she'd learned to study them, craned its head and eyed her with one great black eye. She could sense Jason's gaze through the animal. He was never far away, not so long as he could communicate through his birds.

"You're not surprising me, Jason. Just piquing my curiosity." She refused to give him that sort of small victory. He had won enough from her already, and she had her pride.

Still, damned if she didn't want him. Damned if she didn't like the idea of seeing the man who had changed her into a vampire. She still couldn't say whether or not she was happy with the transformation, merely that she found her abilities useful from time to time.

"I'm coming to see you, Maggie. I know what you're thinking about doing with your priests, but I wanted to let you know that I've arranged to take care of the matter already."

She barely heard his words after he said he was coming to town. Her pulse was too hard in her chest and drowned out the sound of his voice. She licked her lips and made herself remain as calm as possible, fully aware that the birds eyeing her were looking at her for him, letting him see her reactions.

"What if I felt like sleeping with a priest or two? Did you consider that?"

"What if I'm a jealous lover, Maggie? Did you consider that?" Touché.

She shook her head and allowed a small smile to play around her lips. "Who said anything about us being lovers again, Jason? You're the one who left here, not me."

"I hardly had a choice, my dear. Your police there weren't going to let me merely lie around and recover from my wounds." He did a wonderful job of sounding apologetic. She knew full well that he was not, but he faked it like a pro.

"Jason, you should know by now that a woman hardly wants to hear excuses when a man can't find the time for her."

"I always have the time, my dear; it's merely a matter of convenience."

"So now I'm inconvenient?" She smiled again and looked around. The birds were still there, but they were still now, nearly frozen to their spots.

She shouldn't have been surprised by the fact that his voice came from directly behind her when he spoke again. Jason Soulis was very good at managing what should have been impossible.

"You are inconvenient. You are impossible. You are troublesome and tiresome and constantly on my mind." His arms were around her waist before she could even disconnect the phone call. His body pressed against her from behind and his scent, subtle and distinct and so damnably masculine, caught her attention as surely as the feel of his lips against her earlobe. "You are a damnable addiction Mary Margaret Preston." His words nearly burned her skin and she felt her libido respond to him, a moth drawn to an impossible flame.

Damned if she didn't feel herself fall back against him, her body relaxing into his, confident that he would support her weight with ease, that he would not let her fall to the ground, and also sure that he caught her solely because it pleased him to do so.

"You are a damnable addiction and I have missed you so very much."

Had anyone asked her how they got to his hotel room she couldn't have said. All she knew with any certainty was that they were there a few moments later, caught in a darkness that swallowed the world and then released in the luxury of his private place. His hands moved over her and she wanted to tell him to stop, wanted to remind him that she was with Ben and that Ben was important to her, even if she wasn't really sure how important, but instead she found her mouth locked on his, her hands pulling at his perfectly tailored shirt and then his pants, stripping him urgently even as he returned the favor, taking in her body with his eyes and then his hands and mouth and then simply taking her.

Ben became nothing, not even an afterthought. Instead she lost herself in Jason Soulis, exploring his body and being explored. Tasting his flesh and being tasted. It was inevitable that one or the other should bite, should taste blood. Soon they were locked in an embrace that was both pleasurable and violent. It could hardly be called making love and yet it was something more than merely fucking. It was life and she so needed to feel alive, as she always did when she was with him.

The bastard.

***

Dave woke up well before the sun set, and opened his eyes as the waves rocked his new home gently. The three bodies that lay with him did not move yet, but he could sense them, could feel that they were changing as he had changed himself. They were becoming something new, just as he had.

His eyes were still closed, but he could feel them, see them in ways that made no sense. He didn't need his eyes to see them, to see around them. He knew exactly where he was and he understood the connection between them and him. As he also understood the connection between himself and the vile thing that had killed him. Call it instinct, call it whatever you'd like, but he understood that the black-cloaked thing that had killed him had also brought him back as surely as his breath had brought back the ones he'd attacked yesterday. He took from them and then gave back a portion of what he stole with a mere breath and they slept and died and woke again as hungry as he.

If he let them wake. That was the part he had to decide, wasn't it? Would they live? Would they die? He wasn't sure yet.

So he made himself wake fully and rolled over, crawling to his hands and knees in the bowels of the yacht. Two males, one female. They lay about him, placed where he'd set them. They were pale and lifeless when he looked at them with his eyes. They were still, but vital when he closed his eyes and looked again. Even in the near complete darkness of the hold, the light was bright.

They were college kids, all three of them. He knew the type well enough, had been friends with this sort before. And been enemies with more of the same, depending on the day.

Dave ran his hand over the first of the males, the one who had grown his hair into dreadlocks and dressed himself as if he were impoverished. He stank of an easy life and everything about him offended Dave. He was tempted to kill the boy a second time, but refrained. He was beginning to understand how this would work, but he needed time and patience to fully comprehend what was happening. He also needed lab rats to confirm what he believed, so the boy would live. For now.

The other boy was healing, recovering from the wounds Dave's teeth had made on his flesh. The hole in his neck was almost gone and the body looked nearly peaceful. He left the boy alone.

The girl was a different story. She was unmarred—the bones he'd broken the previous night were mended—and he thought her lovely. Waking her was easy; he merely touched her and breathed into her mouth a second time, forcing her lungs to fill with his dark breath. She groaned and moved, opening eyes that had gone as black as pitch, and the breath he blew into her mouth became a kiss that she first struggled against and then accepted. She wanted what he offered; she wanted more. She was hungry, this one, like he was hungry. His hands moved over her face, touching the soft planes and contours, examining her. She was beautiful, and she looked upon him and felt the same way. There was a patina of blisters around her mouth, her nose, and even those were beautiful. They marked her as his.

Once upon a time he would have cared about that. Now he merely did as he pleased. And when he was done, he rose, looking down upon the three of them with an odd curiosity.

The one with the dreadlocks moved, rolled over in his death-like slumber and moaned as the changes tore at his body. His skin was blistered where Dave had breathed into his mouth. The fine blisters spread gradually, a growing pattern on his pasty flesh.

It was hard for him to focus. That was something that he'd begun to understand the night before, when he gave in to his instincts, but now, a full day later, he was fully comprehending that fact.

"Frank." Frank Preston was a good man, a fair man who had taken him in when he was down and out. He wanted Frank to know that he appreciated all that he had done for him. That was true. Frank was also the man who'd sent him to his death, seeking the vile thing that had killed him, fed on him, destroyed and rebuilt him. That too was true.

All of which was secondary to the simple fact that he was once again hungry. Still, Frank was on his mind and he knew where to find the man. He could feel the man, as surely as he could sense the location of the thing that had changed him in the first place.

Instinct. Dave was a big believer in instinct and following it. And so he did. He climbed from the hold of the yacht, hissing in irritation when the girl tried to hold on to him to lure him back into the safety of the darkness.

The sky was overcast, and the faint sunlight was uncomfortable but not fatal. He closed his eyes and looked through his other senses and moved, sliding from spot to spot along the docks, fully aware that the darkness had grown over him as he rested, a protective cover that kept him safe from the worst that the light might have offered.

"Frank." The more he thought about the man, the angrier he became. Frank had to pay, even if he could no longer clearly understand why.

***

The days never got any calmer, which hardly made sense as the slow season was coming up fast. Frank Preston felt an annoying sense of urgency as he finished filling out the forms that were required by law.

Dave Burke was missing and now he'd gone and called it into the police, and they in turn had come out and killed half of his day asking questions. Robert Longwood was courteous enough, but he seemed absolutely uninterested in the answers to the questions he asked, and he hardly inspired confidence in his desire to get to the bottom of the situation.

Dave was a good kid, a little flaky, maybe, but that was understandable. The poor bastard had been dealt some unfair cards. He was good-looking enough, but a lot of girls his age were too superficial to get past the messed-up hand—and didn't Frank feel guilty about insisting on the gloves when the kid was at work—like that hadn't hurt the poor bastard's self-confidence issues. So Dave was lonely, too smart for his own good, and about as socially aware as a jellyfish. The kid could barely even look at Frank's wife when she showed up, and if Maggie had ever come down to the docks, Frank had no doubt at all the boy would have hidden under the boardwalk rather than risk actually talking to her. Frank was fully aware of exactly how attractive his daughter was and had consumed many an antacid as a result of that knowledge. The thought of her dating, the thought of her living on her own, even the thought of her with Ben—who was a good-enough kid—was enough to cause ulcers.

At any rate, he'd lost half a day of work trying to find out what the hell had happened to Dave. He hated worrying about other people. It slowed down the whole get-work-done thing.

Frank heaved himself out of his seat and stretched, easing the pain in his lower back as he stood and twisted. Given a choice between paperwork and walking the docks to handle things, he'd walk the docks, arthritis be damned. Besides, he could smoke while he was walking around outside. It was getting too damned cold out there and he'd have bet fifty dollars on rain coming—his knee always warned him—but it was worth the risk for a smoke and a chance to clear his head.

The sky was surprisingly dark, not quite nighttime dark, but close. Still, he saw the shape when it came for him. It was tall, as large as Dave and that said a lot, but covered in a thick black cloth that draped it from head to at least mid-calf. Under that, there was nothing, not a lick of clothing, and the skin was gray, wet-looking, and dirty. Frank had all the time in the world to notice the cuts on the bare feet, the dirt that had built up on the bottoms, and the long stride that covered far too much space for comfort with each step the form took toward him.

"The fuck? It ain't Halloween yet." He was barely aware that he'd spoken.

"Frank." The voice was hoarse, but he recognized it.

"Dave? Is that you?" His heart stuttered in his chest and Frank realized just how worried he'd been for the kid.

The face was covered with that same coarse black fabric, but he would have sworn he could feel eyes on his face, as the thing reached out for him. Maybe it was Dave and maybe it wasn't but he could feel the menace that came from the thing. Frank twisted his body to the side, ignoring the flare in his left knee, and narrowly missed being grabbed up. He didn't think, but let instinct do what it had to. His fist shot out and smashed into the stranger's face hard enough to rock the man back a step. He followed through with his other fist, punching hard into his target's solar plexus, aiming to knock the wind out of his sails. Forward one step to follow through with his advantage, and his elbow drove into the side of the man's face. By all rights the bastard should have been dropped, that was all there was to it.

Instead the hands that came out from under the fabric caught his wrists and held them with ease.

"Frank. You let me die."

"I...what?" Dave's voice. There was no mistaking it this time, and the words rang in Frank's ears, sapped the strength from him and left him doubting himself. He looked at the hooded face and realized for the first time that the fabric didn't completely cover everything. He could see the lips moving behind the thick fabric, watched them, as they repeated the accusation a second time, and felt the strength leave him. Not merely because of the words, though they would surely have been enough, but also because there was something else going on here, something infernal.

"Jesus Christ, save me." He whispered the words, a small prayer, a desperate cry for help as he tried to reconcile the gray thing in front of him with the boy who was missing. Was it a ghost? It looked like a dead man draped in a loose shroud of black fabric; it sounded like Dave. Was Dave dead? Was his friend dead and blaming him for what happened? The last time he'd seen the boy was when he sent him to find something dead and stinking under the breakers.

It recoiled, releasing his wrists. It hissed, and the breath that came from it stank of rot and decay as surely as whatever had been under the waters a few days earlier.

Tears threatened Frank's eyes and he staggered back, his bum knee almost buckling. "Oh, Lord, Dave? Is that you?" It hissed again and shook its head like a boxer who'd taken one too many to the side of the head. Frank stared at the opened mouth, the teeth that filled that gray wound, and shivered. Dave didn't have that many teeth and they used to be nice and even. Not the jagged blades that filled the gap in the black fabric.

It hissed again, and this time a fine spray of bloody mist came with the sound. The stench was potent and Frank stepped back again, his back pushing against the side of his office building as he tried to step further away.

And before he could make another move, the thing was on him, hissing again, spitting red all over him in a gushing, cold breath. Frank inhaled, not meaning to, and coughed violently as his stomach heaved at the odor.

"It's me, Frank. It's me." Dave's voice came from that abomination, and Frank shivered. His skin felt flushed and hot, and the air was all the colder for it. And the hands that grabbed his throat were colder still.

Dave's mouth lashed forward and bit into his neck, his shoulder, the teeth impossibly long, far too far apart, as if the man's jaw had unhinged, snake-like, the better to bite deeply. Frank screamed again and lashed out, his fists pounding into the stomach and ribs of the kid he'd never once regretted hiring.

The pain was intense, a violation of his body, yes, but more than that, a violation of his soul. He tried to scream again, but the pain dwarfed everything else, stole away his breath.

Dave continued drinking, sucking, feeding, drawing blood and something far more vital from Frank at the same time. Frank fought as best he could, pushing, punching, clawing and even kicking, but it was no good. Whatever Dave had become, he had grown horribly strong.

Even as Frank Preston died, he tried praying to God for salvation. God did not answer him.

CHAPTER SEVEN

Sunrise was still four hours away, and Ben was driving around Black Stone Bay looking for a man who probably would have been perfectly happy watching him drown in the ocean.

His nerves were singing with the levels of caffeine he'd already taken in, and his eyes burned with the lack of sleep, but he kept looking, because some things are more important than others. Maggie happy was one of those things.

He kept telling himself that as he drove, no longer completely certain that he believed it, but as a foundation of his life choices he had no option but to continue.

"Fucking slept with him." He kept his voice low but spoke out loud just the same. Not that it mattered. Maggie wasn't with him. She was out in the night, looking for her father, same as Ben. His hands clenched at the steering wheel with a grip that would have surprised most people. "I can't fucking believe you fucking slept with him." His voice shook. His face was calm enough, but his voice shivered with suppressed rage.

Now was not the time. It might never be the time. Now and then Maggie forgot it was two ways, the connection between them. She could look into him and know what he was thinking, and he knew she had on more than one occasion. He in turn could feel what she felt, whether he wanted to or not. He knew the difference between her enduring a sexual encounter out of some sense of necessity, and having marathon sex with Jason Soulis. She entered the house afterward—showered and fresh at least, so he didn't have to smell the man on every inch of her body—and immediately went to the bedroom, the better to cover herself with her usual perfumes and freshly applied makeup.

He almost followed her up the stairs to the master bedroom, but he stopped himself. Hard as it was, he made himself wait for her, because that was the way it was done. That was the proper thing to do, wasn't it?

They weren't married. They weren't even officially boyfriend and girlfriend, but that didn't mean he felt any less betrayed. He wanted to scream. He wanted to rage. He wanted to find Jason Soulis and gut the bastard, even knowing that the man could kill him without even breaking a sweat.

He'd psyched himself up for a proper screaming match when the phone rang and because Maggie did not answer it, he did. And her mom explained that Frank was missing, her voice on the edge of hysteria, because Frank was predictable. He was always home at the same time and if there was even a slim chance that he would be late, he called.

Had she tried calling him? Of course. His phone went to voicemail. Then the mailbox filled up and could take no more messages. And his car was on the docks, she knew, because she called and then she checked and Frank was nowhere to be seen.

And now Ben was driving around in the bitter cold, looking for a man who was coldly civil to him, hoping to find the man alive and well, because anything else would hurt Maggie to her core—almost as much as she'd hurt him when she went behind his back and slept with that fucker Soulis.

The pale girl who walked up to his car caught his attention. Not because she was pale, but because she was very obviously dead. Her eyes had rolled back in her head, her hair was lifeless, and her mouth hung open, but she attempted to walk seductively, and if Ben wasn't effectively immune to the tricks of the undead she might well have caught him unawares.

Certain benefits existed as a result of being Maggie's what—boyfriend? Pet? He had no idea any longer. Among them was that he was not affected by the simpler tricks that vampires could play to sneak up on potential victims. He needed to be more alert because he needed to protect Maggie. It was really that simple. He supposed there might be a long line of mystical phrases or connections that could be made but he didn't care.

What he did care about was that Soulis was up to his old tricks again. What other reason would there be for a dead girl walking toward him with a smile on her face?

He drove forward, leaving the girl behind him with a confused and annoyed expression on her slack face. How the hell she managed to convey that exasperation with half-lifeless muscles would bother him for a while. That, and she looked almost familiar, though he was sure he didn't know her.

"College towns. You see everyone sooner or later."

Ben pulled his phone from the pocket he reserved for it and called Maggie. She was distracted right now—for more than one reason—and he didn't know if she'd hear any attempts at calling to her mentally. That stuff was tricky at the best of times.

The dead blonde was walking toward him again, still doing her best to look sexy as she strutted her stuff.

Maggie answered on the third ring. "Ben?" Was that relief in her voice? He didn't much care right now. He didn't have time.

"Maggie, I have a vampire coming toward my car. Not like you or Jason. The other kind." The girl was closer again and looked determined to get his attention. The weather was for shit and there weren't a lot of people out, which was basically the only reason he suspected most women would be looking for him. There it was, that negative attitude he was working on. Maybe later, when he wasn't worried about living. He could probably take the blonde, but he couldn't guarantee it. He'd been working out and studying tae kwon do for four years now, but that didn't make him Superman, just in better shape. He wasn't really in a hurry to test his abilities.

"Where are you?" Maggie's voice took on the cold tone he'd grown accustomed to. It was oddly comforting, and he supposed he would have to deal with that.

"Phillips Avenue, near the docks." The blonde reached for the car door and he moved forward again, not at all surprised when the dead face grew angry and the girl hissed at him.

"I'll be right there." There was a bag in the trunk. It carried his workout clothes and his classroom supplies, including a functional sword. If he had to, he thought he could get to it.

He parked the car and popped the trunk before getting out.

The blonde moved toward him in a hurry, and all attempts at pleasantries were gone. Her face was still slack, the skin around the mouth and nose blistered as if she'd been burned with a mild acid, and she stank up close. Christ, her skin was sweating and her clothes were wet.

Ben looked away and pulled sword and scabbard from the trunk. The girl kept coming, her teeth bared, her dead eyes rolling as she looked at him. There was a glimmer from her eyes, and he knew that most people would have been caught in her illusions, but she still looked dead and disgusting to him. "Why are you running from me? Don't you want to be friends?" Her voice was a singsong. She thought this was all a joke.

Ben pulled the blade free, and dropped down into a defensive stance.

The girl laughed, an annoying giggle that was probably supposed to sound cute. Ben gritted his teeth and stayed where he was. He didn't want this, didn't want any of it. But he wasn't going to let her get anywhere near him.

When she realized she wasn't getting anywhere with her attempts at being sexy, the girl hissed again and ran toward him. Ben dropped lower still, then swung the sword forward, aiming at her chest, her neck, any place where he could cause serious trauma.

The blade cut nothing but air: the girl was gone. She hadn't stepped back or ducked, she was simply gone.

Ben looked around carefully, keeping the blade lifted and waiting, knowing full well he'd have a bitch of a time explaining it to the police if they should suddenly show up.

The blonde giggled again, from right behind him. He didn't even have a chance to turn to face her before she hit him. Four years of training. Had he been completely serious about it, he could have worked his way up to black belt by now. He wasn't quite that hardcore, but he was serious enough to take his lessons with more than a grain of salt. Ben staggered forward and rolled, trying to recover from the blow.

His head was ringing and his eyes didn't want to focus, but he still saw the girl as she moved forward again, reaching for him. He tried to move the sword into a defensive position a second time, but his arms weren't working right. He made the usual mental commands to his body, and his limbs promptly ignored him, perfectly satisfied with the notion of simply lying there.

The girl's hand was just grabbing into his hair—fingers cold and damp, and nails feeling like they were made of bone—when she screamed and let go of him.

Ben rolled over and looked at her, his body allowing him that much leeway, and watched as she sailed backward and away from him, scrambling and shrieking as she soared toward the stars. Gravity caught up with her after a few seconds and almost a hundred feet later, and dropped her into the side of a wooden boathouse. Her body bounced off the wood and broke a few boards before landing on the sidewalk.

A person would have been broken, and badly, at the very least, from that sort of impact. The girl fairly leaped back to her feet and charged toward the figure that had thrown her. Not Maggie. Maggie was smaller, shorter, and decidedly more feminine. No, this figure was dressed in dark jeans and a charcoal sweater, and had dark hair that was cut short and professionally styled. Even without seeing the face, Ben recognized Jason Soulis.

Jason turned away from the approaching blonde, his dark eyes looking down at Ben both figuratively and literally. The look seemed to last forever, but couldn't have, because eventually the vampire turned away from him and dealt with the blonde, stopping her with a look.

She screeched, cringed back from him, and cowered, shaking as if he'd been beating her for years and had broken any will she might ever have had.

And a second after that, Maggie dropped from the sky, sliding into a smooth, graceful landing. Ben knew she could fly, had seen her do it before, but he still shook his head, taken aback. There were many things that Maggie could do, most of which she chose not to advertise in public. Sometimes seeing her do any of the things he knew she was capable of was unsettling. Seeing her handle flight as if she were born to it? That was like watching an angel fly out of the night sky, both magnificent and terrible.

The expression on her face was not kind. Maggie stared hard at Soulis, barely even acknowledging Ben's existence for the moment. While the two of them had a staring contest, Ben rose to his feet and picked up his sword, feeling completely ludicrous. Four years of training and he got slapped around like a toddler. He did a slightly drunken stagger over to the car and threw the sword in the trunk. By the time he turned around again Maggie and Jason were locked in a staring contest and the dead blonde was slinking away. He had no desire, nor the energy, to go after her. She'd knocked all his initiative out of him when she tried to punch her hand through the back of his skull.

Maggie turned sharply and grabbed the girl by her hair. The girl screamed, slapped at Maggie's hand, and cursed repeatedly until Maggie took a moment to stare her in the face. Just like that the blonde calmed down from her tantrum and started the shivering act again.

Ben rolled his head a few times and felt along the back of his skull where a lump was forming. He'd be feeling that one for a few days.

It was hardly the first time he'd had his ass kicked properly, but it had never been a one-punch knockdown by a girl who was easily fifty pounds lighter than he was.

As if reading his mind, Soulis looked toward him again, those dark eyes smiling. The expression was placid enough, but it was also a challenge and Ben knew it. Maggie wouldn't see it. Or if she did, she'd ignore it. He knew her well enough to know that.

"Jason, if you want to keep this thing, you'd best let me know now." Maggie's voice was filled with disgust. Five years earlier, around the same time he changed Maggie from a beautiful co-ed into a vampire, Soulis had come to Black Stone Bay for the main purpose of creating vampires to experiment on. By his definition there were two types of vampires, the distinction being that the ones like Soulis and Maggie were living, breathing creatures and far more powerful than the ones created by their casual feeding. Things like the blonde were the by-product of their eating and not cleaning up after themselves. Of course the dead ones also needed to feed and that in turn created still more of the same. It was something of a miracle that the world hadn't succumbed to a vampire invasion yet as far as Ben was concerned. Mostly, however, he knew it was because the newly risen dead ones tended to be sluggish and to die with the first sunrise. There were always a few exceptions, but mostly when Maggie ran across one, she killed it.

Soulis was the one who liked to play with them.

Jason smiled. "I'd rather take this one with me. I want to figure out where she came from."

Maggie blinked, her face showing her surprise for one brief moment. "You didn't feed on her?"

"No. I only got into town today, Maggie." The look he cast her way made clear that he was disappointed she would even consider that possibility.

Ben shook his head. They continued to ignore him, and the thought that rose in the back of his mind was that he wasn't supposed to talk, not while Mommy and Daddy were having a serious conversation. Damn, but he hated this.

Maggie shoved the girl toward Jason, who caught her arm easily. Rather than fight or struggle, the blonde practically wrapped herself around him, holding to his chest like he was a tree and she was trying to make sure she could stay anchored against ferocious winds.

Then Maggie finally looked toward Ben, her eyes softening, her face more like the face he knew and loved, softer, less cruel. "Are you okay?"

"Yeah. Little knot on the back of the head." He pointed. "Jason caught her before she could —" *Kill me. Before she could fucking bite me and bleed me and make me into one of those disgusting goddamned things!* "Before she could get me."

"He's important to you. Of course I protected him." Jason shrugged and put a protective arm around the dead girl, who practically cooed. "You did not feed on this one, either, Maggie?"

Maggie's face worked for a moment. "No. I don't kill if I can avoid it."

Jason shrugged. "To each their own, yes?" He looked toward Ben again, his expression playful and condescending, a deliberate insult. Ben chose not to scream or take a swing. He wasn't feeling particularly suicidal.

Before the already awkward situation could get any worse, the cell phone rang in his pocket and he answered. It was Maggie's mother. They'd found her father. The news was not good.

***

Brad stared out at the tide and sipped at his coffee, feeling the anger baking inside of him, a distant rage that kept coming in and crashing against his soul with the same fury as the waves that threw themselves against the jagged black rocks below the cliffs.

He had spent the night before being interrogated — albeit politely — by the police about the disappearance of his daughter. The same police were currently returning the favor for the bitch he'd foolishly married once upon a time. Both Stacia and Tim were being grilled in return, because Brad's alibi was solid and they'd called in to report him as a prime suspect in the disappearance of his only daughter.

His stomach did another uncomfortable roll over inside of him and he grimaced. The man standing next to him was as calm and cool as Brad was anxious and angry.

Sterling Armstrong was Hollywood handsome and as smooth as a politician. He could have been a star, he could have been a governor or maybe even the president of the United States if you wanted to go off of charisma alone. But, no, he was a lawyer and a damned good one. And a damned expensive one, too. Normally people came to see Sterling at his office, but they'd known each other for a few years now, and Sterling made house calls on occasion.

Of course he charged for house calls. The prick.

"She had every right to make claims about possible suspicion, Brad. Everyone has that right." Sterling stood there looking out at the water, his face calm and collected, his clothes perfect, even after the long drive. "You have the same right." He smiled. "But there are always consequences to our actions, aren't there?"

"What do you mean?"

"I mean she had you dragged away by the police. She didn't say that you should be considered a possible suspect. She flat out accused you of taking Stephanie. That was a mistake."

"Screw that." Brad shook his head. "I don't give a damn about Stacia right now. I want to make sure my little girl is safe, okay?"

Sterling never even batted an eye. "I have four separate private security firms looking into the matter right now. Believe me, we will find Stephanie." He stopped short of saying "*if she's alive or dead*," but the tone of his voice made that fact clear enough. "And when we do find her, should Stacia be in any way, shape, or form responsible for her disappearance, I intend to make sure you gain sole custody."

That was a lovely pipe dream. "Look, just find her, okay, Sterling?'

"We're working on it." Sterling put a comforting hand on his shoulder. "We'll find Stephanie." He made sure that Brad looked him in the face.

Sterling had a preposterous name and chiseled good looks. He was outrageously expensive even for a lawyer, but he damned near always got good results.

That was good. It was important that he have Sterling on his side and working for him, because Sterling and his detectives were the perfect alibi.

After five hours of being grilled and harassed, after dodging the small army of reporters that had come looking for him as soon as his name was mentioned in connection with any shady activity, Brad was about done playing nicely.

This time around the rules were going to get broken, because playing by them had proven a waste of time and money so far and he was done with that shit. You meet the right people, you can get almost anything taken care of the way you need it. Brad had met a lot of people since moving to Black Stone Bay. More than Stacia knew about.

His ex was going to pay for fucking him over one time too many.

***

"Kind of sucks dealing with missing persons right now, doesn't it?" Boyd was gloating a little as he talked to Longwood, and Danny listened, wise enough not to step into that one. Longwood didn't like him. He knew that, he just didn't really care. Longwood was an ugly, uneducated douche bag who took it personally that Danny had old money and all the connections that came with it. The thought pissed him off, actually, and that in turn amused the hell out of Danny.

Longwood moaned and shook his head, the jowls on his face wobbling with the motion. Seriously, he was as ugly as an old man's ass.

Danny poured himself another cup of coffee and listened as the two detectives talked back and forth about the good old days, when the occasional runaway was as bad as it got with the missing person's unit. To hear them talking, the town had been clean and comfortable before the vampires showed up. It had certainly been a little less dangerous, but Danny'd been born and raised in the town and knew all the dirt that even the newspapers couldn't rustle up. Old money has its own secrets. They don't get shared with anyone. Pretty much ever.

Longwood was pissing and moaning about the college kids that were still refusing to show up, and Boyd was commiserating, all in an effort to glean more information than Longwood realized he had, when Jason Soulis walked into the diner.

Danny's hand reached for his service pistol. His free hand slapped the hell out of Richie's arm, because he didn't have time for subtle. Jason Soulis. The fucker was walking around like there wasn't a problem in the world, like he hadn't killed cops in front of Danny and Boyd, and damned if he didn't look just as calm and cool as ever.

"Boyd." Richie looked over immediately. Danny only ever called his partner Boyd when he was serious. Danny was seldom serious.

Boyd looked up and his face paled a few shades. At he same time, he reached out and put his hand on Danny's, stopping him from raising the weapon.

Probably it was for the best. The last time he'd shot the fucker in the chest it just pissed him off.

"Gentlemen." Soulis smiled and stood before them, in the middle of a diner full of people. Full of potential victims to his power.

"You lose your fucken mind, Soulis?" Boyd's voice stayed low. His blood pressure soared, judging by his color, but his voice stayed nice and placid.

"Not at all. I just came to see about cleaning up a mess." He might have been discussing the way his landscapers were mowing the grass against the grain.

Danny kept his hand where it was. He figured if he pulled the trigger he was taking the fucker's balls off. Might not kill him, but he bet it would hurt like hell.

"What sort of mess?" Danny kept his voice casual, which was good, because Richie was looking about ready to start screaming and there were too many people around.

"I'm not really sure. Not yet. I just thought I should pay my respects. After all, you asked me not to come back the last time I was in town."

"No. I think we asked you to lie the fuck down and die." That was Richie, king of the understatement.

"For me these are the same thing. Not impossible, but certainly inconvenient." Jesus, he wanted to pull the trigger. Sure, a dozen people would die, himself included, but it would be worth it to knock the smug attitude off the bastard. Still, he kept his cool, hard though it was.

"So we 'ask you not to come back' and you do anyway. How do you think that's gonna make us feel?"

Soulis looked at Danny and smiled. "I suppose it's enraging you. But you're not a stupid man. Stay out of my way and I won't have to make the same sort of mess I did the last time I was here. I'm just here to clean up a few loose ends, and then I'll leave your lovely town again."

"Sit down for a few. Relax. Make yourself at home." Danny smiled at the man—was he a man? Danny wasn't really sure. "We can play twenty questions and get to know each other a little better."

Soulis's eyes went directly to where the business end of the pistol was aimed at him, and he pulled out the chair at their small table and made himself comfortable, never once flinching from the weapon he knew was pointed toward him. "How can I resist such a pleasant invitation?"

"Do you need those, Mister Soulis?" Danny leaned back, resting the pistol against his thigh, but making sure the muzzle stayed level with his visitor. "I'd heard that your kind couldn't enter a house without an invitation. Or a town, for that matter."

Jason Soulis looked toward the waitress and immediately got her attention. He gestured for coffee and she nodded and smiled. "I was invited here already. Once the invitation has been made, I can come and go as I please. An invitation cannot be revoked."

"Who invited you?" Richie kept his voice calm. It was amazing, really, how calm Richie could be. If you didn't know there was a hurricane inside of him, he looked just as placid as a pond on a windless day.

Soulis looked toward Danny's partner and smiled. "A friend who no longer lives in the area. He moved on to greener pastures."

"Why here?" Danny was trying to be as calm as his partner but wasn't quite managing. Longwood was looking at him like maybe he had grown a third eye, but that was mostly because he'd finally caught on to the pistol aimed at Soulis and was smart enough not to advertise the fact.

"Why not?" Soulis shook his head. "There's no reason aside from I like this place and it suited my needs at the time. And I had access, which always helps."

"So why come back?" Richie again, his eyes were furious, and if he could have, Danny had no doubt his partner would have burned Soulis into dust where he sat.

"Unresolved business. I set certain things in motion when I was here the last time, and they have come to my attention." Soulis stared around the room looking at the faces of all the people around them, his expression mostly bored, maybe moderately amused by the conversation. "My experiments have borne fruit. I must see whether or not that fruit is palatable."

"Why shouldn't we kill you right here and now?" Richie's voice was low enough that Danny had to strain to make out the words.

"What's to stop me from killing everyone in the entire building, Detective Boyd?" The confidence in his tone made Danny hate him just a little more. "I am not here to cause troubles, as I have already stated. I am here to take care of unfinished business."

"Your unfinished business is starting to cause problems again. We don't want any more problems. You getting me?"

Jason Soulis rose from his seat in one fluid motion. He had the same grace as a practiced dancer, which annoyed Danny more than it should have.

Richie stood up, and Longwood stood with him. Danny stayed exactly where he was, barrel aimed at the right testicle of the bastard who was aggravating every last one of them. "One drop of blood. Just one. And I'll kill you." Richie's voice was soft and low enough that Danny was halfway reading his lips.

Soulis allowed a small smile to play around his mouth. "I'll consider myself properly warned. Here's one for you. I'm not responsible for what's happening right now in your town." He paused. "Well, not directly." Soulis shrugged. Though he made the move seem as effortless as anyone else would, he didn't seem comfortable with the notion of shrugging. Maybe it was simply too mundane a gesture for him. "But I'll do what I can to clean up the mess, just the same."

"One drop." Richie stared hard, his face frozen in a mask of quiet fury. Soulis stared exactly long enough to make clear that he wasn't the least bit worried about the detective's threats, and then he made a small bow of concession. Like everything else, it seemed a mockery of proper form. And once again, Danny resisted the urge to pull the trigger again and again until the smile disappeared. It wouldn't be worth the bloodbath that resulted.

"I shall endeavor to handle my affairs as quickly and bloodlessly as possible, Detective Boyd. All the best to you and yours." He stepped back from the table and turned away, not even bothering to look over his shoulder at the three armed men who could have put a dozen holes in him.

To be fair, he'd have just healed the injuries and killed all of them.

Danny put away his pistol.

"Who the hell was that?" Longwood scowled, a puzzled but annoyed expression on his face. He looked constipated. He always looked constipated.

Danny took great joy in watching the man's face while Richie explained the details of their last encounter with the man. He shouldn't have. He should have been terrified. In truth he was, to a certain degree, but he was also excited. Soulis was unresolved business. He hated leaving matters unfinished.

Besides, Soulis he could explain and understand. He was bad news, but he wasn't planning on hanging around. Apparently the bastard wanted to clean up a mess that he had started. Considering the recent problem with the vampires they'd dealt with, that was maybe a good thing.

There was a thought: the notion that Soulis could ever be a good thing. He had no idea.

***

Dave crawled across the ground, slid through the dust and sediment of his new home, and settled himself as the sun rose higher. The sun could kill him, he knew that. It would take a long time, but it could kill him. The shroud that covered his body was a natural defense against that, against everything, really. His hearing was insanely sensitive now, and his vision? In what should have been complete darkness he could still see everything around him. There was a pile of old cigarette butts in the corner closest to him, and there was a child's backpack, complete with several books, resting against the farthest foundation wall. Once upon a time he'd have found the abandoned pack unsettling, possibly even a sign that bad things had happened here in the past, but now that sort of thing was more of an intellectual exercise than anything else. He could smell the old sweat of the little girl on the pack. He could also smell her shampoo, though there were cobwebs and dust trying to hide the backpack away.

He had come to the school building because he had been invited. At least he thought he'd been invited. A child above him had drawn his picture in her little sketchbook and called him Dave the shadow stealer. She seemed utterly fascinated by his existence. One child, one invitation was all that he needed.

Above him, separated by a dozen feet of darkness and a layer of wood and tile and concrete, hundreds of children walked, sat, and suffered through the mandatory imprisonment of a day of schooling. They were young and they were vital.

Though he wanted to rest, to sleep, perhaps, he could not. The feel of them above him was too strong. It wouldn't be right to say that his hunger had returned, but merely that his instincts warned him it would come back sooner rather than later. As has already been stated, the new and improved Dave was decidedly a creature of instinct.

And instinct led him again, told him what he had to do in order to rest.

Dave blew out a long, slow breath, watching with only the mildest curiosity as something more than merely air was expelled from his body. He was aware of the fact that his breath defied most physical laws, spreading through the entire building, moving through floors and walls alike, covering the children, the teachers and administrators. He was equally aware that when he inhaled again, taking in an impossibly deep breath, that the same happened in reverse: he took back from all of them, every living being within the building.

Above him there was little to see, little that changed. The lights in the building flickered for a moment, and a few of the more active children seemed to calm the smallest amount. Anyone looking would have merely thought that the old circuits at the Hartshorn Academy were having trouble taking care of a power surge. Anyone noticing the children would have merely assumed they were lucking into a calmer day at the facility.

No one suddenly grew too tired to move, or came down with an unexpected fever.

That happened later.

After Dave Burke began feeding properly.

Dave settled down and slept at last, falling into a sleep that was mostly dreamless.

***

One of the little girls at the school hadn't gotten onto the school bus the day before. Stephanie Hunter, who was in the second grade and about as cute as any kid had ever been. Lora knew her, of course, because back in the day she'd had a crush on the kid's dad. At thirteen she'd wanted to marry him. Having met him a few times now, she knew his best-looking years were in the past, but he seemed like a nice man and he loved his daughter. And now the little girl was missing and that bothered the hell out of Lora, because they were *careful* at the Hartshorn Academy. They didn't make foolish mistakes and let strangers hang around and they kept watch on all the access points.

The class was subdued, and that was maybe for the best because she was feeling pretty wiped out herself. She could hear a symphony of small sniffles from the kids, and Larry, who was just about hyperactive, was resting his head and looking a little peaked.

For her part, Lora had a splitting headache, the sort she hadn't experienced since her college days when she was working full-time and cramming for finals and living on ramen noodles and a few gallons of coffee every day. She looked at her hands for a moment, studied the fingers and the nails, and watched a very minor tremor shiver through her fingers. Yep. She was coming down with something. That was almost inevitable when you worked with kids, and let's be honest here: the kids were looking almost as icky as she felt.

When the bell rang, the munchkins stood up and moved blearily toward the door, waiting only until she wished them a good day and a safe trip home. Just because she was feeling a little skittish after the disappearance, she went with the main group toward the front doors and looked around the property as they moved toward their school buses and the cars driven by their parents. No one looked the least bit menacing, except maybe Simon Bradford and his uniformed friends, who were all in attendance with a couple of extra rent-a-cops just to be safe. They were pleasant to the kids, they smiled and they nodded, but in every case they were watching the people around them as surely as the crows were once again watching the building. Lora looked up to the spot where she should have seen the crows — just barely visible from this angle — and saw that they had moved. They were on the phone lines above the school, instead, and they were lined up in a silent row, all of them looking toward the front of the school.

Darned if it didn't look like they were watching her. She wasn't sure if that was a comforting notion or an unsettling one. Either way, she shook off the chill and called it a fever from whatever bug she was coming down with. As soon as she was done with work, she was planning on heading home and crawling into bed with a good book and a cup of soup. Everything else would have to wait until she was feeling better. Well, except maybe for *American Idol*.

Chris Henderson looked at her and smiled wanly. He looked about as excited to be there as she felt. Chris was a stocky man who looked like he could break a brick wall with a good head-butting, but he was also one of the gentlest men she'd ever met.

"Feeling okay, Chris?"

"I think we've got a fishbowl scenario here." He grimaced as he spoke, and then tried to smile again. It didn't work that well. Fishbowl was Chris's way of saying that everyone was in the same atmosphere and breathing the same germs. At least three times a year something ran through the school, normally a cold or a minor bug, and at least as many times, Chris talked about his fishbowls. It was sort of endearing.

"Your class, too?" He nodded and shrugged at the same time. He managed to carry it off surprisingly well.

She looked at his gentle face and felt a frown pull at her mouth. His lips had a few minor red marks around them. She'd have sworn they hadn't been there even a minute before.

"I don't know about you, but I think I'm sneaking out early today."

Chris's voice took on a conspiratorial note. "I saw Camille leaving about an hour ago." Camille Lawson was the principal. If she was sneaking out early, it was safe to do so themselves.

"Sounds like a plan to me."

Ten minutes later the school buses pulled away like a great migration of yellow elephants. Five minutes after that, Lora was in her car and heading for home. She felt even worse by the time she made it to her apartment.

When she looked in the mirror as she washed away her makeup, she saw the red marks around her nose and mouth and felt a tremor of fear dance through her stomach. The sores didn't hurt, but they were worrisome. As if she didn't have enough on her plate to worry about.

***

"Seriously, what the hell is this?" Maggie sat at the edge of the couch in her family home, and though she was the same as ever, she felt smaller. Her mom was right there beside her, her face strained by the news, her eyes red from tears shed and the threat of still more to come.

Frank Preston was currently being held at the Sacred Hearts University Hospital, where he was not being allowed to see visitors. Not even family. Whatever was going on with him, it was apparently not the first case the hospital staff had run across, nor did they think it likely that he would be the last.

The Prestons got to hear it just before the news ran on the local TV stations. Something serious and possibly contagious was starting to spread around Black Stone Bay and the Centers for Disease Control was currently moving to limit access to the hospital and to any areas that looked like they might be responsible for outbreaks. The good news seemed to be that they had located a central area for the problems. The bad news was that the infections seemed to be coming from the docks, where her father was the harbormaster.

Until further notice, the docks were being shut down, and an environmental team was looking the area over. The bad news was that there was something going on. The good news, if there could be said to be good news, was that so far there were no fatalities.

The victims suffered from a mild fever, from blistering on their skin, and from a plethora of other minor issues. It seemed likely, according to the voice on the other end of the phone conversation, that the problem was environmental and not a cause for too much alarm. Until such time as anything certain was known, however, all known victims of the infection were being kept isolated.

And Maggie wanted to scream. She was not used to this. After five years of adjusting to a world that was, frankly, very different from the one she'd grown up in, she had become accustomed to her money and her name allowing her certain privileges. Her looks had always afforded her a certain degree of access, but in comparison to what wealth and reputation afforded, that was nothing. Now none of it seemed to matter. Despite her best attempts, she could get no solid answers regarding her father's exact condition, she could not speak to her dad, and even Ben's efforts to hack into the hospital had met with failure.

And that was another problem, another little dilemma she had to deal with. Somehow Ben knew. Before Jason even showed himself to Ben last night, he'd known she'd been with the man.

Ben understood that from time to time she was with other men. He didn't like it, but he understood the necessity of placating the men who had become her source of sustenance. They stopped her from losing control of her darker urges. There had been two occasions since Jason had changed her that had resulted in multiple deaths. She hated thinking about either of them and she knew that they were inevitable. But if she paid attention, if she waited for the signs that she was going to need to feed, she could work it out, she could feed on the willing and make sure that they were unchanged by her needs. That was the plan, and so far it was working out pretty well.

Ben got it. She knew he hated it, just like she hated it, and she knew he understood the necessity.

They had a connection. That was the only way she could put it. When she had needs, Ben knew about them and he responded. When she'd first changed, he'd come for her and saved her from getting caught. He'd found her, taken her home, cleaned her up, and given her shelter when her body was going through transformations that she didn't fully understand even now.

Ben was her protector, even when she didn't know that she needed one.

And Jason Soulis? Hell, Jason was the one who made her into a monster. He came into her life with an offer of easy money, and somewhere along the way he made her into a vampire. She should have hated him, should have wanted him dead. She had condemned him more than once for what he'd done to her, and yet, he came along, he called for her, and she ran to him.

It wasn't love. It was a damned addiction. She didn't even like Jason. She resented his existence and everything that he'd made of her life, and yet, he came to her and she lost her anger — she damned near shivered with anticipation at the thought of his touch.

Ben sighed and shook his head. "No way. The firewalls are too good. I try anything else and they're going to trace it back here and then all sorts of shit goes boom." He shook his head and looked at her mom. "Sorry."

"No. No, Ben. Thanks for trying." She mumbled the words, barely even seeming to know that she was speaking.

Ben looked away from Maggie's mom and stared at her for a moment. He wore his heart on his sleeve. He always had. He was feeling betrayed. And, really, she had betrayed him. She just hadn't meant to. And here he was trying to make everything all right again, like always.

She almost said something, perhaps an apology, or maybe even an explanation, but he looked away too soon and the moment was gone. Did it make sense to let it go? Perhaps not, but it was easier and she had so much to deal with already, didn't she?

Rather than risk speaking, she turned to her mother and put an arm around the older woman's shoulders. There had been a time when it would have been the other way around, but in the last few years something had changed between her and her parents. Somehow the paradigm she'd known her entire life had shifted or at least was in the process of shifting.

Nothing stayed the same. She hated that thought, but there it was, sitting out in the open like a bloated toad.

Ben paced for a moment and then he nodded to himself and walked to the front door of the house where she'd grown up and walked outside. The sunlight was muted, the clouds covering everything as they did almost every time that Jason visited. She was beginning to think he could control the weather. That was a scary thought. He was powerful enough without that sort of ability.

Maggie closed her eyes and thought about the clouds that were scudding across the sky. She pondered them for a moment and then tried to push them away. She willed them gone, curious as to whether or not anything would happen. Though there were windows and curtains in the way, she saw the sky outside brighten and wondered if it had anything to do with what she wanted. It could be a coincidence, after all.

A moment later the clouds came back. She couldn't find the energy to try again. Her dad was in the hospital, and Jason was in town, and Ben was hurting, and somehow she felt responsible for all of that. Really, that was silly. She was only responsible for one of them.

And Ben would forgive her.

He always did.

He always had.

He loved her, after all.

She wished she knew if she felt the same back. Even now, five years along, she couldn't decide.

***

Seeing the girl laid out before him was a delight, and Jason Soulis felt like a child at Christmas must, when the new toys are freshly revealed and ready to be played with. He was looking forward to his new toy. There was simply no other way to put it.

The girl did not feel the same way, apparently, not that he much cared. She struggled and moaned as he started cutting. He shushed her several times, but she didn't stop screaming. It made him glad that he'd bothered to purchase a second home. Maggie would disapprove of his study habits.

Five years had passed since he'd started his experiments and, finally, they were showing results.

Somewhere out there, a child had spent five years growing inside one of his pets and now that child was free. He'd get to it in time, but for right now he was far more interested in the other new thing he'd made from old clay. If, in truth, the girl represented something new.

It was hard to say, as she wasn't fully developed yet.

The dead ones, the vampires that were created from the careless feedings of his kind, were never meant to survive. He was convinced of that. The ones that managed to live through the change were rare, and most died as a result of their own carelessness long before they could become anything significant. They were barely capable of motion when they first rose. He knew, because he'd studied them for centuries. Not constantly because that would have surely bored him to tears, but he did study them.

They came back from the dead. Miraculous, true, but they came back deeply flawed, stunned perhaps by being dead. And given a few days in some cases, or weeks in others, they recovered their sensibilities. After that, they were capable hunters if weak in comparison to his kind.

But this girl? She was only a day old, perhaps two, and she was responding far better than most. She had already mastered the simple glamour that allowed the dead ones to hide their unpleasant condition from the humans. She had more cognitive reasoning than he would have expected, and she understood enough to fear him, though they had only met a short time ago.

She could speak in full sentences, which was often a challenge for the freshly risen. But there was something else going on as well, something new and delightful. And it had been a very long time since Jason had actually seen anything new among his own kind.

Her teeth were wrong, for starters. Normally only the canines extended on vampires, sometimes a few more teeth, granted, but seldom more than that. All of her teeth were changing. It might be a fluke and so he refused to let himself get too excited, but it was an interesting change from what he was used to just the same.

"What are you, my dear? Hmm?" He ran his hand over her flesh. At this stage she should have been rotting. That was what normally happened to the new ones if they weren't fed enough. Instead this one was withering, wasting away like a human in a concentration camp. She was thinner than she had been only the night before, and even now she struggled, tried to escape from the bonds he'd locked her into. Not likely, that. He had been restraining his experiments before her ancestors crossed to the New World.

He lifted her lips and studied the teeth again. There was no denying it. They were all changing.

"Please let me go, mister." She whined at him, trying to generate a fetching pout that had probably distracted more than one boy and won a few arguments for her over time. He was not impressed. First, he could see the decay; second, he was far choosier than that.

He looked at her eyes again and frowned. The pupils were misshapen, changing much like her teeth. "You really are amazing, aren't you my dear? Look at you? What are you going to become?"

Jason Soulis stepped back and settled in to see what would happen next, while the girl struggled. She could smell the food he'd brought for her in the next room: a fine young lad, who even now was gradually waking up from the attack that had knocked him unconscious. Jason was tempted to feed on the boy himself, but this was far more important. He needed to know what was happening here, to understand the metamorphosis.

Three hours passed with only minor changes, after which the progress sped up again. Jason held up the girl's left hand and studied the fingers carefully. The nails were thickening, lengthening into proper claws. Her fingers were also growing longer, which was almost ludicrous when one considered how long her fingers were to begin with. The rings and bracelets she wore were no longer a close fit; instead they rolled around on her fingers and wrists, as if she might be playing with her mother's old costume jewelry.

Her face changed the most. Her eyes grew larger and rounder, and the sockets around them grew more pronounced. Judging by the other changes, it seemed far more likely that her eyes were actually staying the same size, but the loss of facial flesh made them seem larger. He contemplated whether or not it was worth finding a ruler to make measurements and decided against the idea. Really, it was too much effort. The muscles of her face seemed to atrophy, and her skin, already pasty, took on a gray pallor. Her lips thinned a bit, her teeth grew still more pronounced, and her nose withered, not completely falling away but definitely caving in on itself.

She looked, in short, like a corpse merged with a rat. It was not a pleasant appearance.

That wasn't supposed to happen. That never happened.

Jason smiled, delighted by the changes.

Finally, after making her wait long enough, he decided it was time to feed her. The college boy he'd snatched up earlier was awake by then, and would surely have screamed if Jason had not had a tight grip on his throat. Still, he struggled and thrashed and did his best to escape from the vile thing the dead girl had become.

His best was not good enough. She was still restrained, but she lunged as best she could and bit deeply into him with those brutal teeth, tearing flesh and then feeding greedily on what spilled from the boy.

And Jason watched, fascinated, as if he hadn't fed a thousand times himself over the years.

And when she was done, she took in a great breath, drawing the air from the boy's lungs. And then breathed out, spewing droplets of his blood across his face. And the boy whose heart had stopped — and if ever anyone could hear a heartbeat without benefit of equipment, it was surely Jason Soulis — gasped, and his eyes opened again before he exhaled and fell back, his pulse beating slowly within his chest.

"Well, that's delightful, isn't it?" Jason leaned back and let the boy's body fall to the ground. He'd look it over later, after he was done taking care of a few tasks.

For now, he was perfectly happy to leave the new couple alone.

He had so much to attend to, and so little time.

***

The hospital was going just a little crazy. Neil Brighton was still doing his rounds, and Lisa Davis was doing them with him again, but it was all a bit surreal at this point. They were working side by side, taking care of their patients, yes, and trying their best to ignore the small spots that had blossomed on their faces and then dried and gone away. Neil looked at Lisa and studied the angry red marks on her lips and around her mouth in general. A day before they'd been pustules filled with dark black fluids. Now those wounds were gone. The CDC were beside themselves trying to figure out anything at all, and the medical staff they brought along was going absolutely insane trying to understand what was happening. The original victims of whatever this was, were doing no better than before, but whatever they had, it was apparently not quite as contagious as anyone originally thought. He and Lisa were evidence of that. They had recovered from whatever this was, and while none of them were feeling their absolute best, there was no doubt that they hadn't succumbed to the fever and odd changes taking place in the original patients. And there *were* changes. The doctors from the CDC were still communicating with them, still letting them in on some of the systemic alterations that were occurring. Physical changes that seemed almost impossible. If it weren't for the simple fact that every doctor there had seen some of the more unusual physical side effects of disease either firsthand or in books, they'd have thought the changes impossible.

There had been a very real fear that whatever they were dealing with was airborne, but it looked like that wasn't the case. Just the same, most everyone who hadn't shown any signs was continuing to wear protective gear.

On the third day, the first two victims of the disorder died. That was all there was to it. Their hearts stopped beating; their respiration stopped. They were dead.

The autopsies were scheduled for later the same day, just as soon as a proper environment could be cleaned and insulated, in other words. The process took two hours, during which time Neil and Lisa ate a quick dinner and checked in on John Terwilliger, who was not doing well at all. The poor bastard had almost no brain activity, and it was only a matter of time before he was declared brain-dead.

"I have to say, I could use a real day off at this point." Lisa did one of those stretches that was physically impossible for most men, her arms behind her back and her body bent to accommodate the best possible release of tension. Neil watched her with more than one unclean thought, no longer chastising himself for the ideas that ran through his head. After three days in each other's company, he was more relaxed than he usually was around her, and if she hadn't figured out that he had the hots for her by now, it simply meant that she was blind. He still wasn't going to act on it, but there it was.

The smile she tossed his way made it clear she knew. She also knew he wasn't the sort that would try anything stupid. He was safely in the friend zone. Neil made a promise to himself that as soon as he got out of here he was going to start dating. He needed to change his lifestyle enough that being a friend to an attractive woman didn't cause troubles.

"I think I'll just take it the easy way and call out sick for a week when this is done. I'm working all sorts of hours for other doctors, and they'll just have to return the favor."

"I like the way you think." She stood back up and moved across toward the door to Terwilliger's room. Neil made the appropriate notes on the man's records—nothing new to see here—and did the same, but a trick of the light or something else caught his attention and made him look back for a moment, frowning. There was nothing to see, but for just a moment he'd have sworn something was running across the floor. He didn't much feel the need to look under Terwilliger's bed to make sure he wasn't imagining things.

When they entered the hallway the activity was hard to miss. After several days of relative calm—it's hard to have new troubles when no one is allowed in or out of the buildings—all of the staff members stuck in the hospital were active and a few looked a touch panicked.

"What's going on?" Lisa touched the arm of an orderly named Jorge, who stared at her for a second as if dazed and then remembered how to talk.

"Two of them are missing."

"Two of who are missing?" Lisa's voice held an edge, and it was enough to make the orderly focus better.

"The patients. The ones the CDC are here for. Their bodies are missing." He was smart enough to keep his voice low.

Neil wasn't quite so calm. "What?" He already had visions of college pranks going horribly wrong, or of journalists taking pictures of the bodies for one of the sleazier tabloids. The stuff that legal nightmares are made of. Any backlash would surely slap across him in the process, because whether or not the CDC had taken over, he was the attending physician of record. Maybe he was being paranoid, maybe not. Either way, the notion of the bodies disappearing was a nightmare.

Lisa shook her head. "Find them!" She glared hard at Jorge and pointed him toward the morgue. "Now!" The orderly nodded his head and trotted away in a hurry. Deliberate or not, Lisa had the ability to terrify the people around her when she was angry. That was one of the many things he found attractive about her, weird though he thought that was.

Neil was still contemplating that odd sex appeal when he heard the clatter from Terwilliger's room. The man was damned near brain-dead, but that didn't mean he couldn't have a seizure or worse. He didn't think about it, he simply moved, prepared to make the man's last moments in the world as comfortable as possible.

Terwilliger had different ideas. The man was standing up, his legs wide apart, his hospital gown fluttering. After a week of looking at the man prone and dying by inches, seeing him on his feet was unsettling enough, but more than that, there were things inherently wrong with the image. First, he was standing at all, which made no sense as his brain activity was almost nonexistent. Second, he was looking around the room, his eyes flicking from one spot to another. Oh, and third, there was the large pool of blood on the bed that ran across the floor to where the man was standing. The tubes and wires from IVs and monitors were hanging from his arms, his chest, and the man twitched his hands a few times as he took in his surroundings.

Lisa let in a sharp breath next to him, and Neil looked in her direction. For just a moment there he'd forgotten about her being close by. Imagine that, something that could distract him from his obsession. He almost laughed out loud at the notion.

Terwilliger looked at her, too, his face twitching. Not in a way that conveyed emotions, so much as a way that seemed random, like a nervous twitch that had run rampant.

"Mr. Terwilliger?" Lisa's voice was calm, soft. "John? Are you okay? Do you know where you are?"

Terwilliger moved toward the door, his eyes looking them over and dismissing them summarily. Neil might have been offended, but he was far too busy getting out of the man's way. There was something about his moving, about the short jerking motions in the way he moved, that set off alarm bells in Neil's head.

Terwilliger reached for Lisa, and that changed everything. Neil was raised to believe that women should be protected, cherished. Surely if that stood true for anyone at all in his world, it was Lisa. Terwilliger reached and Neil blocked him, the reaction automatic.

Terwilliger slapped him across the room. That was all there was to it. He tried to block the man's path, and the brain-dead bastard backhanded him so hard that he was lifted off his feet and bounced off the closest wall and the medical waste container that had been screwed into the same surface. The metal box received no damage. Neil received a broken clavicle and a hairline fracture of his skull. The box stayed where it was, and Neil slid down to the floor, his head ringing, his eyes refusing to focus.

Lisa tried to fight, but Terwilliger was too strong. By the time she'd brought her hands up he was on her. The man shoved her into the wall and then pushed her to the ground. Lisa tried to scream out a protest, but the impact with the floor knocked the wind from her and left her gasping.

Neil tried to stand up and the room shifted madly. He crashed forward and tried to catch himself on his hands, but the broken collarbone screamed in protest and he fell flat instead. Nausea took hold of him like a terrier after a rat and shook him to his core even as he tried to reach for Lisa.

He got small flashes of her struggle, of Terwilliger crawling over her, his hands groping, pulling at her clothes, and panic seized him at the thought that the man was trying to rape her.

"No! No, you leave her alone!" He gagged and forced himself forward despite the way the world was tilting to the right. His arm screamed, his chest burned, and he moved forward as best he could anyway. Mostly he could see Terwilliger's body over Lisa, his hands on her legs, forcing them wide apart.

The man leaned over her, his face close enough to hers to kiss, and he whispered something to her that made no sense. "Mommy. I found you again." And then he fell on top of her, and Lisa screamed.

And something red and wet dropped from the hole in Terwilliger's back, surely the source of all the blood that covered half the bed, though the angle had prevented Neil from seeing the wound before.

Terwilliger flopped forward, covering Lisa, who struggled and screamed under him, her voice justifiably panicked.

Neil tried to move closer and another wave of nausea slapped him down, forced him face first into the tiles again, where the sharp pain of his broken bone only made matters worse.

Lisa screamed again, this time not merely in panic, but in pain as well.

Her legs thrashed, kicked and shuddered and she screamed, her body bucking hard enough to roll Terwilliger to the side.

Half her body was bared to Neil, a view he would have loved to see if not for the atrocity that blocked the bared flesh. Lisa screamed again, and Neil closed his eyes, unwilling to see what his eyes wanted to show him.

He screamed, too, horrified, and then covered his face with one arm, trying not to see, not to acknowledge what was happening only a few feet away.

Eventually Lisa was silent. Eventually she got up and moved away. By the time anyone ever showed, she was gone, leaving only Terwilliger's corpse and Neil, who refused to speak of what he'd seen.

If he spoke about it, it might be real, and he couldn't abide that notion.

He didn't know how long he lay there, unmoving, not wanting to think or feel. The sound of feet approaching was what finally made him react. Perhaps, just maybe, he would find someone who could help him.

Neil looked toward the sound of the shuffling footsteps, and stared at the draped cloth that fell almost to the ground. The fabric was coarse and ragged, unevenly shredded and dragging the ground in certain spots. The flesh behind it was dead gray and covered with open sores and developing blisters.

He died around the same time the teeth tore into his arm and his leg alike. There were two of them, and they were very hungry.

CHAPTER EIGHT

Malcolm drove back to his house with a nervous flutter in the pit of his stomach. It had now been cleared of any possible contamination issues, but that wasn't the same as actually being safe, not really. Whatever had happened to Randy had happened in the house, and even if the authorities now said it was safe, he found himself wondering what had caused Randy's sickness in the first place.

Behind him he saw the headlights for Chad's Honda. Chad and Lollie had been over studying with Carly when the call came in, and without hesitation volunteered to help. Lollie had stared long and hard at Malcolm, her bottom lip jutting out and trembling, and he had the absurd notion that if he'd said anything at all to her, she'd have broken down in tears right then and there and cried for hours. He didn't know these people, only knew that Carly thought they were pretty good folks. That was enough for him. They followed him toward his house.

Not that it mattered. Not that he was staying. He just needed to pick up a few things and he was out of there for a few more days.

He couldn't be there. Not for long. Not now.

He'd gotten the call on his way back to Carly's after attending school. She was letting him stay for as long as he needed, and he was grateful for that. He was grateful for her. She was amazing.

Even now she sat beside him, and she'd have driven if he'd asked, but the driving helped him clear his head, it always had.

Randy was dead.

Randy was dead, and he wouldn't be getting better, wouldn't be coming home, wouldn't ever bring another girl home to distract Malcolm while he was trying to study. The tears stung at his eyes, wanting to fall, but he was driving, so he forced them back again.

"You okay?"

Malcolm tried to nod, but it became a shake of his head as he pulled over. Grief bit him hard. His little brother was gone. His little brother, the pain in his side who caused so much trouble, who got him in Dutch a million times with his mother, who led with his mouth when he was younger, confident that Malcolm would handle whatever problems came as a result of smarting off. He couldn't count the fights he'd had defending Randy over the years.

No more. Now he wouldn't have to, because Randy was dead.

The next thing he knew he was crying and Carly was holding him, rocking him as he let go a torrent of sorrows. It was embarrassing, or it should have been. He hadn't been raised to cry in public. His mother would surely have been ashamed.

They were pulled to the side of the road less than a block from the house he rented with Randy. It should have been the easiest thing in the world to get over there and pack a bag, but the last thing he wanted was to see anything that made him think of his little brother.

Still, a man has things he must take care of. When the worst of the crying jag was over he wiped his eyes and then wiped the worst of the tears from his glasses and put them back on, smiling a silent thanks to Carly.

They reached the house a few moments later and even though it was dark out, the sun having set, he could see that something was wrong with the place.

Malcolm climbed from the car and frowned. It was autumn; the leaves were turning on the trees, but they hadn't completely turned yet. Two houses down from his yard he could see an oak with flaming orange leaves. The grass in that lawn was patchy, but mostly green. The next yard over was the same way, but about halfway across, the grass withered and died as if it had been starved of moisture. And the lawn at his place was dead. Not sleeping, not withered, but dead. Completely devoid of life. There was no denying it. He wasn't a botanist—he had never much cared for landscaping—but he looked at the grass and understood that it would never grow back. The holly bushes that he kept trimmed and that he hated, were brown and wasted, shedding dried leaves as if they were supposed to go belly up when winter came.

Moreover, the house felt wrong. That was the only way Malcolm could think of it. The house, the yard, the entire thing felt…diseased.

Carly stood next to him and stared at the house, her wide eyes speaking volumes of how she felt about the place. Chad and Lollie climbed from the Civic and stared, too. Lollie's eyes, already wide in her wide face, grew nearly round as she stared. Had he said boo she'd surely have run for the hills.

He wouldn't have blamed her in the least. Something was wrong here. Something was deeply, profoundly wrong.

"Listen, maybe we should come back tomorrow, when the sun is up?" Lollie's voice was a faint thing, nearly ghostly, but still he started at the sound of it.

Nonsense, of course. There was no difference between the place in the daylight and at nighttime. It was still the same building. Just the same he felt himself nodding. There was no part of him that wanted to enter the house in the dark. He preferred the idea of buying new clothes to the concept.

Chad opened his mouth to speak and then turned his head slightly, the gesture making Malcolm think of nothing so much as a puppy looking at something puzzling it had never expected to see.

Carly looked in the same direction, and her eyes widened as she took a step back.

And without thought, Malcolm looked the same way.

And saw Death standing in front of him. The figure was tall and gaunt, covered in layers of black cloth from the top of its head to the ground, and the cloth billowed and swayed in the breeze that came along around the same time the others looked. The fabric covered the head completely, and wrapped tightly around the neck and shoulders, bagging a bit around the torso, draping over the arms and hanging down to the ground, save where it was currently hooked into the dead and dying holly bushes.

He saw Randy's high school ring on the apparition's right hand, the familiar blue gem shining in the light given off by the street lamps. The thing's head was turned at an angle that Malcolm knew well, his body standing in repose the way it always did when he was seriously considering a subject. The hands were misshapen, too thin and too long, with dark nails that looked as sharp as a cat's claws. Ah, but that damnable ring that Randy had always been so proud of was still there. Seeing no features save for the ring, he knew that Randy was under the shroud, and wondered for a moment if he was being visited by a ghost. Surely the hospitals in this day and age wouldn't make that sort of insane mistake, would they?

"Randy?" His voice broke and the tears started. He shook his head hard and willed the tears away. This was Randy. Maybe. But there was a problem. Pure and simple, Randy was giving off the same sort of odd vibe that Malcolm got from the house.

"You let it kill me." Randy's voice was a strained, hoarse whisper but the hatred, the accusation in those words, was impossible to miss.

Malcolm stared at the cloaked figure and shook his head. He had no idea what his brother was talking about. For that matter, he had no idea how his brother could be there. His brother was dead. He opened his mouth to speak, but could think of nothing to say.

Randy moved with impossible speed. He had been standing still, his covered face turned toward Malcolm, and then the next second he seemed to blur forward and his hands reached out and caught Chad and Lollie alike, heaving them off the ground with astonishing ease. Chad was a skinny man, but had to weigh close to a hundred and fifty pounds. Lollie was about the same, maybe even more, and Randy lifted them, held them easily as he turned and looked over his shoulder at his brother.

The front of the shroud covering Randy's face split, the fabric tearing with a simple wet noise that was almost lost behind the sounds of his victims struggling to breathe and to escape. Lollie brought both of her arms down hard, slamming them into Randy's wrist in a move that should have stopped him with ease. Malcolm knew, because he'd taught several classes of girls' self-defense maneuvers, and what she did was a common way to break a man's grip. It should have knocked Randy's hand from her throat and left him exposed to a retaliatory strike. Instead Lollie winced as if her forearms had crashed down on a steel bar. Randy screamed at her, an inarticulate bellow of noise. At the same time, Chad swung one foot up and planted it in Randy's stomach. Nothing. He might as well have kicked a wall.

Carly stared at Randy with raw terror on her face, shaking her head again and again. Malcolm didn't have that luxury. He had protected his little brother countless times over the years, true, but he had also disciplined him when he had to, and despite the insanity of the situation, that was what made sense to him.

"Randy! Stop this!" He moved forward, his hand reaching for his brother, his anger real, his shame just as real. Randy was being a fool, acting like a spoiled brat. They had been raised better than that. He caught his brother's arm and felt the rough fabric and the cold, dead skin, the hardened muscles underneath, and knew in that instant that he was in the presence of evil, pure and simple. Whatever it was that held Chad and Lollie off the ground was no more his brother than the people it was killing. Surely this thing was the Devil's work.

And as he touched, Randy dropped Chad and recoiled as if burned. The bared teeth in the mouth—far too many teeth to be Randy—were stained pink with bloody spittle, and that very spit sprayed the air between them as the thing screamed in frustration.

Chad coughed on the ground, trying to breathe in properly. Malcolm didn't have time to worry about the other boy. He had to take care of Lollie, of getting her free from the thing that hid under his brother's skin. Perhaps he should have been terrified. It's likely he would have been, but Malcolm took comfort where he had always taken it, in the knowledge that the Lord loved him and would protect him.

He grabbed Randy's arm, and Randy screamed, his vile breath wafting from him like the stench of an open grave. Malcolm held on, despite the feeling that he was touching something diseased. "Let her go! You let her go!"

It's true that Malcolm believed the creature was not his brother. It's also true that if anyone had asked him about it and he had answered truthfully, he'd have said that what the thing did was pure spite and exactly the sort of thing Randy would have done when thwarted.

Randy's hand squeezed down and Lollie's neck ruptured, spilling blood across his hand. The blood ran down his arm and flowed toward the ground in a torrent. Lollie barely had time to gasp before she was dead, but Randy gripped harder still until her neck bones broke. Then he threw her body down, a broken doll that no longer served any purpose, and slapped Malcolm across the face, smearing her hot blood across his cheek.

The blow was brutal and Malcolm staggered back and dropped to his knees, his head ringing with a clear white noise.

Before he could recover, Randy turned to Chad and stomped down on the man's head. The end result looked rather like a cantaloupe that had been pulped by a sledgehammer. Chad died instantly but his body twitched and continued to move for several seconds.

Whatever possessed Randy was fast and angry. It spun again, the fabric around it moving like a cape, and Malcolm grabbed at the stuff, trying to stop the thing because he knew what was next, knew exactly what Randy would do if he wanted to hurt his older brother.

He'd thought Carly too busy freaking out to do anything. His mistake. When Malcolm looked toward the girl he'd started to fall in love with, he saw that she was on her cell phone. "Yes, we're being attacked! We need the police!" Her voice was rushed, justifiably panicked.

Randy knocked the phone from her hand as he grabbed for her. Malcolm clutched at the shroud of fabric and felt it tearing, pulling apart in his fingers. He screamed, willed the stuff to be stronger, to hold, to make his brother stop in his tracks before he could hurt Carly. Despite his desperate prayer, this time there was no solace to be found. The black stuff tore and Randy lunged forward, grabbing Carly in his hands.

And then Randy jumped, lifting into the air, the shroud around him whipping and billowing as the breeze exploded into a howling wind. He rose into the air on wings of snapping fabric and took Carly with him. Carly screamed as they ascended. On the ground, Malcolm screamed too. If he could have decided where to go he would have followed, but the two forms were lost in the darkness in mere seconds.

He was still in the same spot when the police arrived.

***

Boyd stared at the kid in the interrogation room and shook his head. He wasn't changing his story. According to him, his dead brother came and killed two people and took off with his girlfriend. There would have been a solid chance that he'd have just locked the kid up, but there was evidence. First, his brother's body was one of the ones that was supposed to get autopsied and disappeared from the hospital. Second, there was the thick black fabric he'd torn from his brother's "shroud." There was no denying that it looked exactly like the stuff that Danny had recovered from under a trashed car not all that long ago.

"We ever get an analysis on that fabric you got from under the car, Danny boy?"

Danny frowned for a moment and then nodded. "Yeah. Hair."

"Hair?"

"Human hair."

"Bullshit."

"I don't make these things up, Richie. I just do my job." He shrugged. "They told me it's the same chemical composition as human hair. You say check on it, I check on it. You don't like the answers, you're gonna have to take it up with someone who can change them."

"Like who?"

"I dunno." Danny looked at him and smirked. "Maybe Whalen?"

Okay. He'd left himself open for that one.

"Danny, does this stuff look familiar to you?" He held up the evidence bag with the cloth that Malcolm Dunbar claimed came from his brother's body.

Danny looked at it for a moment and nodded, his expression quickly moving to serious. "Yeah."

"Go have the lab look at it. See if you can find the tech that did the first one and have him compare. I want to know if it's the same stuff and if it is, if it's the same hair."

"Seriously, Richie, who the hell weaves hair into this sort of shit?"

"Who fucken paints their toenails three different colors? How the hell would I know?" He pointed. "And Danny? Why don't you offer that kid some condolences and get a uniform to drop him off somewhere, okay?"

"What about his girlfriend?"

"That's Longwood, not us." He shook his head. "We have enough shit on our plates."

"What else?" Danny stood near the door, ready to move, but not assuming he was dismissed yet.

"See what Whalen wants to do about the bodies disappearing from the hospital." He shook his head. "No. Never mind. We're just gonna give that to Longwood, too."

"You think there's a connection?"

"Of course there's a connection. I got fifty bucks says this is the shit that has Soulis back in town." He seethed. "Whatever we're dealing with is strong enough to tear up the underside of a car, and to stomp a man's head into jelly. Also, did you see the lawn at the crime scene? Shit was dead as could be. Just like a few other spots we've seen lately."

Danny sighed. "Are we going to look at a house tonight, Richie?"

"No." Boyd shook his head. "We're gonna get a good night's sleep Then we're going to inspect that house in the morning."

"I kind of like that idea better."

"That's two of us."

"We gonna bring maybe a hundred uniforms with us?" Danny sounded so hopeful it almost hurt him to deny his partner.

"Nah. We're gonna do this all by ourselves."

"Can I bring the shotguns at least?"

"That's why we're doing it all by ourselves, Danny. So we don't have to worry about shooting the wrong people."

Danny smiled. "See? All better. Now I get to kill something."

Danny headed out the door and Richie shook his head. Shooting something and killing it were two different things. Soulis had taught them that.

"And Danny?"

"Yeah, Richie?"

"I want you to look up Ben Kirby. I want you to find out where he's staying. We need to have a talk with him."

"Yeah?"

"Yeah. Him and that girl? They know something. Or at least maybe they know something. I'm easy. I'll take whatever I can get along those lines."

Danny smiled. "I know it's cold and all, but do you think there's any chance we'll get to see her in a string bikini?"

"About as much chance as you have of scoring with your grandmother."

"My grandmother's dead, Richie."

"Then it should be easy for you to score."

Danny's smile was bright enough to blind a man. "So there's a chance on the bikini. Cool."

***

There is that time before the night ends and the morning begins when the world becomes astonishingly quiet. Jason Soulis loved that time of night best. Not because it was dark out, but because he could think best in those strange, wondrous moments. Perhaps it was still something to do with the faith of the living. Most people were asleep, and perhaps the slumber stopped them from praying quite as much. He wasn't really sure and in the long run it simply could have been that he liked the quiet and lack of traffic.

He'd been busy for the last few hours. Aside from feeding himself — the girl had not protested and in deference to Maggie's wishes, he'd even left her alive — he'd also been busy checking on his investments and looking over several hundred pages of references to past experiments. Most of those pages bore little but notes on how little anything had changed since he'd started attempting to create a different strain of vampire.

Now, for the first time ever, success. Maybe. He still wasn't completely sure. The changes that had taken place since last he looked in on the girl and her first victim would give him the answer to that question. If the changes that had taken place in her carried over to him then he was on to something. If they did not, then he had wasted another effort.

He moved to the basement of his newly acquired home and opened the door, looking at the table and frowning. She had covered herself with something, a blanket or a sheet, perhaps, which was peculiar because he'd left nothing with which she could have covered herself.

Though she remained strapped to the table, she had covered her body with—

He stopped, his eyes growing wide. It had been a very, very long time since anything at all surprised Jason Soulis, but this? He was stunned.

"Maggie. Come to me please. I need you." He spoke the words and called with his mind, and felt the response from her. Of course she would come. Really, she didn't have much choice. He was polite about it, but he could have forced her appearance if he were so inclined. Regardless of how much freedom he gave her, she would always be his. That was one of the reasons he had created her. She was a fascinating woman and he would always have her.

While he waited he moved carefully around the girl and then looked at her last meal. The man was changing, and though the transformation was hardly complete he was showing the same signs that she had shown. The traits were carrying over. He had, in fact, created a new form of vampire.

Or possibly recreated something he'd thought extinct.

Jason closed his eyes and remembered the times not long after he'd been changed. There had been a castle in, where, Scotland? Perhaps Belgium? It was hard to recall clearly. At any rate, he'd been at the castle and in the protection of the lord of that castle when the plague bearers came.

They'd fallen from the sky, plummeting like stones until they were close to the ground, and then they had spread their arms, and the great sails of fabric that covered them from head to toe had spread like enormous, tattered bat wings and they slowed until they floated above the spoiled, bloodied earth. And then they settled to the ground, tall and cadaverous, but crouching until they seemed only half the size they should have, like broken, miserable beggars.

He'd watched them as they came closer, dark figures, half a dozen at first and then more, not saying a word, not wanting to alert the people on the castle to what he was seeing.

Most of the gaunt creatures had landed in the fields and looked at the castle for a moment before they turned toward the closest village and the burnt, ruined fields nearby. There had been an ugly skirmish and Jason was a guest of the lord solely because he'd helped drive back the attackers. Even at that point, hours after the battle had run its course, there were people out in the fields who were dying slowly and begging for mercy that the lord of the land refused to offer them.

The shapes had moved slowly across the fields, except for one, which moved toward the castle, its shrouded face jerking sharply in different directions as it sniffed the air and then moved forward a few steps.

The thing had stopped coming closer when it saw Jason on the wall looking down. It had looked up toward him and Jason took the time to study that vile face, nearly mesmerized by the thing. Black seeping boils ran across the flesh, dripped gore down the arms and legs, spilled into the soil of the fields, and even from a dozen yards away, Jason could hear the sound of the ground hissing with each droplet. The thing had panted as it looked up at him, its face obscured except for the mouth filled with too many teeth, and dripping a tainted red drool across the front of the hellish form.

Jason's hand had rested on the hilt of his sword, and he'd stared long and hard at the masked face. For a moment he thought they were possibly some form of infernal executioners, for surely the faces were hooded, but when he'd seen the thing as it lurched closer still, he'd seen the glimmer in the covered eyes and understood that this…thing…was related to his kind.

He'd been contemplating trying his luck against it in combat when it let out a mewling noise and backed away from him and the wall. Jason watched as it half-walked, half-crawled after its kin, looking back at him several times before the darkness took it.

Throughout the night the screams and whimpers of the dying soldiers on the field faded.

The next day, the first people in the area came to the castle speaking of the plague and begging sanctuary.

The lord of the castle locked the gates and had his archers drive the townspeople back to their homes. As if that had a chance of stopping the Black Death.

Were they the same creatures? He didn't know, but oh, how he looked forward to finding out.

Maggie knocked on his door within ten minutes. He opened the door and smiled at her, as delighted to see her as ever. She was lovely. She was desirable. She wanted him.

He leaned out and kissed the edge of her mouth. Then stepped aside to let her enter the house.

"You couldn't find a different house, Jason?"

She recognized the place of course. He'd chosen it because it had once belonged to Tom Pardue. "There were certain modifications that Pardue added to this building when he owned it, Maggie. Those included sound-proofing and solid steel doors in the basement rooms. And currently, I find those accessories very useful."

"Why did you call me here?"

He touched her face. "Because I have something to share with you, my dear. I want you to see this. And I want to tell you a story."

"Tell me a story?"

"Absolutely. I want to tell you about the past. A long time ago."

Maggie crossed her arms and leaned against the hallway wall. She was defensive, and he understood why. There were negative associations for her with this particular place. He would fix that when the time was right.

"*Nachzehrer.*" He said the word, rolling it off his tongue.

"Excuse me?"

"Roughly translated, it means 'night eater'. Or 'shroud eater'. There are stories of ghouls that could lie in the grave and eat their shrouds, and as they ate the fabric of the funeral shrouds wrapped around them, their families grew sick and died." Jason smiled, warming up to his subject. Maggie stared at him as if he were discussing something as vulgar as public flatulence.

"What has that got to do with the price of tea in China, Jason?"

He smiled. "Maggie, the stories were real. I've seen them before, the shroud eaters. They are also called plague bearers, because they often carried disease with them and because they hid in plain sight during the plagues. Families would get sick and die, and most people assumed it was the plague. In fact, it was the shroud eaters."

"That's nuts." She shook her head. "Someone would have figured it out, Jason."

He chuckled and hugged her. "Maggie, I have a shroud eater downstairs. I have been trying to create a different strain of vampire, and instead I have recreated one that existed in the distant past."

He studied her face as she ran through the possibilities. He could have read her mind, of course, but there was a lack of excitement in that. Far better to watch, to observe her as she made the appropriate conclusions.

"Wait. Tell me about what makes them different."

"I'll do better. I'll show you." He took her hand in his and led her down the stairs to his impromptu dungeon and lab, delighted that he could show her his newest toys.

And Maggie stared at them for several seconds, repulsed, before she finally pointed to the girl's lips with a shaking finger. "What happened to her mouth?"

"It seems to be a side effect of the condition. I saw her breathe her infection onto the boy on the floor. And within a few hours the blisters appeared on his mouth, around his nostrils. You see? 'Plague bearers,' the unclean." He reached out and lifted the girl's lips. She hissed and snapped at him, but only for a moment before she recoiled from him. He and Maggie were more powerful, and the girl knew it. Her teeth were bared for Maggie to see; the viscous red drool that spilled from the mouth dribbled its way across the girl's chin.

"This 'shroud' of hers, it's a part of her. The best I can figure is it's almost like Spanish moss. It simply grows from her body, drapes over her. I'm not really sure why, but I intend to find out."

Maggie spoke slowly, carefully, and he listened. He could feel it, the rage that was starting to grow inside of her. "Jason, my father is in the hospital. He has similar blisters on his mouth, around his face."

"Then he is very likely infected, Maggie. I'm so very sorry. Perhaps we can find a way to avert this becoming a disaster." He had his doubts, but he also had two specimens in front of him to consider as possible test subjects. And he'd need them, because he could tell by the tone of her voice that Maggie was deeply offended, outraged that her father had become a victim of his experiments.

"You goddamned well better find a way to fix this, Jason. You did this."
He was a patient man, and she was upset. He chose not to take offense.

"I'll see what I can do, Maggie." He couldn't keep the disappointment
from his voice. He'd wanted someone to share this with, someone who
could appreciate the numerous attempts he'd made before. For a moment
he'd let himself forget how young she was, how many connections she still
had to the human world. Some of his kind believed that all family ties
should be killed when one changed, but Jason didn't feel that way. Better
to let them grow old and die of natural causes, the better to appreciate how
fleeting and insignificant they were.

"Maggie, this is an ongoing process." He pointed to the girl and then
to her victim, who even now was beginning a slow metamorphosis. "This
could be little more than the caterpillar stage of a unique evolution. We
don't know yet."

She closed her eyes and took a deep, slow breath, the better to calm
herself. "Jason, this is my father. He is not a butterfly." She looked at the
two vampires he had captured, the fruits of his efforts. "Please find a way
to fix this. I'm begging."

With that she left, and he could feel the turmoil inside her. She was so
very angry with him, so very wounded that her loved one, her father, had
been hurt by his experiments.

She would simply have to recover from her anger. This was important
work, the culmination of decades of efforts. In comparison, her father was
insignificant. Or perhaps, he mused, he was taking her attitude personally.
After all, at the very least he had granted her father immortality.

***

Maggie left Jason's side with her mind moving in unpleasant circles. Five years and she couldn't decide if he was even a friend, despite the numerous things he'd done for her. Five years, and all she knew for certain was that he stayed in her mind all the damned time and it drove her crazy. She'd be fine, going along with her world, enjoying Ben's company and making the best of the life they'd built together—and they had built it together, that was an important thing for her to remember—and then blam! Along came Jason, creeping into her thoughts again, the memory of him whispering in her brain and distracting her from what should have been a good life.

She wanted to hate him. She truly did. If she could have, she would have, She'd have been exactly and precisely as happy with simply forgetting his existence, but that didn't seem to be possible.

The biggest problem was that all of this was foreign territory to her. She'd had a few serious relationships, as serious as they can get in high school at least, and she'd certainly had her share of experience with men, but she was always, always in control of those situations. If they wanted to get too close, she left. It was easier, less messy.

Only now? Now she wanted to leave, wanted to get the hell away from Jason, wanted him to leave her alone in her world, and she kept almost getting that, almost having him gone. And then he'd come back and all the feelings she didn't want to have came rushing back in.

And now? For just one moment she'd let herself think that they could have something. He'd come back to town unexpectedly and they'd had, well, they'd had incredible sex. Again. Like every time they had sex, it was amazing. And she'd let herself think that he'd come back for her this time, that maybe he wanted to be with her, in a real way, not just in a casual fling way.

And he pulls this insanity. New vampires. Worse, one of his fucking experiments had maybe gotten to her father. One of them had changed her dad? Into one of those things? She could almost hear Jason calmly explaining that he would never get old and die as long as he was careful, and the notion made her want to scream. The thought of her dad's face changing, collapsing in on itself, changing like that poor, wretched girl's face had, was enough to make her want to cry, and Maggie Preston didn't cry easily. She'd fought long and hard to reach the point where she could call herself even moderately independent.

She didn't bother looking around, but instead simply soared into the air, riding wind currents with ease. Her mind made the right corrections without any conscious thought. The winds did as she commanded, lifted her high into the skies above Black Stone Bay until the entirety of the town was laid out below her. There, the cliffs and the house she shared with Ben — the house that Jason had given her, but she didn't like to think about that part of the situation — and there, the university where she'd gone to school, where she'd graduated. To the north, if she so desired, she could have spotted her childhood home. Instead she turned toward the universities that faced each other and the hospital that rested on campus.

She had to know if her father was a victim of Jason's damnable experiments. She had to know. She made herself calm down, because losing her temper was a bad thing. When she'd been human it was bad enough but now? Now it tended to lead to rather extreme acts of violence.

Something was different and for a moment she wasn't sure what it was. But finally it came to her. The churches, the houses of God or Faith or whatever you wanted to call it, they weren't repelling her as they had before. They were weakened.

Jason was a man of his word. He said he was handling the churches and apparently he was. Either by using another young woman to seduce the clergy or by some other means, he was destroying the faith of the people in charge of the buildings. It looked like she'd make her cousin's christening after all. That thought damned near crippled her for a moment. Her father would be so proud. If he was alive enough for it to make a difference.

She drifted down to the hospital, fully aware that it was still closed off. Not that it would stop her. Jason had kept a lot of his secrets to himself, but how to move into closed buildings was an easy one for her. She merely concentrated and slid through the wall as little more than a shadow. The notion brought a smile to her face. The first time Ben had seen her do that, he'd nearly wet himself.

Ben. She wanted to talk to him, to explain herself, perhaps, or just ask him to hold her, to offer a little comfort in her confusion, but now wasn't the time.

She moved through the hospital, looking for the unusual and finding it with ease. There were only a few areas of the place that were locked down completely. Besides, the protective gear the people in those areas wore was a dead giveaway. Even if the doors hadn't been locked, even if there hadn't been a zillion biohazard signs to warn people off, she would have taken one look at the figures in their special suits that looked like they'd been designed for moving through the vacuum of space and she'd have known she was in the right area.

As little more than a dark spot she drifted through the glass and stone barriers, ignoring the cameras that would see only a shadowy spot. Finding her father was easy after that. He was the only patient alive in the ward.

He didn't look like the girl; he looked worse. His weight was half what it should have been, and his face bore little resemblance to the man who had raised her. The pustules had broken and spread across his face, leaving blackened wounds and open sores amid a sea of fresher blisters. His mouth was full of the dagger-like teeth that filled the mouth of the girl. His lips had peeled back, and though his eyes were closed, she could see well enough that they were the wrong shape. His skull was changing to accommodate the alterations, and the end result was that he looked almost nothing like the man he'd been.

His head turned, and her father's eyes opened. He looked directly at her, seeing her despite the fact that she hadn't left her shadow state. "Maggie? Is that you?" His eyes were no longer remotely human.

His voice was wrong. Dry and wasted. His black tongue licked across his teeth, and she half-expected him to accidentally cut his tongue into ribbons.

"Oh. Oh, Daddy…." The tears came then, and she shook her head. This was wrong. This was nothing like the transformation that had happened to her. She was changed by Jason, yes, but if anything she was made better. Her father? He was a walking disease, a septic nightmare. She could almost feel the virulence spilling from him.

He sat up abruptly, and she could see that the doctors had been removing the thick shroud-like substance from him, shaving it away, perhaps, or merely cutting it, but there were a few strands of it dangling from his body and layers of the stuff woven into too-thin hair.

"You let this happen." His voice was choked with a sudden anger. "You let him get me and you could have stopped it. I can smell it. You're different. You're not my little girl anymore. You're a demon…." As he spoke he rose from his bed, and though she could see that the bed was designed with restraints, they weren't being used. Perhaps the doctors didn't feel they were a necessity. Maggie had to disagree as her father lunged at her, his face distorted by the sickness and made even more alien by his sudden insane rage. "You're a monster!"

Maggie shook her head one more time and stepped back through the wall, relieved when she heard her father's weight hit the surface instead of merely sliding through.

There were times when Maggie thought that, perhaps, she had lost the ability to feel anything. She could never decide if she loved Ben, could hardly make herself worry if she didn't have contact with her family every day, and even Jason, who sometimes became an obsession, seemed to matter little on a regular day.

Just then she knew that her assessment was wrong. She still felt. At that moment she felt grief, and sorrow and oh, so very much rage.

Maggie rose into the darkness again, sliding away from the building and into the night, her eyes looking at the powerful beacon of the lighthouse at the end of the Cliff Walk as she headed for her home.

She needed to escape from this, all of this. She needed comfort and the only person she could think to go to was Ben.

***

Research, research, research. Wooden stakes, garlic, sunshine, silver, blessings, communion wafers…and Ben had no idea which ones of them were absolute shit and which might work. What he did know, was that he would possibly get exactly one shot at Jason Soulis. More than that and it would only be because Soulis was too busy laughing at his failed attempts to kill him on the spot.

He didn't think Soulis had that big a sense of humor.

Maggie's distress was at the back of his mind. He knew she had left the building, gone out without him, and where she had gone. He also knew that whatever had happened had her angry and worried and sad. He tried to tell himself that it didn't matter, but of course it did.

Still, he had to stop his research for the present time. Maggie might understand and she might not. Either way, she was on her way home.

He deleted the history of his Internet searches and turned off the computer. Some secrets were best left as secrets.

By the time Maggie came through the front door he was waiting for her, half-expecting—what? Accusations? That she was going to break up with him? That she would send him packing? It was impossible to know with her sometimes.

Instead she rushed to him, her face distraught, her eyes tear-stained, and practically wrapped herself around him, hugging fiercely enough that he had to resist the urge to yelp.

And what could he do, really? He held her back, gave her what she needed, the comfort of a body.

And she took that comfort. Before he could fully grasp what the hell was happening, they were in the bedroom and stripped down. They didn't make love. They fucked like animals, rutting and clawing and losing themselves in the moment in a way that seldom happened. For once Maggie didn't feel the need to be in control. She just felt the need. She climbed atop him and rode, her hands clawing and her mouth kissing a thousand times. He returned the favor, mounting her and taking her hard, his hands exploring every part of her, his tongue, his teeth, his lips doing the same until he was panting and exhausted.

And then she took him again, until the entire experience bordered on painful and the lines between affection and violence were completely blurred. And when it was done he fell back on the bed, spent and more than half-numb. And Maggie rested her head on his shoulder and kissed the side of his face, his neck, and whispered "I love you" again and again.

He whispered the words back and could have wept to hear her say them first for the first time in their relationship that he could recall.

Even if they still felt like they might be a lie.

***

Malcolm looked at the house and felt his stomach drop threateningly. He had no desire to enter that building, none at all. But he had to. As surely as he knew that Randy was dead, that whatever wore Randy's body had taken Carly, he knew that he had to enter his house and find the source of the darkness that was creeping from the building and killing everything it touched. Was it logical? No, but faith seldom is.

The house sat where it always had, but it looked different to his eyes now. It squatted there, a bloated thing, looking at him with soulless eyes and waiting for him with a hunger strong enough that it had killed every blade of grass, every tree on the property.

Had he any common sense he'd have called his mother by now, told her what was happening, and waited for her advice. She was skilled along those lines. She knew things, had seen things in her time that she refused to speak of, but he suspected she would have spoken to him now, told him a few stories about why he needed to stay well away from the place where he and Randy had lived and well away from whatever had taken his brother.

That was why he chose not to speak to her, of course. He didn't want to be warned off. He needed to do this. He needed to find Carly before it was too late, and if possible he needed to do something to save Randy, even if that meant killing his brother.

So here he was, ready to enter the house and take care of business, if only he could convince his legs to move forward. That part was challenging. Very challenging. Instead of moving toward the front door he moved around the building instead, circling his prey.

That, or just trying to get his nerve up.

***

The night was dark and wet, and it liked that. The dirt around its body made a delicious nest, and it settled deeper into the hole it had dug. Outside of the house there was a person walking. It could feel that much. This one was not touched by it, and so it could do little more than sense that there was a person above it. A small part of the creature's mind wondered if the person would be dangerous, but mostly it dismissed that notion. The person could hardly be a threat to it where it rested.

Beyond that individual there was a growing web that led directly back to it. Without moving a muscle, without so much as opening an eye, it could feel the network of people who had been touched by its hungers. There was the first, Dave, and there was everyone he had touched, had consumed and released, and from there the numbers were growing in leaps and fits.

Dave rested in the ground now, too, but above him there were children and more children and each of them was feeling Dave's hunger firsthand. Dave was crafty: he fed on all of them rather than on one or two, and the result was that all of them lived, all of them endured the feeding that he did. Hundreds of children giving just a portion of their life to satisfy Dave and, of course, to satisfy it as well.

Every life Dave touched was touched by it as well. The perfect pyramid scheme, the ideal web. Randy fed and Vikki fed and Dave fed, and in turn it was fed. Their victims rose and fed, and they in turn fed Dave and Vikki and Randy who gave a portion of that power to it.

That was good. That was as it should be, because even now its body was changing again, becoming something different, better, perhaps.

It had starved for years and now it would sate itself, and in the process it continued to change, to become a better, perfect predator.

The human continued to move around the house for nearly ten minutes until finally deciding to act. It walked to the front door and unlocked it with a key. Of course. Randy and Vikki had been here with another and that was the one who was back now, the one it had not fed on when it first moved into the house.

The one that had got away.

There was, of course, a reason that he had escaped, though it wasn't really sure how to frame that notion except as an abstract. There was something about the human above that caused it to hesitate. The sun in the sky was too bright, and so it grew the protective layer around its body. The man above was bright in the same way, but the shroud of shadows did nothing to protect from the light spilling from the man.

It searched through its memories desperately, the word it sought at the edge of its mind, but not clear. Then, finally, it understood. Faith. The man had faith. It had believed in God once, and understood that belief could be powerful. Seeing the light that came from the man above, it understood all the better.

Names, places, people, all were abstracts now, more than ever before in its life. There had been people who mattered once, loved ones who were important and took precedence even over self-preservation. Those people were gone now

Teeth biting into flesh, hands holding her body down as she fought, screamed, struggled futilely to defend herself, but he was too strong and he bit her again and again and again, biting, laughing, teasing with a hundred wounds before he dragged her down into the darkness to fester among the other dead things.

Even the memory of those people was a muted thing, colorless and tasteless in comparison to the feelings it received merely by observing the connections it had made through Dave and Vikki and Randy. The memories it had were as disjointed as the colors of a sunset running across the waves. They were there, but no longer made sense and took too much effort to consider. Better by far to focus on the new sensations.

Their hatreds were stronger stuff than the memories it once knew. Each of the ones it created thought of loved ones and blamed them for everything that happened. It thought perhaps that this was a symptom of the change, but how could it know? There was little left to compare with, and in the end, it hardly mattered. Except, in this case, where Randy was concerned. Randy hated the one circling the house. He had but to let Randy know, and Randy would settle the matter. Unless the faith of the one above was stronger than Randy's hatred.

This, too, was an unknown.

It thought it might call to Randy, might have the one above destroyed, but then everything changed.

The one upstairs looking the building over finally approached the front door and opened it, staring around while looking at the threshold, and finally deciding to risk the darkness.

***

The Windbreakers restaurant was a fine dining establishment if ever there was one. Situated on the shoreline with a spectacular view of the water and surrounded by the yachts along the docks, you were guaranteed the very freshest seafood and the finest, freshest vegetables available. The chef had won multiple awards, and the staff was both cheerful and efficient and seemed to have a knack for knowing when they could joke with the customers and when they were to be more formal. The place was hardly for the budget conscious, but the food made up for the cost by being exquisite. All of which was paraphrased from several reviews in restaurant magazines nationwide.

Brad sat in the restaurant and finished his meal, all the time contemplating how he was going to approach the owner about hiring his services for something entirely different.

Demetrius was a very civil man, and pleasant enough to be around as a client. This, however, was a different matter. This was outside of Brad's comfort zone in the worst possible way.

When Jerry, his waiter, came back over to see if he needed anything else, he nodded his head and asked if he could speak to the owner. "Demetrius isn't here right now, Mr. Hunter." The man kept his impeccable smile in place and managed a look of concern at the same time. "I can get the manager if there's anything wrong with the meal."

Brad took a quick sip of his brandy and then gulped down the remainder. There had been stories among a few of his friends, bragging tales of getting things taken care of. With a few simple questions to the right people, he heard that the man who owned the Windbreakers was also into other sorts of business as well. The kind that people don't talk about. There were, of course, protocols for dealing with anything and if you knew the right protocols, you could get anywhere in the world.

Provided you had the cash, of course. Brad was hardly an innocent.

He'd dealt with a few situations in the past, like getting an escort after he and Stacia broke up. Not just a pretty girl to have on his arm, but a pretty girl who did things with her body that were eye opening to say the least. But he had never considered anything this extreme before.

Desperate times called for desperate measures.

And, of course, the right protocols.

"Actually, could I talk to the manager in charge of catering special events?"

The waiter looked at him for a second, his face completely unreadable, and then answered. "Windbreakers doesn't cater, Mr. Hunter."

"I was told that there was a catering manager for special events. Something not on the premises, that has to be discreet?"

"I'll see what I can find out for you, sir. Would you like a refill?" The waiter looked at his glass for one moment and smiled again.

"Yeah. Sure. Thanks."

The man who brought his second brandy was most decidedly not the waiter. He didn't seem overly large, but he also gave off an air of menace that Brad couldn't have faked on his best day as an actor.

He handed over the brandy and stared at Brad for almost three minutes, never once saying a word. After the endless three minutes had passed—and Brad had not, despite his worries, wet himself from the intensity of the stare—the man gestured for Brad to take his brandy and follow him.

He was beginning to feel like he was in a spy movie by the time it was all said and done. The scary guy gave him a pat down as soon as they were away from the customers and back in the offices for the building. After that, he ran a wand-like device around Brad's body and pulled Brad's cell phone from his jacket, opening the back and sliding the battery out. Brad was smart enough not to protest. He also took Brad's Rolex, and Brad let him.

When he was satisfied, he escorted Brad into another room. And in that room, he met Demetrius. The man was just shy of short, but solidly built with salt-and-pepper hair and a tanned complexion that spoke of his Mediterranean origins. Demetrius rose and shook his hand gently and with affection. He had a warm, pleasant smile. He moved around his large desk and offered Brad a chair, and instead of moving back to sit behind his own desk, the man took the other comfortable leather chair in front of the desk and sat facing Brad. He did everything he could to make Brad feel at ease.

And Brad let him, because he had no doubt in his mind that if he offended Demetrius, the man would kill him with his bare hands. Or worse, kill him slowly. It wasn't that he had a mean face. It was the eyes. They were the scariest eyes Brad had ever seen. Had anyone asked him exactly what was so damned scary about them, he would have been at a loss for words.

"What can I do for you, Mr. Hunter?" The man poured himself a snifter of brandy and gently rolled the amber liquid in its glass. He never once took an actual sip of the stuff. Remy Martin. As brandies went, it was about the best and one of the costliest.

"I don't know exactly where to start." He had to clear his throat twice. He felt incredibly parched.

"Let's cut to the business at hand. You would not be talking to me right now if I were worried about a wire. You would not be here right now if I were worried at all. So you can state your business plainly, and we can come to an arrangement."

"My daughter is missing."

Demetrius nodded. "I heard about that. I'm sorry. I lost my daughter a few years ago." He might as well have been chatting about the weather.

"I'm sorry for your loss."

"Let's see what we can do about your loss first, okay? Then we can talk about other matters."

"My wife accused me of taking Stephanie. My ex-wife, I mean. We're divorced." He was normally an eloquent man, but just now? He was making an ass of himself because he was terrified. Demetrius simply nodded for him to continue. "Look. I just want my daughter. I heard you might be able to find someone who could help find her. And I heard you could maybe make sure whoever has her pays."

Demetrius leaned back in his chair a bit, his expression absolutely unreadable.

"If I wanted to hire your services…I…how much?"

"What do you want done?"

"I want my daughter. I want the people responsible dealt with. And."

"And?"

"And I want my wife to go away. I can't deal with her anymore. I want her gone. But accidentally, I mean. So it looks like an accident."

Demetrius stared at him for a long time, long enough to make the earlier staring contest with the man who'd brought him here seem like a passing wink from a cute girl. Finally he spoke. "Do you think you can afford all of that, Mr. Hunter?"

"I can make it happen."

"Are you sure?"

"If I couldn't, it would be sort of insane for me to speak to you, right?"

Demetrius gave the smallest curl of his lip as indication that he'd heard the words. "You have a picture of your daughter? Your ex-wife?"

"Yeah. Of course." He dug into his jacket pocket and offered recent photos of both. Stacia on the beach back in June, looking like a tanned, windblown goddess. And right beside her, Stephanie, who looked up at her mother with a beautiful, angelic smile. Christ, he loved that little girl more than anything else in his world.

"Which is the most important part of this, Mr. Hunter?"

"What?"

"Your daughter? Your wife? Which matters the most?"

"Oh. Stephanie. I need my baby girl back."

Demetrius stood up and extended his hand. Despite a powerful fear that the man might kill him with a touch, he shook. Demetrius had a grip like warm steel.

"I'll do what I can. I expect you to have payment ready within the next two days."

"Two days? How much?" He wasn't sure.

"Two days. Cash. Ask the man who gave you my name how much." Demetrius stayed where he was, but the scary guy — well, scary enough, but not nearly as scary as his boss, thanks — came over and escorted him to the door and then toward the dining room.

When they reached the main dining area, the stranger spoke his first words since meeting Brad. He said, "Dinner's on Demetrius." And then went back the way he'd come.

Brad nodded his head. He dropped a hundred-dollar bill for the waiter on his table and left, trying very hard to remain calm. Hollywood lawyers had not scared him as much as the men he'd just left behind, and he'd never thought any life-form could be as terrifying as Hollywood lawyers.

CHAPTER NINE

Randy Dunbar stood perfectly still and listened to the sounds of the night around him. The air was cold, the wind was sharp, and mostly what he heard was a combination of the leaves skittering and dancing across the surface of the street and the muffled sobs of Carly Winters as she tried to recover.

The way she sounded brought a smile to his face.

The house on Centennial Avenue was abandoned, and had been for months. He had no problem entering it, which was a very nice plus just lately. He couldn't even enter his own home right now, because there was a barrier there that prevented it.

He needed an invitation from the inhabitants before he could enter. Maddening! He lived there, but could not enter.

Vikki squatted in the corner of the dining room, her head resting on her knees, her arms wrapped around her legs, until she looked like nothing so much as a bundle of shadows pulled in on itself. They were not together out of any affection for each other, but simply because it was easier than separating. He could sense her satisfaction. Earlier, she had gone home to see her parents. They had been foolish and let her inside. Currently they were wedged into their closet, unmoving, unfeeling, though that would change.

Carly whimpered in the next room. Randy turned and cocked his head in her direction trying to decide if she was actually trying speak. No. She was merely crying again.

He toyed with moving over to her again, caressing her skin with his fingers to listen to her screams some more, when the summons came to him. If he was a creature of instinct, then surely the summons was as strong as any instinct he had. The image of Malcolm entering the house was powerful, and he responded with an immediate sense of urgency. This could not happen, could not be allowed to happen. This was dangerous!

Vikki lifted her head and then lowered it again. Yes, she heard, but the summons was not for her; it was for Randy.

Randy heard and obeyed. He stepped away from the house, slipped past the For Sale sign, and rose into the air, the shroud that surrounded him billowing in the winds he commanded to lift him and take him home.

Malcolm. Everything that had gone wrong in his world could be laid at his brother's feet if he thought about it. Malcolm, whom his mother loved best, and who was smarter, funnier, and simply better than Randy in every way that mattered. The feelings had never existed before. He knew that. He could look back to before he had been changed and acknowledge that he had felt differently for his brother, but that was irrelevant. Malcolm was all that mattered at the moment, and all that he felt for his brother was a need to make him suffer.

Carly was the first stage of that suffering, or course. She liked Malcolm better, so he made her pay for that. Malcolm loved her, chose her over him, and so she paid for that sin as well. All in an effort to show how much he hated his brother, how much Malcolm needed to suffer.

Deep within his guts he felt a tremor of fear. Malcolm had burned him earlier. Had touched him and caused him pain. Even now he could see the marks on his flesh where his brother had touched. The skin was lighter there, almost bleached.

Black Stone Bay blurred beneath him, and Randy started to descend, guided more by the summons than by any sure knowledge of how to get where he needed to be.

The wind cut at him, moved across his face, his skin, and shifted over angles that felt wrong. He was still adjusting to his new body. His shape was different, his features were altered. None of that mattered, but he was aware of it. All that truly mattered at the moment was getting to Malcolm, drinking Malcolm dry, and making Malcolm suffer in the process.

He started to descend, letting the winds die away and plummeting toward the ground, feeling the air currents adjust to his whims as easily as his hands responded to the commands to move just so.

Everything changed when the first of the crows drove down and cut across his path. The unexpected interruption made him change course, and Randy looked at the black bird, stunned by its appearance. Since he had changed, most animals had avoided him, or actively fled from his presence. Dogs barked, true, but they wanted nothing to do with him as long as he stayed away from their people. He thought that had something to do with the invitation process and little more.

The crow was an exception and an unexpected one. As he let himself fall to the ground in his old front yard, the bird banked and came around again, diving at him and veering off as he reached out to catch it in his fingers.

He hissed at the bird, and in turn it let out a screaming cry that threatened to wake every neighbor on the block.

And in response, a hundred more of the animals let out screams.

"What?" Randy looked around, puzzled more than worried, as the birds moved, flying around him, around the house, calling out to each other and seeming to mock him in the process.

He thought for a moment of entering the house but felt that same resistance that had been there before, as solid as a stone wall, despite the fact that nothing visible prevented his entry. He had not been invited. He could not push through the resistance.

While he was trying, the first of the crows scraped hard talons across the back of his skull, taking part of his shroud from his scalp and revealing the balding, patchy flesh beneath.

He turned quickly and reached for the bird, but it was too fast, already lifting away, cackling as it rose. From down the road, one of the neighboring dogs started barking and roused a few other canines that added to the noise.

Randy stared after the bird for a long moment and then slammed his hands against the air that stopped him from going further.

And as he did so, he saw Malcolm looking at him, his eyes wide in his face.

Randy growled. "Come on then! Come get me if you want your little bitch back!"

Malcolm moved from the house, his dark face showing no fear, only a silent resolve. "Is she okay, Randy? Did you hurt her?"

"She cried, Malcolm! She fucking cried like the little bitch she is!" Malcolm flinched at the words, but came closer, his lips curling down in anger, his hands fisting.

Before he came too close, close enough for Randy to reach him, the birds swooped down, not one or two, but fifty of them in a sudden wave, each plucking at Randy, biting with sharp beaks or scraping with their hard claws. They dropped, attacked, and pulled back almost as one, and Randy swatted at them, knocked one to the ground despite the effort of the animal to get away. He grinned as he looked down at the bird. It was already rising back to its feet, croaking and squawking its outrage.

And while he was looking down at the bird, Malcolm punched him in the face. The fist that hit him was weak, tender. Randy knew how strong he had become, how much he had changed. He understood that his skin was strong enough to let him and Vikki break out of the hospital's morgue with ease, despite the fact that the containers they were in were hermetically sealed and stainless steel. He had felt almost nothing when Carly struck at him, trying to stop him from attacking her earlier. His nerve endings were…muted. He still felt, but not as intensely as before. His body was far more worried about feeding than pain or pleasure. Even the lacerations that the crows had just left on him were minor inconveniences. But when Malcolm hit him he felt pain, real pain, a deep and abiding burning sensation caused by the same faith that had burned him earlier.

Randy staggered backward and Malcolm followed, his eyes locked on Randy. "Whatever you are, get thee behind me." Words. Mere words. But the emotions that were carried with them were like a slap across the face and Randy fell back, hissed in pain, and cringed, feeling his hatred for Malcolm grow in the process. He was stronger now! He was bigger and stronger! Malcolm had to be weaker than him! He had to be!

Malcolm disagreed and hit him again, grabbing for his arms, his chest, and his face. Whatever he was actually reaching for, Randy cringed back and whimpered, hating the fear that was driving him.

The birds nailed him again while he was busy with Malcolm. This time around they bit down harder, clawed with more intent, and opened wounds too large to brush aside.

Randy screamed, lashing out blindly and missing the birds as they darted around him. Even the one he'd hit earlier was back up now and flying away.

Malcolm reached for him again and Randy shook him off, pushing away and running, his body doubled over in an effort to protect himself from the birds and his brother alike. And then he rose into the air, feeling a brief satisfaction as the strong winds staggered Malcolm a bit.

Then Malcolm was chasing after him, calling his name, and the crows were rising, circling around him, calling out their mocking caws and cackling at his retreat.

And Randy ran, terrified and confused. This wasn't supposed to happen. He was supposed to answer the summons and stop his brother and instead he was fleeing, too scared to stand and fight.

Oh, how he would make Carly suffer for that. That was his one satisfaction as he rose higher into the night and outdistanced both the crows and his brother's desperate voice.

***

Malcolm looked on as the thing that had been Randy fled him and the birds that had come to his rescue gave pursuit. They were gone from his view in seconds and there was no hope that he could catch up. There was no sense of satisfaction. He wanted—needed—to stop the thing that had taken over Randy's form. He also needed to know that Carly was safe, which, according to the Randy-thing, she decidedly was not.

Behind him the house he'd been living in still crouched, dark and menacing, and he felt as if the damned thing might actually start to move and come after him if he kept his back to it for too long.

His mother had raised him to believe in God, and to understand that though there were symbols to represent His glory, they were merely symbols. They held no true power. Still his hand moved to the small crucifix around his neck and he took comfort from it.

There was still something in the house. He could feel it, had mistaken it earlier for the very thing that had stolen his brother away. And now that he knew it was there, Malcolm knew he had to face it.

"Randy. What did you let into our lives?" Malcolm's heartbeat was surprisingly steady, especially when he considered that he was surely heading in to face his death.

"Carly." His mother might have disapproved of how he said her name. She might have stated that the way he said his girlfriend's name sounded suspiciously like a prayer. Malcolm would not have been able to dispute her argument without lying.

The key to the door still worked. Malcolm entered his house and was careful to lock the door behind him after he entered. The door did not stay latched, however. Moments after he stepped through the living room, the door opened itself just the slightest bit and the air that slipped through the open door sounded like a sigh.

***

Robert Longwood was tired. He liked working alone, had avoided getting partnered up again after Nancy Whalen let herself get promoted to captain—and she'd let him stay that way mostly because she used his freedom to let her get out and do stuff from time to time.

Currently he and Whalen were sitting in the Silver Dollar Diner—rebuilt after the fire that took it out five years earlier, though it was now staffed with different people as none of the original workers had survived—looking at a growing stack of missing-persons reports with distinct unease.

"You know we're not the only detectives in this town." Bob was trying to be diplomatic. He knew exactly how poorly it would be received.

Nancy looked at him and gave him a crooked smirk. "Oh, yes. Let's call the other detectives off of their work so that they can help Lone Wolf Longwood clear a few cases." She poured herself another cup of coffee. "I can hear Holdstedter now, whining like a little girl."

"Well, yeah," Bob admitted. "But he only does that to get a laugh."

"I know. Thing is, that joke's older than Moses."

"Well, we could always go get some sleep and tackle this in the morning." Nothing ventured, nothing gained, right?

"Not a chance. You think my old man likes me spending all my time out with you and then sneaking in while he's trying to get rid of his mistress?" She might have started a lot of jaws flapping, but the fact was simply that she and her husband loved each other. Neither of them was ever likely to cheat, even if from time to time they considered it.

Longwood knew for damned sure that Nancy considered it. He had never quite understood what she saw in Rich Boyd, but she definitely saw something. Most times they were both good about it, but now and then the sexual tensions between the two of them were strong enough to cut with a knife.

He made sure no one was around and leaned in closer. "So, I saw Boyd and Holdstedter today." He made a point of staring hard at her to let her know he was serious and not getting ready for another Boyd joke at her expense. "They said they thought maybe it was the same problem as before."

She looked at him for a long second, her eyes almost unreadable. Almost. He had been her partner for a few years, and they'd shared a lot of time working together and dealing with each other's horseshit.

"I already have people looking after this Jason Soulis man. If he's in town and dumb enough to use his own name again, we'll track him down.

All on the QT. No one gets told shit about anything."

"That's why we're talking here, isn't it?"

"No. We're talking here because I like the hamburgers."

"Doesn't have anything to do with the fact that Boyd eats here almost every day?"

The look she shot him wasn't quite murderous, but let him know he was skating into a thin-ice zone. "Boyd eats almost everywhere every day. All those two ever do is take over restaurants and call them offices. I've seen them in action a few times."

Bob refused to be terrified of his ex-partner, no matter how scary she was. "I've heard rumors about you seeing them in action. Is it true Boyd gets to be the man?"

Before Nancy could respond, he heard Boyd's voice from behind him. Damn Whalen for being good at not giving them away. "We take turns. I don't let Danny be the man sometimes it makes him all whiny. Kind of like when you and me were partnered, douche."

Bob smiled. He knew there had to be an ulterior motive for Whalen's wanting to meet here. Her face lit up for an instant, and then she composed herself. Had he not been looking at her and wanting a reaction to his last comment he would have missed the change.

Holdstedter looked at the stack of papers on the table. "You supposed to leave that stuff lying around where civilians can see it?"

"You see any civilians here, Danny?" Nancy's voice was strictly business when she spoke, but there was an undercurrent that said she was teasing. Most people would have missed it. The three detectives knew her better.

"Scoot over." Boyd looked right at him as he spoke.

"No. Sit on Whalen's side. I want Danny all to myself." Bob grinned ear to ear as he spoke, and both Boyd and Whalen shot him hard, murderous looks. Just the same, Rich sat next to Nancy. Who carefully left a distance between them. Danny made a noise that could have been a laugh if he'd dared open his mouth.

Maybe he could get to like the kid after all.

"So what are you two doing here?" Boyd looked at Whalen while he spoke. He was deadly good with the poker face when he wanted to be.

"I thought maybe it would be nice if Longwood could actually solve a case or two, so I decided to walk him through the process again and hope it sticks."

"Good luck with that."

Danny looked at the stack and pointed to four of the folders. "Don't waste your time." His voice was completely serious for a moment, and Longwood looked at him with a steady eye until Boyd cleared his throat.

"Let's just call those unsolvable." Rich's voice was very low. It was true there were no customers other than them in the place, but that didn't mean the staff might not eavesdrop.

When the door to the diner opened, they all looked. There was no bell above the door, and nothing to warn them of danger except that the door opened a little too harshly and stayed open a bit too long.

"Halloween's later in the week, hon." The waitress on duty had the dubious name of Lizzie. The name was dubious because nothing about her seemed to belong to a woman with any part of the name Elizabeth. She looked much more like a Mr. Ed, which is to say she was a bit horse-faced. Maybe not the nicest assessment, but Lizzie was also not exactly the nicest waitress. Or the most efficient. Or the prettiest. Her hair was badly dyed a shade of auburn that looked wrong with her complexion and the makeup that belonged to the disco era. Her mouth held the harsh wrinkles of too many years smoking, and her body was thin and slightly stooped. He wondered how it was she managed to carry a tray without breaking. Then again, she hadn't carried a tray yet that he had seen. She hadn't moved an inch since taking their order that Bob could see, and that had been twenty minutes ago.

Bob looked to the door for the same reason as all of them. They were cops, and they tended to look first and then consider if their staring might be rude.

Turned out their staring wasn't rude this time, just common sense. He'd seen a zillion movies over the years and most of the ones about medieval times were among his favorites. Bob fancied himself a bit of a closet historian, and the Dark Ages were among his favorites to study.

His first thought upon looking at the man who walked through the door was that someone had done a lot of research to make themselves look like they had the plague. The man's skin was covered in open sores and pustules, and where the blemishes did not cover him, his flesh was pale and greasy-looking. His eyes were wild and seemed too large in his face, and his hair was wet, plastered to his skin. He was wearing clothes, but he was also covered with a ratty-looking blanket that looked like he was trying to make it into a parka. He'd covered his shoulders with the thing and it bunched up around his neck like a hoodie that he'd pulled down.

The man looked at Lizzie, opened his mouth, and screamed incoherently. There was no indication of pain in the noise, or any attempt — however poorly made — at giving anyone a good Halloween scare. No, the sound that came from that open mouth — and Grandma! What big fucking teeth you have! — was pure hatred.

On second glance Bob was pretty damned sure whatever he was looking at wasn't human. Bare feet, bare hands, and both looked wrong, with digits that were too long and narrow. The skin down on his legs and arms was just as diseased in appearance, and if the bastard was wearing makeup, he'd had it professionally applied.

All that in an instant, as Danny started to stand, his eyes already locked on the man who was screaming at Lizzie.

Bob Longwood considered himself a good cop. He wasn't wrong. What he was not, however, was a man in good shape. He was still standing up while Holdstedter was moving away from the table and drawing his pistol.

The screaming man charged at Lizzie. The waitress, perhaps a little slovenly, was not stupid enough to stand still for that. Instead she stood still and screamed back. The difference being that her voice definitely carried a note of shock.

The screamer slapped a table aside as he ran for Lizzie, ignoring the four cops who were looking at him, including Holdstedter who was screaming, too, bellowing out a command for the guy to freeze.

He did not, contrary to the command, come anywhere close to freezing. The table he'd swatted rolled through the air, losing its napkin holder, the place settings, and the pre-rolled flatware, along with the coffee cups that were waiting to be filled should the need arise.

Damned if it wasn't hard to decide where to look. The table sailed into the acoustic tiles and tried to make its way through to the actual ceiling. It failed and fell back to the ground with an incredible clatter. Lizzie screamed again and started to move, her rail-thin body suddenly very active.

Bob was still trying to decide if the entire scene was for real, even as Danny opened fire. He'd heard from Boyd and from several others exactly how good Holdstedter was on the firing range, and the kid had a few awards from competitions, but damn. Three shots, each squeezed off with remarkable speed, and Bob was lucky enough—though he wasn't sure it could be called luck—to be looking right at the screaming man as they hit him. The first round caught him in the shoulder and staggered him, blew a chunk of him away to scatter across the closest table. The second caught his throat and also took a substantial piece of flesh with it. The third? Yeah, that caught the screamer in the eye and absolutely destroyed his head.

The screamer stopped screaming and crashed sideways into the table he'd just painted with the black crap that should have been blood and meat. All that kinetic force took itself out on the table, and both the man and the furniture crashed into the tiled floor hard.

Lizzie stopped screaming for a moment, her eyes on the dead man who'd been coming for her. Then she took a deep breath and started screaming again.

Danny stayed exactly where he was, looking at the dead guy like maybe he was going to get up and start screaming again himself.

And sure enough, as Bob was turning to ask him if he'd lost his fucking mind, the dead man got back up and started screaming again, half his face blown away, and he was still sounding awfully pissed about the entire situation.

Holdstedter shot him again. And again. And a sixth time. Each bullet staggered the dead thing back a little further, but it kept screaming and making noises all the way through it. After the sixth bullet, however, it decided to fall down and stay there. It did not, however, stop moving.

Lizzie stopped screaming, her eyes bulging as she clutched at her chest and leaned back against the wall. She might have wanted to run, but she was too freaked out. Bob understood exactly how she felt.

Boyd looked at the thing on the ground and scowled. His face was almost chalk white and he was sweating a bit. Bob decided not to say a damned word about the fact that Rich had placed himself between Nancy and the thing on the ground, or about the fact that Nancy had let him. He just chalked it up to both of them being as scared shitless as he was.

"Richie. That ain't what we thought we were dealing with." Holdstedter's voice was surprisingly calm. His face was just as serene. It was his eyes that gave away how much the man wanted to piss himself. Just the same, he kept his weapon aimed at the thing on the ground, which was still twitching and seemed intent on getting back up.

Boyd walked closer to the thing, careful to stay out of range of its arms and legs, and examined it as best he could. Maybe it was instinct that made him cover his face with a napkin to avoid breathing in too deeply. Maybe it was just the fact that the thing stank to high hell and practically gave off a vibe that screamed disease.

It twitched, but did not move aside from that.

When he'd looked it over twice, Boyd nodded his head. "We gotta talk to Ben. Now. Screw waiting for tomorrow. We need to find that boy and have a talk. And we gotta get an APB on Soulis."

Whalen was the captain. She was in charge. She simply nodded her head, looking at the thing as it shuddered and moaned.

Bob tried to speak but couldn't quite find any words to say.

***

Neil Brighton was not used to waking up in hospital beds. It just didn't happen that often and, frankly, it felt like waking up on the wrong side of the mirror. Oh, there was a certain irony and he was aware of it, but still.

Worse was the fact that he'd woken up with restraints on his wrists and his ankles. He wasn't a foolish man; he knew what that must surely mean.

He was infected despite the hope that he had recovered from the worst of whatever was going around. His tongue slipped from a too dry mouth and licked at too dry lips and felt blisters. A great number of blisters.

"What the hell?"

"Doctor Brighton? How are you feeling?"

The man speaking to him was in an environment suit. He was airtight and taking no chances. Though there was little he could make out of the man's body, he could see his face well enough; he had a nice face, gentle and intelligent.

"Why am I restrained?" His words sounded slightly off and he ran his tongue across his lips again and this time caught the way his teeth felt. They were different. They were wrong. They were longer and sharper.

"You know why, I'm afraid."

Neil sighed and did his best to sit up a bit. It wasn't too difficult. They at least gave enough space with the restraints to allow that. "How far along?"

The man's face shifted to a more carefully neutral expression.

"Please, Doctor. Let's not beat around the bush on this. I know I'm infected. I know it isn't going well or you wouldn't have taken such extreme measures." He should have been screaming his fool head off. He should have been freaking the hell out, because he could still clearly see Lisa on the ground with that thing doing the most atrocious damage...and yet, here he was, calm and collected. Intellectually it was a puzzle. Emotionally he found he didn't much care. He rolled his shoulders and felt that, yes, his clavicle was mended.

"Doctor? Have you considered any of the emotional or mental side effects of whatever this is?"

"We haven't really had any patients to discuss that with until now, Doctor Brighton."

"Interesting. I find I am…emotionally numb. That could be shock, of course. I had a rather traumatic experience earlier. Or it could be a symptom. Simply something to consider."

The man nodded his head. "Thank you for that."

"Is it safe to assume that all of this is being recorded?"

"Yes."

"Excellent." Neil looked around the room and contemplated what he saw. He was obviously in an interior room, the walls were blocked by thick plastic, the better to keep the room as airtight as possible. There was a door, of course, but it was impossible to see from where he was.

"What happened to Doctor Davis? Can you tell us that?"

"I'm not completely sure." He tried to muster anything at all, any feelings for the woman he had been infatuated with for as long he had known her, and there was nothing. He felt hollow, and that fact alone caused him less dismay than it should have. "I have to say, I don't think this is shock. I think there's a chemical imbalance going on here. My faculties seem fine, but I can't begin to generate any real emotional interest in anything at all."

"Nothing?"

"Nothing." Neil looked at the doctor for a moment. "Also, I'm extremely hungry."

"Really? Do you think you could eat anything solid?"

Possibly. He wasn't really sure. The idea of solids wasn't quite doing it. "I'm genuinely not sure."

Neil closed his eyes. The man in front of him was situated several feet away and sporting the very latest in airtight anti-germ wear. There were preposterous numbers of sounds around him, his heart monitor, the pumps that were cycling air into the room, the thick caul of plastic that surrounded the entire room and the way it crinkled in the circulating air.

Despite all of that, he could hear the man's breathing, his heart beating. He could hear the man swallowing. Insanity.

"Doctor?"

"Yes, Doctor Brighton?"

"How secure are you within your environmental suit?"

"It's airtight if that's what you're worried about. We're taking no chances."

"Are you sure?"

"Absolutely." Neil looked toward the man and saw that he was frowning in thought. "Why do you ask?"

"I would swear in a court of law that I can smell your blood." Neil paused for a moment. "I don't want to dismay you, but I think the scent is making me hungrier."

Not surprisingly, the doctor was dismayed despite his attempt at quiet reassurance.

***

Jason Soulis let his birds play for a while and then engaged his new enemy on his own. This was not one of his vampires. He could tell a vampire's lineage without even trying and this thing, this shroud eater, was not a direct descendant. There was still a certain affiliation, but if he had to guess there were a few generations of difference between them. Of course that was to be expected as he was dealing with something different. Deliciously, wonderfully different.

Jason left his house and rose into the air, using his ability to see what his crows saw to get him closer to his target. The only specimens he had seen so far were currently restrained within his house—assuming they hadn't figured out how to escape yet — and they were still changing. This was a different entity entirely. This creature had come into its own, and he was delighted.

It floated like a spectre, moving through the air and swatting at his birds, all of which were smart enough to stay away. There was an aura around the thing, a sense of contagion that was reminiscent of the things he'd last seen hundreds of years earlier, but was not quite the same.

Jason observed for several seconds before the creature suddenly stopped bothering with the crows and looked directly at him. From fifteen yards away the thing's face was covered with blackness and still he could feel the intensity of its stare. The hatred it felt for him was almost palpable, a sudden solar flare of emotion from a cold, dead thing. The thought thrilled him.

"Come on, then. Come for me."

What had been a man named Randy Dunbar bristled as if the very fact that Jason would speak to it was an affront. Without a word it charged, cutting through the air like a black dagger as it came for him. He was tempted to avoid it, to let it know how fast he was, but that wasn't what this was about. He needed to know how strong they were, how much they were capable of and whether or not they would be useful to him.

The thing grabbed him with long fingers and sank its claws into his shoulders, cutting through his sweater and flesh with astonishing ease. Jason grimaced; the pain was expected, but the strength was something he hadn't quite been prepared for.

Up close he could see the thing's face better and could see that the diseased flesh prevalent on the ones at his home was far more extensive on the older one. The thing lunged at him, its mouth opening impossibly wide as it tried to bite him. Most of the vampires he had run across had the common sense not to try attacking an undead, but this thing? Either it was damaged or cocky.

Jason slipped out of its grasp with ease, becoming little more than a shadow for a moment and then resolidifying after it pushed through where he had been. The creature looked around with obvious confusion, and while it was trying to understand what had just happened, Jason drove his fist through its back, punched his fist through the creature's chest.

The damage should have been enough to stop it. Most of the vampires he'd encountered would have at least been incapacitated for a few moments. Instead the beast turned its head enough to look at him and spat a stream of obscenities. His arm was in its chest and still it tried to attack, reaching out with surprisingly long arms and clawing at him. The left hand was just exactly close enough and the talons on those long fingers cut into Jason's face.

And while he was distracted by the unexpected pain, the other one attacked him from below. He was too focused on the creature in front of him, too cocky for his own good.

Claws caught his legs mid-thigh and raked down, peeling flesh away from bone and taking muscle along for the ride. The pain was immediate and overwhelming. Jason Soulis was an old vampire, well versed in the ways of his kind and in the ways of the accidents they created merely by existing, but despite his ability to heal, he was not immune to damage or agony.

He lost his concentration and promptly fell, dropping from the sky like a stone.

He saw the two of them above him and shook his head. Stupid. Foolish. Careless. Concentrating was difficult. The trauma to his limbs was substantial, would have crippled a human being in an instant, in fact. Fortunately, he was not human.

Jason shifted into the shadows, pulled himself into the darkness and vanished, leaving the creatures behind.

He reemerged in his home, standing in the kitchen where the blood would easily be mopped away if it became necessary. His legs refused to hold his weight, and he was forced to support himself with his arms.

Concentration was the key. He focused on the damaged flesh and forced it to heal. The pain was just as intense, but only lasted for a few moments. His jeans were shredded, flayed away from his legs, which were once again intact.

And Jason looked down at the ruined pants and laughed, delighted. They were cunning! He'd never expected a second one to show up to help the first. He had assumed that they were almost mindless, as the shroud eaters of the past had seemed.

What a wonderful surprise.

Slightly exhausted, Jason ran his hands over his face and sighed. And froze. His hands checked a second time to make sure that he was not imagining things, and then he went into the bathroom down the hallway to make sure of what he was feeling.

The mirror did not lie. Mirrors never lied to his kind. His face was the same as always, except for the slight red bumps that were forming around his mouth and nose. He willed his flesh to heal and though he felt resistance, the sores vanished. They were gone from his skin, but they were not gone. He still felt them there, burning.

Jason stared for a long time, uncertain exactly how he felt about the possibility that the damned thing had somehow infected him.

CHAPTER TEN

Maggie couldn't sleep. She slipped from her bed and moved through the house as silently as a ghost, lost in thought.

That suited Ben just fine as he couldn't sleep either. Instead of trying, he got dressed in jeans and a shirt and then added a thick jacket as an afterthought. Tennis shoes and car keys and he was ready for the night. Common sense told him he should have been staying in for the evening. The last time he'd been out late at night, a dead woman had tried to eat his face. Still, he'd never been overly sensible. If he had been, he'd never have fallen madly in love with Maggie in the first place.

The Lord knew she was out of his league. She had been since the first time they met and that had never changed. That was the problem, wasn't it? If they were somewhere close to even footing maybe he'd have a chance of explaining why he was so angry. She'd never once said they were exclusive. She'd never once pretended that they ever would be, and if he needed proof of that all he had to do was look back at the times when she'd had to feed her darker urges over the last half-decade.

He left the house and walked along the cliffs for a while, letting the cold air cut across his face and blow down the collar of his shirt. By all rights he should have been shivering, but he barely felt the cold.

He'd walked the majority of the trail and turned around to get back to the house when he saw Boyd and Holdstedter. He remembered them, of course. He'd ignored them the other day at the diner and they'd returned the courtesy, but they hadn't changed much, and they were both the sort of personalities that were hard to forget. Some people might trail away into the distance in a person's memories, but neither of them would ever fit into that category as easily as he did.

He stopped where he was and waited. Let them come to him if they wanted something. And of course they wanted something; everyone did. He was finally beginning to understand that.

Boyd kept a steady pace until he reached him, his cigar burning in the breeze and sending off small plumes of tobacco smoke that were pungent enough to kill small insects. Two paces behind him, Holdstedter nodded amiably, but kept his hands in his overcoat pockets. The biggest change in either of the men was simply that they looked a little stressed. Not even that was much of a change.

"Been a while, Ben." Holdstedter's voice was friendly enough.

"How can I help you gentlemen tonight?" He wasn't much in a mood for company, but he also wasn't stupid enough to antagonize the police, especially when the men already knew about his less-than-sterling record.

Boyd looked at him for a long moment, not speaking, not blinking. "Straight to business, then? Okay. We need to know everything you can tell us about Soulis."

"Not much. He's back in town." His mouth worked, but he couldn't quite come up with the words. What was he supposed to say? That the bastard was in town and fucking the woman he loved? Not exactly pertinent to anything the police needed to know, now, was it?

Boyd's expression changed a bit, just a tiny amount, really, but it spoke volumes. "Danny boy? Give us a little space, will you?"

Danny Holdstedter nodded his head and faded into the distance. There was virtually no chance he could hear the conversation.

Boyd stepped closer. "No love lost between you and Soulis, is there?"

"You could say that."

"I've looked. The house you're staying in belongs to Soulis. He lets you and Maggie Preston stay there. I've also checked on other things. I understand Maggie's father is in the hospital. In the quarantine ward."

Ben nodded and looked out at the water. The cloud cover was heavier out over the sea and was moving in. Another thirty minutes and there would be no chance of seeing the water past the fog bank moving closer.

"You know what the problem is with falling for someone, Ben?"

"No. What's that?" He asked strictly to be polite.

"You fall hard enough and they can destroy you without even trying." Boyd moved over to the railing and looked out at the fog as well, his eyes studying the approaching mists with the intensity of a fortune-teller studying tea leaves in a cup. "I can't remember who it was said it first, but there's a quote I always liked. Basically it says that whoever cares less in a relationship will always have the upper hand."

Ben nodded his head in slow agreement.

Boyd continued. "Just a bit of advice again. Not that you asked. If she's cheating on you, she won't stop. It almost never works after the cheating starts."

"Speaking from experience?"

"You see a wedding ring on my finger?" Ben shook his head. "That's experience in action." Boyd took the cigar from his mouth and studied the cherry as it blazed in the wind off the sea. "But that's not why I'm here and I bet you know that."

"He said his experiments were working out. He came back here to study them again." Ben shrugged. He didn't mean to say anything beyond that. Really, it was all he knew. "I know the thing I saw yesterday wasn't like the ones that were here before, or like Soulis." He didn't mention

Maggie's name. He didn't have to and he knew it. The knowledge of Maggie was one of the things that the men shared, as was the decision not to speak of it. "He took one to study. I don't know where he went. I could maybe find out."

Boyd shook his head. "Nah. You already confirmed what I needed to know. I don't want you getting in any kind of trouble."

"Not on my agenda."

"Try to keep it that way. Seriously. There's enough bad shit going on right now. You shouldn't even be out here at night." Boyd reached into his jacket pocket and pulled out a business card. Without asking, he slipped the card into the breast pocket of Ben's jacket.

"I sort of have protection."

Boyd looked at him for a long moment and nodded his head. "I guess maybe you do." With that, the detective waved and headed back the way he'd come. Danny nodded when Boyd reached him, and Ben nodded back.

"Say, Ben?" Boyd's voice was soft, but it carried.

"Yeah?"

"What kills vampires?"

"You want a list of what's supposed to work? Or a list of what actually works?"

"What actually works would be nice."

Ben smiled and shook his head. "Yes, it would. Unfortunately, I haven't got that sort of list."

"I'll take the other kind." The man sounded a little desperate.

"That card you gave me have an e-mail address?"

"As a matter of fact it does."

"I'll send you the list."

Boyd nodded and started walking again. When the detectives were safely in the distance he let himself sag against the rails. He supposed he should head home. Maggie would start wondering where he was. That thought made him chuckle, but it was a humorless sound. He doubted that she'd notice he was missing.

Hell, if he was lucky, she wasn't with Soulis again.

***

Five minutes after Ben left the house, Maggie left as well. She was tense, angry, and hurt, and though she had certainly enjoyed being with Ben physically, there was nothing to do about the emotion dilemmas surrounding her. Frankly, his turmoil over her almost guaranteed that she would get no rest. The connection they shared let her feel what he felt, even if it was in a distant way, and she couldn't help but feel his sense of betrayal. There was no one to blame but her for that.

Well, and possibly Jason Soulis.

Jason was on her mind, of course, as was her father, or rather the thing that her father had become.

Jason had done that. No matter how she looked at it, his actions were directly responsible for her father being attacked and changed into the nightmare she'd seen at the hospital.

Her entire life she'd always been able to rely on her parents. They were strong, good people, and she'd done all she could to follow their examples. She had fallen short a few times, but she had tried. She could remember looking to her dad for support since she could remember anything at all, and he was always there, always ready to offer whatever assistance he could. The only time he'd ever failed was when it came to the money for college, and that was simply a matter of economics. Besides, she'd figured that out all by herself, hadn't she? Nothing a little whoring couldn't take care of. That thought cut through her depression and added a layer of shame. She tried hard not to think about that aspect of her life, had tried not to think about it while it was happening, but it kept coming back to haunt her.

Ben had discovered her secret in college and never once judged her for it. He'd even accepted that from time to time she had to deal with her old clients for a food source, offering sex in exchange for a quiet way to avoid both discovery and her need to feed. She knew how much he hated that she had to do that. She knew it cut at him every time he drove her to one of her meetings, but he still did it. He was that good to her.

And she'd gone and fucked a man she knew would hurt him. She'd run to Soulis like a little girl running to sit on Santa's knee. Yes, shame was a good word.

Maggie had flown from the house, and now she lowered herself from the sky, settling on the roof of the medical college building. The university was broken into several different buildings, naturally enough, and in this case the classes were fairly small. Most of the classes for the medical college were kept in a mansion that had been built before the university was even a notion. The school kept the place very well indeed, and she settled her weight on the shingled roof without any fear of creaking boards. She wasn't foolish about it. She kept to the darkness and looked around, enjoying the view of Black Stone Bay.

Behind her, out of her view, the hospital where her father was dying and changing loomed like a bad dream. She refused to look at it, tried her best not to think about the words he'd cast at her earlier, because, really, she felt a knife of guilt every time she considered those accusations.

Because to one extent or another she believed he was right.

And she hated the shame that came with that admittance.

Jason Soulis. She thought about him, and all of the anger and shame were there again, magnified and mixed with her sick desire to be around him and to be with him. He was like a drug and she was a junkie and she hated that.

What was it they always said about addiction? Admitting you have a problem is the first step to recovery, or something along those lines.

Well, she definitely had a problem.

Now all she had to do was decide what she was going to do about it.

Below her the campus was nearly completely silent. The night was creeping toward morning, and a thick fog was rolling in from the ocean, covering everything below her in tendrils of white and hiding the worst flaws. Maggie was tempted to drop down into that bank of mist and hope it could somehow work a similar miracle on her, but she knew better. That was part of growing up, wasn't it? Realizing that Santa wasn't real and that no matter what you did, sooner or later you had to pay for your actions.

"Time to start paying up, Margaret." She had to get rid of Jason in her life. She didn't want to, she had to. There was a decided difference. Jason was poisonous. He cared only for himself at the end of the day, and she knew it. He was self-centered, manipulative, and amoral. More importantly, he was a monster who even now was causing the death of her father. Unless there was a way to reverse what was happening, he would be responsible for the best man she'd ever known dying and coming back as something diseased and very possibly contagious.

There was no other choice, really. She had to get rid of Jason.

She just hated that the very notion left her wanting him all the more.

Mind made up, Maggie left the rooftop and rose into the air, higher away from the fog below and the false promise of an easy way to hide her sins. It was time to find redemption, to find a way to save her father if there was any possible way.

***

Dave stirred in his underground resting spot. They were coming back now, the children who'd left him. They were so vital, so alive, and the thought of them coming back roused him. The sun was climbing. In a few moments it would rise properly, and he would have to hide himself, but that wasn't an issue. What mattered was that he was still growing stronger. The morning was upon him, and he was conscious, able to move. In time he might be able to survive the dawn, but for now he had to find other ways around his problem.

He held his hands apart and stared at them, the right with its strong muscles and bones, the thick claws, and the mobility that made it strong: the left with its malformations, sores, and weakened, atrophied state. They were almost nothing alike, but they were both a part of him.

He could feel the sores on his flesh as they healed over, grew again, and ruptured, a slow process, to be sure, but one that continued on. He was, he knew, a walking disease. There were some who would dread that notion, that they might spread illness to the rest of humanity, but he was not among them. Humanity. What a waste. Better to let them fester and die. Better still that they do it and make him stronger in the process.

He could feel the ones he'd created, could tell that they were not doing as well as he was, and that was fine with him. He was not the least bit bothered by their failures. They would prove strong enough to survive, or they would wither and die. In the end, they hardly mattered. What was important was his own survival and the increase in his strength.

With that notion in mind, he once again drew in a great breath, taking in the vital, living air around him and holding it within his chest, feeling the darkness and corruption within him mingle with the clean environment and contaminate it. He did not need to breathe, did not need to exhale, and so he held the breath patiently as the sun rose and the school buses came, disgorging their cargo of living, thriving children. Many of them had left the building the day before feeling "under the weather," but now they came back replenished, refreshed by a night of rest. They were vital, so alive that their mere presence was enough to excite him.

Still he waited. They greeted each other, greeted their teachers and the other adults who were there to supervise them, and slowly, oh so slowly, settled in for another day of school. Even from below them he could hear their murmured excitement. Halloween was coming, was almost upon them, and there would be costumes, haunted houses, ghosts, and, of course, trick-or-treating.

He remembered Halloween. When he'd been younger he'd gone door to door with the other kids and gotten his fair share of treats as well. Those were good times, filled with magic and wonder and the certainty that while monsters were real, if you were careful they could never find you, never get you.

That thought brought a smile to his ruptured, bleeding lips, and he ran his tongue across his teeth, amused by their new shapes. The monsters of the past were not quite as clever as he.

Dave breathed out, slowly exhaling the cloud of disease and death that the people above could not see. Oh, but they could feel it. How well they could feel it. Within the hour almost every child and every adult in the building was feeling the effects of the second breath he'd gifted them with. Many of them were sweating; all of them were exhausted and feeling very little like they had when they'd come to school earlier.

By the end of the second hour, the people in the building had fallen into stupors. While more than one of them thought about calling for assistance, none of them retained the faculties to actually dial the phone or the energy to even lift a receiver. Their skin was wet, and their eyes were glazed; the flesh around their lips and noses was tender, and the blistering had started, black sores covering the areas where they breathed in and exhaled.

By the third hour the situation was even worse, and most had fallen into a proper coma.

Dave smiled and saw that it was good. But he knew how to make it better still. Dave called to his victims, willed them to hear his voice and to obey him. Really, they had no choice. He was so much stronger than they were, as he had already been feeding on their lives and making them his own.

The fourth hour was as silent as the grave. The only exception came from one parent who called the school to see about enrolling her son as they had just made the move to Black Stone Bay and she had heard such good things about the Hartshorn Academy. When no one answered, she decided to call back the next day. Really, there was so much to be done, and school could wait one more day.

It was in the fifth hour that Earl Carter came to see about removing his son from school early. Earl's mother had taken ill, and they were going to head down to Florida to see how she was doing and what needed to be done to take proper care of her. She'd always insisted on taking care of herself, but there were limits to what she was capable of handling, and Mr. Geoffries, the man who ran the assisted living community where she was staying, said she might need to be taken to a facility more prepared to handle a woman who was starting to suffer from dementia.

When he entered the building and found no one in the offices, he thought perhaps there had been a fire drill or some such. They had done those when he was in school, and everyone had to participate. It wasn't until he'd checked the third empty classroom and seen no sign of anyone at all that he started to worry.

By the time he'd gone through entire first floor of the building, including the empty gymnasium and the equally quiet cafeteria, Earl began to suspect there was more to the situation. Every classroom was devoid of life, but showed signs of the students. Book bags, opened books, even a cell phone, though he knew those were prohibited.

None of which was a good sign in his eyes. Earl might be a busy man, but he was hardly distracted to the point of stupidity. Better to face a little embarrassment than to overlook the obvious signs that something had gone wrong.

Earl called 9-1-1 and spoke to the emergency dispatch.

Fifteen minutes later he was speaking with Bob Longwood, a detective, while several uniforms started examining the building. Not much later the first news teams came on the scene and were blocked immediately by the uniforms. But there was no denying that something was happening at the school even if no one knew for certain exactly what that something was.

Stephanie Hunter disappearing was newsworthy solely because she was a child and an Amber Alert had been announced. The celebrity status of her parents made the matter more newsworthy of course. But in comparison to the Hartshorn Academy situation, Stephanie was a minor note. Stephanie attended the academy, and that point was made very clear at the same time that the announcement was made that every member of the faculty and all of the students at the school had disappeared sometime after the first bell rang.

Three hundred fifty students and all of their caregivers gone. Just vanished.

Detective Robert Longwood's day went to hell from that moment forward.

***

Sunrise, and the waiting game was going on again, only this time, just to add to the grins, Nancy Whalen was along for the show. Boyd did his best not to stare at her, which was not as easy as it should have been. Years of acknowledging that she was off limits, years of the both of them flirting and keeping it from ever going any further, and you'd think he'd have figured out how to find something more interesting to look at.

Then she made it easier. She called her husband on the phone and started talking to him. While on the ground in front of them, the thing from the night before struggled, tried to break free from the cuffs that held its ankles together and the other pairs that wrapped its scrawny arms around the base of a tree. Four tent posts driven into the hard ground kept the legs from going anywhere. The thing was as bound as it could be, and even now it was fighting to break the bonds.

That was okay. Danny and Boyd both had guns aimed at the thing. Whalen was watching it and trying to look like she wasn't. The sun started to show itself as more than just a glow on the horizon and the thing let out a slowly building scream. It opened its mouth and drew in a breath and then grunted, hissed, and screamed as it stretched and fought to get free. The black stuff that covered most of its body writhed and slithered, and damned if the stuff didn't act like ivy strands on speed and start crawling up the damned thing's ugly face. The dark eyes squeezed shut against the light, and the black stuff covered the head, but it wasn't enough to make a differ-ence. The sunlight touched the flesh and the black cloak around it, and both started burning. The dark stuff—hair according to the ME—crisped and singed and burned slowly and with a great deal of stench. The flesh under-neath burned faster, especially where the black stuff wasn't. Sure enough the damned thing was trying to grow protection. Boyd hadn't even consid-ered that possibility.

The face beneath the caul started smoking, and the eyes caught fire, and Boyd made himself watch, swallowing the bile that wanted to force its way from his stomach into the sea breeze by way of his mouth. Sour spittle drenched his mouth. He spat to get rid of it but did not let himself look away from the sight, even when Whalen made a surprised noise.

The more the sun hit it, the faster it burned. And that was almost enough to make him smile. "They go up faster, Danny? Or is that my imagination?"

"Goes up pretty damned fast, Richie. Like your dick around—" He had the good sense to stop himself before both Boyd and Whalen would have had to shoot him. "Around my sister." Good save. Boyd decided to let his partner live.

Whalen put a hand on his shoulder. He managed not to scream. On the ground in front of him the thing had stopped moving and was little more than a smoking ruin. The extremities were already crumbling into white ash. "Is it always like this?"

Danny answered for him. "No. This is actually kind of an easy one. Fast, too."

Boyd nodded his agreement and looked at her face as she absorbed that fact.

"So what do we know that kills these things, guys?" Her voice was mostly steady, even if she was looking a little green around the gills.

"You're looking at it." Danny shrugged. "I mean, we've shot the hell out of a few of 'em in our time, and they keep coming."

Boyd scratched at his chin, and the stubble reminded him that he should maybe shave once in a while. Like he should sleep once in a while. Eventually he suspected he would get to both.

"They don't move so good when their heads are gone. But garlic doesn't do anything, and silver is a waste of time."

"They're vampires, right? How about wooden stakes?"

Boyd looked hard at her. "Okay. Here's the thing. I don't normally carry a lot of wooden stakes around. I also don't carry a mallet. And I've discovered that if I get close enough to these fuckers to pound a stake through their hearts, they tend to try to bite my fucken face off. It ain't much of a face, but it's all I've got."

She rolled her eyes. "Your face is just fine, and you don't need to be a sarcastic dick about it."

"He's always a dick. The sarcasm is just a bonus." God love Richie for trying to smooth over the awkward moments in the conversation, but Boyd wanted to kick him in the nuts.

"Well, we can't go handcuffing dead things to every damned lamp post in Black Stone Bay!" Whalen's temper flared. She always looked so damned sexy when she was pissed off. To avoid noticing, Boyd kicked the body in front of him and watched the ashes scatter to the wind.

"Bright boy over there tried a portable ultraviolet lamp. Unless you want one that weighs close to two hundred pounds, we can't get one strong enough to do the job. It's the sunlight or something about the sunlight that does the job."

Danny piped in again. "Hollywood makes that shit look easy, but the batteries weigh a ton, and the vampires don't just stand there when you aim at them. They get really, really pissed off, and they try to bite you." He shrugged. "So far, you shoot 'em enough times, and they at least pretend to die for a while."

"Crosses?"

"We ain't exactly religious types." Boyd scowled and pulled a cigar from his jacket. Whalen didn't much like cigars. For that reason, he bit off the end and put the stogie in his mouth.

"I tried putting a cross out to one of them a couple years back. It just flinched a little and then it tried to bite my face off." He was making light of it, but the night it happened he'd been absolutely horrified. So had Boyd. That particular vampire had been unexpected and very, very hard to put down.

"The goddamned things are like cockroaches. Every fucken time we think we've killed 'em off they come back, and this time they've changed into something else."

"How does Soulis fit in?"

"He said he was here to take care of this mess. I believe him like I believe Danny here will stop staring at teenaged girls."

"What? They wear those little skirts, a man has to look."

"I thought you were serious, I'd cut your eyes out, Danny." Whalen scowled her disgust in his direction as she spoke.

"See? She says the sweetest things, Richie. She's like a really cool mom and a hot momma all rolled into one."

Whalen shot him a one-fingered salute. "What are we going to do here, gentlemen?"

"We need to find out everything we can about Soulis." Boyd finally looked at her and wished he hadn't. She was staring right at him, and he felt the usual mild jolt of electricity. It wouldn't have bothered him so damned much but this was one of those occasions where he could almost feel the attraction was two-way. "I talked to a kid yesterday that met him in the past. Today I say we have to talk to the other one."

"What other one?" Whalen frowned.

"Oh. The other vampire in town." He kept his voice calm.

"There's another vampire in town?" Her voice rose into a shrill pitch. "Since when?"

"Well, we're not a hundred percent sure she is a vampire. But we should maybe question her to find out."

Whalen rolled her shoulders and stretched her neck. "You do what you have to. I'm going home."

"Home?"

"Yeah. I'm tired, Boyd. And I need a shower."

Danny stared at her. "But you want us to keep investigating?"

"Makes up for all the times I ignore you sitting on your asses in the diners." She headed for her car. "Besides, rank has its privileges."

Danny and Boyd both watched her walking away until she had moved to the front of the property.

"Your girlfriend is a bitch, Richie."

"She's not my girlfriend."

"Practically invited you to take a shower with her."

"Fuck you."

"And deprive Whalen? Not a chance."

***

Stacia Hunter was not having a good day. To be fair, she'd expected to have a lousy day at best, but it had gotten much worse than she had been prepared for around the same time the men had come into her bedroom and pinned her to the bed. Her first thought had been that she was about to become a statistic. Break-ins and rapes happened every day in the United States, and while she didn't tend to think of herself as a star, she had a certain level of celebrity and had dealt with a few stalkers in her time.

Instead, the men had taped her mouth shut and then taped her to the chair where she normally applied her makeup. Once they had bound Tim up properly, a man wearing a clown mask sat in front of her on the edge of the bed and leveled the end of a very intimidating handgun at her stomach.

"I'm going to take off the tape. You scream, I kill your boyfriend. Then I shoot off both of your feet and blow your knees out." He looked away from her, his smiling clown face turning to the right to look out the window. "You'll probably live, but the therapy won't be any fun."

Without any more warning, he reached out and pulled the tape from her mouth hard and fast, taking a few layers of skin along for the ride. He carefully wadded up the tape and put it in his coat pocket. He was wearing gloves. So were the other two men with him. Three different masks, too. All the sort that you could buy at any grocery store this time of year. It was Halloween. No one would think anything odd about a few grown men buying cheap masks for a party.

She thought about screaming. She thought about the fact that she had carefully chosen this particular property for the solitude it afforded, and then she thought hard about the threats the man had made. Nothing sexual. Just extremely painful.

"What do you want?"

"We want to know where your daughter is. What you did with her." There were a lot of questions she didn't expect but that was damned close to the top of the list.

"Did that bastard Brad hire you to scare me?" Her voice grew loud and rose in octaves as she thought about his smug face. He wanted to play games? Her baby girl was missing and that cocksucker wanted to play head games? "You tell him to go fuck himself!" She strained against the tape, enraged. He thought this was some sort of stunt she would forgive? He had another thing coming. She would own his ass!

The man in the clown outfit reached forward and grabbed at her chest. His fingers caught one breast for a moment and then slid down to capture her nipple instead. Before she could even properly form a thought that she'd been right the first time, he pinched hard enough to make her squeal in pain and then let go just as quickly.

Stacia stared at him, shocked. Her eyes watered from the slowly fading pain.

"Did you hear what I said before?" His voice was calm, level. "That was your one freebie. I'm a nice man, but this is business and I have a very heavy schedule today. So I'm asking one more time, and if you start screaming again, your boyfriend will get a bullet behind his left ear and his brains will be all over the fucking bed. Think about that before you answer this time. We want to know where your daughter is. Did you take her or do you currently know where she is being kept?"

Stacia stared hard at his face, trying to see any feature at all beyond the clown mask. Even his eyes were lost in shadows. There was nothing. Nothing at all to give her a clue about his identity.

"I—" She could barely make the words form properly. "I don't know where Stephanie is. I thought Brad had her. I've been praying all the time that someone would find her." The tears started. Not because she wanted them to, not even because she missed her baby girl, and she did miss her with every breath, but because she knew that both she and Tim were already dead.

The clown looked at her without speaking at first. "Good. That's good. You should be praying. We are the answer to your prayers. We will find your little girl. If she's alive, we'll bring her home. If she's dead, we'll find the people who did it." He stood up and moved closer to her. She closed her eyes, half-expecting him to once again savage her nipple until it felt like it was bleeding. Despite herself, she started trembling.

Instead, she felt the tape on the chair as it was loosened and pulled away. When she opened her eyes the clown was staring at her. His eyes were still buried in shadow. "We're going to let you go, because you behaved yourself. Mostly." Tim was motionless on the bed, but the man who had been holding him down stepped back and looked him over. "You don't seem too stupid, so listen carefully. We were never here. You're okay. He's okay. Maybe a little sore, the both of you, but no permanent damage. Am I right?"

She nodded vigorously. Yes. Oh, yes. He was so very right No harm. No foul. All was well with the world.

"Good. Excellent. You never saw us. If you call the police, if you tell the FBI, if you decide the local fucking newspaper needs to know how horrible your life is, we'll come back." His hand cupped her breast again, but he didn't squeeze, didn't pinch, and the way she flinched seemed almost embarrassingly like overkill. "And if we have to come back, all those things you thought maybe we'd do? We'll do them. And then we'll get mean. You get me?"

She nodded so fast the room jittered. She also cried again. He let go of her breast, and Stacia cried in earnest, more afraid than she'd ever thought possible. When she was done crying, the three men were gone. Tim was still on the bed, but he was breathing. Whatever had been done to him was not permanent. No worse, apparently, than what was done to her nipple.

Stacia cried again, hating her ex-husband with all of her heart.

***

Ben was asleep on the couch in the living room when Maggie found him. He was still wearing the same clothes as the night before, and he'd half-curled over himself in an effort to stay warm.

As always, he looked so innocent when he was sleeping. She stared at him for several seconds, studying him and wondering why it was she'd let Jason call her away to cause him so much pain.

When she settled on the edge of the coffee table, her knee brushed across his forearm and his eyes opened immediately. His eyes found hers and for half a heartbeat he almost smiled. Then he stopped himself.

Her fingers moved down, touched his face, and brushed through the mousy brown hair on his head. "I'm sorry, Ben." She blinked, almost surprised by the sting of tears that wanted to escape her eyes. "I really am. I'm sorry. I didn't…I didn't mean to. I just…he can make me do things."

Ben didn't move for a long moment, but he looked at her, studied her as carefully as she'd studied him, and finally his hand captured hers and he pulled her fingers to his mouth and kissed the tips. His lips were warm.

She didn't lean toward him so much as she fell, and he caught her. He always caught her. She didn't understand that, never understood that, but here he was again, stopping her from falling too far.

And she let herself be caught, let herself land atop him. He shifted on the couch until they were both prone across, she resting her head against his chest and his arm moving to cover her back, his hand rubbing softly.

Maggie looked to Ben's face and saw him staring out the window, looking toward the view of the ocean that she knew so very well.

"I love you, Ben."

He made no response, save to kiss her temple and lean back down.

"What are you thinking about?"

Ben was quiet for a very long time. Long enough for her to wonder if he was angry with her. "We have to kill him. He has to die." He spoke very, very softly, a whisper that she could barely hear, and when she looked at him with a puzzled expression he pointed with his chin toward the window. When Maggie turned to see what he was looking at she saw the crows that sat perched on the old tree between the window and the distant ocean. They stared back at her with dark intent but made no sound and barely moved at all.

After that they rested together for a while, not speaking, merely holding onto one another, until the knock came at the front door. They were expecting no one. She knew it wasn't Jason. She'd have felt if he were that close by.

For a change of pace it was Maggie who answered the door instead of Ben. The men on the other side of the threshold looked vaguely familiar. There was a short, lean man with a thick mustache, thinning hair, and a few days' worth of stubble, and next to him there was a Nordic god, with perfect skin, perfect teeth, and the bluest eyes she could remember seeing in a long time. She wasn't usually much for blonds, but he was a specimen worth looking at twice. He dressed like the sort of man who could have afforded her back in the day.

"Maggie Preston?" The short one spoke and caught her attention while the blond met her frank stare with one equally unabashed.

As one the two of them flashed their badges. She stared at the two of them trying to decide if she should look at the eye candy or the shorter, meaner looking one.

"You got me. What can I do for you?" She looked at the blond one. If she was going to jail she may as well enjoy the view first.

"We wanted to ask you a few questions about how to kill vampires."

Maggie focused her attention on the short one doing the talking. Suddenly the whole situation seemed a bit more serious.

***

Lora was still in bed when everyone in the school disappeared. She should have been at work but she'd called out. She never called out, but she was feeling truly sick, barely able to muster the strength to make a phone call, forget the idea of getting out of bed and going to work.

Phone call made, she closed her eyes and went back to sleep.

Several hours later she woke up feeling much better. With most of the day lost to her and little else planned, she decided to let her guilt win the day and took care of cleaning the apartment properly. It certainly needed a good scouring. Her iPod went into its cradle, and the volume went up, and she started cleaning to notes of David Gray singing and crooning about life. She loved the man's voice and his passion.

She didn't bother with the news. She seldom did. It tended to be miserably depressing stuff, really. Dishes. Check. Laundry. Check. Bedroom cleaned. Halfway. After that it was time to indulge herself a little and surf the Web a bit. When she got to the homepage of her mail service, she saw the local news and that Hartshorn was now considered a crime scene until further notice. After that, it only took a few minutes to discover that everyone at the school was missing. All of them. Every kid, her coworkers, even the janitors and the security guys. No one was spared.

Lora moved away from her computer, sat on the couch, and stared at the walls as she tried to absorb all of that. People did not disappear. Not like that. Maybe once or twice in history, but not hundreds of people and not without some sort of evidence.

Impossible. It was a stunt of some kind. It had to be. Where would somebody hide that many people after all? There just weren't that many places where you could hide that number of kids.

She thought about trying to call someone, but there was no one she could think to call. If she tried the police, would she be considered a suspect? No. Of course not. Maybe. She wasn't sure. Also, what could she tell them? There had been nothing out of the ordinary that she knew of.

If she called the newspaper or one of the local news stations, she'd get a dozen cameras in her face. She knew from experience. When she was younger she'd seen a shootout between the police and a drug dealer who lived in her neighborhood. The resulting chaos had included several reporters asking her questions and fishing for new angles before they decided she wasn't quite what they were looking for. The dealer's girlfriend, a rail-thin blonde who'd cried her eyes out and screamed about how her boyfriend was innocent made for better sound bites, and she was soon left in peace.

With nothing else to do and no other subject to dominate her thoughts, Lora decided to take a walk to clear her head. For a brief moment a part of her mind warned her that she could get in trouble with the school if she was out playing hooky after calling in sick. Then she remembered that there was no one to catch her. As she walked, she pulled out her cell phone and called the police. Her feet did their thing, and she wandered from the apartments near the school to the park not far from the apartments and then over to the path through the woods that would bring her out at the

Cliff Walk. The view was as amazing as ever, and she wanted a nice distraction.

The woods were haunted according to a few sources. She knew better, of course. There were no such things as ghosts. But she'd heard the stories about how kids had been killed in the woods a few years back at Halloween, and she knew that a lot of her students still thought it best to stay well away from the woods after dark. That was probably for the best. Ghosts might not exist, but there were other types of monsters that wore human clothes and preyed on children.

As she moved through the woods, she spoke first to the emergency operator and then to the local police station, who put her on hold until she could speak to Detective Longwood, who sounded very interested in speaking with her. So interested, in fact, that he said he could meet her along the Cliff Walk if that was her preference. It was. She didn't want to go to a police station or deal with anyone coming to her place. She didn't want to deal with any of this, but she understood the necessity, even if she was dubious about what she could possibly tell him.

The air was cold and getting colder. The day was already overcast, and the winds along the Cliff Walk were not at all gentle as they slashed at her clothes and her face. Still, the view was incredible. The waves drove against the cliffs with fury, as if they sought nothing so much as to put an end to the stones that dared defy them. And the clouds above were mirrored below by a ghostly trail of fog that half-hid the water and seemed to defy the wind and the waves. Cold, yes, harsh, yes, but enchanting just the same.

The man who moved next to her was not familiar, but she wouldn't have minded in the least if he wanted to get to know her better. He wore dark slacks, a greatcoat, and a fedora. On a lot of men it would have seemed out of place, but the outfit suited him just fine. Handsome face, dark eyes, dark hair. He looked like he belonged in a book with cliffs like these and houses like these.

"You looked a little lost out here." His voice was rich and sweet and had a faint accent.

"No, I was just admiring the view."

His eyes never moved from her face, and for that moment she felt she was surely the center of his universe. It was both pleasant and unsettling. "The view is spectacular indeed." She couldn't help blushing just a bit. "My name is Jason. Is it all right if I join you?"

"I... Sure." She had no idea what to say. The Cliff Walks were public, after all. Not that she would complain about a handsome stranger wanting to keep her company.

"I needed to get away from the house myself. The news was simply too depressing." Jason spoke to her but looked away, out into the waters. She nodded her head.

"I know exactly what you mean. The school where all the kids vanished? I work there. I called out sick today because I felt lousy this morning."

He placed a warm gloved hand on her fingers where they touched the safety railing. "How horrible for you."

"I'm supposed to meet with a police detective here. He's going to ask me a few questions." She hadn't really meant to say any such thing to this man—it would hardly make him want to hang around, now would it? But she felt almost compelled to talk to him.

"Well, should you need someone to talk to, please don't hesitate to call on me. I am a notoriously good listener." He smiled softly for her and patted her fingers again.

A moment later he was stepping back. "Where are you going?"

"Your police detective is here. I don't wish to interfere."

For a moment, she wanted to protest. How was she ever going to call him when she didn't have his phone number? But the number was there in her head a moment later, and she wondered how she could have forgotten when he gave it to her.

Before she could give the idea any more consideration, a much larger man shambled toward her. He looked exactly like the sort of man she didn't want to share a few moments with on the Cliff Walk, but he had a pleasant enough demeanor, and he also had a gold detective's shield.

She forgot all about meeting Jason Soulis for the moment. Which was, naturally enough, exactly what Jason wanted. A long line of women through the ages could have told Lora that the man beside her almost always got what he wanted. He was gifted that way.

***

Jason Soulis listened to the woman he'd just left as she spoke to the large detective assigned to her case. He kept one ear on the conversation and did his best to hear everything else going on in Black Stone Bay with the other. There was so very much to hear if one was only willing to listen.

The house where he'd sent his crows after one of the shroud eaters. There was something going on over there. He could feel that much. There was something going on even now, because he might have considered examining the place himself, but he was being stopped. Faith and its consequences. A true believer was in the house even now, and had been for the whole of the day. He could guess who, of course. It would be the man he'd seen last night, the one he'd defended as more of an accident than by choice. He'd asked his birds to keep the shroud eater busy, and in the process they'd saved a faithful man from whatever fate he'd have reached without interference.

He chuckled at the thought that he might have been the answer to a faithful man's prayers.

The detectives he'd had his encounters with in the past were currently with Maggie and her pet human. They were discussing the best ways to kill a vampire. He suspected he knew who would be at the head of the list. That was all quite well. So far Jason had avoided death with little difficulty. His kind were notoriously difficult to kill.

Beneath the surface of his skin there was a war raging, and he still remained uncertain how it would end, though he was beginning to believe he'd have the upper hand. The disease was still there, but its hold was weakening. He could feel the corruptive influence of the one who'd marked him, and through that odd link he believed he was beginning to understand the nature of his enemy better.

If he were to close his eyes and truly concentrate, he believed he could find the thing he'd fought last night. No, not fought so much as toyed with. That had been his mistake and he could admit to it. He'd taken for granted that they were weaker than he was, and perhaps they were, but he'd also been the one who'd wanted to see a transformation in the vampires and now he'd received exactly what he'd been wanting.

They were weaker, yes, but they had a connection, a link that went beyond the physical and stretched to the metaphysical. The more of the shroud eaters there were, the stronger the oldest of them became. Even now, though he fought and was winning the fight, he could feel a small portion of his energies drained from him, stolen by the thing that bore the name Randy. Randy took from him, and likely took from other victims. And each of them in turn would need to feed and would continue feeding a portion of their energies to Randy and to the one that created Randy.

The thought brought a smile to his face. If he could discover how to harness that particular trait and maintain it, he could truly be a terror. Assuming he ever decided it was time to create a greater chaos.

The woman spoke again. Lora. He looked into her eyes and studied her. She was lovely. Short brown hair, hazel eyes, small-framed fashionable eyeglasses. Had she attempted to accentuate and focus on her looks, she would no doubt have been a heartbreaker. Instead she sought to teach and to nurture. The very traits that gave her the most pleasure were the same ones that prevented Jason from ever seeing her as more than a food source. She cared too much for others and too little for herself. Immortality did not mix well with that particular mindset.

Maggie was perfect for his needs because she felt exactly the opposite way. Unfortunately at this moment that was working against him. He'd offended her when he let her father become infected by the plague bearers. She wanted revenge for having slighted her. She wanted him, true enough, he could feel that, and had he been so inclined at that moment, he could have called her away from the meeting she was in and forced his will on her until she forgot about her father. However he was currently spread too thin. He was focusing on too much at one time; his birds and their eyes were a wonderful source of information, but they required a bit of his attention.

He let himself drift away from his body for a moment. The crows were everywhere, and he saw what they saw, heard what they heard. Even as he allowed himself that luxury, he moved his body into the shadows and lowered into the ground.

It was time to see the birthplace of the shroud eaters. He wanted this. Needed this.

Five years ago he'd let the detectives who were with Maggie now destroy the entrance to the cave he'd set up as a safe haven for the newly created vampires. The caves were extensive, and buried deep beneath the cliffs that faced the ocean's fury every day. The single entrance had been the only access point available to human forms, and that had been just fine with Jason. It had served to keep his new toys at bay until he was ready to show them how to leave the caves and let them out to play.

The end result had left the town of Black Stone Bay scarred and pitted. The people in the town were the sort who did their best not to see the dark stains of the past and chose instead to focus on the present and the future.

Those who could not deal with the past had moved on, left their homes and their memories behind and damn the consequences. They left the place and did all they could to forget. Those that were left cleaned up the messes and opened the doors to any and all who would come to replace the ones who'd abandoned them.

New blood. Fresh blood. It was almost always that way. Pave over the bodies and build anew. The house where even now the festering thing that had lived down in the caves had taken residence had been a fraternity house five years ago. Jason had burned it to the ground himself the night that Maggie came into her own. He'd taken the bodies and stowed them in these very caves, watched as they changed and then sent them out to feast upon the town. A surprising number of them had died that night, killed by the people who should have been their meals.

Now five houses covered the same land, and they did so with no concern for the structures that had been there before. That was the way of people. Progress, they called it, as if it were a good thing.

It certainly was for Jason. Progress was another word for forgetting the past. Oh, he'd seen the signs. They gave lip service to the notion of remembering their losses. There was to be a memorial service for the poor wretches Maggie killed at the Phi Kappa Gamma house. No doubt there would be flowers and memorial photos, and surely there would be songs and psalms and prayers to soothe the tortured survivors. And all of it would mean nothing save that a few parents slept better knowing that someone out there remembered their pain.

Meanwhile, Jason would continue on and examine the evidence to see which of the boys Maggie had feasted on was the first of the shroud eaters. He knew it was one of the boys. It almost certainly had to be, because, as with so many vampires, the urge to come home became a powerful compulsion if not held in check.

The urge to come home, and the urge to find the loved ones left behind.

"Better to forget the past. If you cannot forget it, better to destroy the past, thus removing the hold it has on you." The cave walls echoed with each word he spoke. The area was completely lost in darkness, but that no more bothered him than it would any of his kind. He looked at the walls, saw the claw marks that covered them, hundreds of slashes, some feeble attempts and some powerful enough to shatter stone. He smiled in appreciation.

There was little to see, and if there were ghosts to haunt the caves, they chose not to show themselves to him. Still he walked, looking at the few remains of other vampires that the shroud eater had left behind.

The bones, the marks, and the dust all told a story if one knew how to listen. There had been several, perhaps as many as a hundred, vampires left here when the detectives destroyed the caves. He would never know for certain how many. There weren't enough bones left to reveal that particular detail.

The stench of decay in the cave spoke of desperation. Vampires fed on blood. Shroud eaters could feed on life force and on misery if they had to, though he suspected blood was still the best way. Vampires could eat solid foods. Shroud eaters could, too, apparently. Though from what his crows had told him of the first shroud eater's attempts, they could not do so easily. There had been screams and vomiting and bone shards. Had Jason chosen to leave those remains alone, he might have saved the town a great deal of grief. Instead his birds had a feast and destroyed the evidence for him before he ever got back to the town.

The remains here told of desperation. Say there were fifty, for the sake of argument. Say that fifty vampires were captured down in the caves when the detectives blew the opening down and sealed the only exit for the vampires inside. Fifty vampires, all young, most only a day old or less. Jason had dropped bodies here as late as Halloween night, had left them knowing that they would be hours or days fighting their way back to the miserable half-life that was their lot. Say there were fifty and they all awoke as the sun set again. And they awoke to complete darkness, unable to escape, unable to find a source of food.

One lesson that Jason had known even before he became one of the Undead: life will prevail if at all possible. The people he'd tortured in his castle, the women he'd taken, the men he'd locked in irons or left to rot in stone tombs, all had one thing in common. They did all they could to endure, even under the worst possible circumstances. He had recovered from horrific wounds himself, and on more occasions than most would ever know. He'd been broken, bled, flayed, burned alive, and worse, and he had always endured, always come back. The will to live is a powerful thing indeed.

So say there were fifty at first and eventually one of them came to understand that there was no food. Perhaps by that point several of the weaker specimens had succumbed, had fallen too weak to even move, and rather than merely rot away as they were doing, the remaining ones defied every instinct they had and consumed that dead, rotting flesh. There was no blood, to be sure. That luxury would have been long gone.

He supposed they fought, they scrabbled for whatever morsels they could get, tearing at the still struggling, still screaming corpses that were rotting at their feet and chewing at the flesh that wanted desperately to escape them. They gagged on the flavors, to be sure, because most of the lower vampires could barely abide solid foods in the first place and rotting meat would never be a delicacy for them. They gagged, and they cried, and they loathed every shred, but still, it was sustenance. A chance to survive.

And when the first of the fallen were gone, surely they looked toward each other and contemplated who among them was the weakest. And when the decision was reached, they ate again, fighting and killing and feeding on meat that was rotting away and falling from the bones.

And again, until there were fewer.

And again until there was only one.

And that one, that miserable wretch? When it was done with the rotted meat, it must surely have reached the lowest level of desperation. Jason touched a small fragment of a skull and ran his fingers over the deep tooth marks. When the meat was gone it ate the bones.

And when the bones were gone and there was nothing else left, it surely grew too weak to do more than sleep.

And how much later before it discovered how to feed on the distant life above it? Even now, even with the thing gone, Jason easily saw the areas where the lawn above had been destroyed. New sod had been laid, and carefully, but he could see the marks.

How long before it discovered what Jason knew? How to move through stone and earth? How long did it starve?

"How long did you grow hungrier?" He dropped the small piece of skull and looked over the shredded clothing that the thing had made a nest of. The same black cloth that covered the shroud eaters covered the insides of the nest, like silks spun into the remains of a cocoon.

If the shroud eater was the butterfly, the caterpillar must have been a sight indeed.

Jason moved further into the caves, looking for any possible signs he might have missed of what had happened.

The sun was just starting to set when he made his last discovery.

He left before he could laugh out loud.

"Instincts," he chuckled the word to himself as he walked along the cliffs again. "Instincts, indeed."

CHAPTER ELEVEN

Of course he heard the news. He watched the news. There was nothing else for Neil Brighton to do in his small room but watch the news. So far there was remarkably little to report about his condition. According to the Channel 11 anchorwoman, he was one of a small number of people who appeared to have been affected by "environmental issues that were as yet undetermined." He and six others were still being kept in isolation, and their condition was "guarded." By that they surely meant there were guards outside of the room, though he couldn't tell for sure with the restraints on his wrists and his legs.

The hunger was back. One moment he seemed fine, and the next the hunger was screaming through him. He hissed and winced and tried to sit up as best he could, annoyed by the restraints. There was nothing to eat, of course. There was never anything to eat when a patient wanted it. Neil yanked at the restraints, annoyed by them, and was shocked when the high-test steel that anchored them to the bed snapped.

From a logical point of view, he should have called for the nurses and doctors and warned them that he was in the process of breaking free. He knew that. He was a doctor and knew the risks of an infected person escaping their confinement. He just didn't give a damn.

The hunger was everything. He needed to feed, and he needed to do it now.

The room was too bright, this despite the fact that his face was covered with a sheet of some sort. Perhaps there had been changes in the best methods of preventing contagion and no one had told him. He felt the fabric and saw the changes that had taken place in his hands. Again, he felt he should have been worried by the transformations, but there was nothing aside from the simply acknowledgment that he was falling victim to the disease despite all the best efforts he'd taken to stay safe.

Alarms started the moment he freed his ankles and climbed from the bed. The sensors were there to warn about changes in his heart rate, and near as he could tell, his heart wasn't beating any longer. So be it. He would worry about the whys and wherefores after he ate.

Neil had always prided himself on being a rational man, but that went out the window when he pushed through the thick curtains around his isolation room and saw the heavy-duty tent that had been set up to stop him from going any further. Several men and women were scrambling into environmental suits in an effort to stop him from going any further, or possibly just to check on him. In either event he found he did not care. The sight of them sent his hunger to a new level, and his desperation grew exponentially.

The plastic environment tent shredded under his newly acquired claws. The people beyond it were screaming now, their eyes widening in fear of contamination, or just possibly in fear of what he had become, because even without a mirror he knew he no longer looked as he should. It didn't matter. What mattered was the hunger.

Neil reached for the first of them. The same doctor he'd spoken to earlier, the one who had come to take over when he called the CDC. The man died quickly. The sweet red that flowed from him was powerful stuff, and had he been capable of shame at that moment it's possible that Neil would have been embarrassed by his erection as he feasted. The flames of his hunger were not vanquished, merely fanned by the first victim.

He attacked another, a woman who screamed and fought and tried to climb the rest of the way into her environmental suit all at the same time. She failed on all fronts, and his teeth bit deeply as he drank.

There were security protocols in place. Even in an area where they were considered "safe," the people who worked in the contagious diseases area could not easily escape. That worked to Neil's benefit. Long before any doors could be opened, he'd finished feasting. They died bad deaths, violent deaths, and he was fine with that. Before it was done he could almost think clearly again. The pain calmed down, the hunger banked to a low flame instead of a rampaging furnace.

And as the pain subsided, his rational mind took back over.

A look around the area told him how much trouble he was in. The bodies were everywhere, scattered around the rooms and draped like cast-off clothing.

No. This would not do at all.

He had to get away from this. All of it. He just had no idea how to escape the confines of his new tomb. And once the alarms went out and they realized that the security protocols had been breached, there would be hell to pay from somewhere up above.

Panic crawled along the edges of his senses, but not strongly enough to make him react. He shook his head at that notion. This was wrong. He'd just killed people, several people, and he'd just violated the safety codes designed to keep the populace at large safe from diseases. He should have been in an absolute panic. That was all there was to it. Instead there was merely that distance, that calm that should not have been anywhere around him.

There were other tents. There were others like him who were either enduring the rigors of this disease or who had succumbed to it. He could damned near feel them through the walls, which made as little sense as anything else in his world. One does not sense the feelings of others through walls or other barriers.

And yet he could feel them, their cold, patient hunger.

He walked to the closest cell and peered inside. A man, likely close to his own age, possibly even a little older. It was hard to say with any certainty. He could have looked at the patient's files but didn't feel the desire.

"What's your name?"

The man on the other side of the tent cocked his head as if he'd heard him. Annoyed by the security measures, Neil tore the plastic. It wasn't as if the man could infect him or vice versa. They were both diseased.

"What's your name?"

The man looked toward him, his face covered in the same black substance that covered most of Neil. "You smell of fresh blood." The desire in those words was understandable. It was what had made Neil violate the oaths he had believed in for his entire life.

"Answer me, and I can find you something to eat."

"Frank Preston." The voice was cold, but he could sense the growing anger, the hunger. He knew it well.

"You were one of the first ones brought here. You contaminated me."

"I'm hungry. Feed me."

He leaned in closer. As with Neil, the man had been shackled to the bed. The difference was that he had no slack at all. His arms and legs were drawn tight to the surface of the bed. That was their mistake. Someone had shown Neil compassion and in the process condemned them all to death.

Except that wasn't really the case, was it? He could sense the man in front of him. The man was like he was, diseased, contagious and virulent and so very hungry. And the bodies in the other room? They were diseased, too. They weren't hungry yet, but he could feel the disease inside their bodies. Logic be damned. He knew what he was feeling.

"I want to see Maggie. I want to see my little girl." There was no kindness to the words, but there was an attempt at cunning. There was also a deep and abiding hunger. Given the chance, Neil knew, Frank Preston would find his daughter and destroy her.

"Do you love your daughter?"

Preston didn't respond. He didn't have to. Neil could feel the hatred that flared in the man at the very thought of her. No love within the thing that stared at him, but there was hatred in spades.

Neil moved from the cell and stared at the closed doors around him. At least four more according to the news. Four others who were infected. Plus, of course, the ones he'd just fed on himself and Frank Preston.

Neil looked back at the bodies he'd attacked. In each case he could see the blistering starting. Far worse on them than it had been on him at the beginning. Why? Because in his case it had been an airborne attack? Because in their cases he'd transferred the contagion directly to them? He had no idea. He just understood that they would rise soon enough and they would be hungry.

Interesting.

Neil paced around the devastation, ignoring the shrill alarms from the machines that had been attached to him. They would come soon. He didn't know who, but someone would come soon, and they would try to restrain him. Try to restrain the others he'd infected, too.

If he was right about what was happening, they would all wake up the same way, numb to most emotions, possibly capable of little more than anger, which even now he felt, though it was still muted. He thought about Lisa for a moment and, yes, he felt something for her, but it was twisted away from what it had been, perverted by the disease or by the way the disease made him think. He wanted to see her. He almost needed to see her. Given time, he had little doubt that the desire to see Lisa would become an imperative as strong as the desire to feed. Of course, Lisa was, well, Lisa was different now herself, wasn't she? She had her own infection to consider.

He licked his teeth. They felt wrong, and he couldn't help but touch them with his tongue to make sure they were still real. They were. Like the blisters, and the veil that was growing over his face, and the hands that had grown too long and looked nearly arthritic.

Symptoms of a disease, a contagion that was spreading fast and far and that he'd just helped perpetuate. If he let it go, the entire hospital could conceivably be infected within a day. If he let it go and left the hospital, the town could be in serious trouble in the very near future.

"Interesting."

Neil settled himself in the corner of the main room and contemplated the ramifications of what he was considering. The right choice had to be made, of course. He just had to carefully consider which choice would be the right one.

***

The weekend took its own sweet time in showing up, but it had finally arrived. News of the people who'd disappeared from the Hartshorn Academy was the biggest event, of course, and every television station locally and a few nationally were stationed outside of the buildings that had been cordoned off by the police pending a full investigation. The continued issues of quarantined people at the hospital was still high on the list, and even the missing child of two B-rate actors stayed in the news, though in comparison to the other problems the town was dealing with, Stephanie Hunter was chump change.

Not to her father, of course. Brad Hunter carefully counted the money he'd managed to get together and put it in an envelope. Then, just to be safe, he counted it again. His little girl was worth it and more. He kept telling himself that.

He fervently believed it, too.

The first thing he needed to do now was remind himself that the situation was being handled.

That was a challenge.

The phone call helped to distract him. The voice on the phone was familiar enough, though he honestly hadn't expected to hear it. "Your wife doesn't know anything about where your daughter is."

"How can you be sure?"

There was a long pause. "Trust me on this. I'm sure." Was it wrong that he felt a certain satisfaction from that answer? He couldn't help hoping there was some pain involved in getting the answers they'd extracted from the bitch.

"So what happens now?"

"You pay me. I make reports when I know anything." The connection was killed that quickly.

He hated not knowing. He hated waiting. Brad paced the house, feeling restricted despite the size of the place. All he could do was wait.

He hated waiting.

***

The night came on quickly and swallowed the house where Malcolm had lived with his brother, and as the sun set, he opened his eyes again and tried for the hundredth time to free himself from the madness that surrounded him.

He'd walked through the front door of the house and tried for the lights, but failed. He found the light switch. He found the lamp in the living room, but neither worked. He'd paid the bills, he knew that much for certain. So whatever had happened was not his doing.

When he'd stormed into the house he'd been filled with righteous anger. Whatever was in the house had caused his brother harm, had made his brother into a monster and in turn had led to Randy taking away Carly. He'd planned to find whatever was in the house and tear it apart with his bare hands if he needed to. And maybe he would have, but the darkness was complete and the lights didn't work and as he tried to feel his way around the wall until he could find another light switch, he tripped and he fell and now he had no idea where the hell he was. He only knew it was hard to breathe and that he couldn't move his body from the painful angle it was stuck in. And all that anger he'd felt earlier? It was gone now and had taken his confidence with it.

His arms were bound to his sides, and his glasses were mashed into the side of his face in an uncomfortable angle, and his legs were wrapped with something too strong for him to budge, no matter how hard he tried. Had he been lying prone, he might have actually been afraid that he'd been buried alive and that the air would fade soon, but he had been here for a long time, and so far he was still breathing just fine. Mostly, he really had to answer the call of nature. Desperately.

And the darkness seemed like it was alive around him. There were noises, small ones, that filled his senses as he waited for whatever would come next.

Fear was not a part of his day-to-day makeup. Not because he was overly brave, not because he was a police officer or a man of action. No, but because he was usually too damned busy. He had school to consider, and he had his brother to look out for, and there was the time he wanted to spend with Carly and the time he needed to handle his studies. Randy almost never did chores, so he took care of those too, and before you knew it, his days and nights were filled.

The lack of anything to do? It made his imagination go crazy. Or maybe there was something to be afraid of, because the sounds outside of the dark cubby where he was currently situated were getting louder and more chaotic.

The darkness was complete, near as he could tell. He couldn't see anything, whereas earlier there had been at least a little illumination, enough to let him know he faced a white surface.

Voices. He heard them now, distinct and gravelly, low and urgent. The sound of a doorknob rattling came to him, and Malcolm let out a low moan, unable to stop the noise from coming. Something, someone, was here.

The world fell out from under him, and he rolled backward, falling, falling.

The scream that escaped him was, perhaps, inevitable.

***

Falling Rastafarians were not on the agenda, but one fell on Danny anyway. The man screamed and so did Danny. He tried to catch him, he did, but the drop was unexpected for both of them, and the next thing Danny knew there was a man sitting on his face and chest and screaming bloody murder.

The good news was that he had his gun. The bad news was that the man's weight had his weapon and trigger finger pinned to the ground.

"Getthefuckoffame!" He fairly roared the command.

"Aaaaaaahhheeee!" Was the only response from the man currently sitting on him and squirming.

Then Richie was grabbing the wailing Rastafarian by the hair and hauling him out of the way. Danny didn't think his partner actually aimed for the dreadlocks, but there were a lot of them and they were wiggling and they got caught in his grip as he pulled at the man and the bed linens that covered him.

Freed from the closet he'd been locked in for God alone knew how long, the man scrambled and fought his way from the sheets, screeching the entire time. Danny stared at him, not certain if he should laugh or shoot and deciding to wait a while before making up his mind.

When he was finally standing up and was done giving the house a wild-eyed stare, the man finally looked toward Danny and Richie. Richie had taken a few moments to pull his detective's shield. Danny took the same amount of time to aim his pistol at the Rastafarian's face. Dreadlocks adjusted his glasses, looked at the shield, the gun, the shield, the gun and finally stuck his hands into the air.

"What the fuck are you doing here?" Richie's voice was all loud and boomy. He did that better than any one his size should have been able to do it. The number of perps who almost wet themselves when he started barking was substantial.

Dreadlocks looked at Richie for a second and then focused on the gun again. Not the dumbest man Danny had ever met, even if he wasn't looking very calm. "I live here!"

"What's your name?"

"Malcolm Dunbar."

"Danny?"

"That's the name on the lease, Richie."

"Can you tell us what you're doing locked in the closet here?"

Dunbar looked at both of them and half-lowered his hands. Danny opted not to shoot, what with it being his place. "I'll answer any questions you'd like, officer. But please... I really have to use the bathroom."

Richie shrugged. "Go. Take care of business. We'll be right here."

The man bolted down the hallway, and a moment later a door slammed. Danny figured he had to know the place pretty damned well, because the only lights currently on were the two big flashlights he and Richie had brought with them. Two minutes later the man came back out accompanied by the sound of a toilet flushing.

By that time Richie had found the fuse box in the kitchen and fixed the circuit breakers so the power came back on. Danny had to give him that one. He had no idea in hell how anything electrical worked, and he was just fine with remaining ignorant.

The kid was nowhere near as scary-looking in the regular light. He was tall, muscular, and dark, with handsome features and the sort of hair that had to take years to get fixed up properly. He pulled a hair tie out and pulled his dreads back, and Danny watched, absolutely fascinated.

"How long it take you to grow your hair that long?" Richie shot him a look. "What? I'm just asking is all."

"Any idea what happened to you? Or why you were locked in the closet, kid?"

Okay. In hindsight, Richie's question made a lot more sense to the investigation.

Malcolm Dunbar looked at the two of them with an expression that spoke a great deal of loss and fear. Just that fast Danny decided to calm down his attitude and listen. Richie was right there with him.

"Please. Before we do anything, I need to look the house over. I need to know if there is anyone else here." Danny and Richie led the kid through the entire house, room by room, and then down into the basement. They found nothing unusual until they reached the basement and looked around carefully. Someone had punched a hole through the cement retaining wall behind the water heater, and it looked for all the world like a giant mouse hole back there. A great deal of investigation with drawn guns and flashlights revealed that the spot was empty. It would have been a lie to say Danny was upset about that.

"What's next, Richie?"

Richie looked over their new friend for a moment, his eyes scrutinizing. "We're gonna buy Mister Dunbar dinner and he's going to talk to us about what he knows."

"I am?" The kid sounded dubious.

"You are."

"My girlfriend is missing."

"All the more reason to talk to us."

"Why are we going to eat while we talk?"

"Because I'm hungry and I'm betting you are too."

Dunbar thought about that and nodded. "I could eat."

"So let's talk."

Richie led the way out of the place. Dunbar locked up like there was any chance in hell that anyone would want to rob it. There wasn't. The house looked okay, but it was creepy as all hell.

They ate at the Silver Dollar, but noticed that the waitress was brand new. Looked like Lizzie maybe had switched to the day shift or moved on.

No loss. She was a lousy waitress. They ate a lot, and while they ate Malcolm Dunbar explained his story to the best of his ability, and the detectives listened and asked a few hundred follow-up questions. Along they way they expressed their condolences for his loss and explained that, yes, they believed his brother was beyond saving, much as he did. He seemed surprised by their willingness to believe his words. They got that a lot these days.

"So the police are aware of what's going on in this town?" Malcolm's voice was soft, and his eyes were very alert. He struck Danny as a sharp young man, give or take the dreadlocks, which, as fashion statements went, simply did not fit into Danny's lifestyle in the least. It was just possible he was jealous, but he couldn't be sure.

Richie fielded the answer. "We're police officers, and we're aware of the situation. The police force at large? Not so much."

"Why not?"

Richie popped a fry into his mouth and ruminated on it before answering. "Did you call the cops when you figured out what was wrong with your brother?"

"No." Malcolm frowned and shook his head.

"Why not?"

The kid figured it out and nodded his head silently. Danny poured himself another cup of coffee. Some people got it, and some people didn't. You could scream all you wanted, but only a few people would actually accept what was going on around them without concrete evidence, and even then, there were a few hard-asses who would refuse. There were still people who refused the notion of space travel and trips to the moon despite the fact that cell phones worked in conjunction with satellites that ran all around the damned planet.

"So what happens now?"

"We're still working that part out." Richie swirled his next fry around in the trails of ketchup. It was just possible that the bottomless pit had filled up.

"I would work fast."

"Why's that?"

"If the thing that was done to my brother is contagious, there will be a lot of these things around in a very short amount of time."

"So why didn't your brother take you out, Malcolm?"

The kid looked at his plate for a moment and then looked Richie in the eye. "God protected me."

"You a true believer, Malcolm?"

"Yes, I am."

Richie smiled. "How would you feel about meeting a few people?"

Malcolm got a puzzled look on his face. Danny did, too, for a second, and then he smiled.

Oh yes, this could get interesting.

***

At eleven forty-seven in the evening, three men broke into the house of one Warren Connor, who lived by himself three blocks from the Hartshorn Academy. Warren was a person of interest to the police as he had been involved in a few cases of child pornography in the past. Detective Robert Longwood was currently waiting for a search warrant to obtain the right to seize computers and examine the contents of Connor's house.

The gentlemen who broke in did not bother with search warrants. They were quiet, they were efficient, and they found Warren Connor in bed by himself. They also found the room where he kept his new friend Stephanie.

At that point in his new career as a pedophile, Warren Connor was still building up the nerve to go beyond taking pictures and fondling. He had not actually consummated the relationship with the girl that he wanted to have.

He did not get the chance. One of the gentlemen who entered the house very carefully carried the girl outside, a task made easier by the fact that she had apparently been fed sedatives with her last meal.

The other two men carefully and meticulously went about the business of murdering Warren Connor. They bound him and gagged him to avoid any possible screams.

In order to avoid being connected with the relocation of the child, the men in question arranged for her to be dropped off at Saint Joseph's hospital. She was examined and treated for minor injuries and for dehydration. Her parents were notified as soon as the girl told them who she was and where she lived.

Both mother and father were at the hospital in very short order, and while the media was eventually alerted to the situation, they did not find out for several hours. By then the tearful reconciliations were taken care of, and the police had come along to take statements.

Robert Longwood might have had a few doubts about exactly how this miracle occurred. It's very possible and even highly probable that he did. He did not, however, do anything about those doubts. He had in excess of three hundred other cases to handle and was not feeling overly frisky about pursuing possible shady connections as long as the missing person was returned mostly unscathed. He marked the case of Stephanie Hunter in the "win" category and left the celebrations and explanations to his police captain and any glad-handers that might want the media's attention for a few minutes.

Brad Hunter and Stacia Hunter barely acknowledged each other's existence. They were exactly as civil as they had to be for their child. Being a mostly sensible man, Brad made a visit by the Windbreakers restaurant very early the next morning and dropped off his envelope. He did not shortchange the people who took the money. He did not see Demetrius, but he saw the scary man who'd led him to the offices.

***

The night was not only for children taken from their homes. More to the point, the nights in Black Stone Bay became the property of creatures that had not existed only a few weeks earlier.

It crawled through the comfort of its home and listened to the children it had created, and to the progeny that they in turn had created, and it reveled in its new position of power.

Having considered the need of memories and names, it had decided it needed none of those things. Names were an inconvenience, and the past was mostly a blur of black and endless miseries. Better by far to dwell in the new and the present and the future than to waste time with the past.

It was changing, becoming something more than what it had been, and that was a good thing. Like a spider it spun its webs and waited. For five long years, it had known hunger and deprivation, and it had learned one thing above all else. Patience. There were creatures beyond its control who were involved now, and more of them involving themselves in its business. That would have to change, but all in good time.

It was home, and comfortable and glad to watch the night change around it, to watch the world come alive with new awareness.

Each of its children was a connection to the world outside of its new home. What they felt, it felt; what their children felt, it felt. Not as strongly as something experienced firsthand, but that was insignificant, really. It was learning more all the time. Each child was a thick strand on the web it was creating and each of their children a thinner strand that spread further and further. Information, influence, and sustenance all combined in the growing tapestry of its power. And that was good, because as it was rapidly coming to understand, it was always hungry.

The first child was Randy. Randy was angry. Randy wanted to kill his brother. The hatred Randy felt was irrational, but it could also be used to the advantage of Randy's creator. The brother of Randy was powerful. His belief in a benevolent God was a potent thing, and it had already experienced a brief searing pain upon contact with that power. Being near the faith was enough to make it flee the house it had chosen as its own. It had only barely managed to cover the man in cloth and roll him into the closet before it had to escape the searing light that came from him.

Randy's hatred was strong. Possibly even strong enough to let him kill his brother. That would be for the best. Even if Randy failed, he might injure the brother enough to eliminate him as a threat.

The second child was Vikki, who even now was preparing to leave Black Stone Bay. Her family was in another place, and she wanted to get to them. Like Randy she felt an unnatural hatred toward her family. It was beginning to understand that hatred; the hatred was merely a wind to help pollinate the world. His children would move further, go forth and multiply as the Good Book had said must be done. The Holy Bible. It had no fear of the Word of the Lord, and yet the faith of Randy's brother could burn. No. Enough. That would be a concern for later. Now it wanted to finish the thoughts before it became distracted again.

Vikki was leaving, going to a distant place. When she got there she would feast on her family and they, in turn, would rise and feast and spread the gospel of its nature. Disease, darkness, death. These were the weapons of its will, the way to grow stronger.

Because it would need its strength.

There was another connection, one it could not escape though it wanted to and desperately. There was the creator, the one who had brought it death and rebirth and then left it to wither and die in the darkness for eternity. It could sense that creator, and with all of its kind, there was a powerful, irrational hatred brewing inside its every atom.

The creator had to die, but before that happened, it would need still more strength.

The best hope it had for that was Dave, who was almost as endlessly hungry as it was.

Dave, who had created most of the children so far, and had taken more to feed on than any other.

Dave, who even now was watching and waiting as all that he touched was corrupted and reborn. Dave was strong. Dave was patient. Dave was so very hungry.

***

"Here's the thing, assholes: my three hundred and fifty kids takes precedence over your dead people. Fucking deal with it." Longwood was gloating. Sort of. Mostly he was just being Longwood. Boyd could accept that. He didn't have to like it any more than he liked spending his time searching the grounds of the Bayside Academy—also called Hartshorn, but he liked Bayside better and so that was what he called it—when he could have been getting a little sleep, or maybe trying to find out how to kill Jason Soulis.

There was no doubt about it in the eyes of the ones in the know: Soulis had to die. Unfortunately, that wasn't exactly an easy task. He had first-hand experience with that particular dilemma, and in a good month the memories only gave him nightmares about three times a week.

As cranky as he was about the idea of walking the grounds, it was looking like the best possible place for everyone to meet. Everyone in this case meant Nancy Whalen, Longwood, Danny, of course, and their new pet holy man, Malcolm. Just for grins, Ben Kirby and his girlfriend were there, too.

Sort of. Currently Maggie was standing fifteen feet away and looking around the place. She wasn't actually joining them for two reasons. First, Nancy Whalen didn't know about the vampire in residence, and Maggie wanted to keep it that way. Second, as Boyd deduced in a matter of seconds, Malcolm made Maggie uncomfortable. Very uncomfortable. She kept averting her eyes from him, like staring at him was as uncomfortable as staring directly at the sun on a bright, clear day.

Interesting. Good to know. He stored that fact for later.

Danny in the meantime kept casting looks toward Maggie that had nothing at all to do with police investigation. It wasn't just curiosity, either. He pretty much wanted to nail her. He wouldn't, because she was with Ben and because she was also capable of killing him with ease, but he wanted to.

That thought made Boyd feel all warm and fuzzy.

Whalen cast the beam from her flashlight at the ground in front of her and sighed. "We get it, Bob. You can't handle the pressure of a few missing kids. Now quit your crowing and commence to looking around. I'd like to see my husband this year."

Danny opened his mouth, and both Boyd and the captain shot him the sort of look that could freeze a river of lava. He saw and got all pouty-looking. Boyd nodded his head. Whalen looked his way for a second and looked away. Damn it.

He pushed thoughts of her aside and looked around. "So what places haven't been searched on this property?"

Longwood looked at him for a second, frowning. "What do you mean?"

"I mean we're out here, freezing out collective privates off, looking for an entire school full of missing kids. Where have you actually looked, Bob? Where the fuck have you looked, and where haven't you looked?"

Danny looked his way and again said nothing. He could guess, though, that his partner would have made a snide comment about how lack of sleep made Boyd all cranky.

Longwood stared hard, and Boyd could see him fighting against a desire to say something stupid. "Sorry. I'm tired. Where have you looked?"

"Everywhere. Most of the woods. The stables, the barn, the school buildings." Bob's voice was cool but in control.

Boyd considered the structures he knew about for the place. That seemed to cover most of them. The place was called Bayside for a reason, though. "Looked at the boathouse yet?"

Bob shook his head. "There isn't enough space there to hide that many people."

Boyd rubbed his hands over his face and shook his head. It wasn't that Longwood lacked detective skills. It was more that he was an optimist. Even after all the years they'd known each other and worked on the same police force, Boyd was surprised by that fact.

"No, Bob. There is enough space there to hide that many people. Just not if they were alive."

Longwood closed his eyes and then looked down at the ground. "I haven't looked at the boathouse. It was closed."

Boyd nodded and oriented himself. "Got ya." He pointed to Danny. "That way. Let's go." The entire group turned in that direction. There wasn't any actual enthusiasm for the investigation; instead there was a certain dread. If the bodies hadn't been found anywhere else, and only one structure hadn't been carefully examined, then it stood to reason, didn't it?

"So. Talk to me about where we stand on everything else." That was Whalen. She made sure to look at someone other than Boyd. In this case, she focused on Malcolm, which made sense because the kid was a good-looking guy. She wasn't ordering off the menu, but no harm in looking.

"According to your detectives, vampires are real. According to my own experience, my brother is now a vampire." Malcolm spoke calmly enough. His eyes looked carefully around them, which made perfect sense. The grounds were dark, and the woods were thick enough to be intimidating. Being with a handful of cops might take some of the apprehension away, but the kid had already dealt with a vampire or two, and so far he wasn't having a lot of fun with them.

"So what do we know about vampires?" Nancy was doing her best to sound calm and collected, but she wasn't having fun. She hated this shit. Boyd knew, because she'd said so on a dozen or more occasions.

Danny spoke up. "Let's see. They drink blood. They don't like sunlight. They usually smell bad and look even worse." He cast his eyes to where Maggie trailed behind them. "There are exceptions."

Before Danny could say anything else, Ben added his own feed. "These aren't traditional vampires. According to Soulis, these are something different. He called them shroud eaters and said they were either responsible for the Black Plague or they took advantage of it, or both. The quarantine at the hospital is probably a part of it, but no one can get close enough to find out and the CDC isn't exactly making announcements about what they've found out so far."

Whalen nodded. "I can probably get more information on that at least." She waved a hand for Ben to continue. Which he did.

"The shroud eaters that Jason saw in the past didn't have to touch a person to feed on them. They didn't have to drink blood. They can suck in the life force, or the soul. They go after loved ones first, at least the ones that existed in the past did."

Danny and Boyd both looked at Malcolm at the same time. The kid was shaking his head, his face set into a dark expression.

"So what do we know about these shroud eaters?" Whalen looked at Ben and then at the trees around them. The wind was picking up, and the trees were rattling and creaking and adding a level of unease that was not at all pleasant to consider. "Anything about what can hurt them?"

Ben shrugged. "There's a lot he doesn't know. He said he encountered them a couple of times back in the past, but aside from that he wasn't exactly forthcoming."

That one stopped Boyd in his tracks. "Wait. He encountered them before?"

Ben nodded. "Yeah."

"When? Back when the plague was popular?"

"I don't know." Ben shook his head and looked toward Maggie in the distance. "He didn't really give a lot of details. He just sort of brought it up."

Longwood spat. "What the fuck are you even talking about? Can you hear yourselves?" He shook his head. "Let's just save this shit until after we look at the boathouse, okay? We're here." He pointed, and just over a small rise to the left Boyd could see the shingles of a roof.

"So let's look, Bob. Lead on." Boyd let the man take over. It was Longwood's investigation, anyway.

Longwood stomped his way over the small hill and headed for the boathouse. It was a large building, certainly large enough to store the boats and all of the equipment needed, but he could see why Bob hadn't really considered it previously. If you were looking for a large enough structure for a few hundred people it definitely wasn't the right spot.

Not if the people you were looking for were alive. The problem was, as Boyd was all too aware, that vampires didn't tend to leave people alive. They killed them. It was in their nature.

Bob had stormed toward the building in a righteous fit. Not because he was feeling all that righteous, Boyd knew, but because he didn't want to deal with the idea of vampires or shroud eaters or even little green men from Mars. Bob didn't like any of that stuff. The closest he ever wanted to get to the supernatural was to look at the decorations on a Halloween cookie before eating it.

Sucked to be Bob.

Before he made ten paces down the small hill, he'd slowed down, and three more paces saw him coming to a stop as he stared at the boathouse.

It was just a building. Not even an impressive one: a squat, fat building with a recent paint job and little else to mark it as anything special. There was a long dock, wooden slats over a long tongue of steel, and concrete that had been built to last. The water probably wasn't very deep, but it led to a tributary that ran to the bay proper. Nothing remarkable and nothing to send off warning bells, unless you were the sort of person who trusted your instincts.

Cops tend to trust their instincts. If they don't they either leave the force by choice or in a body bag. A cop without instincts is like a car without tires. Doesn't go very far and takes forever to get there.

Danny stopped right next to Boyd, his hand resting on his hip, right above his pistol.

Bob Longwood sighed and looked over his shoulder, eyeing each of them with a nervous expression. He didn't want this to be bad. He didn't want to trust what his instincts were already telling him. Boyd understood, because he felt exactly the same way. His instincts were screaming, letting him know that this was a bad place, unclean, possibly even unholy.

Whalen coughed into her hand and stared hard at the building. The windows, black and sightless, seemed to stare right back with malevolence. It wasn't just the night. Someone had covered the inside of the windows. He couldn't decide what with, but there was something between the glass and the interior of the building.

Malcolm and Ben stood near each other, both eyeing the place like it might suddenly rear up and try to take a bite of them. So it wasn't just cop instincts. The place felt bad.

Malcolm coughed into his hand. "Well, this has been fun…" He was trying to make a joke. It went over poorly. In his defense, everyone looked a little too ready to piss themselves for a joke to go well.

Ben spoke loud and clear. "Fire."

"What?" Danny looked at him as if he might have just grown a second set of eyes.

"Fire. For killing them. That's what they used on a lot of the bodies during the Black Plague, right? Maybe that was how they got rid of the shroud eaters."

"Makes sense. Kind of causes a lot of property damage, though." Boyd shrugged. "I mean, I can see it, but the delivery has to be careful or you wind up with a serious problem."

While they were talking, Maggie headed for the boathouse.

***

Give us a kiss.

The thought crept into the back of Maggie's head, the voice a distant memory of a grandmother she barely remembered. When she was very tiny, only a toddler, she'd had a frail grandmother: a tiny woman, to be sure, but to Maggie she'd seemed as gigantic as every other adult. The old woman could barely speak and wore an oxygen feed half the time. Whenever she saw Maggie she always said the same thing. She'd smile her toothless smile and reach out with her withered, bony hands and say, "Give us a kiss," and Maggie, far too young to make her fear known, cringed inside every time the old lady touched her.

The place was creepy, no two ways around it. The difference between Maggie and the others was simple enough and almost elementary from her perspective. She was already a vampire. If there were more of them inside the building, there was remarkably little they could do to her that hadn't already been done.

Give us a kiss.

It looked good on paper, at least.

The door to the boathouse was barricaded from the inside. That was hardly a deterrent. She pushed hard and felt whatever was on the other side of the door slide backward far enough for her to force her way inside.

The darkness held no surprises. The boathouse was a different story entirely. What had blocked her entrance was one of the boats. It had been forced against the door to make room in the center of the place for the heap of bodies that rested in the place. Maggie tended to think of herself as cold, and she might have been right, but that didn't mean she was immune to emotions, especially shock. She's prepared herself for the possibility of bodies. But there are degrees, aren't there?

The children ranged in age from roughly five to eleven, and they'd been tossed into the center of the room with the same respect one might show a heap of dirty laundry. Bodies fell across each other with absolute disregard. The arms of one were pressed under the midsection of another, while legs pressed against the face and midriff of two others. All of them wore school uniforms in differing stages of disarray, and it would have been possible to convince herself that she really was looking at a pile of laundry if not for the faces. Some peered between arms and bodies, others were staring directly at her, but the faces all stared, eyes wide and dull, mouths often open in a mute scream. The faces all stared, the eyes looked, and she knew they were looking, could sense that they were seeing her and that they were…repulsed by what they saw.

She didn't see children often. Maggie's world was deliberately isolated, because she had only lost control of herself once, really, but she was always scared of the possibility that she could lose control again. The first time, she'd killed a dozen or more people at a party. What if she did that to children? She didn't think she could forgive herself, and yet here she was looking at bodies thrown aside with utter contempt. Children. Innocents.

What kind of monster would do that to hundreds of children? She already knew the answer, of course. The man who'd done this to her. The man she still wanted.

And was it her imagination, or were the children starting to move? She couldn't tell; she was too busy trying to look everywhere at once.

Give us a kiss, Maggie.

None of them moved, nor did they breathe. The dead do not need such things. She could see the teachers, the guardians of the children, heaped in the center of the boathouse. They slumped against the walls, slack-jawed and empty-eyed, as lifeless as their charges, the dark eyes seeing her, she knew, seeing everything, but they were not done changing yet. They couldn't move, could not defend themselves. This would be the one chance the detectives had to destroy these things before it was too late.

The children, the adults, all of them showed the same signs of corruption. Their skin was gray, save where the blackened blisters marred their flesh. Plague bearers. Shroud eaters. Might as well simply call them what they were: Black Death. Seeing them merely added to the notion of the Grim Reaper as shown in old illustrations. The only thing missing was a massive scythe for each of them to swing as they harvested their human wheat.

In the distance she could hear Ben talking about the cleansing benefits of fire. She completely agreed.

"Margaret Preston?" The voice was completely unexpected. She turned to find the source and backed away quickly as she saw the shroud eater that had been Dave Burke.

The girl she had seen before had appeared almost like any of the things Jason left behind when he was done eating. There was no mistaking that this was a different beast entirely. The gray skin, the gaunt form, the bleeding pustules that spilled a dark red ichor across flesh and the ground alike. This was a vile thing, pestilent and malevolent. Had she ever met Dave Burke she would not have recognized what he had become. She had barely recognized her father and she had known him since she was born. This thing? This was as far from human as anything could be while remaining humanoid.

It stepped from the shadows and moved toward her, appeared almost to glide a few steps forward. The room had a high ceiling despite the squat appearance it gave; still, he gave the impression of stooping as he came toward her.

Had she thought herself incapable of feeling dread? Of fear? She was so very wrong. Maggie stepped back again as it came closer, and it hissed, baring teeth that seemed impossible in a mouth that was too large. Though the shroud covered much of the face, she could feel its gaze on her, and there was nothing of mercy within the thing. It wanted her dead, hated her on sight. And for some insane reason, it recognized her.

Now there are a lot of people on the planet who would have backed down immediately upon seeing the thing in front of her. Maggie was not an exception. She turned and ran for the door. The thick claws on the thing's hand raked across her back and shredded her coat, her blouse, and the flesh beneath them with ease. The impact sent Maggie staggering, and she ran through the door she'd used to enter the place, propelled by the force of the blow.

And the vile thing followed her, stepping into the night and spitting a stream of reddish mist from its mouth as it came for her. Maggie did not stand still and wait for it. She hauled ass, doing her very best to clear as much distance as she could. Being a member of the Undead, Maggie's best was pretty spectacular. She blurred as she moved, and didn't stop until she was at the top of the rise, over which she and the others had come to see the boathouse in the first place.

Half of the people who were with her did their best to follow her progress. The other half faced the thing that was after her.

The faithful one, the one she could barely even look at, Malcolm, stood his ground and stared at the thing. He was scared, she could see that, sense that, and yes, even smell the fear on him. He still stood his ground. The light that burned inside of him grew brighter if anything. She knew that none of the others could see it, but she could, and she could feel it as well, a heat that blazed warmer than the sun. It was both comforting and terrifying. She saw it. So did the shroud eater. The creature looked toward Malcolm and roared as it tried to block off its view of the man. It did not run, did not flee, but the presence of the man was very obviously as uncomfortable for it as it was for her.

Malcolm looked at the creature and moved forward, shaking his head. "Randy? Is that you?"

The shroud eater moved, its left arm lashed out, and the palsied hand grabbed Malcolm by the face, lifting him from the ground.

Malcolm screamed as the thin, malformed fingers of the thing's left hand squeezed down, digging into his flesh.

The thing screamed in return as the very same fingers began to smolder and then to actually burn; still, it did not let go, it clutched all the harder at the young man's face.

Bullets flew. A couple of the police officers opened fire, while the others looked for an opportunity that wouldn't risk killing Malcolm in the process.

Malcolm screamed again, and the shroud eater shook him, baring its teeth and hissing again as its flesh burned and the hand blackened. Finally it could stand the pain no more, and Malcolm sailed through the air as it threw him aside, yowling like a cat at the pain in its ruined limb. And the bullets? They hit again and again but seemed to do very little actual damage.

Maggie moved on instinct. She sought to grab Malcolm before he could bounce off the tree he was headed for, and she meant to see him safe.

Unfortunately for the both of them, his faith was as strong as ever, even if his body was failing him. She couldn't reach him. Try though she might, the same light that made him a beacon also burned, and she was forced back before she could touch him.

Malcolm ran into a tree, doing a little better than thirty miles per hour. His bones shattered on impact. His scream stopped immediately.

Without the burden of a hostage to slow them down, the detectives did their best. They opened fire on the shroud eater, and the bullets drove into the creature again and again, staggering it backward and pinning it to the wall. Aside from that impact, they seemed to do little to slow the monster down.

That bright light, the very glow that had weakened her and kept her from saving Malcolm, vanished. It did not fade away, but disappeared completely as his life force faded.

Maggie looked at the thing and felt her rage bloom. She sought to keep human life; even when she had to feed, she did her best to avoid killing. The shroud eater on the other hand seemed to revel in the idea of death. The children she'd seen in the building behind it had seemed a horrible sight, but now she was beginning to fully understand what she'd seen. They weren't props. They were people the same as the man she'd just seen so casually killed.

The anger roared through her, and Maggie attacked, not worrying if she were revealed before anyone, not concerned about her possible safety.

Her hands sought the shroud eater as it stalked toward the detectives. She grabbed the thick stuff it wrapped itself in and hurled the beast into the side of the building with all of her strength.

The shape drove into the wooden building, and the boards shattered under the sudden force. Maggie followed, not done yet, not wanting this finished. She wanted it to suffer, because the horror of what she had seen was digging deeper and deeper into her psyche.

"Dead! All dead! You killed them!" She was screaming, her voice shrill, but she barely even noticed, hardly felt the raw scraping of her throat as she yelled. Maggie pushed and felt the cold, dead thing fighting back, felt claws ripping at her flesh, carving wounds that should have been agony but hardly seemed to matter.

The shroud eater roared, spraying her with its bloody spittle, gnashing with its teeth and biting into her shoulder, her neck, even as she forced its head back and pushed, drove into the building with all of her strength.

The wall collapsed around them, and they were inside among the bodies, falling into the piles of flesh, the uniforms, the cold, staring faces. Anger and fear mixed in Maggie; revulsion sent shivers through her as she thought of the cold flesh she felt press against her. Worse still was the conviction that the cold flesh was moving on its own. She knew it was true could sense the mockery of life within the bodies, and contact with them made her want to run, to hide away. They were vile things, no longer innocent flesh but walking diseases, things that ate and destroyed and would only become as bad as the very thing she was fighting.

Small fingers moved into her hair, touched her face, her arm, and Maggie let out a small whimper. She felt those fingers trying to clasp onto her, trying to stop her from moving. Her skin would have crawled if it weren't already pulled into gooseflesh.

The shroud eater struck her hard, a savage punch that sent her backward. A second later it was on her, before she could even consider recovering. The hard flesh, the blisters leaking their vile toxins, the teeth gnashing at her face, Maggie felt panic growing even stronger within her and screamed a second time. The burnt, ruined stump of the creature's left hand pressed against her throat as the thing tried to claw at her face with its undamaged fingers.

"Give us a kiss, Margaret." She heard the creature speaking, heard the words that came from its mouth and felt revulsion creep through her entire body.

And Maggie tried to fight back, even as the bodies behind the shroud eater started moving.

CHAPTER TWELVE

Jason Soulis heard Maggie's screams and toyed with going after her, but decided against it. She had offended him, sneaking off with the detectives and her pet boy, meeting with a man whose faith was damned near blinding, and most of all, conspiring to kill him. Really, it was almost enough to make him want to kill her himself.

Instead he decided it was time to hunt down and examine one of the older shroud eaters. The ones in his basement were maturing, changing, but he needed to find the one that had marked him, because he could still feel the damnable disease burning inside of him, and he didn't like that notion in the least.

Besides, there was a chance that they would become competition, and he couldn't allow that. One thing to play around, to experiment, and quite another to risk your place as the dominant species.

He finished dressing and left the house, taking to the air and letting his pets look for what he needed. Spotting one of the vile things took almost no effort. They tended to lack subtlety.

The thing he found was lurking in the woods near the interstate, heading from town to who knew where. It wanted to migrate, to spread its contamination in other places. Unacceptable.

Jason came down from the sky and did not waste time toying with his prey. Instead he drove his feet into its skull as he landed and watched the creature's head drive into the dirt. This one had been female. It was not the one that had poisoned him. Pity. He'd have to take care of that one later.

The thing grabbed at him, but Jason stepped back, shaking his head. "No. Not this time."

"What?"

"Never mind. I'm talking to myself." He kicked the creature in the chest and drove it back against a tree trunk. The thing hissed, and the tree groaned under the impact. The damned wounds within him seemed to respond to the creature, almost as if they were drawn to it. He could not tolerate that notion. The shroud eaters were vile, little more than vermin if they were the same creatures he'd dealt with when he was younger. He had to consider this experiment a failure. The thought was almost depressing.

He kicked the thing a second time, a third, and felt bones break with each impact. It tried to defend itself, and while it was fast, it had no experience. Jason Soulis had centuries of practice at combat. Four more deliberately brutal kicks and the creature was broken and harmless, for the moment at least.

Jason reached down and caught the thing's jaw in his hand. He strained and pulled and the jaw ripped free. After that it was easy enough to separate the head from the rest of the body. Once it was properly incapacitated he called his crows to finish the job.

And while the great swarm of birds began tearing and feasting, he dialed an international exchange on his cell phone.

"Hello?" The voice was familiar. Despite himself he smiled when he heard her accent.

"Hello, my dear. It's Jason."

"I recognize the number. How can I help you?" She was being distant. He couldn't think of anything he'd done to offend, but it was best to play carefully.

"You aren't happy to hear from me?"

"You never call on me unless you have a need for information, Jason. I am not now, nor have I ever been, an encyclopedia for your convenience."

"I only call on you because there is no one else I can trust to be honest with me. You know that." He smiled as he looked at the birds tearing into the remains of the shroud eater. It still tried to struggle, to fight back, but they were persistent.

"What is it you need, old fool?" She said the words with a certain affection. He accepted that the affection was twisted and hollow, but it was still there.

"Can you remind me how we got rid of the shroud eaters?"

"We didn't. I believe they died out on their own."

"No. I remember fighting them."

"Do you?" She paused, and he could imagine the pout on her perfect lips. Had any woman ever been so lovely? He couldn't recall one.

"Well, it was a long time ago. But I know I fought at least a few of them."

"Beheadings to incapacitate. Burnings to destroy their infections. I believe it was the Templars who finally destroyed the last of them."

"I thought you said they died out."

"I might have lied for the sake of convenience, Jason." She paused, and he could almost hear her thinking through the connection. "Why are you asking these questions, Jason? Have you found one alive somewhere?"

"Not quite. I think I found new ones."

"They are not playthings. They are like cockroaches. They are almost impossible to get rid of. If you should actually find them, I would recommend killing them quickly, before they can spread too far." Her voice said all that he had to know. She at least suspected he was up to mischief again.

She knew him as few ever would.

"Fire?"

"Fire. Beheading. I suppose one could try that nonsense with shoving rocks in their mouths to stop them from chewing on their shrouds, but I don't believe it ever really worked."

"Do you know, I'd forgotten about those attempts." He shook his head.

"Of course you did, Jason. Remembering requires effort, and you are infinitely lazy."

"Nonsense. I merely prefer to discover things all over again. It keeps me young."

"The blood of virgins keeps you young, you swine."

"That, too." The birds were done. Little remained except bones that he knew would burn in the sunlight. He sent them on their way, and they left, mostly sated. "Thanks for the help."

"When are you coming to visit me?"

"Likely soon. I'm almost done here." He killed the phone call. It was true. He was almost done. He just had a little pest control to take care of before he left.

"Fire. Why is it always fire? Why can't it ever be a good rain that cleanses everything?" No one answered his questions, except a crow that let out a loud caw. He ignored the bird. Most of the time they just liked to gossip anyway.

***

It had settled itself deep within the cave it had once again claimed as a home, and it had wrapped itself within the fibers that grew from it, half-cocooning its body as it allowed the changes to occur.

The changes were part of whatever this process was. This metamorphosis. It could feel the changes happening, the slow twisting of bones, the gradual swelling in size, but there was no need to worry. The pain was minimal, and there was plenty to keep it relatively sated.

And then Vikki died. The attack was sudden and violent, and by the time she was truly aware that she was being assaulted, it was too late, and one of its three children was dead.

It stirred, but did not allow itself to waken. This was too important, and Vikki had barely even managed to feed herself as she prepared to leave the area.

This had to happen. This was meant to be. Vikki's death changed nothing.

And so it let itself drift back into a distant sleep again as the changes continued.

***

His little girl was safe. That was all that mattered, wasn't it? Brad Hunter hoped that was all that mattered at the end of the day. It had to be enough.

He packed quickly, because he had places to be, and those places involved, by and large, not being in Black Stone Bay for one minute longer than absolutely necessary. He had places to be.

The suitcases were shoved into the back of the car, and he even remembered the charger for the phone this time, which he counted as something of a miracle, really. He almost always forgot the damned thing.

As he locked the door he turned his back on the driveway for only a brief moment. When he finished the simple, menial task, there was a man standing on the porch who hadn't been there a moment earlier.

"Ah. Jesus Christ." His heart stuttered in his chest, and Brad took an involuntary step back as he looked the man over. Casual clothes. A decent jacket over a button-up shirt and denim. The guy was wearing a good pair of running shoes, and he was looking very relaxed. Too old to be selling magazine subscriptions. He didn't even manage an embarrassed smile when he saw that he'd startled Brad.

"Sorry. You have me confused with someone else. My name is Buddy Fisk." The voice was calm and casual.

"What can I do for you, Mister Fisk?"

"Man I work for asked me to find your little girl and get her back safely to you. Did that work out for you?" He looked at the stranger again. He was lean, maybe even a little older than Brad had originally guessed. He could be upwards of his mid-forties, but if so, he kept himself in excellent shape. He had a mustache that looked just a touch too perfectly groomed. You notice that sort of stuff when you work in Hollywood long enough. If it was a fake mustache, it was very high quality.

"Yeah. Yes, it did. Thank you so much for finding Stephanie."

"She's with her mom, right? Tonight? She's with her mother?"

"Yeah, yes, she is." His heart was still beating too fast. The questions seemed innocent enough, but, really, they didn't sit well. "What is this about, Mister Fisk?"

"That's sort of what we wanted to know. There was an agreement, wasn't there? An amount you were supposed to pay?"

"Yes, absolutely. I paid it."

Fisk shook his head. "No. You paid a good portion. You didn't pay the entire amount."

"I paid what I was told would settle the matter, Mister Fisk."

"See, we thought maybe there would be a matter of miscommunication, so we checked. You're an actor, right? I thought maybe you were thinking there was some sort of agent's fee included in the price and because you didn't actually have a middle man in this transaction, you decided to just cut that part out of the total. Stranger things have happened. Sometimes people make mistakes." Fisk stepped just a few paces closer. He was exactly out of easy range for touching. Brad had taken a few fighting lessons, of course. You almost had to if you wanted to work in Hollywood as an actor, and before his looks went away, there had always been the chance that he would grow into the sort of actor who did action-adventures. It hadn't happened, but he'd studied a bit, just in case. Still, he wasn't anywhere near dumb enough to consider swinging at the man in front of him.

"I think there must be a mistake."

"That's my point, right? I told my employer that you always struck me as a straight-up guy. I mean, you know, you can only tell so much about a guy when you've never met him, but you have an honest face." Fisk looked around, his body not really moving so much as his head made a slow turn and his eyes took in everything around them. "I was telling him you didn't seem like the sort that would deliberately try to fuck him over for fifty thousand. Not when it came to seeing to the safety of your daughter."

Fifty thousand dollars. It was a lot of money. An insane amount, really. Worth it if the man had done everything but not if only half of their arrangement was handled.

"I thought that part was for handling the other matter we discussed."

"Your wife?"

"She was supposed to be handled, too."

"She will be. You wanted it to look natural. These things take time."

"Oh. I thought I was supposed to pay after."

"No. That would look bad, wouldn't it? You pay out a lot of money when your little girl disappears, and no one even blinks. You take out money after your wife has a bad accident, everyone notices and wonders. See?"

"Of course. I can get the money for you. It might take a couple of days."

"Where were you planning on heading off to, Mister Hunter?"

"I have business on the Coast. The West Coast, I mean. California."

"You might want to delay that." Fisk took two steps back. "Attend to your business here, first. That would be my suggestion."

He was about to answer the man, to say that he would, of course, handle whatever needed to be handled before leaving—and he meant it, too—when something moved from the shadows of the street and headed for them.

Panic. Sometimes it gets the best of a man. "I will! I will! Just tell your friend to calm down!" He didn't mean to yell, but the guy coming from the street was moving fast, and he looked like he meant to do some damage.

Fisk looked toward the street, drew a firearm, from thin air as far as Brad could tell, and opened fire. The shape had just reached the porch and was fairly sailing up the steps when the gun went off. The report from the weapon was thunderous, and Brad recoiled, dropping his keys and covering his head with his hands as the flashes from the muzzle changed the night to day for an instant and then did it three more times.

Each flash of light revealed the thing coming from the darkness. He didn't see it very clearly, but he saw enough. Teeth, claws, blood. The thing had been coming in fast, and it flew backward, screeching as the bullets pounded through it and took enormous pieces of flesh with each shot. Four rounds. The thing took all four and then flopped to the ground, twitching and smoking where the bullets had gone through.

And Buddy Fisk pointed the pistol at Brad. "What the fuck was that?"

"I don't know! Jesus! I don't fucking know!" He prayed the man believed him. He was telling the truth, but he had never so desperately wanted to make sure that someone believed him in his entire life.

"Get the money. You know where to deliver it. Do not leave this fucking town without paying." Fisk stared at the thing on the ground, his voice once again calmer. Across the street a couple of lights came on. Down the block a dog started barking its fool head off.

The thing lying in the front lawn got back up. Fisk pointed again and blew the head off of the thing. That was all there was to it, really. It was like a magic trick. There was a brilliant light, a phenomenal boom and then a corpse hit the ground.

Fisk kept walking, barely even looking around.

And Brad watched him go. His hands twitched a few times. His eyes watered. When he could finally manage to move, he grabbed his key ring and opened his front door and climbed back inside before he locked it.

When he was safely inside and could see that the thing in his lawn was not moving and didn't seem in any particular hurry to suddenly get back up a second time, he called the police.

Stephanie was safe. That was what really mattered. He kept repeating that to himself while he waited. He also kept a careful watch on the dead thing in his front yard.

He also took the time to wash his face. Some of the thing's blood had gotten on him, though he was damned if he knew how.

***

Impossible!

The transforming sleep ended abruptly. It opened its eyes and stared at the darkness, seeing not the distant walls of the cave but the images that were the last Randy ever saw. Randy was fast! Randy was strong! Randy was cunning enough to meet with one of the strongest creatures it had ever met and to survive.

And Randy was gone. The body was still there, still feeling, but there was no sight, or smell or sound or taste. There was only the sensation of lying in a lawn and fading into nothingness.

Impossible!

It did not want to move, did not want to rise from its rest, but there was no choice. Something was wrong now; something was happening that could not be permitted. Its children were dying. Two were dead and the third?

Dave was in danger.

This could not be allowed to happen.

It strained, pulling at the anchors that had secured its safety, and felt the walls around it shudder.

No more.

This would not be allowed to continue.

***

Maggie screamed and Ben moved, running toward the boathouse for all he was worth. It had nothing to do with love, or perhaps it did, but this was stronger. He needed to be with her, to keep her safe, regardless of the consequences.

He wasn't carrying any weapons, but even that didn't matter. He looked around the area, spotted a large enough section of broken board and swept it into his hand as he kept running. Behind him Boyd and Holdstedter both called his name, but he ignored them.

Maggie needed him, and that was all that mattered.

Maggie and the shroud eater had broken through the side of the building, and that was a faster access point than the door so he took it, stepping over the shattered wood and carefully placing his feet. Rushing headlong was one thing, but tripping and braining himself before he could help Maggie would be pointless.

Ben ignored everything but the black spectre that was attacking Maggie. The thing was pushing her back, forcing her against one of the boats and biting her, biting at her neck, her face.

Ben charged and lifted his weapon high above his head. The sharp point of wood came crashing down, drove into the back of the thing, and it reared back, screeching.

He didn't let himself stop. Instead Ben grabbed the wooden board and pushed it deeper, even as he hauled it to the side, forcing the shroud eater off of Maggie, freeing her from taking any more damage.

And the damned thing bucked and writhed, throwing its weight wildly, forcing Ben down with its struggling weight. Ben rolled to the side, throwing the damned thing's weight and using the training he'd had over the last few years to his advantage. The shroud eater hit the floor hard and continued to struggle.

Ben pushed the makeshift weapon in harder, the wood groaning in his hands and several splinters pushing into his fingers and palms. The thing on the ground in front of him stood back up, and lashed out with its left arm, slapping him hard enough to send him staggering backward.

It wheeled and charged at him, forgetting all about Maggie, all about everything, apparently, but ripping Ben in half.

***

Richie and Danny moved for the boathouse, pausing only long enough to switch the clips in their pistols, while Whalen dropped next to the poor bastard who'd been slammed into the tree. That was fine with Boyd. He didn't want to look at the kid, didn't want to see anyone else who'd been mangled by the dead.

Really, he should have gone to look after Malcolm. It would have been easier.

They found the kids. That was all there was to it. He looked at Ben and the freak the kid was fighting, he looked at Ben's girlfriend, who was recovering from being torn into by Ben's newest enemy, and then he saw the dead kids who were maybe not as dead as they should have been.

Danny was staring. He was having trouble soaking it in, and Boyd couldn't blame him. His partner was insanely good in combat situations, but this? This wasn't a fight, it was a catastrophe and they were too late to stop it from happening.

Boyd took careful aim and fired at the shroud eater's head. His partner was a better shot, but he was pretty damned good. He nailed his target on the first shot and sent the thing staggering back. Never let it be said he hadn't learned from the best. The bullets were hollow-points. Completely against department policy and he didn't care in the least.

The monster threw something at him, and he felt a hot flare of pain across his forehead. A second later there was blood trying to blind him, but he ignored that and shot it again.

Before the thing could consider recovering, he shot it a third time. Then a fourth time. It felt so good he just kept aiming and firing until he was out of ammunition. His face felt wrong. It took him a second to realize he was grinning ear to ear at the mess he was making.

Richie slapped him on the shoulder to get his attention and pointed to the hole they'd both climbed through to get inside.

"Leave!" Boyd tried to make sense of what he was talking about, but right then he just wanted to shoot the fucken thing on the ground a few more times. Oh, right. No bullets.

Danny pushed him toward the exit. He thought about arguing, but he needed to gather his wits. He knew himself well enough to know he wasn't exactly being rational anymore.

Ben grabbed his girlfriend and was dragging her toward the same exit. And while they were doing that, Danny stepped in further.

Richie didn't like the look on Danny's face. He didn't look at all right. There was no humor. No human emotion. He looked like a statue given the ability to move, he was so damned expressionless.

Still, Ben and Maggie were urging him back, and there were the bullets to consider.

Boyd stepped back into the night air and took in a deep, brisk gasp of air. He hadn't even realized he'd been holding his breath.

Bob Longwood was shaking his head, his face set in a deep scowl. He grabbed Boyd's arm and hauled on him, physically lifting him from the ground. Sometimes he forgot how damned big the man was. He wanted to tell the bastard to put him down, but his ears were ringing too loudly and he had no idea why.

He looked around and saw Nancy Whalen, and she was running toward him, and naught but a couple of feet from her Malcolm was standing up, his face bloodied, his arm hanging limply, but alive.

Maybe there was such a thing as miracles after all, because he'd have bet the poor kid was dead.

Whalen was saying something, her eyes wide and horrified, but she wasn't looking at Boyd, she was looking behind him.

Behind him, where Ben and Maggie and Danny were still hanging around.

He started to turn his head, but he didn't make it very far before the explosion lit up the night and knocked him through the air.

***

Danny didn't much care for his job these days. Truth be told, he was seriously considering retiring, because this was just getting to be too goddamned much. Dead people? Okay. Sucks, but there it is. Vampires? Not fun, but, hey, he'd dealt with them before. But this?

He looked at the piles of dead kids and froze. It was too damned much. He didn't have kids, but he had a nephew, and he loved that twerp. He had cousins who were the same age as some of the ones he was looking at. The ones who were covered in open sores and staring with dead eyes.

And moving.

They were fucking moving. He thought the occasional moving corpse at sunrise was about as bad as it was going to get, but, no, not even close.

The thing Boyd had shot to hell was on the ground and making noises, shaking and shivering and pulling itself back together. He could see the holes in the damned thing. He could look through its chest and the gaping wound in its head and see the fucking stacks of moving dead kids on the other side.

Oh, yes, there were going to be some serious nightmares in his future.

Danny looked around to make absolutely sure that no one else was alive in the boathouse. He got lucky. There was no one.

That was good, because he didn't know how much longer he could remain rational.

The dead kids were moving now, not thinking about it, but actually starting to get up and head in his direction. They were gray-skinned and their eyes were black and glistening and they rolled off of each other and crawled, or simply climbed over their buddies as they noticed him. A nice, living meal, just what they all seemed to want.

Boathouse. Same one he'd frequented when he went to the Hartshorn Academy. Oh, there were fresh layers of paint, and probably a few of the boards had been replaced over the years, but a lot of the shit floating around the place might actually have been the same stuff that had decorated the interior of the boathouse when he attended all those years ago.

Back then Eoghan Guinness had run the place. He'd been a cranky old bastard, but if you treated him with just a little respect, he'd let you hang around after school and maybe even go out on the water in one of the rowboats. He only had a few rules, really. The biggest ones involved respecting him enough not to think he was stupid and to avoid smoking in the boathouse, because it was also where the school kept a lot of supplies they didn't want to leave on the campus proper. Supplies like old paint, old equipment, and a few gallons of gasoline for the backup generator that never got used.

It was nice to know some things never changed.

Danny looked at the dead things heading toward him. Most of them were a little slow, and that was good, but a couple of the fuckers were starting to look lively enough to make him worry. Normally the notion of a few kids coming his way didn't cause him to worry, but in his defense, they were eyeing him like he'd make a good snack, and they had that whole disease thing going on.

Danny hated germs.

He moved to the cubbyhole where the ancient supplies were kept, and he did it fast, because there wasn't a lot of spare time here. The freak in charge of the other freaks was healing up too quickly for his comfort. It was standing up now, and it looked like most of its head was back where it was supposed to be.

Oh, and the little ones were creeping along just fine now, heading for him and licking at their too long teeth.

He threw a paint can and nailed the first kid in the chest. The can bounced and popped its lid and spilled institutional green paint all over the little bastard's dead face. The kid hissed at him like a damned cat, like that shit wasn't creepy at all. "What the hell is with the hissing? Can't you fuckers ever just talk?"

"Is that you, Daddy? Can you tuck me in?" The voice came from a little girl, maybe six years old. She had blisters over most of her face, and her eyes were black and weeping from a few open sores.

Okay. Maybe they could go back to hissing.

He grabbed another can. This one felt about half-full, and he hurled it as hard as he could at the little girl. She slapped it out of the air and shrieked at him.

Turpentine. He opened the top of the thing and threw it. The fumes were vile, but not as bad as the smell coming from the dead things heading his way.

He looked away from them for just a moment, long enough to see a rusting gas can. He twisted the lid off and threw that next, watching the contents slosh around and spray across the boathouse floor and a few of the little darlings.

The can hit one of the kids in the head. The little one staggered a bit and then charged at him, running hard and fast.

Not a chance.

The bullet hit the kid with enough force to send her sailing backward, a massive hole where her stomach had been. He didn't let himself think, but instead fired at the can and blew a hole in it. And then he fired again. And nailed another kid that was getting too close. The smell of gasoline and paint and dead, diseased flesh filled the air.

Danny ran for the opening in the wall and fired again. This time the shot skimmed along the gas can and made it bounce. It also managed to get a streak of sparks going.

And after that, the air caught fire.

***

Neil was done thinking. It was time to act. He rose from his position along the wall and tore open the plastic from the tenting that was supposed to keep him safely away from everyone else. It wasn't doing much good, anyway, as he'd already killed all of the attending doctors and medical staff. Oh, to be sure there were more out there, but they were very likely trying to decide what should be done. They might even have called the police, but he also knew that the police wouldn't come waltzing into a hot zone without checking with the CDC first.

The first rule of human nature: People want to survive. They might overlook that fact in certain circumstances, like the occasional war or if they worked in emergency services, but by and large people tended to want to live as long as possible, and that meant they didn't kick down the doors into areas that were contaminated with unknown contagions unless they absolutely had to, and even then they wore protection. So, no, he wasn't sweating about anyone interfering.

"What are you doing out there?" Frank Preston's voice was querulous. He wanted answers, and he wanted to get free to kill his daughter, not necessarily in that order. Also, the dead man wanted food.

He called back to the man in his small room. "I'm setting us free, Frank. Don't you think it's time to get out of here?"

"Just unlock these damned cuffs. I'll get us out of here."

"What will you do when you get out of here, Frank?"

"I need to see Margaret! I need to have a talk with my little girl." The tone of his voice made clear that talking wouldn't be on the agenda.

Neil moved around the area and began opening the valves on all of the canisters of oxygen that had been set aside. There were several as the area was meant to be contained and airtight.

"Frank, do you love Margaret?"

"What kind of fool question is that?" He could hear the attempt at cunning in the man's voice.

"I know you did love her. But I bet you don't anymore. I bet you hate her, don't you? For doing this to you?"

"She needs to be punished!" There it was: the anger that he knew had to be there.

He was feeling it himself now, and he understood it. "Funny thing about diseases, Frank. They like to find ways to spread."

"What are you talking about?"

"Hear me out. I'll explain. You love Margaret. She's your little girl. Maybe she's been disappointing a few times, but that's almost inevitable. You'd forgive her in most cases. But what's happened to us isn't allowing that. Do you know how I know that?"

Frank didn't answer for a moment. He knew he was mostly talking to hear himself talk, but he liked having an audience. That was one of the reasons he'd chosen to work at a teaching hospital.

Finally Frank decided to play along, most likely in the hopes that Neil would let him go a little sooner. "Fine. How do you know anything at all?"

"Because I was wrong. I thought there wasn't anyone in my life for me to love and so there wouldn't be anyone for me to blame. But it turns out my mind has decided to blame Lisa. You might not remember her, but she was doing rounds with me when you came in."

"So? Maybe it's Lisa's fault!"

"No. I thought about that. Lisa was dead when this happened to me. I shouldn't blame her but I do. And I figured it out. The disease—this contagion that we have?—it wants us to blame our loved ones, so we can go after them and spread the disease even further. It's an interesting way for a disease to work, don't you think?"

Medical supplies galore in the area. Alcohol for cleansing wounds and sterilizing flesh. Plenty of other flammable materials, too. Neil opened packages of gauze and soaked them. He poured more of the rubbing alcohol on the plastic tenting materials, and then on the bodies he'd left lying around.

"That doesn't make any sense." Frank was still sounding petulant, but at least he was still playing along.

"Of course it does. The disease is smart. It wants us to infect our loved ones. Then they find other loved ones to infect. And it spreads out faster and faster."

"When are we getting out of here? I need to find Margaret."

Neil took a deep breath of the highly oxygenated air. He didn't need to breathe, but he found he still wanted to. "We're leaving right now, Frank." The good thing about hospitals: there's always plenty of medical supplies if you're willing to look.

Neil found an electrical outlet and he shoved a pair of stainless steel scissors into the opening. The electrical arc ignited the air with ease.

The resulting explosion took out three floors of the hospital.

CHAPTER THIRTEEN

Detective Boyd was on the ground and shaking off the worst of the impact. The lump on his head was still bleeding, but he was moving, and that was a good thing. The police captain crawled on the ground next to him, the expression of worry on her face made it very clear to Malcolm that she had feelings for the man.

Not far from them, Detective Longwood was looking around and calling for Holdstedter. A bit further away, the woman who was avoiding him—and he wasn't foolish, he'd figured by this point that she wasn't quite human—was standing guard over her friend Ben.

The boathouse burned, and from within its confines he could hear the screams of the damned. He knew they were damned. He could feel the same darkness coming from them that had come from Randy.

Malcolm stood where he was and watched the fire. He hurt everywhere, but he needed to know that they died, all of them, because they were abominations. They should not have existed, and they needed to cease tainting the world.

He wanted to fall, but stood his ground and waited.

It would come out. He knew that.

And so it did. The shroud eater threw itself from the burning building, flames licking at the black cloak that covered it. It was not foolish. Rather than coming for him, it threw itself into the water and extinguished the blazes threatening to devour it.

And Malcolm started for the water, his head ringing, his arm a useless, aching weight.

The thing crawled from the water and rose, a cascade of vile fluids falling from the cloth that covered it. The thing looked toward him and scowled, baring its teeth to him. It only had one hand now, and he could see that no ring adorned the fingers.

Not Randy. It was not his brother. And that was just possibly a blessing.

Malcolm grabbed at it with his good arm and pulled it to him, holding on for all he was worth. Just as with Randy before him, the monster shied back and tried to escape from him, but he could not allow that to happen. It had to be destroyed.

There was no fear in him, not the least bit of dread. This was what had to happen, and if he were to die in the process, then he had to die. The thing fought him, struggled and pushed and shoved him backward, but Malcolm held on, his fingers catching in the black cloak it wore to protect itself. Pain flamed along his broken arm, and his skull throbbed, and still he held to the beast as it screamed and lashed out.

"How many did you kill? How many of those poor children?" He hissed the question against the vile thing's face as it clutched at him, pulled him closer in an effort to break his neck, perhaps. Surely its grip was strong enough, and he felt himself starting to black out from the crushing pressure it exerted.

"All of them! Every last one!" There was no regret from the monster. It reveled in what it had done.

And Malcolm held onto it, felt it burning against him, the ruined arm of the beast pushing against his own broken limb, felt the claws of the thing digging into his chest. But he felt more than that. He also felt the way it withered and burned as it continued to touch him. Not because of anything that he did, but because the Lord willed it. He was already dead and he knew it, accepted it. His death meant nothing as long as he could stop it from killing anyone else.

Malcolm screamed, and the thing screamed with him.

And as Malcolm fell backward, the thing screamed once more and fell back from him, burning even as it collapsed back into the waters it had emerged from.

***

The boathouse burned, and Maggie watched. Malcolm fought the beast that had almost killed her, and Maggie watched that, too, unable to get any closer. If Malcolm's faith had been a beacon before, it blazed like a funeral pyre while he held onto the plague bearer. And then that light faded a second time and the monster he held on to landed in the waters and dissolved as she watched.

And a few of the things that had burned in the boathouse attempted to escape; burned and ruined, they fell into the waters and tried to get away, driven by instinct to seek shelter.

And Maggie killed them as they attempted to scurry away. Ben lay on the ground, and she left him there to destroy every one of the things that attempted to escape. They were nothing, insignificant. The thing that had created them had been powerful, but they were so weak in comparison.

She just reminded herself that they weren't really children, not anymore.

And she paused in that endeavor exactly long enough to pull the handsome blond cop from the water's edge and lay him out on the land. The other cops moved to him and worked on him, fighting to save his life while she took care of the disease that wanted to destroy her home.

She paused only once, almost letting one of the children escape her, when she felt her father's death. And if she cried while she finished her grisly work, she didn't allow herself to acknowledge that fact.

***

It screamed in outrage when Dave died, deprived of the last source of nourishment. This was too much! There was no choice but to rise from its slumber completely and to free itself from the cocoon it had created. Whatever it was becoming would have to wait until it had taken care of the damnable things that sought to stop it from finding peace.

Rising through the earth was easy enough, but severing the ties it had created with the earth was not as easy, and the cliffside shook as it rose from the caves. Above it the lawns and trees withered and died in an instant, and within the tides that caressed the cliffs every fish that was unfortunate enough to be in the vicinity perished as it ripped the life force from them.

It hungered, and it would feed.

In the air above the cliffs, seagulls and crows alike plummeted to the ground, struck dead as it took their lives as well.

It roared, and the sky shivered. It howled, and the wind howled as well, blasting shingles from roofs, shattering windows in the mansions along the Cliff Walk, and throwing aside trees that had just died as if they were little more than twigs.

The earth shuddered again, and the ground cracked. The waves were shattered as the cliffs crumbled in several spots.

It rose from the ground, no longer solid, no longer merely a physical entity. It had changed, and it had grown, and it was filled with rage.

In five houses along the Cliff Walk, the families that had lived for generations in Black Stone Bay were extinguished. Every individual in those buildings at that precise moment died, as their very souls were ripped free and consumed. And still it rose and hungered and roared its outrage for all to hear.

And Jason Soulis looked upon his enemy and wondered if just possibly he had let matters fester for too long.

He remembered the plague bearers of the past and had studied the new creatures at his home, and the thing before him was decidedly not the same creature. Or possibly it was. Surely the shroud eaters of the past had worked together, had come to the castle and the surrounding land and fed on the misery and suffering they created. But it had never occurred to him that they might have a leader.

And surely this thing, this shadow that rose from the ground and ripped what it wanted from the living, was undeniably the first of its kind.

The thing looked to the heavens and roared again, and then it turned its attention on Jason Soulis. Perhaps it realized that there was a kinship. Perhaps it understood that he had caused its creation, or perhaps it merely sought to feed on him. He would never know for sure.

He simply knew when it tried to feed. It reached for his life force and sought to wrest it from his body. The infected wounds that he had hidden within his body throbbed as the shroud eater opened its mouth and drew in a breath, and the air around him shivered, and the crows that circled around him as his escorts died in an instant, withering and crumbling to dust as they fell from the sky.

And that was far too great an insult to be tolerated.

Jason Soulis attacked.

There were many things that Maggie suspected about Jason, and several of them were absolutely true. He could control the elements.

He often did, summoning clouds and rain to hide him from the sun and allow him comfort. From time to time he called forth snowstorms to keep his victims at bay, and he'd even been known to alter the weather on an occasional battlefield, the better to assist whichever side he felt like helping.

There were other applications, of course.

Jason called forth the lightning from a clear sky, and the lightning answered, blasting the glowering thing that tried to feed on him. The undead were not like other vampires. Jason had explained that to Maggie and a few others in his time. They didn't much like sunlight, but they could tolerate it.

The shroud eaters were unlike other vampires as well. They were far more sensitive to the light. So sensitive, in fact, that they generated the shrouds that earned them their names in an effort to protect them from the light.

The lightning burned brilliantly and lanced through the thing that sought to fight against Jason. And the shroud eater screamed as it burned.

Just like the two creatures Jason had experimented on screamed when he electrified them.

There were witnesses that night. A few people actually saw the pyrotechnic display along the Cliff Walk and spoke of it later, though none saw it from close by. Those who could have witnessed the event from nearer to the cliffs were dead by the time Jason Soulis cut loose, sending searing bolt after slashing tongue of lightning into the creature that screamed and burned before his fury.

He continued on until his newest creation was completely destroyed, taking no chances. Summoning a storm took a great deal of power, but some things have to be done, and he could not afford to take any chances. The shroud eaters were simply too virulent to allow them to continue.

When he was done, Jason looked upon the burnt remains of the thing and cast them into the wind. Ashes and little more. What was that old rhyme from the plague days? "Ashes, ashes, we all fall down...."

Exhausted, Jason headed away from the cliffs and away from Black Stone Bay. He could not stay, no matter how much he might want to. For the time being, he was too vulnerable, and it wouldn't do to let Maggie or any of the locals who knew of his existence catch him in his present state.

He rose into the night sky and left the town behind. Later he could always come back and take care of the rest of his affairs.

Later.

Another time.

***

The sun rose on numerous disasters, and there were plenty who demanded answers. Boyd and Holdstedter were not among the officials who offered any answers. Both were hospitalized — at St. Joseph's in this case. Boyd had a concussion, and Holdstedter required a few days' observation as a result of nearly drowning in the waters and damned near blowing himself to kingdom come. He came out of it with a concussion of his own and several sprains.

Whalen and Longwood were both in better shape, medically speaking. The captain managed to recite a few lines for the press, and the detective spoke about the ongoing investigation regarding the incidents at the Hartshorn Academy. All that anyone knew with any certainty was that a college-aged man had died in the night and that his identity was being withheld pending notification of his next of kin. There was no known correlation between the man in question and the disappearance of the entire student body.

The police force had a bit of egg on its face. The FBI had come in to assist regarding the disappearances, but much like the police, they had little to say regarding the missing children.

Ben and Maggie listened to the news from their home, both of them aching and bruised, not just physically but emotionally, as well. The news made much of the explosion at the Sacred Hearts University Hospital, and for several days speculation continued as to whether or not there might have been a terrorist attack involved. The investigations eventually pointed to a faulty oxygen tank and bad wiring.

And while the investigations went on, Maggie waited as best she could, sensing the distance between her and Ben and dreading what it might mean. For several days and nights he moved around the house like a ghost, seldom speaking to her except to answer questions and acknowledge the arrangements regarding her father's funeral service. There was no body to bury: like everything else within the west wing of the hospital, he had been incinerated, but there was still a service, and he attended with her. He held her when she cried, and he supported her mother, as well.

And when she could no longer take the silence, she broke down and asked him flat out. It was nighttime, and the funeral was over and done with, and Halloween was over. The world around them prepared for Thanksgiving, though many families in Black Stone Bay would be struggling to find reasons to be thankful during the season.

Ben was in his office and working late, his face locked in a scowl, when she came in and sat on the edge of the desk, worrying her lower lip while she stared at him. He eventually looked up, his face taking on the slightly dazed expression he often wore when she interrupted his work.

"Ben? Are we okay?" She could barely make herself ask the question. The answer might well destroy her as near as she could figure.

Ben looked into her eyes for a very long time, not speaking at all. When he finally did respond, he looked away from her. "I don't know. I guess that depends on you."

"What do you mean?"

The look he shot her said exactly how dense he felt she was being. "You have needs. I get that." He looked into her eyes again, and she saw the hurt. "Jason Soulis is not a need. And if he is, then we're not okay. That's for you to decide. You need to speak to him from time to time, and I get that. But if it goes further than that, I won't be here the next time you come back."

That was the last he spoke of the matter on that occasion. He did not bring it up as Thanksgiving approached, nor did he bring the subject up over Christmas, though they were still together at that point.

The snows came to Black Stone Bay not long after Thanksgiving, and they brought with them the same false promise that snow always brought. The world was washed in white and made pristine, at least on the surface.

Brad Hunter celebrated Christmas with his daughter. She enjoyed Thanksgiving with her mother and Tim, but not long after that, the couple died in a car wreck, sliding on a patch of ice, apparently, and falling off the bridge that led out of town. Apparently they'd made plans to do some shopping in Newport, though they'd said nothing of it to Stephanie.

There were tears, of course. That was inevitable. Brad was there for her, and he hired a nanny to take care of her as well. After the events that had taken place in the past year, he decided that Stephanie was better off being homeschooled, and he found a teacher to take care of giving her a proper education. Lora Dowling had taught Stephanie before and had managed to miss the disaster at Hartshorn solely by virtue of being sick when everyone disappeared.

Stephanie needed a familiar face, and Lora needed a job. It was a win-win as far as he was concerned.

Brad considered himself to be the luckiest man in the world. He had his beautiful daughter back, his business connections in Hollywood were bearing fruit, and he had dodged a bullet in the health department, apparently. The man killed in his front yard — and according to what he told the police, the man had been attacked by complete stranger who happened along when Brad was being assaulted by the diseased wretch — had been extremely contagious at one point and should have been in the hospital. All he knew for certain was that he developed blisters the day after the attack and they went away on their own within a day.

Sometimes though, late at night, he could still feel the spots where the blood had covered his skin, and he could almost feel the blisters rising on his face. When he woke in the morning, they were always gone. Damnedest thing. He wasn't alone, of course. Apparently several people had dealt with similar problems and had recovered from them. Lora, for one. She had gotten sick at the Bayside campus and called out the day the kids disappeared. Like him, she sometimes felt like the blisters were just waiting for the right time to come back. Also like him, she had avoided any outbreaks recurring.

Lucky. That's all there was to it.

Some people were not as lucky. Carly Winters, for example. The poor girl had vanished from her home one night and not been found for almost a week. When she was finally located in an abandoned house she had been tortured and tied in place. Whatever was done to her, she had not recovered well at all. She remained in a catatonic state, and seldom responded to anything at all, except for the darkness. As soon as the lights went out, she started screaming. Eventually it was decided to leave her in a well-lit room at the facility where they kept her. It was best for her and for the rest of the patients.

Not long after Christmas the body of Doctor Lisa Davis—who had disappeared from the hospital two months earlier—was found in the woods near the Cliff Walk. She was freshly dead and had apparently been attacked by wild dogs or possibly even a bear. Her body was mostly intact, but her lower abdomen had been torn to shreds. Evidence in the case led the medical examiner to believe she might have been pregnant at the time of her death, though her husband claimed she had been on birth control and had not, to the best of his knowledge, been with child.

Around the same time that her body was discovered, Black Stone Bay had the first documented case of a missing person since October. Ms. Paula Lawrence, a college student, disappeared shortly after having an argument with her boyfriend, Mark Owens, also a college student.

Mister Owens swore that he dropped her off at her dorm at the end of their date. The only unusual thing he knew was that Paula claimed she was being stalked by a pregnant woman who kept calling her "Mommy."

And through it all, Black Stone Bay endured.